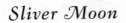

Sliver Moon

JAY BRANDON

Sliver Moon

A New Chris Sinclair Thriller

FORGE®

A TOM DOHERTY ASSOCIATES BOOK

NEW YORK

SLIVER MOON

Copyright © 2003 by Jay Brandon

This book is printed on acid-free paper.

Edited by James Frenkel

A Forge Book
Published by Tom Doherty Associates, LLC
175 Fifth Avenue
New York, NY 10010

www.tor.com

Forge® is a registered trademark of Tom Doherty Associates, LLC.

Library of Congress Cataloging-in-Publication Data

Brandon, Jay.
    Sliver moon : a new Chris Sinclair thriller / Jay Brandon.—1st ed.
      p. cm.
    "A Tom Doherty Associates book."
    ISBN 0-312-87436-7
    1. Sinclair, Chris (Fictitious character)—Fiction. 2. Parent and adult child—Fiction. 3. Bexar County (Tex.)—Fiction. 4. Public prosecutors—Fiction. I. Title.

    PS3552.R315S58 2003
    813'.54—dc21

                           2003041766

First Edition: July 2003

Printed in the United States of America

0 9 8 7 6 5 4 3 2 1

★

Once again,
this is for Dorene Brandon
and Robert Brandon,
with love and gratitude

Sliver Moon

★ The Santa Rosa Hospital stands on the western edge of downtown San Antonio. The hospital has grown to become a small complex, much of it devoted to the treatment of children. One of the newest buildings, twelve white stories, holds doctors' offices. Recently, psychiatrist Anne Greenwald had moved her office into this building, after years spent in the hospital building itself. Anne had liked being part of the action of the hospital, close enough to hear the emergency room doors opening to admit a rolling stretcher, but she finally admitted to needing larger, more modern rooms. Some of her patients hadn't liked entering the hospital to see her. In fact, as Anne readily admitted, many of her patients didn't like coming to see her at all.

On this Friday afternoon her waiting room stood strangely empty. Within the suite, Anne hummed as she moved around her office, deftly stepping over or around stacks of files. Anne wore a slight smile and her green eyes were lively. She couldn't have said what made her happy, and wouldn't want to try. A good mood shouldn't be analyzed to death. She was getting away early on a Friday, taking Chris out of town. That was enough.

She carried her thinnest briefcase, one not big enough to carry a weekend's worth of guilt. Anne rarely took off a whole day from work. This weekend she should be writing two reports for court, one other for the state Human Resources Agency, and several private evaluations. But she had decided only to take one little file—if she could find it.

She picked up the stack closest to her desk chair and lifted it up to the desk, began going carefully through the tabs, checking the names on the files. As she thumbed through the cases each name seemed to reach out for her. Every file evoked a memory or the thought of what she might be able to do to help the people, mostly children, whose lives lay embedded in these files.

The humming had stopped. Anne sighed. Then her determination to have a good weekend reasserted itself. "This empathy crap has got to stop," she muttered to herself.

Just as Anne found the file she wanted, and pulled it triumphantly from the middle of a stack of similar folders, the telephone on her desk rang. Anne looked startled, though on most days the phone rang all the time, and directed a glare in the general direction of the outer office, where her receptionist had been given instructions not to send back any calls except emergencies. The phone jangled again, sounding innocent. *Pick me up*, it seemed to pipe. *Maybe I'm just a friend calling.* Maybe it was Chris, calling to confirm their travel plans.

Anne lifted the phone. "Anne Greenwald."

The pause that followed sounded sinister. But then a child's voice said, "Hello, Dr. Greenwald, this is Meg."

It took Anne a minute to place the name, because Meg was a new client who had only come in twice so far. But they had gotten along well; the girl didn't seem to resent the visits at all.

Child Protective Services had recently taken Meg from a home that featured an abusive father and an alcoholic mother, with nine-year-old Meg functioning as the parent-in-fact for her two younger siblings. She had been placed temporarily in a group home with six other girls from similar home environments. In spite of her background, Meg seemed like a cheery, bright girl, always on the lookout to make a new friend. Maybe it was just an act, but it was a good one.

"Hi, Meg. How are you, honey? Is there a problem?"

"No problems," Meg chirped. "It's a good day. I'm just calling to tell you happy birthday."

"Thank you, sweetie, that's very nice. But it's not my birthday."

"I know," the girl chuckled through the phone line. "It's my birthday. I called to wish you a happy *my* birthday!"

Anne's eyes grew suddenly moist. "Oh, how nice, Meg. Happy birthday! Is it a good one so far?"

"Oh, yes," the girl said, but Anne knew better. The poor girl must be calling everyone she knew trying to elicit some recognition of her special day. If Anne, who had only met Meg twice in a professional way, had made the girl's list, it must be a short, depressing list.

Anne had a cheerful, congratulatory conversation with the girl for five minutes, then wished her a good day again and hung up. Immediately she made two more calls, to the group home leader and to Meg's caseworker, so they could do something to acknowledge the birthday. Was there any family member they could bring to see her, an aunt, maybe her little sister? The caseworker, overwhelmed with crises, said she'd do her best, and the group home leader promised a celebration with cake and ice cream. But still Anne hung up feeling she had to do more, picturing the girl smiling through a birthday in a group home. In Anne's professional life, the angry kids made life difficult, the withdrawn ones took the most work, but the cheerful ones broke her heart.

The jurors sat in their box looking shy and mean. For the most part they kept their heads down, unwilling to look at the lawyers or the courtroom audience, as if they had done something shameful. But when a juror would shoot a glance around the room, it was defiant. Collectively, the jury in its box looked like a small, fierce animal that had retreated deep within its burrow, that wanted only to be left alone but would attack in another moment.

Chris Sinclair used to think of juries that way, back when he had been a young trial prosecutor. Now he always made a point of looking at jurors as individuals. Sitting at the State's counsel table as if relaxed, he watched them. Chris shared the jury's feelings. He wasn't proud of this week's work, but it had been necessary.

He listened to the last few stanzas of the defense lawyer's closing argument. Harry Price was saying just what Chris had known he must say in behalf of his client. The defendant, a young woman with lank brown hair and deep circles under her eyes, slumped listlessly at the defense table, apparently unconcerned about her fate.

The defense lawyer stood directly in front of the jurors, his hands on the front railing of the jury box. "You have found this woman guilty. She accepts your verdict. It took some very good investigative work by the District Attorney's Office and the medical examiner to determine that a crime had occurred, but as soon as they did she confessed. She didn't try to hide the truth. She admitted what she had done. The worst crime we can imagine a woman committing: killing her own child.

"She admitted it because she couldn't help herself. Just as she couldn't help the killing. It hadn't been a decision to commit murder; it had been an irresistible impulse. When Marilyn did what she did, she was in such a deep hole of depression that she didn't see a chance of ever climbing out. She thought the whole world was buried in that blackness. She's tried to explain to you what she felt, that she was doing a kindness for her baby: taking her out of this world so that she would never have to feel the despair that her mother felt constantly."

The defense lawyer turned and looked at his client, who didn't seem to be listening. She appeared more sunken and listless than ever. Price turned back to the jurors and concluded, "I've never been in that pit of depression and I hope none of you has either. But you know it was real for Marilyn. Don't take vengeance on a woman who couldn't help herself. That won't help anyone. Sentence her to probation and let her get the treatment she needs. Thank you."

He sat next to his client, putting a sympathetic hand on her shoulder. The defendant didn't respond.

Chris Sinclair watched the young woman too. He wanted to go to her, lean down close to her face, and say, *Pay attention.* Instead he stood briskly and approached the jurors in his turn. They watched him covertly but attentively. Chris Sinclair, the district attorney of Bexar County, looked younger than his thirty-five years and moved gracefully. As he walked, he buttoned the jacket of his brown suit, which made him look thinner. In fact, as usual during a trial like this, he had dropped a couple of pounds. The stress diet. Chris made sure he had the jurors' attention and began seriously.

"Mr. Price has been eloquent in his client's defense. But

what he has just argued to you is essentially what he presented in the first phase of trial, an insanity defense. You jurors, though, have already rejected that defense by finding the defendant guilty of murder."

Which accounted for the jury's hangdog but glaring attitude. Many of them obviously believed that the young woman had been suffering from mental strain when she held a pillow over her baby's face for ten minutes. But they also believed the act had been murder. Murder required punishment, which was what Chris Sinclair and the defense lawyer were arguing over this morning.

Chris assumed a conversational air in jury argument. He felt the jury's dilemma. He shared it.

"So what punishment fits this crime? As Mr. Price said, the worst crime we can imagine. A mother killing not just her child, but a helpless, blameless, completely innocent three-month-old infant, one who needed her for nurture and comfort and protection and instead ended her life screaming and choking as her mother's weight bore down on her.

"But Marilyn Lewis suffered under her own weight, of clinical depression. You've heard from the experts for both sides about whether she knew the difference between right and wrong at that moment, but certainly she suffered from depression. We can see it now. We want to pity her as much as condemn her."

Chris walked close to the slumped defendant, which made her defense lawyer look up warily. Chris stared down at the young woman. "She looks helpless, doesn't she? Pathetic. But how much more helpless was her baby?" He held his hands cupped upward, only a few inches apart. "A tiny, tiny baby who was not responsible for Marilyn Lewis's depression. No—Marilyn was responsible for that baby. She had made the decision to get pregnant, the decision to bring that child into the world, the decision to stay home and care for her.

"And at some point illness began to descend on that young mother. But where was that point? Think about it. No one wakes up suddenly clinically depressed. She must have had glimmers that something was wrong, back at a time when she remained rational. What did she do? Did she seek help? Did she realize, *I'm losing it, I need to do something to protect this child from me*. No. She did nothing. Even after she was prescribed an antidepressant, she stopped taking it."

Chris stood in front of the jury, still with his hands cupped, sounding as if he had earnestly tried to understand the case himself. "We can compare Marilyn Lewis to a drunk driver who runs into a pedestrian. No, he didn't mean to kill that pedestrian. He didn't have control of himself or his car because he was drunk. But at some point he wasn't drunk. He made the decision to keep drinking, knowing he would soon be driving. *That's* the person we punish, the one who made the fatal decision while still in his right mind, before drink or depression had deprived him or her of judgment.

"It's my job in this proceeding to ask for the maximum punishment, life imprisonment. Mr. Price has done his job and asked for the minimum, and I'm supposed to urge the opposite extreme. But I'm not going to do that. I'm just going to ask you to do what you think is best. Because no matter what you decide, it won't be enough. She'll serve her probation or her prison term and someday she'll emerge again. But her baby will be dead forever."

He turned quickly on his heel and resumed his seat. Moments later the jurors filed out. They didn't look at Chris Sinclair and he didn't look at them, as if they were conspirators who couldn't acknowledge each other in public.

Anne Greenwald found Chris Sinclair in the courtyard of his condominium building, a pleasant space of bushes, flowering plants, and a narrow pond where mosquitoes bred. The late afternoon in early May had uncharacteristically been only warm, not oppressively hot. Chris looked comfortable sitting on a green metal chair with a suitcase next to him. He rocked back in the springy chair, staring up past the roof of the two-story condo building toward the sky. Anne smiled at the sight of him, and her tread grew softer. Five-and-a-half feet tall, Anne could give an impression of smallness. She seemed to crouch down within herself as she crossed the courtyard and knelt right behind Chris, who didn't seem to have heard her. But he didn't startle when she spoke.

"You must have good eyes," she said, "because I can't see a damned thing you're looking at."

"The blameless sky."

Anne put her arms around him from behind. "Let's go to the country. You can tell me all your worries in the car."

"Yeah, but then I'd have to listen to yours, right?"

Anne laughed. "Me? Worries? I don't have any worries."

Ten minutes later they were driving through the northern outskirts of San Antonio, Anne at the wheel of her dark green Volvo. Anne glanced at Chris as he stretched out his legs as much as the seat would permit and did seem to relax. Already he had abandoned his trial mode. His blond hair fell down across his forehead, and his hands lay still on his legs. He had changed out of his suit before Anne's arrival, into soft light brown jeans and a green sports shirt that Anne had once complimented him on.

"Where's Clarissa?" she asked lightly. Clarissa was Chris's sixteen-year-old daughter from, as the enlightened say, a previous relationship, and Anne always kept her voice light when speaking of her. The girl lived with Chris now, an arrangement that had taken a good deal of adjusting to on everyone's part.

"Her grandparents came to visit for the weekend."

"Well, that worked out nicely."

"I don't think coincidence had any part in it," Chris said, looking out the window. "Almost as soon as I mentioned this weekend to Clarissa, she got a phone call from the grandparents. I don't think she wanted to come along, so if I check the phone bill next month I'm sure I'll find that she made the first call. But I won't."

Clarissa had her mother's gift for manipulating events. In a sixteen-year-old, it was cute.

Anne was dressed in colors similar to Chris's outfit, quite by coincidence, in soft-soled brown suede shoes and a green dress. One of the seven deadly sins of love, dressing color-coordinated. She hoped her father wouldn't notice and think they'd done it deliberately. Then she remembered how profoundly color-blind her father was and relaxed on that score.

But Chris seemed to have picked up the subject of her thought. "Going to see your father, huh?"

Anne nodded.

"The same father I met before?"

Anne nodded again. "I decided to renew his contract for one more season."

Chris sat back in the seat and folded his arms. "Well, that's good. We got along so famously, I wouldn't want to have to start over again charming someone new."

Though Chris and Anne had been seeing each other for more than a year, and Anne's father didn't live far away, Chris and Morris Greenwald had met each other only twice, on rather formal occasions that hadn't given them a chance to get to know each other. But then, Anne had only seen her father one other time in the last two years.

"Why am I doing this, exactly?" Chris asked.

Anne shrugged. Somehow she felt excited about this weekend's prospects. Taking her beau to see her father at the family home seemed so old-fashioned and silly that Anne enjoyed the idea. Even the possibility of drama and tension exhilarated her. The mere change of pace from her usual life alone made the idea pleasing. She answered Chris's question: "He invited me. Which, believe me, is rare enough to make it a special occasion."

"I understand why you're going to see him," Chris said. "My question is why am I?"

But he wouldn't have missed it. Chris, too, felt secretly happy—that Anne had invited him along, that she felt him that much a part of her life, and like Anne, just at the idea of getting away for a weekend. Their daily lives were stressful enough that any change seemed like a relief.

Chris could have asked Anne about her father. He knew a little—that they'd had some estrangement in the past, but not the reason. Maybe this invitation represented Morris's reaching out. Maybe he'd resent having Chris along on the trip. But Anne had wanted him to come. Chris knew she'd get around to telling him what she wanted to say in her own time.

Anne, on the other hand, knew that Chris had to be prompted ever to say what was on his mind. "So what did she get?"

She meant the young mother who'd killed her baby. Chris said slowly, "First they sent out a note asking if they could give alternative sentences. None of us knew what that meant, and the judge just sent back an answer saying no, they had to reach one verdict on punishment. A few minutes later they came back and gave her twenty-five years."

Anne's eyes widened as she watched the highway. "More than I would have guessed."

"Me too," Chris said. "But I think it was a very carefully calculated sentence. She's twenty-four years old. After she's served half her sentence, as she'll have to do before she becomes eligible for parole, her child-bearing years will pretty much be over."

"Not quite," Anne said. At thirty-four, she had made some personal calculations along those lines.

"No, but given her having to work her way back into society, form a new relationship—at least she couldn't have a lot more babies. I think that's what the jury was thinking."

"Did you find out what they meant by alternative sentencing?"

"Yes. They told the defense lawyer and me afterwards that if she would have agreed to have her tubes tied they would have given her probation."

They rode in silence for a mile or two. The twenty miles of highway between San Antonio and the town of their destination, New Braunfels, never really turned rural. Subdivisions, the Retama race track, stores, restaurants, and a cement plant occupied the frontage road all the way. In the near distance, though, grazing cows populated the rolling fields. Anne and Chris breathed more deeply.

Just before they reached the city limits of New Braunfels, Anne exited the highway and turned west on a looping road that widened and narrowed seemingly at whim. Here, too, occasional neighborhoods bloomed out of the rustic environment, but for the most part trees filled the view. Most of them were evergreens, or oaks that hadn't lost their leaves during the winter, but here and there newly blossomed trees shone bright green.

Chris looked over at Anne to find her glancing at him. "Your father didn't strike me as the rural type," he said.

Anne started to answer, changed her mind, and smiled. She put her hand over Chris's on the seat and drove on. Two miles farther on she turned off the road onto a smaller, narrower one for which the trees barely gave way. Not far down that lane she turned right into a gravel trail. Almost immediately a gate stopped her. Anne rolled down her window and punched numbers into the code box standing beside the drive. The metal gate jerked and rolled out of the way.

"You still remember the code?" Chris asked.

"He gave it to me with the invitation."

They rolled down the trail, which very quickly opened out into a wide parking area. On the other side a long, wide lawn sloped up to an imposing two-story house, wide and defiantly white, with no effort to blend into the landscape. The house had dark brown trim, tall arched windows on the ground floor, and wide, high double front doors. Three chimneys rose from the roof.

Chris whistled. "You never told me you were Anne of Green Gables."

They got out of the car and stood close, looking over the grounds, which were extensive. Off to the left and behind the house Chris saw a gazebo, and he would have bet on finding a pool in the back. Anne stared at the house almost disdainfully, as if its lavishness embarrassed her. "I didn't grow up here. This isn't the old family homestead. Dad bought this place about ten years ago. Probably in a fire sale of some kind."

"That's too bad," Chris said, bumping her shoulder with his. "I was hoping to see the room where you spent your girlish years."

"Oh, they re-created that."

He couldn't tell whether she was joking.

They crossed the parking area and the lawn, and as they approached the front door Anne shamelessly took Chris's hand, which surprised him, here at her father's house. Anne didn't often act this way publicly. But she kept hold of his hand as she rang the doorbell.

A pause passed, long enough for Chris to make up stories in his mind: an empty house, a burglar, scurrying conspirators, or a man who'd never extended an invitation at all. Then one of the heavy double doors opened and a man blinked out from the dark interior. Morris Greenwald's head rose barely half as high as the tall doors. He had white crinkled hair, almost gone on top. His face showed deep creases in the cheeks and fine lines around his eyes, but his temples and a spot just above his forehead were surprisingly smooth and shiny. Mr. Greenwald looked compact and careful in his movements, but then his face and posture changed.

"Annie!" he cried, holding out his arms.

"Hello, Daddy." Anne stepped close to him and her father put one arm around her shoulders. They stood in a very tentative embrace like acquaintances posing for a picture. Anne, slightly taller than her father, bent to put her cheek against the side of his head.

Chris smiled at them. Anne quickly stepped away from her father and said, "You remember Chris."

"Of course." They shook hands, the older man gripping Chris's tightly.

Morris waved them into the house. The entryway was less impressive than Chris would have guessed from the outside, just a small foyer with a hallway leading straight back. Morris Greenwald put his arm around his daughter's waist. Anne turned on an overhead light and reached back for Chris. Morris led them toward a staircase. On the left Chris glimpsed a formal dining room. On the right side of the hall a dark door stood closed. From the other side they could hear voices, too indistinct to pick up words.

"Someone here?" Anne asked.

"Oh, you know, some people," Morris answered dismissively. Chris thought he was hurrying them up the stairs.

"I've made some changes. You'll like it."

Upstairs another short hallway to the left led to another set of double doors. Morris quickly opened them and waved, presenting a large sitting room, an elegant but less than formal living area with scattered chairs, love seats, windows on two sides, and a small fireplace with marble mantel.

"Oh, this is nice, Dad."

"Thank you. I designed it." Morris smiled at Chris, as if to say he hadn't forgotten his guest, and waved him in too.

"Very nice," Chris said, feeling inane.

"Somehow I like being up high when I relax," Morris explained. "Like I think a flood is coming, or an angry mob." He laughed at himself.

"You could be right about the mob," Anne said over her shoulder.

Morris shrugged self-deprecatingly, as if she had complimented him. "I'm not nearly as involved as I used to be."

Chris strolled around the room, trying to give the father and daughter room to speak privately. He discovered that one of the floor-length windows was actually a French door that gave onto a balcony. Chris stepped out onto it and found himself at the front of the house, standing above and to the right of the front doors, from his perspective looking out. Chris had missed seeing this balcony as he and Anne had walked up, thinking it was just ornamental filigree on the face of the house. The balcony was no more than five feet deep and ten feet wide. Bushes that decorated the front of the house reached high enough that their leaves brushed the underside of the balcony, like the outstretched fingers of that mob Morris Greenwald had fantasized about. The sides of the balcony were dark wrought iron in the shapes of twining leaves. They blended into those bushes from below, another reason Chris hadn't spotted the balcony.

Across the lawn Chris saw two more cars in the parking area than there had been when he and Anne arrived, making a total of half a dozen. People seemed to be arriving, though he didn't see anyone. Had Mr. Greenwald invited Anne for a special occasion?

He left the balcony and stepped back into the sitting room to see Anne and her father across the room looking out another window. Mr. Greenwald smiled shyly in a way that made him look much younger. Anne smiled back at him, but Chris knew her well enough to see the effort.

"Want to see your room?" Morris asked cheerfully.

Anne nodded. Chris cleared his throat and said, "I think I'll look around a little, if that's okay."

Morris gave him a curious glance, more than just perfunctory, as if Chris had announced an odd intention. Then the host said, "Sure." He took his daughter's arm and led her away, Anne trailing a long look at Chris. "Thought you wanted to see the room," she said in a voice with undertones.

Chris walked out after them. Hearing their voices down another hall, he went back downstairs, away from what he assumed to be the house's private rooms. He and Anne had brought overnight bags, prepared to spend the night here or in New Braunfels, but they were less than half an hour from their own beds. Morris's invitation hadn't been very specific.

That one dark door downstairs was still closed. Chris couldn't hear voices from behind it anymore. He went through the dining room, a beautiful, coldly elegant room that had obviously been furnished as a unit, rather than piece by piece over the years. Cream-colored, gilt-edged plates stood at attention behind the glass panels of the china cabinet.

Chris pushed through a swinging door and found himself in a kitchen standing almost nose to nose with a stone-faced man in a dark suit. It could have been a statue Chris had almost bumped into for all the man's expression changed. Chris brushed past him and they stood looking at each other. The older man had iron-gray hair, a somewhat fleshy yet hard face, and bright gray eyes. His wide shoulders carried his suit like a uniform and he stood with one hand behind his back in a stance that made Chris feel threatened. Under the dark suit the man wore a black dress shirt and dark tie as well. On his lapel a small dark-blue circle with a golden eagle gleamed, appearing like a piece of great ornamentation on the man's deliberately drab outfit.

The man said, "And you would be?"

Such a question always inspired in Chris the urge to give a ridiculous response—*You mean if I could be anyone I wanted?*—but he resisted that. "My name is Chris Sinclair. I'm here with Anne Greenwald?"

The man didn't look as if either name meant anything to him, but after a moment he thawed and said, "Sorry, sir. You weren't on my list."

"You're not on mine, either," Chris said, and walked out of the kitchen, deliberately giving the man a view of his back.

Strange little incident. It seemed characteristic of Morris Greenwald's compartmentalized house. The man's mention of a list made him sound like a servant, but he didn't look like one. Chris forgot about him as he explored the grounds. Morris might not be a rancher or a huge landowner, but he certainly didn't have to see his neighbors. This was on the edge of what Texans called the hill country, though Appalachians would have laughed at the slightness of the folds of the earth. But the land had a pleasant, rolling aspect, both isolating and liberating from Chris's vantage point. The land was wooded, too, with oaks and mesquites, hardy trees that couldn't be driven out by flood or drought.

That was the view. Closer at hand lay the pool Chris had predicted, a few steps beyond the back door of the house. A deck surrounded the water; the space looked as if it had been designed for parties rather than exercise. Chris walked around it and to the right, looking up at the house. From behind, the house looked smaller than he'd first thought, though still impressive, like grand dreams built to a practical scale.

Chris returned to the front of the house. Another car had added itself to the small herd. Apparently people kept slipping in without his seeing them. That made him want to remain outside. He was also trying to give Anne time alone with her father, perhaps even more than she wanted. That front of the house still looked elegant and large. Anne said she hadn't grown up here, but she had grown up in similar circumstances with Morris and her family. Chris studied the house as if studying Anne herself. She had sneered at its lavishness; she lived in a very different way from this now.

The sun declined toward the western hills. It must be six o'clock, but May and Daylight Saving Time held dusk at bay. Hands in his pockets, Chris walked up the lawn and around the house again to see that gazebo he'd spotted earlier. It was a classic affair, thin white columns supporting a decorative roof. It could have been a Victorian contemporary of the house or been ordered from Home Depot last month. As Chris approached it, he saw someone waiting for him. Morris Greenwald was standing in the gazebo, leaning on its rail, smoking a cigarette. So he hadn't spent much time with his daughter after all.

Chris would have turned back to the house, but Morris had

obviously already seen him, so Chris walked on and joined him.

"Like the house?" Morris asked impersonally, as if they were both guests.

"It's beautiful."

Morris shrugged. "I lose my perspective after a while. Can't really tell what it looks like until other people are here."

"Looks as if you're having several guests tonight."

"Yeah, some people are dropping by. You and Anne can meet them. Well, she knows most of them, I think."

Morris Greenwald opened what looked like a decorative plant holder on the inside wall of the gazebo. Inside was a metal ashtray with a lid, where he carefully put out the cigarette. Then he looked at Chris more directly. "So I hear you have a daughter."

"That's right. She lives with me."

"So you know what it's like. Being responsible, worrying about her."

"I certainly do."

"How long have you and Anne been together?"

They were standing a few feet apart, the older man leaning out of the gazebo, Chris below him with one foot on the step. Chris felt bemused. He had never been in a conversation exactly like this. Morris Greenwald didn't sound hostile or prying, but in fact rather detached. "You're very direct, aren't you?" Chris said to him.

"I used to be a lot more circumloquacious, believe me. Thought I could talk my way around anything. Always thought I was the smartest person in the room, too, so I knew I'd get what I wanted eventually. Nobody could read me but I could look at somebody and know what he was thinking."

Chris laughed.

"What's funny?"

"I didn't know attitude could be hereditary."

"So you think Anne's like that?" Morris asked with an unmistakable hint of pride. "How can you put up with her then?"

"It's easy, believe me." Chris fell into a momentary reverie, but the old man recalled him to business.

"So are you telling me you're in love with her?"

"No. I'm trying to avoid telling you anything. Am I being interviewed?"

"Excuse me for being interested. I think it's okay for a father in these circumstances to ask some questions."

"What circum—"

Chris heard a footstep close at hand and turned to see Anne stepping through the lush grass. She had obviously been there long enough to hear part of the exchange. Her arms were folded and she smiled. To Chris she said, "He's afraid of having blond, blue-eyed grandchildren and disappearing from the face of the earth."

Morris answered seriously, "I'd like to have some kind of grandchildren."

"You would?" Anne sounded genuinely surprised.

"What do you think I want out of life, just this stuff?"

"Yes."

The Greenwalds looked at each other exploringly. Chris could see Anne's determination in her father's face, a similarity in the curve of their shoulders, and perhaps more family resemblance than either of them had ever noticed. Chris coughed and said, "I'd slip away and let you two have some privacy, but I keep doing that and you keep following me."

Morris's face softened toward his daughter. "I'm curious, baby. It's been a long time since you've brought one of your boyfriends to meet me. I figured—"

"It's still been a long time, Daddy. I didn't bring him to meet you; I just brought him." She glanced at Chris. "Sorry, did that sound like an insult?"

"No," Chris laughed.

"I like having him along." Anne sounded embarrassed, so she shifted back to her father. "This grandbaby thing, have you talked to Bruce about it?"

Morris made a dismissive sound. "Bruce. All your brother cares about is making money, not babies."

"I wonder where he gets that?"

Morris turned to Chris and sounded philosophical. "Your children, it seems like each one just takes on one aspect of your personality. None of them's willing to embrace the whole, you know?" To Anne he answered her last remark. "I did both at the same time, you know."

Morris came down from the gazebo so they were all on the same level. Chris looked back and forth between them. "She's biting her lip, Mr. Greenwald. I think she's refraining from saying something."

Morris looked at his daughter contemplatively. "Probably a good thing."

"I guarantee it."

Morris took Anne's arm, she slid her other hand into Chris's, and the three of them began walking back toward the house.

"So what's the occasion, Daddy? Who's coming?"

"Just some old friends dropping by."

Anne squeezed Chris's hand.

Half an hour later Anne entered her father's upstairs sitting room to find company. The guests who had arrived by twos and threes had come out from behind closed doors and assembled. They weren't a large crowd, but the room felt full because the twenty or so people had spread throughout it in small groups and pairs. At first no one looked familiar to Anne. The men wore suits, so did most of the women, except one who wore a long dress. It looked like a formal cocktail party; that was probably what kept Anne from recognizing anyone. But then one face, that of a solemn-looking man talking to her father, grew familiar. Before Anne could place him, a voice spoke her name.

An elegant-looking lady in her sixties smiled broadly at Anne. "Why, little Anne, I haven't seen you in years. How are you?"

The lady claimed to have watched Anne grow up, but Anne barely remembered her. Across the room she spotted Chris, listening politely to a large man in a gray suit. Chris didn't glance over at Anne, but she felt his awareness.

She excused herself and crossed the room, nodding and smiling, until she came to her father, who beamed at her as if delighted and then said, "You remember Ben."

Anne had noticed the person in conversation with Morris mainly because of his sports coat, which was a striking cream color, almost yellow. In the room of dark suits it made him stand out, but it also stole attention from his face. Anne had taken him to be an earnest young man in his twenties, but in fact he was about Anne's age, as she knew well. Ben Sewell had a long, expressive face, with eyes that went soft as he looked at her and a mouth with a great number of white teeth. "Hello, Anne," he said, quietly as if giving a punch line. He continued watching her, smiling, waiting for her exclamation.

The two men obviously expected Anne to be startled, and she was. "Ben," she said rather loudly. She held out her hand to him and then changed her mind and clasped his arm instead. "Why, Ben, it's been ages. Do you live here?"

"In Austin," said the tall young man.

Anne looked back and forth from her father to Ben Sewell. "And are you two still—?"

Morris and Ben glanced at each other and Morris smiled. "Now and again," he said.

After a minute of chat, Morris excused himself, claiming hostly duties. He walked across his sitting room, smiling and nodding, stopping for a sentence or a laugh here and there but not letting anyone detain him until he reached Chris. "Ah, there you are," Morris said, with a joviality that sounded false. Chris thought it could be that Morris's expansive mood was real but that he had lost the sincerity necessary for expressing such a mood. Morris took his arm and said, "Let me introduce you to someone. Nick, do you know Chris Sinclair? Nick Winston. I thought you two might know each other, both being elected officials. Nick is on the Railroad Commission."

A thin man with alert brown eyes and a mouth that seemed to be suppressing amusement turned around to be introduced. Nick Winston stood almost at attention, an impressive presence of tall calm in the chatter of the sitting room. For a long moment Winston devoted all his attention to Chris, undistracted. Under scrutiny like this Chris tended to go all innocent-looking. Winston looked at him deeply enough to give the impression of seeing through this pretense. He shifted his drink to shake Chris's hand. "And you?"

"I'm the district attorney of Bexar County."

Winston dipped his head as if impressed. "Of course. You put Malachi Reese on death row."

Chris went a little stiff. "Friend of yours?"

Nick Winston shook his head, still appearing on the verge of laughing. "I thought it was a good career move for Malachi. Made him famous." Winston put a friendly hand on Morris's shoulder. "And what brings you to this old sinner's house? Is he trying to suppress a prosecution?"

Morris said congenially, "Chris is Anne's friend."

"Oh." Winston looked across the room to where Anne and Ben Sewell remained in conversation. "And there she is talking to her old friend. I guess it's been a while, hasn't it, Morris?"

After a slight pause Morris Greenwald said to Chris, "Anne and Ben over there used to date. Years ago."

Chris nodded as if uninterested, aware of the other two watching him for reaction. He glanced over at the man talking to Anne. "Not everyone can wear yellow," he said of the young man's sports coat. Nick Winston laughed.

Morris continued explaining as if Chris had asked. "Then Ben and I went into business together. I don't know if that's what drove Anne away from him, but . . ."

Chris again looked across the room at Anne and Ben Sewell, almost involuntarily, because he still felt the the sidelong scrutiny of other two men. Anne stood looking up at the taller Sewell, laughing, what looked like her genuine laugh, not the obligatory one. Ben Sewell looked very gratified at having amused her. Chris knew the feeling.

Making conversation, he said, "What's the occasion, Mr. Greenwald? Just an ordinary weekend at your house?"

"Pretty much," Morris said, looking around with a self-satisfied air. "Few old friends dropping by."

They were both being disingenuous. Chris recognized one state senator and had been introduced to a man whose name he recognized as a well-known political consultant in Austin. Here and there a conversation looked more serious than cocktail party chitchat.

Nick Winston, by contrast, stood very much at ease, not

appearing to have any hidden agenda. He still wore that amused expression, especially since Morris's answer to Chris's question. Morris excused himself to be hostly and Chris found himself standing with his newly met acquaintance. It seemed remarkable to him, now that he thought about it, that Nick Winston didn't have anyone accompanying him. Railroad commissioner was an important, though archaically titled position in Texas; among other things, the Railroad Commission regulated the oil industry. But Winston seemed at ease on his own and showed no inclination to move on to someone more important than Chris. He glanced again across the room to where Anne and her old boyfriend remained in conversation.

"So how long have you and Anne been whatever the word is?" Winston asked.

"People keep asking me that tonight. I don't think duration is as important as depth, do you?"

Winston laughed, then answered seriously. "Old friends exert a certain pull on us."

"Is that what you are, an old friend of the family?"

"Morris and I've known each other a long time. Since the old days when he was important."

Looking around the room, Chris would have thought Morris Greenwald was still important. He could certainly draw a nice crowd to his house.

But before he could follow up with a question, something happened. Chris didn't know what, but it took Nick Winston away from him. Winston had a politician's trick of giving his full attention to the person with whom he was speaking, creating an instant feeling of intimacy. But now he looked over Chris's shoulder for the first time and something captured his attention. He lost his secretly amused expression, his eyes moved swiftly around the room, and he set down his drink on an end table.

"It's been nice meeting you," he said abruptly, taking Chris's hand again. Winston's was long-fingered and soft, and he didn't make a gripping contest out of the brief contact. "I hope we'll see each other again."

He gave Chris a swift but deep glance—the politician's habit again, possibly—and then strode away.

Chris couldn't see what had caught his attention. The room didn't appear to have changed, except that one of the double doors now stood open slightly. Someone might have signaled to Winston from there and then disappeared. No one else in the room seemed to have noticed anything; they went on with their drinking and talking.

Chris stood slightly at a loss, not wishing to intrude on Anne and her old friend and not seeing anyone else he wanted to meet.

"Bored?" Anne said.

Chris turned and looked at her. "Not now."

He had a way of making her feel beautiful, or charming. Anne still sometimes felt the beginning of a blush when he looked at her, especially in the midst of people like this. She took his arm and they strolled around the room, nodding and smiling.

"Do you know everyone?"

"About half," Anne said. "Though I keep running into people who claim to know me a lot better than I remember them."

"Maybe you've blanked out a large, unpleasant portion of your life."

"Maybe it just doesn't seem important anymore."

They stepped out onto the balcony to see the night, which

was fine, cool and clear with a sky full of stars, undimmed by city lights. Across the lawn more than a dozen cars filled the parking area, among them only a couple of sport utility vehicles standing tall. These guests seemed to be a traditional crowd, favoring Mercedeses and Cadillacs. A man in a dark suit was moving among the cars. He didn't look like a parking lot attendant. Chris frowned.

Anne leaned close against him and he forgot about the parking lot. "Is there a plan? Are we spending the night here?"

"Do you want to?" Anne's voice had that husky undertone again.

"That depends," Chris said carefully. She laughed.

"I think this is breaking up soon. Some of them are leaving, some are going into town for dinner. Daddy invited us along."

They went back inside. There did seem to be fewer people in the room. Even the host had left.

"Your old friend seems to have left, too," Chris observed.

Anne didn't sound guilty. "Someone told you about Ben?" She sighed. "It made me feel very odd seeing him. Like I owe him something. Not an apology, but attention . . . or more interest than I gave him before. Poor old Ben."

Chris liked the sound of that. "Do you want to go to dinner with them?"

Anne turned to him with a smile. "Not really. What else do you have in mind?"

Anne had to search through the house to find Morris, finally having to knock on one of those closed doors. Morris emerged looking grim and harried, and didn't appear upset by the news when Anne told him that she and Chris wouldn't be joining him for dinner. "Come back after," he said, patting her hand. "We'll have a drink and a chat."

"Are you all right?"

"Oh, sure." Morris rolled his eyes. "These people—you can't get rid of them. And everything has to turn into politics. I'll see you later, sweetheart."

Chris, getting the car from the largely depopulated parking area, didn't see the dark-suited man anymore. He started the car with a slight wince, thinking of gangsters and bombs, then drove around to the front of the house to pick up Anne. She emerged looking thoughtful, but soon put it aside.

"Tell me all about this great love affair you had with Yellow-jacket."

"Can't I keep any of my secrets?" Anne said lightly.

"Sure. Let's talk about you and your father instead."

Anne settled back in her seat. "I met Ben in college. We were both at Baylor in different majors. And he kind of followed me around like a puppy, until one day I took him home and my father made me keep him . . ."

Later, when Anne and Chris were coming back from pizza in New Braunfels, the house seemed more isolated than it had before. Chris almost missed the turnoff from the road. Inside Morris Greenwald's gate the road was composed of caliche, a white rock that made the road shine in the darkness, a broad pale path. This road took perhaps a quarter of a mile to reach the house. As Chris drove, Anne leaned against him and laughed, but above her amusement he heard or sensed something outside. He slowed down and steered the car to the edge of the path. Seconds later a black sedan, looking cloaked in the dimness, hurtled toward them. Chris moved the car even farther aside, edging off the road. The heavy, dark car didn't slow down. If anything it went even faster as it passed them, throwing up shards of caliche in its wake. Chris turned to look at it as the car passed a mere foot from him, but the moment went too quickly; he couldn't see anyone inside the car. There had been several such cars at Morris's earlier.

Because the car had seemed to be fleeing, he half-expected trouble at the house, but it stood unalarmed as they came within sight. Chris drove up to the front door of the house. "Shouldn't you—?" Anne started to suggest.

"Oh, are we staying? That's fine, that's fine. Why don't you go on in and sound out your father and I'll park."

Anne realized that Chris kept trying to throw her together with her father, but she didn't object. She stepped out of the car and Chris drove it around the circular drive and up toward the parking area. Anne stopped for a long moment in the cool night air and breathed in the country scents, blends of new grass and decay. The stars were bright but the moon didn't give much light. Anne looked for it and found it more than three-fourths of the way up to the peak of the sky, a bright but narrow slice of white. The moon hovered in its last phase before going dark altogether, a sliver of a moon that looked like a scimitar cutting through the night sky. An atmospheric decoration, but ineffective as lighting.

Her hand on the doorknob, Anne suddenly became aware

of voices. It must be a loud argument going on, if she could hear it through the closed door. Then Anne realized the voices were carrying too distinctly. She looked up and saw two men on the balcony. Light spilled onto one end of the balcony from inside the room, but the men were standing in the shadowed part, smudges against the pale wall of the house.

As Anne peered upward she recognized Ben Sewell, partly by his distinctive jacket. She started to call to him, but he was engaged in a confrontation that she didn't want to interrupt. The other man on the balcony yelled at Ben that he was an idiot. Ben protested, and the argument became physical. The other man pushed Ben back against the wall. Ben, tall and rather soft-looking but strong for all that, stepped forward and shoved the other man back, almost to the railing of the balcony.

The scene changed character abruptly, and Anne felt unable to move. The other man's teeth gleamed in the moonlight, a fierce snarl. He sprang forward and grabbed Ben's collar. Ben, looking frightened, slapped at him, which further infuriated his attacker. The man's hand disappeared, then emerged again—Anne could see the hands because they were white against the dark background of the man's suit. He pushed something hard against Ben Sewell's head. Just as Anne realized the object was a gun and drew in her breath to scream, a sharp crack broke the night. Ben slumped and collapsed on the railing of the balcony.

Anne did scream. The killer stepped back, into the light from the sitting room. Nick Winston stared down at her from the balcony. Though obviously startled to find himself observed, his eyes quickly narrowed and focused on Anne. Then he moved swiftly, coming toward her.

He was thirty feet above her, a safe interval, but Anne still recoiled. Winston looked so fierce it seemed he could leap the distance between them. Anne turned, flung open the door of the house, and ran toward the stairs.

After Chris parked the car he thought he saw someone in the gazebo, wondered if it could be Morris Greenwald, and began walking that way, then thought he might be interrupting a private conversation, so he turned back in the direction of the house. So he approached it from the opposite side of the balcony. He couldn't see the front door; the bushes blocked his view.

Chris walked along slowly, hands in his pockets, looking at the ground. Then a sound drew his attention, a sound so sudden and startling he couldn't immediately place it. He looked up quickly, toward the front door of the house. He saw nothing unusual, and began walking toward the house. Again he scanned the front of the building. This time his attention was drawn to the balcony. Half of it was dark, and in that dark portion someone moved. Chris focused and recognized Ben Sewell standing there alone, very recognizable in his height and his yellow jacket. He seemed to be looking out toward Chris, or the parking area. Then he lifted a hand to his head, his hand in an unusual position. He held something. In the next moment Chris heard a loud retort, the sound startling and echoing in the night. Chris realized a gun had been fired, and that that was the object in Ben Sewell's hand. He had just shot himself in the head as Chris watched.

The man fell forward over the railing of the balcony, which hit him at the waist. His legs lifted high, then turned as the body continued to fall forward. Sideways, the legs came forward over the balcony railing, like those of a high jumper barely missing a jump. The body dropped into the tall bushes just below the balcony.

Chris stood stock-still for a long moment, unable to believe what he'd seen, waiting for the night to fill with sounds of response. But he heard nothing else. Chris began running. He couldn't see Anne or anyone else alive, and felt very alone in the night.

★ Chris fought his way through the bushes below the balcony. They were thick, resistant cedars, with many small branches that scratched his face and hands. No light or sound guided him, but then he heard the noises of something moving ahead of him. He pushed through and found himself in a clear space just underneath the balcony. Ben Sewell lay there on his back, his yellow sports coat looking even more ridiculous in its disarray. A blackened wound on the right side of his head corresponded with what Chris had seen happen on the balcony.

A man knelt beside the body, reaching a hand toward it. At the sound of the bushes parting the man turned, and Chris saw it was Nick Winston, the guest he had met earlier. The man had completely lost his sardonic amusement. The paleness of his face, emphasized by a long scratch across his cheek, made his eyes look darker. His hand shook as he withdrew it from the body.

"Should we move him? I—I don't know what—what you're supposed to . . ."

Chris moved forward, stooping to replace Winston at the body's side. He put his hand first to Ben Sewell's neck, then to his wrist. He felt no movement within the still, doughy flesh.

"No," he said. "He's dead. Let's leave him right where he is until the police come."

"God," Winston said shakily, drawing back.

Chris stood up, feeling officialness settle over him. He had seldom been in on the beginning of a case, but he had often, as a prosecutor, wished he had been. Like most lawyers, he'd always thought he could manage a crime scene better than the police officers who usually became his witnesses. His mind raced with thoughts of what to do. Don't disturb the body—or the scene, to the extent possible. And obtain witness statements immediately, before they had time to think or compare notes.

"Let's get out of here and make a call." Chris took Winston's arm and guided him past the body. Along the front of the house the bushes had been cut back to leave a path. Branches crossed it, but not as thickly. Chris guided them through that, looking for footprints or other signs, but it was too dark to see anything that small. Besides, Chris knew what had happened. He had seen it.

When they reached the porch, under its light Chris saw scratches on Winston's thin, aristocratic face. Chris's face probably bore similar marks, from his plunge through the bushes. Taking a phone from his pocket, he said, "Where did you come from?"

"I was walking around the house," Winston said at once. "I'd just had a—well, never mind, it's not important, but I was walking around thinking when I heard the shot. I looked up and saw Ben go over the railing, so I ran in here."

"Through the bushes?" Chris asked.

"I guess—no, I think I came along that path, because it

wasn't hard, I got here in a matter of seconds. He was lying there, and I thought I heard him breathing, or moaning, so I bent to see if I could help him. Then you came out of the bushes and scared the shit out of me."

Chris nodded. Into his phone he said, "My name is Chris Sinclair. I'm at the home of Morris Greenwald, out off Ruekle Road. We have a dead man here. . . . Yes. It's all right, I'll stay here. I'm a prosecutor, I'll keep people from—Yes, ma'am. Thank you."

He clicked off and he and Winston looked at each other. What Winston had said corresponded with what Chris had seen. He tried to think of more questions. "Did you see Ben Sewell up on the balcony, before you heard the shot?"

Winston raised his eyes over Chris's head, thinking. "I think so, but I'm not sure. I didn't even see Ben's face, I don't think. I recognized him by that jacket."

Chris nodded.

"Then of course on the ground I saw his face," Winston concluded. He shuddered.

"Did you see anyone else up on the balcony?"

Winston didn't answer. "Did you? Who do you think—?"

"Nobody," Chris said. "He shot himself. I saw it."

"Ben?" Winston stared. "But why would he—? Oh, damn!"

"What?"

"I—nothing. It would just be speculation, I can't—Let's go inside."

Chris put his hand on the front doorknob, then said, "Oh, hell."

"What?"

"The gun. Did you see it?"

Winston shook his head again. Chris felt torn, wanting both to go back into the bushes and up to the balcony. He didn't think anyone else would come along to find the body, though.

If they'd heard anything they would have been here by now. "Let's go up."

Inside, Winston put a handkerchief to his mouth, mumbled "Excuse me," and went into a bathroom. He looked as if he might throw up, and Chris didn't blame him. He, too, felt the physical revulsion of touching the dead body. But it wasn't his first time.

The ground floor of Morris Greenwald's house sat empty and silent. When Chris had left here two hours ago everyone had supposedly been leaving. Had Ben Sewell remained behind, or come back by himself? And what about Winston? But these questions only sprang from his habit of re-creating events. He had seen what had happened here. Case closed.

Winston returned, his face damp but looking more composed. He and Chris went hurriedly up the stairs and along the hall to the sitting room. Its double doors were thrown open wide. As they approached Anne came running out, her eyes wild. She drew to an abrupt halt, sucking in breath. Her eyes changed from frightened to glaring.

"Good, you got him," she said to Chris. "Don't just stand there with him. We've got to—"

She raised her right hand and for the first time Chris saw that she held a pistol. She pointed it straight at Nick Winston.

Chris stepped between them, which took a lot of nerve, because Anne's hand holding the gun trembled slightly, and Chris could see the hammer cocked back. "What the hell are you doing?"

Anne looked puzzled, even as she moved to try to keep Winston in her sights. "Don't you know? We've got to arrest him, Chris. He killed Ben."

Chris stared at her. When he found his voice, he spoke very calmly. "No, Anne, he didn't."

The moment stretched out. Anne turned her head to stare

at Chris. He felt the skin along his shoulders and arms crawl with the expectation of something horrible happening. Chris glanced back over his shoulder. Nick Winston hadn't moved. His face had grown, if possible, more pale. Chris felt Anne's hand shake, making the gun barrel vibrate near his arm.

He stepped closer and whispered to her. Anne didn't seem to understand what he said. "Do it," Chris said more loudly.

Anne suddenly dropped the gun to her side and walked quickly away. Winston drew a shaky breath. "What the hell was that all about?"

"I don't know," Chris said. He looked at Winston strangely. Again the scene on the balcony passed through Chris's mind, Ben Sewell suddenly raising a gun to his head and firing. Chris's own head jerked as he seemed to hear the sound again.

He and Winston went into the sitting room. Winston took out a cigarette. He stood very self-contained, turned slightly away, his eyes moving back and forth but apparently not seeing anything.

Anne's footsteps sounded, returning quickly along the hall. Winston turned and then flinched as light flashed in his face. He stared again, startled.

Anne lowered the camera, looking triumphant. Everyone paused.

Then Chris said, "Take some more, Anne. Of all of us."

As Anne raised the camera again, Winston didn't exactly pose, but he stood still, face unshielded. He looked across the room at Chris. This was how the young district attorney had distracted his girlfriend from shooting Winston. After a moment, when Anne stopped snapping his picture, the trace of a smile returned to Winston's face, aimed in congratulations at Chris.

★

District Attorney Andrew Gunther strode into Morris Green-wald's entrance hall. Gunther must have had a good relation-ship with the sheriff's office, because he arrived on the heels of the deputies sent in response to Chris's 911 call. Gunther planted his boot-shod feet firmly on the hardwood floor, put his fists on his hips, and said with satisfaction, "I've always wanted to see the inside of this place."

Gunther stood about six-two, with a large head that nar-rowed as it rose. His stomach extended impressively and solidly. He was used to dominating a room and so didn't work at it. He turned to Chris Sinclair, who had opened the door for him, and said, "Andy Gunther," extending a meaty hand. In his other hand he carried a small paper sack.

Chris introduced himself and Gunther said, "Good to meet you, Chris." Actually they had met two or three times in the past, at conferences, nothing memorable. Chris knew Gunther as the district attorney of this county and by reputa-tion, which was that of a good old boy who'd become pretty well known in high school and college as a football player and parlayed that fame into elected office. Chris remem-bered a defense lawyer saying, "It's easy to underestimate him, but sometimes it's a mistake. Only sometimes, though."

"So what's the story?" Gunther asked, looking around the entry hall. He took Chris aside into the dining room, so they had a private moment.

"Have you talked to the officers?" Chris asked. "Seen the body?"

Gunther shook his head dismissively. "You saw it, didn't you?"

"Anne and I—Anne Greenwald, the daughter of the man who lives here—Anne and I were coming back from having dinner in town. I dropped her off, then I was walking back here from the parking area up there and I saw the dead man,

Ben Sewell, up on the balcony. He put a gun to his head and shot himself."

Gunther nodded. He'd obviously already heard the story. "Where is everybody?"

"Upstairs. I tried to keep everyone together and out of the way."

Gunther led the way back to the entry hall and up the stairs. Chris said to his back, "I barely knew the dead man. I'd just met him this evening."

Andy Gunther turned with an amused expression, stopping so suddenly that Chris bumped into him. Grinning, Gunther said, "I knew Ben Sewell, and I know who Anne Greenwald is. I know what they were to each other a few years ago, too. You'd be a good suspect for this, if not for who you are." Gunther winked. A man who loved his job, loved his position in the world, liked holding secrets.

They walked into the sitting room. A sheriff's deputy stood there, not talking to the others, just watching. Morris Greenwald was sitting in a chair, a woman who looked about his age close to him. Anne was standing in the center of the room. She glared across it in the direction of Nick Winston, who leaned against the wall near the balcony, his arms folded and his eyes watchful. He didn't return Anne's stare.

As soon as the two district attorneys entered, Winston pushed himself off the wall and came toward them, as Morris Greenwald stood up. Both began speaking, but Andy Gunther turned toward Nick Winston, who said his name. The two men shook hands. Winston still looked pale and troubled. One's first dead body will have that effect for some time, Chris remembered.

"Hello, Commissioner," Andy Gunther said heartily. "How'd you get mixed up in this?"

"Is he really dead, Andy? I mean, Mr. Sinclair and I

checked him, but we only had a moment, we didn't—"

"Oh yes, he's dead. Gunshot to the head will do that about nine times out of ten. I understand you found the body?"

Anne said loudly, "He knows very well he's dead. He killed him."

The district attorney looked at her, then turned back to Nick Winston with a raised eyebrow. Winston shrugged, as if he'd already put up with too much already. Gunther turned and walked slowly to Anne, looking her over speculatively. Chris followed. He wanted to advise Anne to take that high, hard look off her face if she wanted to sound credible. Gunther said, "What's that, ma'am?"

"I saw the murder."

Chris interrupted. "You know, you should interview the witnesses separately, that way—"

"Oh, I don't think we need to follow all the procedures," Gunther drawled. "We all know them here, don't we? Go ahead, Ms. Greenwald."

In a very controlled voice, not looking at anyone except Gunther, Anne said, "I was standing at the front door, about to go in. I heard men's voices and looked up and saw the two of them on the balcony, Ben and Mr. Winston. They were arguing. They started pushing each other, then suddenly Mr. Winston pulled out a gun, put it right to Ben's head, and fired. I screamed, and he saw me." She shot a glance at Nick Winston.

Gunther obviously began to take her more seriously. "Come show me."

Anne was eager to do so. She led him to the balcony, and the two of them, along with Chris, stepped out onto it. Below they could see three sheriff's deputies on the lawn. They had finished photographing the death site and collecting evidence, and stood together chatting and smoking.

"Where were you?" Andy Gunther asked.

"At the front door," Anne repeated, pointing. Gunther looked down there, measuring distances.

"And the men? Where were they exactly?"

"On this end of the balcony. Closer to me."

"But out of the light. Was there some other light that's been turned off now?"

"No," Anne admitted.

Gunther looked down toward the front porch again. "And you could see over the bottom of the balcony—it didn't block your view? And the men were here in the dark, but you recognized them?"

"Well, I knew Ben's voice, and he was wearing this jacket you couldn't miss. I didn't recognize Mr. Winston until after he'd shot Ben, when he stepped into the light from the room."

"Which would have taken him back here." Gunther walked backward. "I can barely see the front door from here, ma'am."

"Of course you can," Anne said adamantly.

"What about you?" Gunther asked of Chris. "Did you see anything like that?"

Chris shook his head unhappily. "I was over there, coming from the other direction. I couldn't see Anne from where I was. And like I told you . . ."

Gunther let Chris tell his story again without interruption, until the end.

"Then, when you got through the bushes, Nick Winston was already there. He said he'd been walking around the house, you said."

Chris nodded, seeing the implication Gunther had already caught. Gunther turned to Anne. "In the few seconds between Chris seeing the shot and his getting through the bushes, I don't see there was time for Nick Winston to come all the way down through the house and through those bushes himself, if he started where you said he did. Plus he would have had to come right past you. Did he?"

Anne shook her head. "But he did it. I saw him."

Gunther looked at her with the speculative look back on his face. He made an odd sucking sound with his mouth, a sound that could be taken for speculation or derision. "Let's go hear what the others say."

Back in the sitting room, Gunther asked, "Was anybody else inside the house at the time the shot was fired?"

The deputy answered, pointing his chin toward Morris Greenwald. "They were."

Morris had been waiting for his chance to speak. He patted the hand of the lady who seemed to be with him and came forward. "Yes sir, I was in here. In fact, I must have just been coming back up here from downstairs when the shot was fired. I'm not sure; I didn't hear it. I had been downstairs seeing off Mrs. Pettigrew, when she realized she'd left her coat up here, so I came to retrieve it. I heard some noise or confusion out on the balcony, but when I looked out there I didn't see anything."

"All that's true," the lady on the settee said suddenly, and came to stand beside Morris. She was the lady, Alice Pettigrew, who had remembered Anne hours earlier. Mrs. Pettigrew still looked elegant in spite of the evening's events. She had a way of raising her chin slightly so that she seemed to be looking down questioningly at anyone with whom she talked. Her blue eyes fluttered frequently. She looked to be sixty or so, but well kept.

"Morris was seeing me out. We didn't hear anything. He

came up here to get my jacket. I thought it was taking him too long, that perhaps someone had taken the coat by accident, when the front door flew open and Anne came rushing in. She ran right past me without seeming to see me and ran up the stairs. I followed, of course. When I reached this room, she was out on the balcony. I couldn't see what she was doing. When she came back into the room she had a gun in her hand."

"Yes, the gun," Gunther said. He opened the paper bag he'd been carrying all along and pulled out a pistol inside a plastic bag. The pistol was a black revolver, with a very textured hand-grip. It looked rather small in Andy Gunther's large hand, but Chris knew from experience that it would be heavier than it looked.

"This is the gun," Gunther said. "Whose is it?"

No one answered. Gunther looked at each of them in turn. Then he smiled grimly. "Well, that will be bad for somebody, when I find out who owns it."

"Maybe it was Ben Sewell's," Nick Winston suggested quietly.

"Wait a minute, let me see it," Morris said. Gunther held it out, still in its plastic bag. Morris peered closely.

"It might be mine," he said. "I've got one like that. I think it's downstairs in a desk drawer. Or was."

Gunther shot a glance at Chris, who tried to keep a neutral expression, though he knew what his fellow district attorney was thinking. People who don't keep track of their guns tend to get themselves in trouble.

Turning to Anne, Gunther said, "And then you came up here and picked it up. Haven't you ever seen any crime shows on TV? Didn't you know you were supposed to—"

"I'd just seen a murder," Anne said hotly. "And the murderer saw me. I didn't know where he was. When I saw a gun I picked it up, yes. For protection. I realized it might be evidence, but I also didn't want to get killed, thank you."

"I understand. But of course you understand that in the process you probably ruined any fingerprints the gun might have held." Gunther scratched the back of his head. "What I will want to do is run paraffin tests on everyone's hands, especially Mr. Winston, since you've been accused, and Mr. Greenwald, because you were inside."

Chris gave a small cough and Gunther turned to him. "Winston went to the bathroom before we came up here," he said apologetically.

Gunther put his fists on his hips again, which had the effect of banging the pistol in its plastic bag against his leg. Gunther didn't seem to notice. "You gave him a chance to wash his hands?"

"I didn't know he was a suspect. I told you what I'd seen."

Gunther shook his head in exasperation at his fellow district attorney.

Anne stepped up to the discussion again. "I'd like to know how much evidence you need before you make an arrest? You've seen the body and you've heard me. I saw Nick Winston commit murder. What more do you need?"

Gunther looked as if he were trying to be unaccustomedly delicate. "Well, ma'am, there are some contradictions. And given Mr. Winston's position, I don't think he's going to flee the state. He should be safe enough while we investigate."

"And what about me?" Anne said.

Gunther looked at Winston, who lifted his hands, palms outward, and looked like the least dangerous person in the room. "Get a restraining order on me, whatever you want. I'm not going near her. Besides, I live in Austin. And I'd like to go back there tonight if that's all right, Mr. Gunther."

The district attorney glanced at Chris as if silently asking his advice. Chris didn't say anything. Gunther said, "That's fine, Mr. Winston. Just stay in touch, all right? And I'd appreciate it if you could give me a written statement. Starting with what this meeting was all about."

"Just a party," Winston said coyly, regaining some of his earlier attitude. He shook his host's hand, said, "Thank you, Morris, for a lovely evening," and quickly walked toward the door, before anyone could call him back.

"I'll walk out with you," Chris said suddenly, to everyone's surprise. Winston shrugged and didn't protest. The two men left the room together.

In his wake Andy Gunther said, "Let's go over this one more time."

"You're letting the murderer walk away!" Anne said loudly. Gunther looked at her as if she were being pushy.

Chris returned in only a couple of minutes, by which time Gunther had heard Anne's story again. His face showed that he remained unconvinced. The district attorney moved on.

"Let's go over a few things. First of all, I want a complete guest list. Who else was here?"

Morris Greenwald answered, "At the time Ben was shot? Nobody."

It seemed to Chris, looking at the side of Morris's face, that the older man studiously avoided looking back at him. Chris thought about that parking area filled with cars. Who had lingered behind? How many cars had been parked there when Chris had returned from dinner? He couldn't remember.

And what about that black sedan hurtling down the caliche road when Chris and Anne returned from dinner? It had looked like someone fleeing a crime scene, but the crime hadn't happened yet. From what had the people in the car been running?

★

"I'm just saying you're not going to get anywhere that way," Chris said.

"You don't believe me, do you, Chris?"

"I saw something different," he said apologetically.

Anne put her hands on her hips and stood in the center of the sitting room just looking at Chris. He was watching her as well. Anne's cheeks were red with anger. She had witnessed a murder, accused someone of it, and been roundly ignored. The murderer was driving home to Austin, while Anne stood in her father's living room being interrogated.

Chris turned to Morris Greenwald. Again Morris was sitting on the love seat, now alone, Mrs. Pettigrew having finally gone home, though with obvious reluctance. Her presence had seemed to annoy Anne as well, but Anne's temper hadn't improved when the lady had exited.

"What was this evening about, Mr. Greenwald? What did Ben Sewell and Nick Winston have an argument about?"

"I don't know. I wasn't here."

"Who else was here? Were there any late arrivals after Anne and I left?"

Morris looked up at him levelly. "No."

Something tugged at Chris's memory, but he couldn't bring it up. "Everything will come out," he said. "Andy Gunther has to decide who he believes, and lying to him is going to arouse his suspicion."

"I'm not lying." Morris still looked guileless.

"I don't believe you," Chris said flatly. "And I guarantee the district attorney of this county doesn't either."

"He doesn't believe anyone in the family," Anne said to her father.

Chris turned back to her. As clearly as Anne, he knew what he had seen, and he had no reason to distort matters. He didn't know Ben Sewell or Nick Winston. He barely knew

Morris Greenwald. Anne knew them all; she went back years with them. "How well do you know Nick Winston?" Chris asked.

"I hardly know him at all. But I know what he looks like. I can recognize him when he's staring down at me from a balcony."

"That's not what I'm talking about." Chris turned back to Morris. "What about Winston and Ben Sewell? Did they know each other well?"

Morris shrugged. "I don't think so. But they both lived in Austin, maybe they saw each other there. I think I introduced them, though, and that was only about six months ago."

"Why?"

"Why? Ben and I were involved in a couple of projects together, and I knew Nick. It never hurts to know people. Get them together and see what clicks. That's what I've always done."

"They didn't click too well tonight." Chris remembered something. "When I told Winston I'd seen Ben shoot himself, Winston seemed to think of something that would have given Ben a reason to do that. What was that?"

"I have no idea."

"Damn it, Morris, you're sounding guiltier and guiltier!"

Chris exchanged a look with Anne. She didn't believe her father either.

Morris stood up from the love seat and gestured with his hands. "Ben and I were talking to Nick about one of our projects. Nick's a railroad commissioner, he was in a position to help. But of course you don't just put it to him like that. But Ben was a little too—pointed. He wasn't very good at introducing ideas subtly. Nick told him so." Morris shrugged his shoulders again. "It made Ben look a little silly, but it certainly wasn't humiliating. Nothing to kill yourself over."

"Or reason for Nick Winston to kill him," Anne interjected. "No, certainly not that."

Anne had renewed the controversy between herself and Chris. He looked at her seriously. "How is it possible for both the things we saw to have happened?"

"I don't know." But she began to sound more puzzled than angry.

"I saw Ben Sewell alone on the balcony, and you saw two men. Is it at all possible—just think about it, Anne—that it wasn't the two you thought it was?"

Anne gave the idea some consideration. But she could still picture the scene too vividly. "No. I'm sure."

Chris thought of angles and lines of sight, of the possibility of Nick Winston stepping into the light from the room, rather than from the balcony.

"Maybe it's the time sequence we don't understand," Chris went on. "I didn't see you there, you didn't see me. Maybe we saw things at slightly different times."

"Then Ben died twice. Or—" Anne thought. "It could have happened the way I thought, except Winston didn't kill Ben. I didn't see the gun actually against Ben's head when he fired it. Maybe he just did it to scare Ben, or maybe he just grazed him. Then Winston left, I ran inside, and you walked up. Ben came to . . ."

Morris said, "And was so embarrassed that someone had tried to kill him that he shot himself in remorse?"

"Plus that doesn't explain why you didn't see Winston coming downstairs through the house," Chris added.

"All right, I tried," Anne said. "So one of us is wrong."

She and Chris gave each other a long look. Then Chris spoke to her very seriously. "Where'd you put the camera?"

★

Outdoors, the thin sliver of a moon had risen higher. Its light and the starlight lay softly on the earth, like frost. The house spilled light, but a few steps away the night deepened. The woods seemed to have encroached nearer. They could no longer see the parking area or the gazebo.

"What are we taking pictures of?" Anne asked. She was holding her father's camera that she'd used earlier, a small 35 millimeter film model with automatic focus.

"The view from the front door to the balcony, first of all. Good. Take one more. Now let's take some of the bushes. Get as close as possible. Is there enough light?"

As Anne took more photos, Chris explained. "The deputies probably took pictures of all this, but they thought they were working on a suicide, so they might not have been too thorough. I want to make sure we have everything."

"Everything like what?"

"Broken twigs," Chris answered, indicating one on a bush limb. "See which way they bend. What about footprints?" Chris pointed the flashlight Morris had also loaned him at the ground and Anne willingly snapped more pictures. This job of investigation appeased her.

"Why did you go out with Nick Winston? What did you say to him?" Anne asked.

"Not much. It wasn't him I wanted to talk to. When I got outside here I made sure the deputies took a picture of him, too. That might be more official than the ones you took."

"Why?"

"For evidence. To show what he looked like tonight. How his face was scratched."

Anne gazed at him more fondly than she had in hours. Obviously, Chris took what she'd said seriously. In his methodical way he was going around trying to prove something, rather than to talk her out of what she thought she'd seen.

Anne took photographs, feeling professional and productive. The task obviously didn't provoke the same feelings in Chris. When she ran out of film, he was standing back, staring up at the house. Feeling Anne's eyes on him, Chris said, "Something went on in this house that neither of us saw. This wasn't just a social occasion. Your father knows what it was. Maybe it would be better if you talked to him alone. He might tell you. After all, he wanted you here."

"He's never told me a secret in his life, Chris. He'd be more likely to tell you."

Anne and Chris decided to spend the night, to be on the scene in case Morris sobbed out a confession in the middle of the night. That didn't happen. Instead Anne woke up during the night. She'd made a joke about her father re-creating her childhood bedroom here in this house where she'd never lived, but in fact it *was* furnished with the furniture from her old room, and a few pictures of Anne and her brother at various stages of growth. It felt eerie to wake up there, as if she'd caught an eddy of time and been caught up in a whirlpool that swept her through different years.

The room held no photos of her mother, but what could she expect? It held enough to comprise a block of the past.

After it became clear to Anne that she couldn't fall right back to sleep she got up and slipped out of the bedroom door, padding quietly down the hall in her bare feet, wearing a silky, pale-blue, knee-length nightgown, not old-ladyish but not her sexiest number, either. She remembered her father keeping his house very cold, but that wasn't so anymore. The air felt cool but too close.

The house held reminders of the guests from the evening before. Anne almost thought she could hear them. She hesitated for a moment before opening the sitting room door. But the room inside lay empty and dim. She sat down for a moment, near where she had had her last conversation with Ben Sewell. Feeling as if she could turn her head and see him, or sit very quietly and hear him talking, Anne realized she had focused too much on Ben's killing and the murderer, and not enough on Ben himself—what he'd felt during that last evening, what his last moments had been like. While she'd talked to him, Anne had felt Ben inclining toward her. Maybe that had only been a matter of nostalgia, but possibly it reflected genuine longing. Ben had never gotten what he'd wanted from their brief relationship. Neither had Anne, except out of it. She felt now that she'd been too abrupt.

A tear grew in the corner of her eye. The dead always make the living feel guilty. Anne stood up and walked to the door to the balcony. She found it unlocked. Morris probably seldom locked this second-story door; he didn't really fear that imaginary angry mob he'd mentioned. But the bushes grew right up to the underside of the balcony. An agile climber might be able to make his way into the house through this passage.

Nevertheless, Anne opened the door and stepped out onto the empty balcony. Here she did feel crowded by ghosts, not only of the dead but of the living. She felt Nick Winston's eyes on her. Looking down, she even imagined herself at the front door, looking up to here. Had she really seen what she thought she had? Anne had been emphatic to others, but inevitably, as the memory receded, she grew less certain.

Suddenly she shivered, seemed to feel eyes on her again, and went back inside. She locked the door and walked quickly back to her bedroom. She moved toward the bed, starting to feel foolish, like a little girl about to hide under the covers, when she gasped. The bed was occupied.

Chris sat up. "I was afraid I'd startle you if I followed you out onto the balcony."

"So you preferred to startle me here?"

"I hoped it would be more like a pleasant surprise."

Anne lay down beside him. In the narrow twin bed they were very close. Their legs entwined. Chris wore only pajama pants. His eyes closed, he still seemed drowsy, but his hand moved along her hip.

"There's something about a girl's bedroom," he murmured. "Were you a teenager here? Is this where—?"

Anne laughed. "Shut up, you idiot. I told you this wasn't really my room."

Chris's hands gently tugged on the nightgown. He touched her bare leg. "But we can pretend," he said.

★ Chris Sinclair had a secret he would never have shared with anyone, even Anne: he liked Mondays. He woke up exhilarated, ready to jump out of bed before his alarm went off. Early Monday meant he had a long week before him in which to do the work he loved. He liked weekends, too, especially since Anne had come into his life, but work gave him his strongest feeling of self-worth, and he was usually glad to return to it.

Clarissa had some inkling of his secret. Clarissa, Chris's sixteen-year-old daughter, had come to live with him only a month or so earlier; sometimes they were still surprised to see each other in his condo. On Monday mornings he always had to call her name several times, even on late-spring mornings like this one when the sun was well up before Clarissa was, until she dragged herself out of the bedroom, older and grimmer and much more tired than she'd been the evening before. She looked even older than Chris remembered her mother when he'd first met her.

He knew better than to be chipper on such occasions, but couldn't stop himself. "Good morning!" he called from the kitchen, making her hesitate in the doorway as if she were deciding whether to turn around and go back inside. Clarissa was wearing the white blouse and plaid skirt required by her private school, but somehow made it look like a costume. At sixteen she had long legs, a thin frame, and an elongated, high-cheekboned, ethereal face. Or perhaps only Chris saw her that way, because she had appeared in his life already almost grown. He saw so many ghosts in her face, including his own.

"Hi, Darling." He gave her a gentle, one-armed hug and let her pick her own cereal. As she crunched it moodily she began to lighten up, but she glanced at Chris a few times, obviously annoyed or alarmed by his cheerfulness.

"Doesn't it make you look forward to being an adult?" he said cheerily. "To think of being glad to wake up in the morning?"

"No, so that I can sleep as late as I want."

He dropped her off a block from her high school—Clarissa wanted a car, but they hadn't agreed on the conditions of that yet—and watched her walk away. Clarissa had a sway to her hips that made the plaid skirt look inappropriate, but twenty yards on she turned and waved to him and smiled a big, sincere grin. Chris smiled back. Such moments made him easily able to put up with Clarissa's grumpiness at other times. He knew a good kid lurked in there, and that she loved him, even if she resented the idea.

Before Clarissa, Chris used to often be the first person into the Cadena-Reeves Justice Center on Monday mornings. Now the place was half-filled by the time he arrived. To Chris, the five-story building that held the criminal courts and the District Attorney's Office still felt new, in spite of being more than ten years old and crowded almost from the day it opened, because he had begun his legal career in the much, much older courthouse next door. The sturdy stone box of the Justice Center still looked like a bold kid next to the slouching old gothic courthouse across the street.

Chris found his way to his office in one of the top corners of the building, saying Hi and being greeted. From the speculative looks he got, some people apparently already knew the story of his adventure in New Braunfels. Of course, the looks could also have been because of the scratches that remained on his face from the branches of the bushes through which he'd pushed to find the body of Ben Sewell. "How was your weekend?" one of his assistants asked, thinking herself sly. A dead man was just something to talk about here, another file on a desk. Chris began to forget the weekend as he reached his own desk. In his office he felt happy, useful, and in control. Often, this Monday morning feeling lasted as long as half an hour.

Chris was standing beside his desk, glancing over the day's agenda and notes for his meeting with the county commissioners in the afternoon, when his first assistant, Paul Benavides, slouched into his office. Paul was one of those tall men who seemed embarrassed by his height. With his dark-rimmed glasses and perpetually solemn face he looked better suited to being a scholar than the basketball player nature had intended. Without a greeting, he dropped a two-inch-thick, bound stack of papers on Chris's desk. "Malachi Reese has filed his writ," he said.

"Good morning, Paul. And is it devastating? Does he make us all look like fools and scoundrels?"

"Mostly only you, I'm glad to say. My name isn't mentioned

at all, although the office as a whole does not come off looking our best."

Paul's humor was much more effective for never sounding as if he intended or understood that anything he said might be funny. Chris looked at the thick stack of pages, which he knew his first assistant would have scanned before delivery. "What's the worst of it?" he asked.

"Your testifying against him, in violation of several rules. Not only should his case be reversed as a result, but you should be disbarred."

Chris nodded. They had expected that. "And selective prosecution and seeking the death penalty for racial reasons," Paul continued.

"He won't get anywhere with that. Anything that does have a chance for him?"

"Enough to at least get a hearing. He'll be back in town."

Malachi Reese had been a well-known crusader in San Antonio, a political operative with innumerable connections and a national career set to blossom, until Chris had prosecuted him for capital murder and obtained a death sentence from a jury. Reese had proven himself far from powerless even on death row, however. He would be looking forward to returning to San Antonio for his writ hearing. He would be stretching out his invisible fingers now to see if he could still pull any strings.

And if Reese did manage to get his conviction reversed, Chris would have a very hard time re-trying him, because his main witness was dead.

"Let me see our response when we have one," Chris said mildly.

"Yes, sir. And how was New Braunfels?"

"You have a good network, Paul."

Paul smiled faintly. "There was a story in the New Braunfels Sunday paper, and in an office where three hundred people work someone would have seen it. Do you need any help there? Should we offer Andy Gunther assistance?"

"He wouldn't want it. I'm barely involved, anyway. Just a witness."

Chris remembered the experience of being a witness against Malachi Reese. Look how that had turned out. If this case somehow went to trial, he and Anne would contradict each other from the witness stand. Again Chris wondered how they could have seen such different events in the space of only a few seconds.

Later in the morning, still at his desk, Chris received a call from Judge Peter Thompson's clerk. Almost whispering, the young woman said the judge thought it important for Chris to come down to his courtroom, right away if possible. This was a strange call in a variety of ways, one of which was that Judge Thompson was a civil judge, who didn't handle criminal cases. What could he want with the district attorney? Chris was intrigued enough to go downstairs and walk through the underground tunnel to the old courthouse. On the fourth floor, inside an expansive district court courtroom, the clerk waved him back to the judge's chambers. The door stood open, and Chris saw two people in the visitors' chairs. A lovely young woman turned and gave Chris a smile, which she did very well. The smile started quickly with her wide lips, then crept languidly up her face, brushing her eyes with sincere interest. She wore a short, blue, sleeveless dress that her legs justified. Her dark hair fell to her shoulders. As Chris entered the office she continued to watch him, as if she knew him or had heard of him. It took a moment for Chris to turn his attention to Nick Winston, the railroad commissioner.

"Hello, there, Chris," Peter Thompson said. He sat behind his desk divested of robe, a florid, jovial man who made every meeting an occasion. "Thanks for coming. You know Nick Winston, don't you? And this is the lovely Celine."

Chris bent at the waist to take the long hand she offered. He repeated his name and said, "Celine?"

"I'm trying to cultivate the one-name thing. Or maybe it's just the habit of being a school counselor, where you want the little monsters to find out as little as possible about you."

Nick Winston, on his feet by now, wore a dark suit and a more sober expression. He shook hands. "Sorry about this, Chris. I dropped by to see Peter, who's an old friend, and he thought it was a good idea for us to meet again under less bizarre circumstances."

"I'd think the judge would have some qualms about getting witnesses together pretrial," Chris said, trying to make light of the meeting as he glanced at the judge.

Thompson waved away his concerns. "Oh, that thing's not going to trial. I've heard all about what happened. Anyway, it's certainly not a Bexar County concern. Excuse me a minute. Let me make sure I don't have anybody waiting for a decision. Marcie!"

He stepped out the door of his office. *That was subtle,* Chris thought, but Winston too looked embarrassed at being forced on him.

"Hope everybody's okay," he said uncomfortably. "You know, at Morris's house and all. I don't suppose they grilled him all night, what with your position—"

"No, it wasn't bad. We're just waiting for what happens next."

"Yeah." Winston shook his head regretfully. "I've been

thinking about Ben. I guess we all have. Remembering—you know, what you'd asked me about, what happened a few minutes earlier."

He glanced at Chris as if asking whether Chris had already heard about this, then specified: "The argument he and Morris had. You know Morris's precarious position. Well, Ben was the same way. They were like two drowning men trying to save each other. Then Morris got mad at him over something Ben hadn't handled very well, and yelled at him to get out, that he didn't want him coming near him again. You know, the kind of thing Morris is famous for screaming at people. Now it seems like . . . And seeing Anne again, I don't know how—*She's* not feeling guilty, I hope."

Celine stood up, putting herself on their level, and perhaps telling her escort they should be on their way. She still had a playful expression around her lips and eyes. Not having been at the party, the death was undoubtedly less real to her. Picking up on the remark about Anne, she said, "Does she have that kind of devastating effect on men often?"

Chris hesitated, having no immediate answer. "I see the answer is yes," Celine said, smiling more broadly and putting her hand on Chris's arm as if to apologize for teasing him.

"Well, um." Winston seemed ill at ease, not nearly the confident man he'd appeared the night Chris had met him. He waved a hand indicating the awkwardness of the situation. "Sorry about all this. I was in town for a meeting, dropped by to see Peter, and he insisted."

Chris said to Celine, "And why weren't you at the party?"

"That's what I keep asking. Nick told me it was going to be some boring political thing. Next time I'll know better than to believe him."

When she turned away toward the door, Chris saw her left

arm for the first time. Celine was wearing a short jacket with the sleeveless dress, but it had slipped down when she'd stood up. Just as she shrugged it back up over her shoulders Chris saw what looked like smudges on her upper arm. Having worked as a prosecutor for years, Chris had seen such smudges before. Bruises. Celine might have been at a wild party herself Saturday night. Looking back from the doorway, she gave him another small smile that her friend Nick didn't appear to see. They left the office and Chris waited to exit until he heard them leaving.

As Nick Winston and Celine walked out of the Bexar County Courthouse, down its long stone steps, Celine said, "Isn't there anybody else we should drop in on casually?"

"I can't help having friends," Winston said, almost sullenly. "It just happens—"

She laughed and took his arm. "It doesn't just happen, sweetheart. You're charming, that's all. Everywhere you go you leave a string of friends."

He shrugged modestly.

"And what else?" Celine asked, still smiling but with her voice taking on an edge. "Friends and what else?"

He gave her an innocent look, so blatantly phony that they both smiled again. "I think you're not going to any more parties without me," Celine said comfortably.

They held hands all the way to the car, but sat mostly silent during the hour-long drive to Austin. She didn't ask him any more questions.

Treating sullen teenage boys ordered to see her as a condition of juvenile probation usually comprised the most difficult part of Anne's practice. Their shells were tough to break through because they were more than shells. Bad attitude was a part of the boy, the essential component of his character. Dig through a layer and you often found something worse underneath. Or nothing.

So sixteen-year-old Ronnie Harris should have been a welcome relief. Ronnie, red-haired with freckles over his nose and an endearing crooked smile, sat tall in the visitor's chair and looked straight at Anne as he said earnestly, "I just don't want this to ruin my chance of getting into college." He leaned forward and laced his fingers together. "I know I made a mistake, but I want to make sure it doesn't mess up my life."

"Good," Anne said. "Because you have a lot of life ahead of you. Why are you here, Ronnie?"

"The judge ordered me to come. I know that's not the only thing you mean. I had a problem. I went a little crazy over this girl." He blushed at having used the word "crazy" in a psychiatrist's office. Anne smiled to tell him it was okay, but her tone remained firm.

"It sounds as if you were the problem. Who's Lauren Salem?"

"The girl. She was new to school this year and everybody kind of liked her. Well, I did, anyway. I started talking to her before class and in the halls, you know, and I could see she liked me. Finally I asked her out but she said no; her parents said she couldn't date yet." He gave Anne an exasperated look to show what he'd had to deal with. "She was only fifteen. She said they said she had to wait until she was sixteen. Can you believe that?"

"Yes. Why didn't you?"

Ronnie drew his long legs up close to the chair. He sat with his legs close together and his hands still holding each other, a posture of imposed self-control. "Oh, I did, at first. I kept talking to her, and she kept letting me know she liked me, y'know—"

"How did you know she liked you, Ronnie?"

"From the way she'd talk to me. You know, she seemed shy, she wouldn't look at me most of the time. She'd be messing with her books in her locker, but then she'd shoot me a little look, just for a second, but it was like, well, you can tell, y'know, Doctor?"

Anne knew. But she didn't think Ronnie did. He had an open, friendly air that invited Anne's sympathy, even her friendship. Anne suspected that Ronnie expected everyone to like him. She was willing to do so, but not necessarily on his terms.

"So what did you do?"

"Nothing."

"'Nothing' doesn't get you in front of a judge, Ronnie."

"It's just probation. In fact, it's—what do you call it?"

"Deferred adjudication?"

"Yeah, that's it. The judge said if I behave myself I won't even have a record."

He was also required to fulfill the terms of his probation, such as cooperating with his court-appointed therapist. At least Ronnie had motivation to succeed at this.

"So what did you do?" Anne asked again.

"I just—watched her. At school, you know, and then I like saw her at the mall and stuff, and one day I saw her walking so I followed her and saw where she lived. And I started leaving her notes in her locker once in a while."

"Did you sign them?"

"She knew they were from me. I was the only one, wasn't I?"

An earlier generation might have called this puppy love, but Lauren Salem's parents had called it stalking, after the boy started spending about four days out of seven across the street from their house, and his notes got stranger. Poor teenage Lauren had felt that she couldn't leave her house, or even have any real privacy in it. The few friendships she'd begun to develop with other girls in school had withered as she became a prisoner of Ronnie's obsession with her. After Mr. Salem warned Ronnie away and the boy persisted, though more furtively, the Salems had managed to convince a police officer and then a prosecutor that Ronnie was more than infatuated. They had gotten him put on probation for stalking, a relatively new offense in Texas. The probation was more of a stern warning to the boy than the outcome of a criminal case. The judge had told Anne she just didn't want this kind of thing to become a pattern for the boy, who came from a good family and did have a bright future if this case didn't blight it.

"So what was the mistake you made, Ronnie?"

"I just came on too soon. I know that now. I should have waited until her parents said we could date." He shrugged ruefully. "Now they probably won't let me even after she turns sixteen."

Anne wanted to laugh. *No, Ronnie, Mr. and Mrs. and Mrs. Salem probably won't be too keen on having you date their daughter after they've gotten a court order that you stay away from her.*

Anne listened for the rest of the fifty-minute hour as Ronnie talked freely about his life, other girls he had liked, his father's strictness. He seemed like an easygoing kid and the case one of the easiest Anne had. After all, the judge had practically told her just to rubber-stamp the kid's file "cured." But somehow free and easy Ronnie, who so openly acknowledged his mistake, made Anne uneasy.

After he left she made the phone call she'd been thinking

about all day, to her father. He'd said very little to her in his home. Anne thought he might be more forthcoming if they weren't face-to-face. No experience of her life made her believe that, but she wanted to try.

"Hello, Daddy, are the police still around?"

Morris Greenwald laughed. "You know, I couldn't have arranged this better, Darling. I guess getting you involved in a killing was the best way to ensure that you call me all the time."

"Who would you have killed if you'd known, Daddy?"

"I can think of a few." Morris chuckled again. He seemed in remarkably good spirits, which Anne took as a bad sign.

"Have you heard any more about the investigation?"

"I'm not sure there is an investigation. I know that district attorney greatly preferred your boyfriend's story to yours. Maybe that will be the official explanation."

Anne started to respond, hesitated, and moved on. "What was that evening all about, Daddy? Why were Ben and Winston there?"

"I just invited people I knew, people I thought might be able to help each other out."

"How?"

"Just in general." Anne heard testiness growing in her father's voice. She pictured him standing now, pacing around impatiently with the portable phone held tightly against his ear.

"I can tell when you're lying, Daddy. I've heard it before."

"Listen, my dear daughter, I don't have to—"

"Why was Nick Winston there, Daddy? You hate him more than anybody I can think of."

"You can't go on like that," Morris said patiently, as if trying to complete her education. "Maybe he thinks he owes me because of what happened before. Maybe I can turn him into a friend instead of an enemy."

"When did that become your philosophy?"

"Annie, there's so much you don't understand."

"Does it matter to you at all that Ben is dead?" Anne shot back at him.

The line went silent for so long that she thought her father had hung up on her. Then Morris said very softly, "Yes."

"What did you get him involved in that got him killed?"

"Nothing," her father answered in a small, sullen voice.

"Daddy, there were people meeting behind closed doors. People Chris and I never saw. Did you tell the police about them?"

"That always happens when people get together," Morris said, not answering her question. "Everybody thinks they have secrets to whisper about. Closing doors makes them feel more important."

"Who?"

"I have to go now." The testiness returned to his voice, erasing any trace of regret over Ben's death.

"Daddy, let me ask you just one thing. Do you believe me? Do you believe Nick Winston murdered Ben?"

Another long pause grew. Then Morris Greenwald said, "Yes," and hastily hung up.

Anne put her phone down and stared at it as if it had an expression she could read. She didn't know what that last affirmation from her father meant, but it had made the whole difficult conversation worthwhile.

Generally speaking, the district attorney can sit in his office, summon anyone who works for him, and be assured that that person will appear promptly. Chris had grown accustomed to doing that. But sometimes he needed to get out of his office. Going to look for someone betrayed his restlessness and desire for action. So when Chief Investigator Jack Fine looked up and saw his boss standing over him, Jack knew that Chris had gotten personally involved in a case again. Sometimes that happened because Chris did have a personal involvement, such as in his last big trial, which had involved Clarissa and her mother, but more often the facts of a case just grabbed him. Jack still marveled at Chris's willingness to care.

Jack Fine had passed fifty a few years earlier but shrugged off the milestone, possibly because he'd looked that age for years. Jack had a thin build, a narrow, creased face, very sharp eyes, and an expressive forehead. He had been a detective, a twenty-five-year veteran of the San Antonio Police force who had left the department because of a triumph of investigation in which he had discovered that a few fellow officers were stealing from a charitable fund. This had earned Jack the undying gratitude of no one, and a "promotion" into a dead-end job designed to isolate him from the rest of the force. It hadn't taken Jack long to get what was happening, and to get out. His tenacity impressed newly elected District Attorney Chris Sinclair, who offered him a job. Jack took it with an apparent reluctance that still infused his relations with his boss, but he retained his investigative stubbornness, oddly coupled with a hard-core cynicism.

"What's up?" Jack said. He rose from his bare metal desk, knowing Chris would want to walk. They went out into the white hall with the scuffed linoleum floor.

Surprisingly, Jack hadn't yet heard about his boss's weekend adventure. When Chris sketched it out briefly, Jack paid him the tribute of raised eyebrows. Not much surprised the investigator, but this clash did. "You saw the guy kill himself and Anne saw somebody else kill him?" Jack immediately went investigative. "Which of you knew the victim better?"

"Anne. She'd known him for years; she used to date him. I barely knew him."

"Did she know this Nick Winston that well, too?"

Chris wondered how well anyone knew Nick Winston. He had seemed like such a different man this morning in Judge Thompson's office. After what Winston had told him about Ben Sewell's situation, Chris's view of what had happened had been reinforced. He shook his head in answer to Jack's question. "Only slightly. I don't think she'd seen him for years before Friday."

Jack pursed his lips. "That's a wash, then. She should be more positive of her ID of the victim, but not the killer. Say, maybe you came up—"

"I've already spun the possibilities, Jack. I want to know which way the cops and D.A. are leaning. Do you know anybody in the Comal County Sheriff's Office or District Attorney's Office you could ask, off the record?"

"I'd have to think about it. Seems like I ought to know somebody who left the S.A. force and moved to New Braunfels. Why don't you just ask the D.A. yourself?"

Chris said slowly, "I will, but I don't know if I'll believe what he tells me. Do you know him, Jack—Andy Gunther?"

Jack shrugged. They stopped speaking for a moment as they turned a corner. Their conversation wasn't exactly secret, but instinctively both men wanted to know who might be nearby. Jack said, "I remember him coming here on a few cases when he was only a lawyer." He said this last slyly, as if the elevation from plain lawyer to district attorney were enormous. "He seemed like an easy-way-out kind of guy, didn't want to do all the work to get to the end. Like he just wanted to take the case and charge over left tackle with it, if you know what I mean."

Chris nodded. He had gotten that impression himself. "That's why I'm a little leery about him. The easy way out is to believe my version and just drop the case."

Again Jack's eyebrows went up, creating endless ridges on his forehead. "And don't you believe your own version?"

This was why Chris had wanted to walk, why he couldn't sit still in his office. "I know what I saw. But Anne's positive, too. I want to make sure her side gets fully investigated."

Jack went silent for a few paces, mulling over his boss's motives.

"I just want to know," Chris said stubbornly.

"I've heard that before."

The weariness in Jack's voice—entirely feigned for the purpose of making his point—put the first touch of amusement in Chris's morning. He clapped his investigator on the shoulder and said he'd make the call to New Braunfels. Chris walked away with longer strides, apparently reinvigorated by having talked to his investigator. Jack couldn't think why.

It took a while to get through to the district attorney of Comal County. Chris called, left a message, waited around, wondering whether Andy Gunther was busy, hiding out from his staff, or had no desire to talk to the district attorney of Bexar County. But Gunther himself called back in less than an hour—none of this having the secretary phone for him—and sounded hearty enough. He was also clearly talking to Chris on a speakerphone.

"Christian Sinclair!" Gunther boomed. "I remembered you later. You spoke at that seminar on extraneous offenses. Kept telling us to be careful about using them. A couple of people afterward were wondering whose team you were on."

Chris didn't know what to say to that. "How're you, Andy?"

"I'm good, I'm good." Gunther's voice grew fainter. He had turned his head away from the speaker. Chris felt the irritation of listening to someone through a speakerphone. On the other end Andy Gunther could have been practicing his putting or even holding another conversation—in any case paying scant attention to anything Chris had to say. But then Gunther's voice boomed through the line more animatedly. "Been digging up some interesting stuff on that scene you were part of the other night."

"Oh, yes?"

"You bet. Young Ben Sewell was going through some hard times. Business reverses. I've got his income tax returns for the last three years and it looks like a playground slide. Swoosh, straight to the bottom!"

"Well—"

"Not just that. There was talk about a grand jury investigation in Austin over unauthorized lobbying Sewell might've done."

"Really."

"Well, he wasn't a registered lobbyist, and if you're not, you got to be careful talkin' to those guys in the capitol. Aw, probably nothing to it, really. You know old Ronnie Earle in Austin, always lookin' for some legislative scandal to prosecute. Keep his name in the news. Still, it's got to be something that would worry a guy, especially when he's got other troubles."

"Hmm," Chris mused. But Gunther wasn't the kind to leave the obvious unspoken.

"The kind of things that would make some guys think about killing themselves."

"Sounds like you're gathering evidence fast, Andy. What about Nick Winston?"

A pause came over the line. Again, Gunther could have been talking to someone else in his office in New Braunfels. Then his voice turned bland, like someone else's. "What about him?"

"Have you dug up any reason for his animosity to Ben Sewell?"

"Not a thing, my man. I don't even know why he was there, except it seemed to be a politician drop-in kind of night." Gunther's tone of genial contempt for "politicians" obviously excluded Chris and himself, elected officials both, from such company. "I haven't heard of any past dealings he'd had with Ben. Have you?"

"No." Chris remembered Winston's speaking of Ben Sewell earlier that evening, in a perfectly genial tone of voice, apparently interested in him only for entertainment or gossip value. Then this morning Winston had seemed genuinely remorseful, trying to puzzle out the mystery of Sewell's suicide.

"I thought old Greenwald might've confided in you, since you're practically family. Oh, and speaking of Morris, he and Sewell did have a lot of connections. And not just that Sewell was engaged to his daughter once upon a time. No, they were working together these days. In fact, that so-called lobbying young Sewell did in the legislature—?"

"Yes?"

Andy Gunther picked up the phone, so his voice came much more clearly and directly to Chris's ear. Gunther obviously knew a punch line before he delivered one. "It was on behalf of Morris," he said.

Chris asked haltingly, "So is that grand jury—?"

"Uh-huh," Gunther said slyly, clearly enjoying himself. "Now they might be looking into Morris Greenwald, too. Except he didn't talk to any legislators himself. And nobody can say he told Sewell to. Not now, anyway."

"Hmm," Chris said again, and this time Andy Gunther mimicked him. "Hmm." He stripped the hum of its inherent thoughtfulness and instead made it sound jolly. It must be wonderful to enjoy one's work so much.

"I guess I'll have to ask Mr. Greenwald about that," Chris said.

"Thought you might. Fact is, I might ask him myself."

They dropped into the banalities of farewell, each done with the other. When Chris hung up he continued to picture Andy Gunther's face and relaxed posture. He seemed to be the way Jack had described him, laid back to the point of laziness, but he had obviously moved fast on his investigation.

For all his hearty bluffness, Gunther had a sly way with sleight-of-voice, too, the way he had elevated Chris into intimacy with the whole Greenwald family yet at the same time mentioned that Anne had been formally engaged to Ben Sewell at one time. Not exactly the short-term, casual relationship Anne had implied. That didn't matter. Probably not to this case, and certainly not to what Chris had with Anne. They hadn't met until they were in their thirties; of course they had pasts. Part of Chris's had intruded forcefully into their lives before, but Anne had kept hers very much in deep background. Her family, her boyfriends—she'd always said talking about that stuff bored her. Chris had thought this a strange stance for a psychiatrist, but he'd let her maintain it.

That was fine.

Everybody lies. They lie outright or they lie unknowingly. They deliberately, solemnly lie about major events, and they casually, almost unknowingly lie about who took the last doughnut. This had been one of the first lessons of prosecution, that the nicest people could not be trusted, even when they looked you in the eye or put their hands on Bibles. Sometimes a good falsehood sounded more elegant and made more sense than the ridiculous truth: you couldn't judge veracity by the sound of it.

In daily life what people say doesn't much matter. People lie with a word, a greeting, a nod, a smile, any small gesture that says *I like you, I find you worth saying Hi to*, when the truth is quite different. But so what? Little courtesies grease the day, let civilization proceed smoothly. But when a crime happens, it becomes important to learn the true facts, and people cannot give up their habits of deception. Sometimes they even let their own eyes lie to them. When trying to solve a murder, this easygoingness about the truth can be disastrous.

Late that afternoon, Chris jogged through Olmos Park. Not really a joggers' place. It was a gloomy park, a sunken hollow, low-roofed by the leafy branches of old trees. Sunlight had a hard time fighting through to the ground. The park was never crowded with children or picnickers, so it could have been a good place for running, except that there were few paths and the undergrowth threatened broken ankles by covering up unnumerable fallen branches. It was an especially dangerous place for a runner not paying attention to his footing.

So Chris took a turn through the park to get his mind off his thoughts and onto his feet. He could have jogged around the track at Alamo Heights High School, a few blocks from his condo, but running around a track seemed not far removed from doing it on a treadmill, and he didn't like either. To inspire Chris to run, he needed the illusion that he was getting somewhere.

A couple of men had parked in the park, dozens of yards away from each other, and each stayed in or near his car. They looked at Chris and then away, both furtively. If Chris stayed here and went into hiding, he could probably gather evidence of some crime he wouldn't want to prosecute. He ran out of the park, onto the road, and back to thoughts of what had happened at Morris Greenwald's house in New Braunfels. He needed to talk to Anne again, but wasn't sure she'd want to have the conversation. No: he *was* sure.

Running didn't give him any new thoughts, and as six o'clock in the evening approached he ran toward home. Time to start cooking dinner for Clarissa. But his thoughts stayed dark, as dark as that night in the country when the moon had barely shone and the trees and shrubs could hold innumerable secrets.

Everybody lies, Anne thought as she looked at her father's face. Morris Greenwald stood in his second-floor sitting room, speaking earnestly to her. Earnestness was his worst mode, the one that made her trust him least. No, come to think of it, she didn't trust him when he was being casual and offhanded, either. *That* was his worst posture for convincing her of anything. But when he tried he was almost as bad. Anne was standing with her arms folded across her chest, letting him talk.

"Of course Ben and I had some business dealings going on. What do you think I do with my time? I had other lines in the water, too, but the deal Ben and I tried to make was the most promising. It was about that land, you know, the land right outside Austin, right where the city would naturally grow, if the damned legislature hadn't 'protected' it from development because of that little yellow whatchamacallit."

His face reddened as he remembered, and Anne recalled, too, that a few years ago the discovery of a tiny yellow bird had helped bring down her father's fortunes. Apparently the bird nested nowhere else in the world except on some valuable land owned by Morris and a few others. Conservation-minded Austinites, of whom there were many, had convinced the legislature to preserve the birds' habitat. So Morris's investment lay there as wildland, paying him nothing and costing him taxes. Anne thought he'd given up years ago on trying to recoup that loss. She should have known better.

"And Nick Winston might've been able to help, if we could've convinced him."

"Daddy, that doesn't make any sense. Wasn't he the lobbyist for the conservationists in the first place?" Anne remembered her father cursing Winston's name with even more than his usual passion.

"Yes, because he was paid to be. But that was over, and maybe he thought he owed me a favor."

"Even so, how? He's a railroad commissioner now. He doesn't have anything to do with land regulation."

Morris shrugged. "Who knows? We were just reaching out anywhere we could, making friends who might have other friends."

Now he sounded casual again. Anne's eyes narrowed.

"You're right, Annie. Everybody at that party could have done me some good one way or another. And I could've done something for any of them, too. That's how life is, didn't you know? But there was nothing big that was just about to pop. Nothing on my horizon, anyway."

On the last sentence he put his hands in his pockets, looked down at the carpet, and suddenly appeared old. The skin under his eyes sagged.

Anne reached out, rested her wrist on his shoulder next to his neck, and touched his ear. "Daddy, I'm sorry. I wish—"

He looked at her a little moistly, but Anne's mind had engaged again. "I wish you wouldn't lie to me," she concluded.

"What?"

Anne turned away, pacing, hands on hips, and said loudly, "Because if nothing big was going on there was no reason for Winston to kill Ben! And he did! I saw it! Even if—even if you believe what Chris saw, *some*thing had to have happened for Ben to want to kill himself. It wasn't just an ordinary little party full of ambitious people."

Her outburst didn't seem to bother her father. Morris still stood with his hands in his pants pockets, so his whole body moved when he shrugged again. His clothes looked a little too big for him. Anne saw him shrinking before her eyes. She had never thought that before, even after his reversals of fortune.

"Ben talked to me about you after you and Chris left," Morris said quietly. "It really affected him, seeing you. He said, 'Just think, Morris, if things had worked out like they were supposed to, Anne and I would've still been here together tonight. And we were.' He seemed to be going off into some fantasy alternate life.

"But then you left for dinner, he kept drinking, and he didn't want to talk any more. I've thought about it a lot since then, what I could've said. . . ."

Anne had thought of the same thing, how wistful Ben Sewell had looked while talking to her. His expression had made her reach out to him more than she would have otherwise, touching his arm and laughing at his ever-so-slight witticisms. She wondered if her father had told this story to the district attorney here. It added more weight to Chris's version of what had happened. Ben growing listless, thinking of what he'd lost. . . . As far as Anne knew, this would be the only man who had ever killed himself over her.

But that's not what had happened.

Morris began, "Would you like to go into town and get a little—" But then his phone rang and he crossed to the table to answer it. "Oh, hi. We were just—Yeah, I could do that. What's up?"

Morris glanced toward the French doors that led out to the balcony, which seemed odd. While he concluded his call, Anne found her purse.

"I'm sorry, honey," he said, as he hung up. "I've got—"

"That's okay, I do, too, Daddy. Another time."

He accompanied her only as far as the top of the stairs, and stood there and waved as she let herself out. That struck Anne as odd, too, as if her father were confined there, as in a nursing home, or under house arrest. She stood on the front porch of the house for a moment and looked up at that balcony. It stood empty and silent. Anne didn't even see ghosts re-enacting what she'd seen. She tried to picture the movements and hear the words again, but the memory had already begun to fade, as even the strongest do.

She had parked right in front of the house after coming here on the spur of the moment, calling her father on the way. As she put her hand on the car door handle, something made her stop. Someone had put something under her windshield wiper, like the handbills kids pass out at shopping centers. But this was the wilds of Comal County; no kid could have come by.

Anne bent forward to get the square of shiny paper, but before she looked at it she turned, as if her gaze were being drawn by a strange force.

Up in the parking area, fifty yards or more away, Nick Winston stood watching her.

Light had faded to dusk, and he was farther away than he'd been the night of the murder but she still recognized him. He stood in the open door of his car, silhouetted in the weak light from the car's interior, dark eyes staring at her. A breeze ruffled his thin brown hair. Anne saw, or imagined at this distance, the slight, sardonic smile Winston habitually wore, as if he were waiting for a delicious surprise that only he knew was about to occur.

Anne stood rigid, penetrated by his stare and his presence. Then suddenly she doubted that he would be alone. She rapidly pivoted her head right and left, looking for his people. She saw no one. Then Anne remembered that she'd left her car unlocked. She opened the driver's-side door, which turned on the interior light, and she quickly scanned both the front and back seats and the floorboards. She wouldn't be stupid enough to put herself into a trap like that.

The car was empty. Then she realized that her watchfulness had given Winston time to cross the distance between them. She turned back quickly again, but saw only the car. His car door was closed, and no one was inside. Where was he? Anne looked around, beginning to breathe more shallowly. This was a man she had seen kill someone, and she was the only witness against him. She jumped into her car and slammed and locked the door.

As she groped in her purse for her keys, a sound drew her attention back to the dark sedan Winston drove. The sound was the car's engine. The car's taillights flared, momentarily flashed white as well, then went dark as the car started forward. It had been parked with its back end toward her, positioned to leave quickly, and now it did. The car rapidly gathered speed on the caliche road, kicking dust up high.

Anne sat in her car, forcing her breathing to slow, waiting for her heart to stop bumping her ribs. It had been one of the strangest encounters of her life, feeling Winston just stare at her. She couldn't even say he had been threatening, except by his presence, his obvious knowledge of where she would be.

Anne still held the square of glossy paper in her hand. She

turned on her car's dome light to look at it. The object was a photograph. At first Anne had trouble orienting herself to what the picture showed, then her own face jumped out at her. The photograph had been taken from below, and it took a long moment for her to realize that it had been through a window, because one side of the frame barely framed the picture itself. Anne stood looking out, above and beyond the camera, indifferent to it—or, as she knew, unaware of being observed. She recognized this as a back window of her father's house, partly because of the blouse she was wearing. This appeared to be a recent photo, yet she had been here so rarely she suddenly remembered the occasion: earlier in the afternoon the night of the murder. She had gone to the bedroom and changed clothes. That's what the picture showed, in excellent focus: Anne at the window unbuttoning her blouse. She had almost fully undone the blouse, the shirt falling open, her fingers appearing to linger. The picture showed a lacy white bra and a wedge-shaped slice of her abdomen. One of her hands reached just inside the fabric's edge as the other hand undid the last button. Anne in the photograph appeared to be teasing the cameraman, pausing overly long in the last step of removing her blouse.

But Anne knew she hadn't had any idea that she'd been observed. She remembered looking out that window, at the tops of the trees and the fields beyond the house's yards. The photographer must have been behind one of those trees, hidden for some time, with a powerful lens focused upward on Anne's second-story window. How long had he stood there waiting for her? He must have known which room was Anne's, as well as that she was in the house. A room called hers even though she didn't enter it from one year to the next.

She shivered, reached for her keys, and started the ignition. By appearing here and leaving the picture, Nick Winston obviously meant to send her a signal. He had. More than one signal, in fact, including one he didn't intend. Winston was guilty. He wouldn't threaten her this way if he didn't have good reason to fear what she could say about him.

Anne tucked the picture away in her purse. She drove very carefully back to the highway and home, looking in her rearview mirror more often than normal.

★ Anne stood in front of the desk of District Attorney Andy Gunther. By noon of this day in late May, the air outside already seemed like the dead of summer. Anne felt drying sweat under her white blouse. She had called Gunther that morning and he had agreed to meet her at lunchtime, which showed more consideration than Anne would have expected. It might have been a professional courtesy to Chris, by proxy.

Gunther's office was larger than Chris's, but also older and less well-decorated. Old-fashioned venetian blinds admitted sunlight and a view of the street one floor down. Old, dark, and slightly warped paneling covered the walls. Behind and above Gunther's head, a large deer's head was mounted on the wall. It seemed a strange placement: Gunther couldn't see it most of the time; instead the deer stared at his visitors, as if the D.A. had an enormous bodyguard standing behind him. If Gunther had known another effect of the trophy, he would have had it removed: sometimes, when Gunther toyed with a paper clip on his desk, or just appeared not to be listening, his face suffered by intellectual comparison with the thoughtful expression of the dead deer.

But the district attorney watched Anne carefully enough most of the time. He lounged back in his old-fashioned swivel chair, displaying one large alligator boot. Without getting up, he invited Anne to take a seat, but she preferred to stand. Before saying anything, she handed him the photograph of herself that she'd found under her windshield wiper. Gunther perused it very carefully while Anne waited. As she did, she realized another consequence of Winston's leaving this photo for her. It constituted evidence of some kind; obviously Anne would show it to people. As the district attorney studied it much longer than necessary to identify what the picture showed, Anne crossed her arms and felt herself starting to blush.

Gunther glanced up at her from under his lowered brow, then returned his gaze to the picture. Anne wanted to snatch it back. After a minute Gunther turned the picture over, which made Anne grateful. Gunther looked for identifying marks, treating the photo as just a piece of evidence instead of as a keepsake Anne had handed him.

She knew he wouldn't find anything, except the brand name of the manufacturer of the developing paper. Anne started talking. "Nick Winston left this on the windshield of my car when I was at my father's house late yesterday afternoon."

"So this is the new evidence you said you had against him," Gunther said neutrally. "Nice," he added as he handed the picture back and gazed at Anne, obviously retaining the image in memory and comparing it to real life. He smiled at her.

"Look," Anne insisted, angry at feeling herself continuing to blush. "He's obviously trying to intimidate me. I wanted you to know what he's—"

"How do you know it was Commissioner Winston? Did you see him leave it?"

"No, but he was there. He was standing there watching me when I found the picture."

"Are you positive of that?" Anne thought he sounded sarcastic, but maybe only she would have thought that.

"Yes, I'm certain it was him. Well—not positive, not like the other night. He was farther away, and it was getting dark, but yes, I'm sure it was him. He has that way of standing, you know—"

Gunther frowned. "Yesterday afternoon? What time was this?"

"Sometime after six. Six-fifteen, maybe six-thirty, but I don't think that late. I had driven up from San Antonio after work—"

She stopped because the district attorney had begun shaking his head. "It wasn't him."

Anne put her hands down on his desk. She leaned toward Gunther, which made him glance down from her face, and Anne stood up straight again. "What makes you say that?"

"Yesterday between six and seven Nick Winston was at a reception downtown here honoring a Republican candidate for judge of the Austin Court of Appeals, Randy Pease."

"How do you know? Is he faxing you his itinerary every day?"

New Braunfels was not a large city, but Anne's father lived on its outskirts, several miles from downtown. Winston could certainly not have been here in the central city and outside Morris Greenwald's house within a few minutes' time.

"I was there too," Gunther said. "I saw him."

Mentally, Anne sagged. Winston had set her up again, somehow.

Gunther stood up. He asked again, "Do you still say it was him?"

"I told you I wasn't positive. I thought so, but—if it wasn't, it was someone who deliberately looked like him, someone he sent to confuse me."

A shift of Gunther's lips showed what he thought of that explanation. "Or it could have been someone else entirely. You're a psychiatrist, aren't you, Ms. Greenwald?"

Even though he knew the answer, Gunther still wouldn't use her title. Anne nodded.

"You've treated people with criminal records, people who are—" Gunther made a gesture of groping for a politically correct term but didn't strain very hard. "—deranged in some way or they wouldn't be coming to see you in the first place, right?"

"Most of my patients are children."

"And you've been practicing for a while and children grow up. You've had some of these patients follow you before, haven't you, or otherwise develop some fixation on you?" Gunther began to sound as if he were in court, the country-boy patterns falling out of his speech.

"I suppose so."

"I'm asking about your own personal experience, Ms. Greenwald. You know you have. Couldn't this man watching you have been one of these patients or someone like that?"

Anne stared at him stonily. "That would be an odd coincidence, wouldn't it, that someone else starts following me around just after I've accused Nick Winston of murder? And what about the photograph? That's a room of my father's house. I was there Friday and Saturday for the first time in a long while; the picture was obviously taken then. That's when Winston was there as well. He must have—"

Anne faltered. How long would the photographer have stood out there behind a tree waiting, very likely in vain, to get a shot of her standing at the window? It couldn't have been Nick Winston, since he had been inside the house during that time. Or had he? Anne hadn't seen him until the party, when everyone gathered in the sitting room. Before that she assumed he'd been in one of those closed-door meetings. But he could have been strolling around the house as he'd claimed to be doing later. He could have just spotted Anne at the window then and on impulse snapped the picture.

Because he happened to be carrying a camera with a long lens.

Gunther saw her frowning at her own chain of illogic and appeared satisfied. "I don't think that was taken by a still camera," he said, apparently helping her out. "I think someone had a video camera trained on that window and took a lot of footage, just on the chance someone came to the window." Gunther glanced at the picture again, obviously thinking of the glimpse of Anne's skin. "He got lucky."

"But why—?"

"Frankly, what you're showing me makes no sense for Nick Winston. Anyone could have done that. It might have come from a security camera of your father's."

"My father wouldn't have kept a picture like that of me. He certainly wouldn't have had someone put it under my windshield wiper."

"Someone else could have gotten hold of the footage. Don't ask me why."

From the gleam in Andy Gunther's eye, Anne knew he had thought of one reason, one that had nothing to do with any case. Gunther's guess about the source of the photo meant something else, too. Someone had video of Anne, and had chosen this one still frame from it to pass to her, letting her know that he had more, that he had also seen the next frame and the ones after that.

"Don't you see what it means? This is an obvious effort to intimidate me. He's telling me that if I don't change my story he'll be watching me. I'll be in his power somehow."

"And I'd think that was a good theory except for what I told you. I was with Nick Winston yesterday at the time you saw him."

"Where was this reception?"

"I told you, downtown here. At a law office."

"What time exactly did you see Winston there?"

Gunther said exasperatedly, "It wasn't a crime scene. People weren't checking the time every five minutes. But he was there, I promise you. Lots of people saw him."

Anne looked at Gunther intently, developing her theory. "Suppose he *was* at my father's house, looking at me, then he drove like hell down here, parked wherever he could, and rushed in and acted as if he'd been there all along. He came later than other people, I'll bet. You check, you'll find that he got a parking ticket while this event was going on because the parking was all gone by the time he got there and he had to park next to a fire hydrant or in a red zone."

"Nick Winston's car has license plates that say 'State Official.' Nobody would waste the county's paper by putting a parking ticket on one of those."

"Yes, you see. That's how he could drive so fast on the highway without worrying about getting stopped." Anne said this triumphantly, as if she'd just proven her case. But Gunther continued to regard her as if she were slightly deranged herself.

"I'll check on it," he finally said insincerely, rising from his chair. "Meantime, I'd better keep that picture for evidence."

Anne had been standing with the picture in her hand, but when Andy Gunther reached for it she drew it away. "No, I'll hang on to it. Let me know if you need it."

The two gave each other long, cool looks, until Gunther smiled slyly, which made Anne turn on her heel and hurry out.

"Going to see that idiot was a total waste of my time."

Chris nodded. He sat on the sofa in Anne's living room, watching her as she rode an exercycle. They could hear Clarissa moving in the spare bedroom, supposedly doing homework but first needing to call a friend to "get the assignment." So far the call had lasted longer than it would take her to do the work.

Anne's house was old and furnished in an old-fashioned way, with a scattering of rugs over a richly gleaming hardwood floor, a massively thick-legged dining room table behind Chris, and in this living room the sofa, two armchairs, lots of bookshelves, and one wooden wall devoted to photographs and art objects, clustered together. The first time Chris had walked into this room he had found it uninviting, but now he loved it.

"It probably was," he agreed, about Anne wasting her time. "Talking to Gunther wasn't a very productive use for my time, either, except I got a higher opinion of his investigative skills. I was surprised by the amount of material he'd already turned up."

"Such as?" Anne asked, slightly out of breath. She rode the exercycle hard, as if she could get somewhere on it.

Chris sketched for her the background of her father's business dealings with Ben Sewell, and the latter's decline in fortune. Anne listened attentively, not changing expression when Chris mentioned the dead man to whom she'd once been engaged. During the telling of the story she only made one comment: "Sounds like my father."

He concluded by stating the rather obvious. "So Ben did have motives for suicide, the classic ones." Chris didn't mention the dead man's just having seen his former fiancée again, or what emotions that visit might have inspired.

Anne had been staring straight ahead. After a pause grew into silence she glanced up, surprised. "That's it?"

Chris had not suggested how the story implicated Morris Greenwald as well; he knew Anne would have understood that. So that wasn't what she meant when she implied that Chris should have learned more. "That's all Gunther told me."

"So he hasn't found out anything about Nick Winston, what kind of dealings he had there, what his motives for murder might have been."

"Not that he told me," Chris said neutrally. He got up from the couch and walked closer to Anne and to the closed door of the room where Clarissa was.

"Do you get it?" Anne asked.

"You think Gunther's making no effort to corroborate your story of what happened. He's not going to pursue that at all."

"That's one explanation," Anne said. "The other is that he's not as great an investigator as you think. Somebody's feeding him the information they want him to have."

She didn't have to add whom she believed to be the source of this information. "If you have any way of checking, see if the Sheriff's Office is digging up this material for Andy Gunther or if he's getting it from outside."

"I've already got Jack checking on that," Chris said thoughtfully. He put his hand over Anne's on the handlebar, just let it cover hers for a long moment.

Behind him the bedroom door opened. Clarissa was standing in the doorway looking at them. Chris didn't draw his hand away from Anne's guiltily, but he did turn to look at his daughter. Clarissa was a lovely girl, tall and long-waisted, with long legs. Blond hair, paler than Chris's, fell to her shoulders. At times Clarissa projected a forceful beauty, lips pursed, chin thrust forward, as if she wanted to be seen through, wanted to shrug off the burden of prettiness. In the first moment Chris looked at her she wore that face, but then her expression lightened.

"Is anybody going to eat?"

Chris walked over and gave her a quick hug, not demanding anything in return. Sometimes Clarissa seemed so uncompli- cated and sweet—such as when she was hungry—that he wanted to do that. Other times he wanted to hold her because she looked so incapable of being comforted.

"Let's go get something," he said.

He didn't add an invitation to Anne, but Clarissa did. "Want to come, too?" Clarissa displayed very mixed feelings toward Anne. Sometimes the girl confided in Anne, sometimes she obviously didn't want Anne near her father, interfering with the growing relationship between Chris and Clarissa, or with memories of Clarissa's mother.

Anne smiled but shook her head. "It would take me too long to get ready, and I know how important it is to get you food right away when you've announced that you're hungry."

Clarissa laughed, a sound that thrilled through the nerves in Chris's arms and shoulders. Clarissa's mother used to laugh in just that way when she'd been struck by an idea for a scheme that would be both fun and dangerous. But Clarissa's young face showed no such sinister intentions. "Let's go," Chris said, and after Clarissa had gone through the front door gave Anne a quick kiss. For a moment they looked into each other's eyes from only inches apart. Neither blinked. Chris caressed her cheek and left.

Over dinner at a Luby's cafeteria, Clarissa asked, "That school I'm in is supposed to be a good school, right? You have to be smart to get in?"

"Smart or rich," Chris answered. "They'll forgive a few points of GPA if your parents can pay full tuition."

Clarissa looked thoughtful. "He doesn't seem that smart," she murmured.

Chris hadn't been a parent long, but he knew better than to ask an immediate prying question. While Clarissa looked off into space, he glanced down at the plates on their Formica-topped table. He'd allowed Clarissa two desserts—pecan pie and Jell-O—as long as she had two vegetables as well, and she'd eaten it all, as well as a generous serving of roast beef. Chris felt no guilt about indulging her in food, even sugar. Clarissa had that teenage metabolism that could absorb any amount of calories without lasting effect.

Chris remembered those days but no longer enjoyed their powers. His plates held the remains of fried fish, broccoli, and mashed potatoes without gravy. At Clarissa's age, the meal he'd just eaten would barely have served as an appetizer.

Jean, Clarissa's mother, had had the same power, but not just over food. She could absorb any experience without apparent effect. No person or situation intimidated her, and no plan seemed too grand. Her confidence had been scary at times for lesser people, like Chris.

Clarissa didn't seem to have that invulnerability, and Chris prayed she'd never need it. Surely she'd suffered enough tragedy for one lifetime. He had the parental hope of making the rest of Clarissa's life a smooth ride. Still, Chris knew the vanity of that hope. Clarissa was, after all, a teenager, so heartbreak and humiliation lurked as the potential outcomes of every day.

"Sometimes you can't tell who are the really smart ones," Chris said, as if musing to himself. "They disguise themselves. And I'll tell you something else, even though I know you won't believe me. Once you're grown, it doesn't really matter all that much. I mean, sure, the richest guys on earth are probably pretty smart, but so were some of those guys you see pushing shopping carts down the street."

Clarissa looked at him skeptically. "Have you talked to any of those guys?"

Chris looked alarmed. "No. And don't tell me you have."

Clarissa nodded. "And believe me, it's not excess brain-power that put them where they are."

Maybe Clarissa had her mother's resilience after all. Chris sometimes forgot the wide variety of experience that life had imposed on the girl in only a handful of years. Her mother had dragged her along in a nomadic life, on the edge of the criminal underworld, for a decade and a half before Chris even learned of Clarissa's existence.

He suddenly felt a surge of pride in his daughter, just for having survived what she had and managing still to seem like a normal kid most of the time. She had been through a lot without any help from Chris, without his even knowing she existed, but that hadn't been his fault, and he intended to make up for that by keeping her as safe as a president's child.

"So are you still the new kid in school?" he asked.

Clarissa shrugged. "I've made a few friends. But I'm not the newest anymore anyway. When kids transfer in in the middle of a semester the other kids get curious. You know, is your father a Southwestern Bell executive who just transferred in from somewhere, or did your parents just get divorced, or did you get in trouble at your old school?" She saw Chris look at her with concern and added quickly, "It's not that bad. That's how you get to know some people, because they want to find out about you. Then some newer kid comes along and the pressure's off you."

Clarissa didn't seem to mind the scrutiny. She knew the rules of new-kiddom as well as anyone. Chris felt proud of her again, and hoped Clarissa saw that in his expression as he gazed at her. Maybe she did, because she bumped the back of her hand against his on their way out of the cafeteria, and smiled up at him shyly.

Chris hadn't forgotten her muttered remark about the new boy in school who didn't seem particularly smart. But Clarissa had already taught him the ineffectiveness of direct questioning. Chris had managed to teach her, he hoped, that he loved her no matter what. Between them they continued to learn, daily, how to be a father and daughter.

That Sunday, large type on the front page of the *Austin American-Statesman* blared, WHO KILLED BEN SEWELL? The *Statesman* chronicled the doings of legislators and lobbyists and other denizens of the state capital assiduously, and so enjoyed a good political scandal more than any other paper. So readers who had never heard of Ben Sewell looked at the headline and knew politics of the clandestine kind had been involved in his death.

Most of the principals had declined to talk to the reporter who wrote the article—Anne only vaguely remembered the message that he had called, and Chris had decided not to give the newspaper his version of events, because of the conflict with Anne's—but the reporter had managed to get information from a few off-the-record sources. For the rest, the story played innuendo for all it was worth.

Chris learned more about Morris Greenwald from the story than he'd known. The reporter came up with this thumbnail sketch: "Once a political contributor at the top of most Democratic lists, with his circle of best friends including governors and senators, Greenwald has fallen into relative obscurity in the past decade. Still, his name was well-known in political circles, so that if he sent out a summons to a meeting, some would respond. That was the case two Fridays ago when a railroad commissioner, a state senator, two local judges, and a flock of the politically invested came to Greenwald's mansion in Comal County."

The newspaper went on to describe these people, omitting only the supposed star of the story, the one featured in its headline. That turned out to be deliberate. The story essentially asked why any of these powerful people would care about Ben Sewell, a nobody in political terms. The answer must lie in skullduggery. At this point the supposed grand jury investigation came to the newspaper's rescue, allowing the story to sensationalize Sewell's death, if not his life. He'd obviously been involved in some shady business. On behalf of whom?

Continuing with the guest list, the newspaper story noted the presence at the gathering of Christian Sinclair, district attorney of neighboring Bexar County. "Sinclair declined to speak for attribution, but this reporter has learned that Sinclair was an eyewitness to the killing, and that his version of what happened differs markedly from that of other witnesses.

"Anne Greenwald, daughter of the host of the party, has told investigators that she saw Railroad Commissioner Nicholas Winston fire the shot that killed Ben Sewell. However, Ms. Greenwald's story is completely contradicted by District Attorney Sinclair. And thus far investigators have not uncovered any connection between Winston and the deceased that would provide a motive for murder."

From this point it became clear that Winston had spoken to the reporter, unlike most of those involved. Just reading his words, Chris could see Winston's face, with that look of concern that nevertheless harbored a slight smile, showing his confidence in himself and the judicial system. "I was amazed to hear that Ms. Greenwald had accused me of killing Ben. Luckily, I was in a position that made this impossible, and have witnesses to that effect. If I hadn't been fortunate enough to have witnesses close by, I might be in serious trouble by now."

Actually, Winston had only one exonerating witness. That one sat at his desk on a Tuesday morning reading the newspaper story from two days earlier. Chris's eyes went more and more hooded as he read, as if the story were losing his attention. That was not the case at all.

He wondered how much more of the story the *Statesman* reporter had gotten. The next paragraph told him: "This reporter has learned through sources who insisted on anonymity that Anne Greenwald has continued to accuse Winston. Since the party she has gone to District Attorney Andrew "Andy" Gunther to say that Winston has in effect been stalking her and taking pictures of her partially disrobed. Gunther confirmed the existence of such a photograph, but said its source could not be determined. Again, Winston is saved from this accusation by an alibi. At the same time Anne Greenwald insists that she saw Winston outside her father's home in Comal County, Winston was in fact attending a political fundraiser in downtown New Braunfels.

"Asked for comment, Winston sighed as if beleaguered, but also seemed to take this second accusation from Dr. Greenwald lightly. 'Anne Greenwald is a psychiatrist, so she would know the term for her behavior better than I. Would it be "fixation"?'

"Asked by the *Statesman* what motive Anne Greenwald would have for making false charges against him, Winston would only reply that she might be acting on behalf of her father. He declined further comment."

Wise move, that, since Winston had already used the story for everything he wanted. The tone of the story's conclusion might have come from Winston, too, though he would have been sure to distance himself from it. For the ending, the reporter returned to the murder in the mansion and to D.A. Andy Gunther, portraying him as leaning back at his desk and crossing his hands behind his head as he said, "Don't worry, we've almost got this case wrapped up." "However," the story concluded, "many observers believe that the Comal County District Attorney's Office lacks the resources to uncover the truth behind this sad death, a truth that may go back years and involve even more sordid secrets."

The last line was a bid to sell more newspapers. Chris hadn't had to buy the Austin paper, though. Within a few days other newspapers around the state had picked up the *Statesman* article, including the *San Antonio Express-News*. Chris finished reading it at his desk on Tuesday morning, and wondered why his phone hadn't rung yet.

Here came the answer. Just as Chris's phone buzzed with a message from his receptionist, a figure appeared in his open doorway. She stood there dramatically for a moment, posed with hands on hips and eyes opened wide. "How does it feel to be dating a crazy woman? Maybe we should stop it; my disease might be contagious."

"Nobody called you crazy, Anne."

Her eyes flashed even more angrily. "I'm the mental health professional here. I think I should be the judge of that. Believe me, they called me crazy—in a subtle enough way that maybe I wouldn't understand what they were saying, since I clearly don't have all my wits about me."

She came toward him and Chris rose from his chair to meet her, but then Anne veered aside to pace around the office. "You and I should probably revise our policy about not speaking to reporters. Nick Winston talked to this one and managed to twist the whole story. Now it looks like *I'm* stalking *him*! The man is beautiful, you've got to admit it."

Chris refrained from saying that if he had talked to the reporter he would only have made Anne look even worse, since Chris had seen something quite different from what Anne reported. He was also Winston's alibi witness, since he and Winston had been together in the bushes one floor down from the balcony seconds after the fatal shooting.

Chris cleared his throat. "Anne?"

As soon as he spoke her name, Anne turned quickly to face him, eyes narrowing. In spite of her scrutiny, Chris continued. "How positive are you that it was Nick Winston standing there when you found the photo?"

When she only stared at him angrily, Chris went doggedly on. "How sure? Because this time he was farther away and no one else saw him. Maybe he planned it that way. And this time it's not just one person who gives him an alibi—me—it's a whole crowd of them. A politically powerful crowd at that. It's as if he planned it."

"He did," Anne answered emphatically. "You can be sure of that. He's raising the stakes. He wants to make me look crazy because he knows I'm the only one who saw him kill Ben."

Chris nodded soberly. "So don't help him. Don't try to retaliate. Stay away from him."

"Now *you* think I'm pursuing him?"

Chris ignored the silly question, although Anne's expression made it clear she took the answer seriously. "Stay here. Everything bad that's happened so far has been in Comal County. If Winston's going to come after you any more, make him come here. Believe me, you have a much better chance of getting him arrested for stalking here. You've got friends in high places."

He didn't smile, he waited for Anne to smile first. She didn't. But she took a deep breath as if rising up from sleep, and afterward she looked more like herself. Chris walked over and put his arms around her. She sighed again and hugged him back, head on his shoulder.

"Maybe that story will light a fire under Andy Gunther," she said. "It made him sound as if he doesn't know what he's doing. Or was that too subtle a message for him to get?"

No, Chris thought, Gunther probably understood the implication of the story's conclusion, or at least had had it explained to him by now. When the reporter mentioned the limited resources of the Comal County D.A.'s office, he meant intellectual resources. The story's ending challenged Gunther to solve the case, with all these political hotshots involved.

Chris didn't tell Anne, but the idea of Gunther's accepting that challenge—to solve the case publicly—made Chris very nervous.

After Anne left, Chris returned to his review of police reports and reports from his own Intake section, the department of the office where prosecutors decided whether to indict people and for what crimes. This review took Chris's mind off his more personal case for a while, but occasionally put details of it into sharper focus. He made a call to the Juvenile section, then went to find another of his assistants.

Judy Darling ran the Victims' Assistance Department of the District Attorney's Office. A nonlawyer who had spent years working in the judicial system, Judy related to victims better than most lawyers did. Her very name seemed to put victims at ease, and her manner did the rest. Short, pale, with thick black hair and a few lines around her eyes, Judy looked fragile, but the way she acted proclaimed otherwise. She could be brisk and efficient, or she could sit and listen to a sobbing parent's story for forty-five minutes without fidgeting. Nearly all the people who came to her, most of them frustrated by their involuntary involvement in criminal proceedings, left believing that Judy Darling was their ally against the system.

Chris knocked on the doorframe of her open office door. Judy, talking on the phone, waved him in while barely looking up. She was almost ten years older than Chris and treated him with casual respect and no subservience. Some days Chris felt as if he were working for her.

"Yes, ma'am, Tuesday. Yes, we do need you here. I know, I know your whole day got wasted last time, Mrs. Torres. Damned lawyers. What can I do? But this time—I understand. How about if I talk to your boss?" Judy winked at Chris. "Yes, ma'am, I'll be glad to do that. I think I can make him understand. What's his number? All right, I'll call him in a few minutes. . . . Yes, ma'am, you certainly can."

Judy hung up and said to Chris, "Bastard resents her taking time off work to come testify that someone murdered her daughter."

"You'll turn him around," Chris said, dropping into a chair. If an office pool had been started on how long it would take Judy Darling to have the boss give his employee all the time off she needed, and be calling Judy "Ma'am" in the bargain, the entries would have run only into seconds. Judy smiled as if complimented and sat looking at him, waiting.

"I was looking at a stalking case," Chris said. "One of the few we've ever indicted. You talk to a lot of people. Do you think—?"

"That it happens a lot, without anyone's getting arrested? You bet."

"I know why people don't report them, I think, and I know why we don't indict very many. It doesn't seem like that terrible a crime at first. Following somebody around, trying to get their attention, that's something—"

Judy shook her head. "You sound like a defense lawyer, Chris. You know they're more serious than that. We don't call it 'stalking' unless the victim feels threatened. Believe me, it's frightening, thinking you're never alone, that someone's always watching."

Judy spoke as if from personal experience, but Chris didn't think so. She had absorbed so many victims' stories, they had become part of her.

"That's what I want to know, Judy. What percentage of these stalking cases turn into some worse felony? Do we have any statistics on that?"

"I have some informal ones, from our own cases. People tell me their stories, and that's how a lot of crimes started: murder, assault, kidnapping. He follows her around because he's jealous or lovestruck or whatever, until he works up the nerve to do something more."

Chris understood the gender terms Judy applied to her hypothetical situation, and she knew he knew.

"I've read a couple of national articles on the subject, too," she added.

"Let's see if we can put together some more formal statistics of our own. I think this may be the next hot crime that needs to be spotlighted. Get people to report it more, see if we can head off—"

"That's an excellent idea," Judy said. "I should have suggested it myself. What Mothers Against Drunk Driving did to

DWI in the eighties, we can do for stalking now. I'll get on it."

Chris rose from the chair, feeling he had passed a test by gaining Judy's approval. "Good. And maybe one of these days, Judy, we'll have a conversation where I can finish my thought—"

"Before I'm thinking the same thing? Sorry, Chris, I'm just a fountain of empathy."

And perhaps a mind-reader. Chris roamed his way back through the halls, something tugging at his mind. Not any of the stalking cases he'd been reading about, or Anne's problem. An image lurked just below his consciousness, not yet focused.

The newspaper story had reminded Chris of the political nature of the party at Morris Greenwald's house. That reminder stayed in the back of his mind as he went about his round of courtrooms and meetings. About mid-afternoon he went to see his first assistant. Just as Chris lifted his hand to knock on Paul's door, the door opened swiftly and Paul Benavides stepped out, so that it looked for a moment as if Chris would punch him in the throat. Both men looked startled for a moment. Paul's surprise quickly fled, but Chris remained standing with his hand raised, a faraway look in his eyes. He didn't respond when Paul said his name.

The coincidence of the door's opening reminded Chris of pushing through the swinging door into Morris Greenwald's kitchen and finding himself face-to-face with the stone-faced man in a dark suit who had studied Chris as intently as if he were a suspect in a lineup.

Then Chris remembered an event from hours later that evening, a dark sedan speeding away from the Greenwald house, as if fleeing a crime scene, but *before* the murder happened. Chris hadn't forgotten either of these events, but they hadn't seemed significant because he hadn't put them together. Now, in the instant of the door's opening before he could knock, Chris's mind put together the two earlier scenes. He remembered another detail, the small eagle-decorated lapel pin the stone-faced man had worn.

In Texas, protection of high-ranking government officials and their families is provided by the Department of Public Safety, a statewide law enforcement agency that also includes the Texas Rangers and the highway troopers who give speeding tickets. That small band of DPS troopers who provide the protection for government officials don't wear uniforms. They wear dark suits. Only a few small details give away their function: a radio receiver that might be taken for a hearing aid, a wire down the inside of a jacket sleeve that ends in a small clipped-on microphone at the cuff—and a dark blue lapel pin with a gold eagle. Chris had noticed these details and had them explained to him during a fundraising event at which the governor of Texas had appeared. An affable young trooper had been pleased to share these secrets with the district attorney, and Chris had found the trooper's job more interesting than the governor's.

The troopers, of course, also drove their protectees. Remembering the lapel pin, Chris also remembered the car speeding away from the Greenwald house, and understood its significance. Someone else had been part of those meetings, someone who had been taken away in a hurry when trouble seemed to be brewing.

But who had the trooper been protecting, and how had he known that a killing was about to take place? Had he foreseen it, or in some way inspired it?

Chris knew where to start looking for an answer.

★ Anne listened to the tale that seemed to be told by an idiot. The eleven-year-old girl with thick, glossy hair, very black eyes, and round cheeks explained earnestly that she had thrown the rock through the school window in self-defense. Sylvia had been caught when she confessed to the deed, and now she'd been through the whole system: juvenile court, a finding of delinquency because she had committed criminal mischief, and a court order that Anne evaluate her as a condition of her probation.

For their first meeting Anne took the girl across the street from the Santa Rosa Hospital to the playground in Milam Park. The city had recently upgraded the park into a pleasant place for children to play, with groupings of slides, swings, and climbing forts, and lots of benches from which tired parents could watch or ignore them. Anne often brought kids here and walked with them as they talked. It put them more at ease than sitting in Anne's comfortable, cluttered, but undeniably clinical office.

Sylvia continued, "My daddy brought me to the school playground at six o'clock on Sunday because that's where my mother's supposed to get me from him at the end of his week-end. The judge said for them not to go to each other's houses anymore, because there's too much chance for trouble. If Mommy's boyfriend is there especially. But sometimes there's nobody else at the playground. I think the judge should pick a different place, like maybe McDonald's, where there'd be people around."

In a perfect world, no child should ever use the phrase "Mommy's boyfriend." In Sylvia's world, Anne knew, the girl was lucky to have both a mother and father, and know who they were. As Sylvia talked about her playground scene Anne looked around the real playground and seemed to see too many strange adults not attached to a playing child. Most looked burned-out from weariness, but at least one was watching her. Anne could feel it, though so far she hadn't caught anyone's eyes. She stood straighter and concentrated on the small girl at her side. Sylvia idly climbed a small set of monkey bars until she was sitting at eye level with Anne. At first the girl's face showed little emotion as she talked. She had told the story too often.

"So I was swinging, and when Mommy came, Daddy said something to her and Mommy stopped coming toward me and said something back to him and right away they started again. Just like when they were married." Sylvia's eyes slid away from Anne's as she obviously remembered that time. The little girl didn't shudder. She sat very still, as if wanting to disappear.

"I called to Mommy that I wanted to go home, I was hungry, but they didn't hear me. I was so afraid he was going to hit her like he used to, or she'd scratch him. If she did . . .

"But nobody was around! The judge should have picked a different place," Sylvia insisted again.

"I'll talk to the judge," Anne promised. She leaned forward on her forearms on a bar and stared earnestly at the girl, concentrating. Sometimes the only help she could give her patients was the attention they didn't get anywhere else. "So you got mad? That's when you picked up the rock?"

"No." Sylvia seemed surprised by this interpretation of events. "I wasn't mad, I was scared. I would have screamed, but I didn't think anybody would hear me. And if I ran away they'd catch me. So I broke the school window with a rock to set off the alarm. I was pretty sure the windows had alarms.

"After I threw the rock they both started yelling at me. But the alarm started ringing and Daddy yelled, 'Take her!' and ran off toward his car and my mother grabbed my hand and pulled me to her car and fussed at me all the way home."

"But he didn't hit her. I kept him from doing that."

Sylvia sounded proud. Her chin came up, her lips set in a line impervious to any lecture. Anne didn't feel like scolding her, anyway. It sounded as if the girl, who stood under five feet tall and didn't weigh ninety pounds, had made an excellent adjustment to what life demanded of her. Anne thought the rock-through-the-window solution ingenious.

But the judge probably wouldn't want to see in Anne's report that she had complimented the girl on destroying school property.

Instead, Anne said slowly, "Nobody caught you, Sylvia. You got away. Why did you tell your teacher the next day that you were the one who threw the rock through the window?"

Sylvia sounded surprised at Anne's slowness. "So they'd send me to Juvenile." Anne raised her eyebrows and the girl continued. "So I'd be put on probation, and have a probation officer, and maybe have CPS come around the house." CPS stood for Child Protective Services, the agency that often took children from abusive parents. Sylvia dropped the terminology easily. In her world, having a P.O. was as common as graduating from high school. "So I'd get to talk to someone like you," Sylvia concluded triumphantly.

With one rock, the girl had acquired a set of guardians who, while ostensibly monitoring her behavior, would also oversee her household—and notice bruises.

After climbing the monkey bars to be at Anne's level, the girl had shown no more interest in the playground. She hugged herself and scanned the other people. At six o'clock, the park had begun to empty out as working people went home. Anne joined the girl in looking at the remainders. One man close to the far sidewalk stared at Anne, maintaining eye contact, then abruptly threw down his cigarette, stepped on it, and walked away. The Hispanic man with deep-set eyes would never be mistaken for Nick Winston, but his eyes had brought to mind the other man.

"Let's go in," Sylvia said, beating Anne to the thought. Anne took her hand as they walked back to the tower that contained Anne's offices, and the girl seemed younger than her years as her little fingers nestled inside her psychiatrist's. "Next time can we stay in your office?" she asked.

"You bet," Anne assured her. Anne had no trouble at all putting herself inside the little girl's skin. There on the hard steel playground, Anne's empathy worked like a charm. The kind of charm that conjured up an evil genie.

An hour later Anne arrived at her house, briefcase in one hand and two bulging files under her right arm, a fast-food pita sandwich hanging in a plastic bag from that hand, groping with her left for her house keys. The sun had only recently descended; the house wasn't dark, though no lights illuminated it. Inside, Anne clicked on a floor lamp from the switch beside the door. She dropped everything but the sandwich bag on the couch, and carried dinner to the kitchen. The house felt unused and dusty with heat. Anne turned down the thermostat and went into the bedroom. Her blouse hung damply on her from the day's humidity. She discarded it in the bathroom hamper and walked back into the living room. There, in her long living/dining room, she noticed how open to the outside world her house remained. She liked it like that; she had arranged it that way. Some of the windows, such as those in the living/dining room that faced the doorway and the side of the house next door, didn't have shades of any kind.

Anne returned to the front door and locked it; she hadn't had a free hand to do that when she'd come in. The central air-conditioning's pumping masked the small sound of the lock's click. Anne stood with her back to the door for a moment and surveyed the house. It was just as she had left it that morning. Except that the door to the extra bedroom was closed tight. Anne usually left it ajar, or fully open. The coming to life of the air conditioner might have pushed the door closed; it sometimes had that effect. Anne opened the bedroom door, pushed it wide, and looked in. The room held a twin bed, a dresser, and the remains of what had been Anne's home office before she'd re-converted the room into a bedroom. A computer desk and two filing cabinets stood in a corner of the room as if disgruntled at having been shoved aside for bedroom furnishings.

Anne didn't look into the room's closet or under the bed. Paranoia didn't have that strong a grip on her. She just wanted the door open, so the room could join the rest of the house. After a quick glance around, she returned to her own bedroom and finished changing clothes, into cutoff jeans and a dark blue T-shirt that carried the seal of the Bexar County District Attorney's Office over the heart. She seemed to pick the shirt at random, but if a patient had told her that, Anne would have grimaced. She pulled her hair out of the neck of the shirt and thought, as she always did in early June, about cutting it short. Anne's bare feet padded almost soundlessly on the hardwood floor as she walked to the kitchen. The wooden floor and the hard white tile of the kitchen floor remained cool even in the dead of summer, one of the subtle luxuries of a house built before air-conditioning.

Anne ate the sandwich with a glass of skim milk, sitting at her dining room table looking out the side windows, watching night erase the neighborhood, the house next door, and finally everything except the room in which she was sitting, as the black windows turned reflective. She had set the air conditioning too low; it had finally brought the temperature down. Anne felt cold in her summer outfit—she should get up and turn on the outside lights—but for a brief spell she felt paralyzed. Evenings of a single life: as often as she and Chris were together, she still spent many nights like this, wondering how best to use the hours until bedtime. She had a list of *should*s: exercise, review those files, read the newspaper. But if she sat and read files or a textbook she would have no break from work at all. In fact, the dinner sitting alone at her table had felt much like her working lunch, a sandwich eaten at her desk. Anne liked her work, but there should be an end to it sometime. Once she had enjoyed this, having so many hours at her disposal to do her job. Now she vaguely wanted a second part to the day, one she didn't have.

She didn't need constant rewards. But when the workday never ended between dawn and sleep, her mind never lifted from its normal paths. That was the way to grow rigid and narrow. She had counseled people to that effect, but of course telling people how to live was always easier than changing her own habits.

Anne didn't need to rise and walk through the house to review her options. She didn't even have to turn her head. The exercycle wouldn't be enough of a break. That, too, was work.

She had chosen this life, more than once when someone had offered an alternative. The price of self-indulgence is loneliness, but Anne had always been ready to make that bargain. She liked her own company; usually she could entertain herself better than other people could. But inevitably nights like this intruded on her satisfaction. She remembered Ben Sewell, not regretfully, just imagining lonely nights he must have spent because—in a way—of Anne, and of nights they had spent together, some of them fun and interesting. Up until a month ago he had seldom crossed her mind, but she hated thinking of him gone from the world, all his possibilities narrowed to a single point.

Shadows moved behind the reflections in the windows. How could there be shadows at night? Yet undeniably the darkness wasn't uniform; it held patterns of paler and deeper dark. Anne stirred in her lethargy, took her dishes to the kitchen, and padded out the back door. Her backyard was large but tame, with an old mulberry tree and two oaks that gave ample shade and provided fragrance and sounds as well, leaves that the breeze could set whispering. Anne didn't garden except in fits of Saturday flower-planting, and that remained confined to the front yard. Back here only grass prevailed. A twelve-year-old neighbor boy kept it trimmed for a ridiculously cheap $10 a pop, but he compensated by mowing the yard more often than Anne would have liked. She would have appreciated a little wildness back here, but this grass lay thoroughly cowed.

Her back porch was only a small concrete slab. She stepped

down off it into the grass, cool under her bare feet. All the yards on this street were surrounded by chain-link fencing. At the back of Anne's yard a six-foot-high wooden fence kept her and that neighbor from seeing each other's houses. There was a dog back there that sometimes barked fiercely, but it had grown deaf to Anne's scent and stayed quiet tonight. Anne didn't have a dog of her own, though Chris occasionally urged her to get one. She had enough responsibility in her life, and usually enough companionship. But a canine friend in the yard would have been comforting tonight.

The moon had risen, close enough to full to create moving patterns on the ground below the trees and to allow Anne to see the yards on either side. Her neighbors didn't have their yards artificially illuminated tonight, either. In fact, no one seemed to be home at either house. Anne stood feeling comfortably alone. She crossed her arms and looked up through the trees. Sometimes home ownership quietly reassured her of belonging somewhere. She didn't know how Chris could stand to live in a condominium at his age. He talked about buying a house, but spending time at hers seemed to fulfill that urge. Anne smiled, thinking of Chris. She wanted to call him, but wouldn't. He'd be busy with Clarissa, or work of his own. She could certainly let one day and night pass without talking to him.

A stray cool breeze, adrift from a different climate, raised gooseflesh on her arms. A sound to Anne's left made her turn quickly in that direction. There was nothing to be seen except the dark yards fading into impenetrable night. Anne stood staring as if another sense could reach past that blindness. Moonlight dappled the grass and trees. She felt as if someone were standing there just beyond the reach of her vision. Why, she couldn't have said. She took a few steps deeper into the yard, for a different angle, but saw nothing. "Hello?" she called, half to break the silence and half-hoping that dog across the fence would hear her and start his stupid yapping. But the dog didn't respond and the silence quickly swallowed her one word.

This was stupid. She should put on the lights. She knew exactly what she feared, and why she didn't fear him enough to cower indoors. Twice she had seen Nick Winston staring at her, one of those times just after she had seen him kill another man. But she hadn't feared Winston either time. He stood too cool and poised to do anything as messy as touching her. And if anyone hurt Anne now, he would be the first suspect. Though she had been angered by his presence, and by the photo he'd left, she refused to let him cow her.

Nonetheless, it seemed a long way back to her back door. She reached it, pulled open the screen, twisted the knob of the heavier inner door—for a moment it resisted as if locked—and hurried back inside. The door slammed shut behind her. The air conditioning did that, Anne thought. She locked the door, turned on her back porch light, hurried through the kitchen and the living/dining room, and beside the front door flipped the switch turning on the front lights as well. Her suddenly bright driveway lay empty of any car except hers. She turned both locks on the front door—hadn't she done that already—turned to put her back to the door, and let out her breath in a giggle. She felt silly. These few minutes had certainly been a break from her workday routine. The sudden build and release of tension had accomplished what she needed, lifted her mind to a wholly different plane—one where only staying alive mattered.

Still smiling to herself, she stepped away from the door, glancing at the clock high on the wall above the kitchen doorway, caught something wrong from the corner of her eye, then turned to her right and stopped dead.

The door to the second bedroom stood closed tight.

Anne had opened that door only a few minutes ago—she knew she had. This time the damned air conditioning had not closed it, because the air conditioning had been running for more than an hour now, not causing any sudden gusts. Besides, she had left the bedroom door wide open.

She didn't have a gun in the house. She stood barefoot in shorts and T-shirt. Anne could walk out her front door, but she would have to keep walking. Her car keys sat in the kitchen, her purse with her driver's license and money in the bedroom. She could probably reach the phone in the kitchen, to call 911 or Chris, but either might end up making her look silly.

But silly beat dead every time. She walked softly to the kitchen, listening for the sound of that bedroom door opening behind her. She stepped onto the cool tile floor and stood there with the swinging door leaning against her back, picking up the wall phone just inside the kitchen door. She dialed Chris's number, thinking no one would answer, but someone did after only two rings.

"Clarissa, Hi. Is he there? No?" Anne bit her lip. "No, it's OK—Wait. Yes, you can. Listen, Clarissa, can you do this? I'm going to put down the phone. If you hear me yell or something, call 911 to come to my house. Do you know the address? . . . Nothing, I'll tell you later."

Carefully, Anne set the receiver down on her dining table. She walked—more quickly than before, because she felt Clarissa waiting tensely—across the room, quickly turned the knob of the bedroom door, and flung it open. The door banged back against the wall with a sharp crack, not the dull stop of hitting something soft, and came back toward her. Anne stopped it with her hand. The noise of the door had broken the quiet. Anne raised her voice to keep it broken.

"Come on in, I'm pretty sure I've got it here in this filing cabinet. No, it'll just take a minute."

She pulled open the creaky drawer of the old metal filing cabinet while looking all around the room, which was empty of humanity. After the file drawer stood open, Anne swiftly pulled open the closet door next to it. Her idea was that if someone were standing inside the closet she would push the door closed again, and even after he opened it the file drawer would still be blocking his exit, giving her time to run toward the phone and scream.

The closet, which held her winter coats and long dresses, looked full. Anne couldn't see behind the clothes at first. It took her almost a minute, reaching tentatively and then more and more briskly, to be sure that no one was hiding there.

She exhaled again, put her hands on her hips, and surveyed the room. It occupied the front corner of the house and so had four windows spread across two walls. From where Anne was standing she could see the windows were still fastened. Besides, they had alarms—like her little client's school's windows—because of a previous problem like this. That left only the bed for a hiding place. Anne went resolutely toward it, raising her voice again to say something silly and meaningless, keeping up her own courage more than anything else. She inhaled deeply and bent suddenly to pull up the dust ruffle of the twin bed.

By the time she returned to the telephone, Clarissa was calling her name. Anne quickly answered reassuringly. "It was nothing, dear. Thank you. No, I was just being silly. I needed your help, though. Thank you, Clarissa. Will Chris be home soon? . . . No, I mean for you. Do you have his cell phone number? . . . No, I have it, I just wanted to make sure you did. All right. Good night, Clarissa . . . No, it's nothing to worry about, believe me. Don't tell Chris." She almost said, *Let it be our secret,* but Clarissa was too old to fall for that little-kid secretiveness.

"I promise, I will. Keep this to yourself and I'll explain it the next time I see you. Promise."

Anne hung up the phone, feeling the outside world recede as she did so. She stood there for a long moment looking around at the doors of this room. She felt reluctant to approach any of them. The house no longer felt like hers. If some bastard had wanted to accomplish that, he had done a good job. On the other hand, Anne might have done this to herself, which would be a much bigger problem, if she kept letting it happen.

She consciously relaxed, letting her shoulders broaden and slump and her eyes narrow. She started growing angry, a common reaction Anne could easily have explained psychologically, but she didn't try to analyze it to death. She welcomed the reaction.

Still, she had a very fitful night's sleep. By the time she lay in bed the alarms were set on the front and back doors; no one could get into the house without waking Anne and alerting the police. But the fear that kept pulling her back from the edge of sleep was that he was already inside. Not just inside her house, inside her head.

Chris got lucky with the website of the governor of Texas. The website wouldn't provide the governor's daily schedule—his security officers would insist on keeping that information unavailable—but the governor apparently had a very active webmaster who updated the site at least weekly, providing a broad outline of the governor's activities. Chris had gone to the website rather idly, but found just what he wanted. Two weeks ago, for four days, the governor of Texas had attended the Southern Governors' Conference in Atlanta. The site chronicled the event with photos, including several of the Texas governor standing prominently among his peers.

The second day of the conference had been the Friday on which Morris had held his party—the gathering that had turned out so tragic for Ben Sewell. At the time of the shooting, the governor of Texas had been speaking to hundreds of people in the Atlanta Civic Center. No way the governor could also have been in New Braunfels, Texas.

Chris wasn't sure who else drew protection from the Texas Department of Public Safety, but the governor's wife had been at the conference with him and their three children were grown, probably not getting daily protection. So when Chris went to Austin looking for the stone-faced man he'd seen in Morris Greenwald's kitchen, he had a good idea where to start.

On his way out of town he stopped to see Anne, and caught her between appointments. She remained sitting and blinked at him tiredly for a moment as if trying to place Chris as a fourteen-year-old shoplifter.

"What's the matter with you?"

"Nothing," Anne said with a little edge in her voice, as if she'd been fending off this question all morning. "Just didn't get enough sleep."

Less than eight hours' sleep was undoubtedly a regular event for Anne, but Chris had seldom seen her look this distracted and irritable.

"I'm on my way to Austin, want to come?"

"You know, Chris, to do something that spontaneous I'd need about three weeks' notice. Anyway, the short answer is No, I don't."

He sat on the side of her desk and leaned toward her. "Watson could always drop his practice when Holmes told him the game was afoot."

"Watson's practice was fictitious and probably just a front for a bordello with a woman to run it for him. Mine is a little more hands-on. *There* it is." She pulled a file out from under Chris's leg with more effort than the job strictly required, as if she wanted to slide Chris off the desk at the same time. He obliged by standing up.

"Are you all right? Clarissa said you called last night."

"If you were so concerned, why didn't you call me back?"

"She said you said not to."

Anne frowned up at him as if she'd finally realized who he was but didn't like what she saw. "So now you do everything I tell you to do? Or not to do?"

"What's the matter with you?"

Anne sighed and consciously relaxed. "I told you, I didn't get enough sleep. But the main problem is I've still got the little sociopath I just interviewed in my head, and I'm about to have another kid sitting there who really isn't a bad kid, just doesn't realize all his options, and when he arrives I'm supposed to look like I have all the answers, and it takes a few minutes for me to get there."

"So you're a Method psychiatrist," Chris dead-panned.

Anne gave him a long stare that turned more amiable the longer it lingered on him. Chris understood that that long friendly gaze turning slightly intimate was the most she could give him in this place at this time, so he smiled back, said he'd see her that night, and 'Bye.

As he opened her office door, Anne said, "Chris? What's in Austin?"

He turned. "Sorry, Dr. Greenwald, if you're too busy, then you don't get the reward of being the first to know, after me. Anyway, the short answer is I don't know."

He slipped out the door, leaving behind for a moment his hand giving her a jaunty wave. Anne smiled and waved back, as if Chris could see through walls. Five minutes later she nodded along as the teenager caught shoplifting told her his story. Within minutes after that she had entered his world, her own worries left completely behind but waiting until she came up on the other side.

The eighty-mile drive to Austin, straight up Interstate 35, was so familiar to Chris it could almost lull him to sleep. This was the trek he had made almost monthly while going to school at the University of Texas fifteen years earlier, and he had had regular business in Austin ever since, especially as an elected official. The state capital, centrally located close to the heart of Texas, routinely attracted all the politicians in the state. This had helped give the town a sense of importance out of proportion to its size. In recent years Austin had grown a silicon link to the West Coast, with several computer and Internet companies moving to Austin or starting up there, so that the city's income had finally caught up to its ego. In Chris's college days Austin had been a very nice place to be poor; now it almost demanded wealth, the newer the better.

Driving in from Austin's south side, though, Chris could forget those changes. He took the Riverside Drive exit just before the Colorado River, turned west and then north again, so he approached the capitol building from Congress Avenue, the building's front door. The Texas capitol was a near-replica of the national one, except a few feet taller if you counted the statue on top of the dome—which Texans did because it allowed them to claim the tallest capitol building in America.

The capitol looked white and beautiful and the Avenue prosperous as Chris drove up Congress. A few years earlier a blight had killed the majestic live oaks that used to line the drive up to the capitol, but state gardeners had replaced them with elms that looked less ancient but more elegant. Chris parked at a meter and walked up that drive, through the park that surrounded the capitol complex. Chris didn't have an appointment with anyone or even a good idea whom he might see, but he had a destination he felt confident of finding. He entered the capitol like a tourist, stopped on the star in the middle of the large foyer, and stared up inside the dome like every other out-of-towner come to visit, then walked into the building's interior.

The capitol featured extremely tall ceilings, wood molding and trim, and many doors, as if a crew of elves worked in a building designed for titans. As Chris strolled around, his imagination made him feel guilty, as if he were plotting a crime. The building could have been full of people with such plans. Chris hadn't had to pass through a metal detector to come in. Department of Public Safety troopers were standing in the halls at regular intervals, conspicuous in their khaki uniforms and cowboy hats. These men had watchful eyes even when talking desultorily to each other; their gazes seemed to grow even more alert when Chris passed the same spot more than once. He felt sure more troopers would be stationed inside the more important offices of the capitol. They made Chris's own office security look lax.

He finally consulted the information desk and learned that the office of the lieutenant governor lay behind the Senate chamber, the body over which the lieutenant governor presided when the legislature was in session. The Texas legislature meets for only 150 days every two years, so in early June most of the legislators had been gone—back to their districts—for a month. Another oddity of Texas government is that legislators are paid a pitiful salary, roughly $4,000 a year, but can hire several full-time staff members, so the bureaucrats could govern year-round, while the people's elected representatives had to go find jobs.

The lieutenant governor was an exception, one of a handful of full-time public officials elected statewide. While the governor of Texas had very little constitutional authority—the power to make some appointments, issue stays of execution, and offer legislation—everyone inside the capitol knew that the lieutenant governor wielded more actual power by presiding over the Senate, a position from which legislation could be guided to approval or killed without ever coming to a vote.

And she rated protection from Department of Public Safety troopers who wore suits rather than uniforms. Since Chris had determined that the governor of Texas had been somewhere else the night of Morris Greenwald's party, the lieutenant governor was the only other official he knew of who would have brought such a protector to the house: a man like the one Chris had encountered in Morris's kitchen.

Chris walked through the empty Senate chamber and through a door up front that led into a wide hallway. Across this hall, the heavy outer doors of the lieutenant governor's offices stood open. Beside one of them a discreet bronze plaque announced the current holder of the office: "Veronica Sorenson, Lieutenant Governor of Texas."

Chris tried to remember all he knew about the second-term lieutenant governor, and found very little except the standard bio: Mrs. Sorenson had been raised on a central Texas ranch, but spent much time in Austin and Dallas, acquiring an excellent education, including a master's degree in psychology. Her private life consisted of a stable marriage and two teenaged children kept out of the limelight. Veronica Sorenson was said to work wisely and without fanfare behind the scenes of government, but every election year her profile grew, because she was always mentioned as a strong possibility for higher office: the United States Senate or even the Vice Presidency.

Chris tried to remember some personal details about Mrs. Sorenson's life and couldn't, except a joke, that she was "Ronnie" to her supporters, "Mrs. Sorenson" to her intimates. One thing voters admired about her was that she was relentlessly unflamboyant.

Chris had worn a suit for this occasion, and had picked it out with more than usual care. He straightened his lapels, put on the frown of an important personage, and strode boldly into the lieutenant governor's office and up to the receptionist's desk. To her polite inquiry, he said, "I'm sorry, I know this is unusual. My name is Chris Sinclair, I'm the district attorney of Bexar County."

"Yes, sir, Mr. Sinclair, I recognize you."

Probably not true, but flattering to say. The young woman gave him an attentive smile.

"Thank you. I wonder if I could see the lieutenant governor for just a very few minutes. I know her day must be full, but this would only take—"

"May I ask why?" The receptionist continued smiling, showing lovely even teeth. Very politely she asked the question that had to be asked, without yet revealing whether Veronica Sorenson was even in the building.

Chris hesitated. He had a lie prepared but under the receptionist's open gaze he decided to abandon it. "Just say it's about Morris Greenwald, please."

The receptionist didn't blink or otherwise show that the name meant anything to her. But she rose from her chair and said, "Let me see if anyone can help you."

As she started out the door behind her Chris began, "I don't think anyone except Mrs. Sorenson could—" The receptionist smiled again, as if he weren't speaking, and said, "I'll just be a minute."

Chris waited that minute and more, leaning on the tall, dark wood counter that separated the waiting area from admittance to the inner office. He felt observed. After a minute he turned suddenly, thinking this would be the scene where a small army of people came through the outer door and hustled him away. But the waiting area remained undisturbed. A uniformed DPS trooper was standing near the door, but he had been there all along and hadn't moved. Chris nodded in his direction, but the young trooper didn't seem to notice.

The receptionist returned, leaving open the door behind her, and said, "Ms. Wright will be glad to see you, sir. She's Mrs. Sorenson's—"

"No, I'm afraid no one else could help."

The receptionist reached behind her and closed that inner door. "I'm sorry. Perhaps you could leave your card."

Chris took one out and turned it over to write on the back. "I'll be in Austin the rest of the afternoon. If the lieutenant governor finds a minute to spare, this is my cell phone number."

Moments later he found himself standing back in the hallway. During this brief episode there hadn't been a moment's unpleasantness or any attitude displayed except utmost civility, but he had been brushed off as effectively as if those imagined armed guards had burst in and hurled him outside. In fact, Chris had been kicked out so efficiently yet politely that Veronica Sorenson could still count on his vote the next time she wanted it.

Chris was left thinking that he had probably made a mistake about the lieutenant governor's attendance at Morris Greenwald's house the night of Ben Sewell's death. If she had been there, she would know that Chris had been, too, and

would have responded to his coming to her office with at least
a brief interview, to find out what he knew. Besides, he hadn't
seen the stone-faced man in the black suit. His assignment
must be elsewhere, which meant Chris was wrong in thinking
it was the lieutenant governor the man had accompanied that
night in New Braunfels.

But he had come all the way to Austin, and wouldn't give up
even a mistaken idea so easily. Chris took up his post out in
the entry hall on a backless bench, took out a book, and settled down. Surveillance was the most boring task an investigator ever drew, and required resources most people didn't have:
the capacity to do nothing for a long time. Jack Fine had
taught Chris this among other lessons: "The thing about surveillance is," Jack had said, "when you're just sitting there for
so long you have lots and lots of opportunities to tell yourself
this is a waste of time. The body wants to move, and after a
while so does the mind, so you have to constantly argue yourself into submission. Most of the time, watching somebody's
place doesn't pay off, and you know that, so sooner or later the
vast majority of people manage to convince themselves that
there's something much more efficient they could be doing
somewhere else to break the case."

"How do you argue yourself out of leaving?" Chris has
asked curiously.

"I imagine that just after I leave the guy I'm looking for
walks out and sees I'm not there and laughs at me."

Chris didn't imagine Veronica Sorenson laughing at him.
But he knew very well he didn't have anything else to do this
afternoon. He sat and read.

At 12:45 he was rewarded with a glimpse of the lieutenant
governor. A woman came out of the office doors, speaking
back over her shoulder. Then a DPS trooper's brown-shirted
back blocked Chris's view of the next person who emerged,

but Chris craned his neck and as the small party turned he caught a glimpse of Veronica Sorenson's face. She stopped to answer back her staffer, felt Chris's attention, and glanced across the hall at him. Then she stopped.

Chris had seen the lieutenant governor's face in newsprint many times, and had briefly met her once. Around forty years old, Veronica Sorenson technically looked younger—her skin smooth, no sag to her jaw or neck—except that she radiated experience. She had very dark hair with lighter highlights that framed her face, which looked thin and elegant, though full-mouthed. Brown eyes lit on Chris briefly and seemed to take in everything significant about him.

Another trooper—obviously one, though he wore a suit—emerged from the office behind her, and Mrs. Sorenson even put a hand lightly on this man's shoulder to move him aside so that she could study Chris. Chris stood up. He recognized her, but Veronica Sorenson couldn't possibly remember him from their one brief meeting in a reception line. If she remembered seeing him, it could only be as he was driving back to the Greenwald house while her car was speeding away from it.

He took a step toward her. But if he'd thought Veronica Sorenson wanted to speak to him, he was mistaken. She turned away and her party hurried down the hall, leaving Chris alone. He hurried out into the Senate chamber to stare after the lieutenant governor, but she didn't look back.

He almost gave up then, but didn't. Chris got a sandwich from the capitol's cafeteria and returned to his self-assigned post on the bench. Now he was going to stay here as long as it took. If this trip was a waste of Chris's time, he was going to waste it right. His posture took on a grim attitude as he hunched over the second of the two paperback books he'd brought along.

Around five o'clock he felt the building begin to empty out

all around him. Small rustlings and footsteps grew larger collectively as most of the clerical staff left together, including half a dozen people from the lieutenant governor's office. Chris wanted to join this exodus, but stayed on. At five-thirty the DPS trooper in the dark suit came out of the lieutenant governor's office. Chris thought he must be accompanying Mrs. Sorenson again, but this time the young man walked out alone and kept going, out into the Senate chamber and away. Chris almost followed him but didn't, luckily.

Chris decided to take one more stab at getting in now that most of the lieutenant governor's staff had gone. He walked quickly to those tall front doors, and just as he reached them a man stepped out and blocked his path. The black-suited man looked to be in his fifties and was a couple of inches shorter than Chris, but appeared formidable. His shoulders seemed to widen to block the doorway. He clasped his hands in front of him, clenched his jaw, and gave Chris a stony stare that seemed familiar. It was the same one Chris had received in Morris Greenwald's kitchen from this same man.

"Excuse me," Chris said perfunctorily, stepping to the side.

So did the trooper. "No," he said.

Chris stared at the man harder. "My name is—"

"I know who you are, sir. But I'm afraid the lieutenant governor doesn't have time to talk this afternoon. I came to tell you not to try to intercept her."

"Isn't she curious about why I came?"

"No." *And neither am I*, the man's face said clearly.

Behind him, the inner door opened. Chris looked past the black-suited trooper and saw Veronica Sorenson emerge from the inner office, again accompanied by three other people, including a younger man in a dark suit. The trooper in front of Chris seemed to sense her presence and stepped forward, moving Chris out of the doorway.

Mrs. Sorenson came through the doorway ahead of the others. For the second time that afternoon her eyes caught Chris's. She blinked and paused. "Ma'am," Chris said distinctly, "this would only take one minute."

Chris didn't move, but the trooper in front of him put out a hand as if he had.

Veronica Sorenson sighed. "Mr. Sinclair, I'm afraid I have no help to give you. I'm sure Morris Greenwald has said he knows me, but I'm sure you understand that a lot of people say that when in fact I don't remember them. If I knew anything about what happened at his home that night I would come forward, believe me, but I don't."

"As a matter of fact, Morris hasn't mentioned you," Chris said levelly. He felt all the pairs of eyes on him. The lieutenant governor's turned slightly curious.

But she had discipline. She had made a decision and she would stick with it. "I'm sorry," she said, and turned away. The black-suited trooper held his ground in front of Chris, who realized that a shoving contest would be silly and futile.

"Trooper—What is your name, by the way? You know mine."

"Smith," the man said flatly.

"All right, Trooper Smith, do you think this is really the best way of protecting her, having her not talk to me so I have no choice but to go to authorities to tell them what I know?"

"I don't make those decisions, sir. And I don't think you know anything. She wasn't there that night."

"Then why were you?"

Trooper Smith took two or three slow breaths while deciding whether to answer. "I have several assignments, including temporary duties at times."

"I'll check on that," Chris said, intending a threat. The trooper didn't flinch. He stood there silently for a few more seconds, until he judged that his protectee had gotten safely away from this intruder, then the stone-faced man turned and walked quickly away. Chris wanted to call after him but couldn't think of anything to say. His interview with the lieutenant governor had ended.

But he felt more certain than ever that she was hiding information. At any rate, now he had something to ask Morris Greenwald.

After Chris knocked on Anne's door late the next afternoon he decided she wasn't home after all, because he stood for a minute without the door's opening. But he felt observed, then heard unfamiliar noises. The door swung open, revealing Anne's face. "Hi," she said with a strange, unfamiliar tone. She might as well have said, "May I help you?"

"What's the matter with you?"

"Nothing," she answered, still with the bright, false tone. Anne swung the door open wide, showing she still wore the long-sleeved pale yellow blouse she had worn to work, but had changed into white shorts. "What's up?"

"'Hi'? 'What's up'? Who are you, what've you done with Anne?"

Anne laughed, more like herself. "I'm sorry, I guess I was—thinking about something else. Come on in."

He did, happened to glance at the doorframe as he passed through it, and frowned anew.

"Where's Clarissa?" she asked.

"Went home from school with a friend. I'm supposed to pick her up in a little while. If she's making friends, great, but I'm afraid she's just trying to give me . . . Never mind. What happened here?"

"Nothing. What do you mean?"

"I mean before you let me in I heard your little fingers tapping on your alarm pad, turning off the alarm, and taking off this brand new chain lock, after you'd had time to look out and see it was me standing on your porch. Most of the time you forget to turn on your alarm, and never before you go to bed, and you usually just fling open your door to whoever knocks. Plus you called me a couple of nights ago and Clarissa said you sounded weird. So what happened here?"

"Nothing."

"Anne—"

"No, I mean it, nothing happened. That was the weird part." She folded her arms as if chilled, pretty much an impossibility in San Antonio in June. Chris went to hold her but she stepped away from him. Over her shoulder she said slowly, "I'm sure somebody was here, but he didn't do anything."

"Why didn't you tell me?"

"Because it was literally nothing. Nothing happened except I got scared."

"Was it him? Winston?"

"I don't know. I never saw anybody." But that was a lie too. Anne had felt his presence, his handiwork. If Nick Winston hadn't been in her house, someone acting for him had been. "I can't even be positive anybody was here, Chris." She gave him a very brief account of her possible intruder two nights before. "But nothing happened, nobody took anything, nobody left me a threatening note."

"Except by implication." Chris's face had darkened with blood. He walked across the living room and looked through the open door into the second bedroom. It looked not only undisturbed but pristine, a museum exhibit of an early-twenty-first-century bedroom. The rug on the floor lay diametrically centered, the twin bed not only made tightly but made out invitingly as if by a hotel maid. "You know that's what he was doing—sending you a message of what he could do."

"No, I don't." Anne spoke firmly. Now her folded arms projected stubbornness. "Maybe all he wanted was for me to make another report that would turn out to be obviously false. I haven't checked on where he was that night, but it was probably miles away with lots of witnesses. I thought maybe he just wanted to make me look—unreliable."

"So you didn't even tell me?"

"You're the district attorney."

Chris looked as if she had slapped him. The thought crossed his mind in an instant: *Is that all?* Anne suddenly looked anguished as she stepped toward him. "No," she said loudly. "But you are, Chris. Wouldn't you have to report it? Wouldn't you start investigating? Look at you, that's what you're planning to do right now. And that means somebody else will find out what I thought, and I won't be able to prove it and I'll look nutty again."

Chris stood still, his eyes on her but his thoughts elsewhere. Of course he planned to investigate this. Anne was right about that. Maybe he would do it quietly, unofficially. But Anne already knew his thoughts. She looked at him imploringly.

"Don't you see? That's his game. He has to discredit me."

"Or worse," Chris snapped.

"No, I think I'm safe," Anne said quickly. She had obviously thought about this a lot, perhaps obsessively. "He can't really hurt me. If anything happened to the one person who's accused him of murder—No, he's not stupid enough for that. He's a lot more devious. He's proven that."

She stopped suddenly, shooting Chris a sidelong glance. He turned away, walking toward the door as if to examine the lock. She hadn't mentioned her father's balcony, but he knew what she meant. Their different sights of what had happened still lay between them, though never discussed anymore.

"Look," Chris said authoritatively, turning back to her. "This is why I told you to stay in San Antonio. Now it's happened in my territory. This is good. I'll send an investigator out here, at least dust for fingerprints—"

"You think he'd be stupid enough to—"

"But it doesn't matter. If we can't prove anything, we don't say anything. We bide our time."

Anne watched Chris, knowing how much he'd like to have proof. She felt herself longing to prove something, anything, to him, and hated the feeling. This was why she'd hesitated to open the door.

"Listen . . ."

And someone knocked at the door. A quick rap, as if the door stood ajar and the rapper had been listening to them. Chris turned quickly and pulled the door open. A tall but doughy man stood there with a blank face, eyebrows raised at the sight of Chris. Even with what could have been taken as a surprised start, the man's brown eyes remained flat. He was about Chris's age, with dark hair combed straight back, revealing a strong widow's peak between receding hairlines. He kept his arms at his sides.

"What do you want?" Chris snapped.

"Bruce!" Anne said as if in answer.

The man turned to her and said coolly, "Hello, Anne." Then he looked back at Chris as if their business weren't finished or he was waiting for an explanation of Chris's presence.

"What is it?" Anne asked the newcomer, drawing his attention back to her.

"Hello to you, too," the man repeated. "I need to talk to you."

"That's what I'm asking you to do, Bruce." Anne sounded

exasperated, as if taking up an old conversation with old irritation.

Again the man looked openly at Chris, obviously waiting for him to offer to leave. When no one moved, the man—Bruce—sighed, turned back to Anne, and said, "Dad's in trouble. He needs your help."

"How?"

Bruce waited a beat for emphasis, and said flatly, "He needs to be bailed out of jail."

"What? For what? What did he do?"

Bruce looked at Anne as if she were being deliberately stupid. "For murder, of course. They've arrested him for killing Ben Sewell."

The tall, pudgy man looked back and forth between Anne and Chris and seemed neither pleased nor surprised with the startled looks he'd produced.

★ Anne and her brother rode through the endless Texas dusk. In June it seemed as if the sun would never release its hold and drop below the horizon. The yellow light at nearly eight o'clock at night gave an impression of suspended time. So did sitting beside Bruce in a car while he drove, fast but casually, only his wrist atop the steering wheel. Anne sat on a cream-colored leather seat cooled by air conditioning. Bruce's car was not her father's Lincoln Continental—those huge black cars Anne remembered from her childhood, so autonomous they made the world seem like a passing scrim on the windows. Bruce's car was a discreet silver, and smaller than the Continental used to be, but still a heavy, thick, smug American car. Bruce wore an expensive suit, too, and treated it as casually as sportswear. With his suit coat flung into the back seat, he looked older, in his rumpled white shirt and dark tie pulled tight. He looked like a very successful man happily approaching middle age, eager to shed the signs of youth. Anne had no idea whether Bruce really had achieved financial success, though. The car could be the heaviest load of a deep trough of debt; Bruce could be living in a one-room apartment the size of this car. She would never ask, and he wouldn't have told her anything if she had.

"Why'd he send you, Bruce? Why didn't he just call me? They do still give you one phone call when you get arrested, don't they, or is that just on TV?"

Bruce shrugged. "You'd know better than I, wouldn't you, with your—?"

He nodded back twenty miles, in apparent reference to Chris. Anne had insisted that Chris not come. He'd wanted to, had almost said he would in spite of what she said, but Anne thought this was a family problem. Somehow having Chris smooth their way would make her feel worse, and her first sight of Bruce in four years had brought out her stubbornness.

"I happened to be in San Antonio on business that Dad knew about. He called me at my hotel and asked me to get you. Thought you knew more about the case, or who to call, or something. So I came."

What had Morris been thinking? If he wanted Anne, why hadn't he just called her? If all he needed was bail money, didn't Bruce have it? Anne kept her questions to herself, which also reminded her of childhood. Morris as usual, even under arrest, had schemes going.

"What else did he tell you?" she asked.

She felt Bruce turn and look at her, she pictured the slight lift of his lip, as if he had something on her because she had to ask a question. Maybe she was doing her brother a disservice imagining him this way, but that's how the picture looked out of the corner of her eye, and she didn't want to turn to confirm it.

"Nothing else."

They sat mostly in silence until Bruce took the highway exit for downtown New Braunfels. "Do you know where the jail is?"

"Turn here—No, wait. Let's try the District Attorney's Office. It's on Seguin Street, in the courthouse annex."

The trip didn't take long, and Anne's hunch had proven right. Though the building sat quiet and still, they walked through the empty receptionist's office to find District Attorney Andrew Gunther at his desk. He seemed to be going over papers, didn't even look up at once, but was obviously unsurprised by Anne's appearance.

"Ms. Greenwald," he said complacently. "How are you?"

"This is my brother Bruce. We came to get my father out of jail, and thought maybe you could tell us the procedure."

"Sure thing. Hi, Bruce." Gunther stood up and the two big men shook hands. Anne turned away from the gripping ceremony. In spite of his soft-rich-boy appearance, Bruce could change to fit the occasion, including hearty handshakes, thumbs hooked in the belt, even spitting if the situation seemed to demand it. If exposed to Gunther long enough, Bruce would start to drawl, and Anne would have to walk away.

"Looked forward to seeing you again, Ms. Greenwald," Gunther said. "Sorry it's under these circumstances."

Anne felt sure Chris had called him. Of course, Chris would have done that even if she asked him not to come along. In fact, he might be here now, waiting for them at the jail.

He wasn't. Gunther drove them to the county jail and shepherded them through the process of arranging bail. "Kind of a professional courtesy," he said at one point, and Anne knew he didn't mean to her.

"Nobody's set bail," Gunther said, "but I could probably dig up a magistrate to do it if you really want to get him out tonight."

"Please," Anne said.

Gunther sat on a bench in the holding area where they

waited for Morris to be brought. The room had cinderblock walls, a very scuffed linoleum floor, and large insulating tiles on the ceiling that brought it lower and made the room seem even more like a box, as if all of them were confined already. Bruce stayed by the door as if wanting to be the first one to bolt when it opened. But Gunther seemed at home here, as he did everywhere. He gazed up at Anne. She thought she felt something proprietary in his gaze, and knew why.

"All right. I'll call a judge. Sometimes I tell the families it might be best to leave them in jail at least one night so they can think about how they got here."

Anne gave him a look, two steps nicer than smoldering because he had been very cordial, but Gunther understood. He shrugged, punched numbers into his cell phone, and after a minute said, "Judge Phitzer. This's Andy Gunther. Yes, sir, very sorry about the call, but we've got Morris Greenwald down to the jail and his children would like to bail him out. Could you . . . You didn't know? Yes, he's here. Thank you, sir. We'd all appreciate that."

When he hung up, Anne said stiffly, "Thank you very much. I'll have to thank the judge for coming, too."

Gunther winked at her. "Don't worry about it. Judge Phitzer'll be glad to come down. Sometimes they like to, you know, like to get in on the ground floor of a case like this, that people'll be talking about. Especially since I just let him know he's been out of the loop so far. He's doing you a favor, but I just did him one, too."

Anne nodded, trying to show interest she didn't feel in Gunther's musings. He hauled himself upright, knocked on the door, and when a deputy opened it said, "Change of plans, Billy. Can you have Mr. Greenwald brought to the courtroom? Little bail hearing. Thanks."

He ambled off down the institutional hallway, Anne and

Bruce following. Bruce leaned over to say, "He seems to like you." Anne watched the shambling figure of the district attorney. She had seen Chris several times on his way to court, and he always appeared wound more tightly. Even when Chris projected confidence, the prospect of trial made him grow more watchful and tense. Andy Gunther, on the other hand, appeared to be falling asleep as he walked. He carried nothing in his hands and didn't seem to need preparation.

The jail included a small, informal courtroom for just such occasions as this. They waited, with very little to say to each other. The judge arrived in a remarkably short time, a short middle-aged man wearing khaki pants and boat shoes, with a vinyl jacket thrown casually over a T-shirt. He had a high forehead and a prominent nose that made his eyes appear sunken. He addressed everyone cordially but didn't offer to shake hands. As soon as he had seated himself—the room had a desk for him, not a traditional bench—another door at the back of the room opened with the rattle of a key and Morris Greenwald appeared. Morris's nose looked larger too, as if he'd lost weight, and his eyes hid deep under his brows. He stopped still at the sight of Anne, then shuffled forward.

Her father looked terrible. He wore an orange jail coverlet with short sleeves and a white T-shirt underneath. Paper-thin jailhouse slippers were on his feet. Worst of all were the handcuffs that weighed down his arms in front, making them look stretched and skinny. Anne turned away, embarrassed for him.

Andy Gunther frowned, first at the prisoner, then at the tall, alert deputy accompanying him. Gunther nodded at the handcuffs and said, "I told you that wasn't necessary, Billy."

The deputy replied, "Murder, Andy." A defiant apology, almost whining. The deputy made no move to remove the handcuffs.

Gunther turned back to the seated judge and quickly

sketched the charge. The judge nodded impatiently. If Morris Greenwald had been arrested, Judge Phitzer knew what for. He quickly made sure the prisoner understood the charge of murder, and asked, "Do we have a request to set bail?"

Morris Greenwald stood staring straight ahead, obviously not intending to reply. "Yes, please," Anne said for him.

The judge nodded, then lost his assurance. "Uh, first-degree felony, the guidelines, I believe . . ."

Gunther stepped in. "Judge, we don't think Mr. Greenwald is a flight risk. He's got property in the county and he's—well, you can see, sir. You want to stay and fight this thing, don't you, Mr. Greenwald?"

"Of course."

Gunther said casually, "I think the State would ask for no more than a hundred thousand, your Honor."

The judge looked up at the prisoner like a pawnbroker appraising an offered item. "Is that all right, Mr. Greenwald? On a hundred-thousand-dollar bond, you'd have to pay a bondsman 10 to 15 percent of that and put up property for the rest, to ensure that you'll appear for trial."

"Cash bond," Gunther said, as if offering a favor, though Anne didn't know what he meant.

"Really, Andy?" the judge asked. "All right. Mr. Greenwald, that means you could deposit 10 percent in cash, $10,000, into the registry of the court, which will be refunded to you after trial. That way you don't have to pay a fee to a bondsman. Can you do that?"

And then everyone looked at Morris Greenwald for an answer. It seemed to Anne, glancing at Andy Gunther out of the corner of her eye, that the district attorney was watching more intently than the rest. Gunther had set the amount and the terms, allowing the prisoner the opportunity of freeing himself for a relatively modest amount of money. But now it looked as if the procedure had been a test, or an elaborate way of embarrassing Anne's father, forcing him to admit the real shallowness of his resources.

Morris cleared his throat. "Of course, if I have time—" he began, and Gunther seemed to smile slightly.

"I'll post it," Anne said quickly. "What do I have to do, your Honor?"

The next forty-five minutes passed slowly, with repeated assurances that release was imminent, but also continuing needs for paper and signatures. The district attorney faded away without farewell, though Anne saw Bruce shaking hands with him, which seemed incongruous. The realization had begun to hit home to Anne that this slouching, amiable schemer would soon be prosecuting her father for murder—a murder Anne had seen another man commit.

But that prospect seemed remote tonight. Remote as well, but achievable, hovered the goal of getting Morris out of this place. Darkness had fallen and deepened by the time he emerged from the interior of the jail, back in his own clothes and no longer shuffling. Morris looked rather dapper, in fact, in sharply creased navy slacks, a bright-yellow shirt, and a light-blue silk sports coat, as if someone had called to alert him about his imminent arrest and he had dressed for the occasion. He came striding up to Anne as if they were meeting here by appointment.

"Sorry you had to get involved in this, honey. I'll get your money back to you by the end of the week."

Anne didn't answer. Bruce came up on the other side and took their father's arm. Morris didn't look at him but seemed to have expected his son to be there. The little family unit went out the glass doors and down the steps onto a downtown street of New Braunfels, deserted at ten o'clock at night.

"How did this happen, Daddy?" Anne asked as they walked to the car.

"Politics," Morris said. "It'll get dismissed, trust me. They just want to put some heat on me for a while."

"Why? To make you do what?"

"You have to know everything, don't you?" Bruce said, as if he did know everything himself. Anne refrained from pointing out that neither of the two big shots walking with her had had bail money handy, and if not for her Morris would still be in jail.

"You need to attack this thing right away," Anne said. "I've seen how these things work. The more aggressive you get from the beginning the better. Don't wait to be indicted. You have to get a lawyer right away."

"Sure," Morris said, nodding decisively. "I need to know who's best and who knows their way around here, and I don't. Why don't one of you call—"

He stopped abruptly, both his voice and his legs. Morris stood on the sidewalk just approaching the zone of a street-light, so his legs appeared bright but his face remained shadowed. He stared out as if he saw someone approaching from the darkness on the other side of the light.

"What is it?" Anne asked, alarmed.

Her older brother, showing a brusque tenderness, took his father's arm again and steered him along the sidewalk. Quietly to Anne, Bruce said, "He started to say, 'Call Ben and ask him.'"

Morris didn't answer, so it must have been true. Morris didn't speak again for a long while. With his first genuine realization that his longtime associate was dead, his confidence seemed to have disappeared as well.

★

Chris was standing beside his desk. His office looked as if he had been away on a long vacation and the staff had cleaned and tidied the place every day. On the large surface of his desk only two folders and a legal pad lay on the blotter, neatly aligned. Across the room the love seat and two chairs carefully faced each other as well, and coasters on the small end table had been stacked. The appearance of the room bore evidence that Chris had been thinking for a while before he placed this call. Sometimes while mulling over a problem he tidied up, quite unconsciously.

His voice came out hearty and casual, like that of a man leaning back in his chair with his feet up on the desk. But, in fact, Chris was standing at a corner of the desk, stiffly, one hand on the desk. His face looked stern. The effect was incongruous, as if he were a ventriloquist, or the ventriloquist's dummy, but no one was there to see it.

"Andy, you're amazing," he said. "You get a big murder case, you hear two versions of what happened, and you go a third route entirely. You've got nerve, man. Nobody can fault you for that."

He spoke admiringly. On the other end of the line, Andy Gunther, who *was* almost reclining at his desk, knew he was being played but couldn't help enjoying the words. "Well, you know," he drawled, giving the opening line of an old prosecutors' joke, "anybody can convict the guilty. I like a challenge."

"You shocked old Morris, I'll tell you that. Gonna cost him some money, too." Chris developed more of a Texas accent himself as he talked. He had decided that in dealing with Andy Gunther a stick would be useless and a carrot not much better, but a stick of Juicy Fruit might help. Chris wouldn't come right out and ask for information or a favor. Gunther and Chris would be opponents on this case—they both knew that. But they could maintain a friendly connection—and Gunther did enjoy the sweet temptation of gossip. If he gave a little, Chris might tell him a little about how things were going in the opposition camp.

"Sorry about that, son," Gunther said with feigned gravity, "but you know the old man's going down. I'm not fooling here."

"You didn't like Anne's story?"

"There's a lot about her as a witness I didn't like. No offense. But, of course, she's Morris's daughter, so there's motive to cover up. I'm not saying she did, I'm just talking about how it'll play to a jury. And there's that old business with her and Morris and Winston—good reason for them both to hate Winston and try to set him up. Just all in all, I wasn't looking forward to presenting her and frankly I'd rather see her as a defense witness. Besides, your story kind of cancels out hers."

"But you didn't like mine, either." Chris's voice flattened.

So did Andy Gunther's. "I'm sorry, Chris, but the suicide story just won't wash. Trust me on this. I don't know what you saw, but it didn't happen that way."

Chris didn't dig for any more. So, as so often happens, Gunther tossed him a little extra. "Oh, and of course there's the other thing, that you already know. The gun."

"Yeah," Chris said, not a question.

"The murder weapon. It was Morris's, of course. And he didn't admit that to me right off. I told him that'd come back to bite him."

Gunther ended the conversation on an odd, regretful note, as if the thing were just too easy. "Listen, man, you and your sweetheart should just stay out of this as much as possible. No use wrecking what you two have over a lost cause. Of course, your kids will have to visit Grandpa in prison. I've had guys like that. One guy, perpetual thief. Nothing violent, never did hard time. Then one day when he was sixty-two he shoplifted a tube of Crest from Walgreen's. Habit of a life-time. But he got caught."

"Yeah, I've had guys like that too."

"So he got convicted as a habitual and now he's doing twenty-five in the penitentiary because he couldn't stop. That's Morris Greenwald. He just couldn't quit."

Chris felt Gunther's offer of friendship. With gruff, comradely farewells the two prosecutors hung up. Chris decided he didn't want to be friends with Andy Gunther. On the other hand, he didn't much want to be on Morris Greenwald's team, either.

Nevertheless, later he made a call to Anne's office. Her secretary said Dr. Greenwald was gone for the day. Since it was almost five o'clock, that shouldn't have seemed odd, except that it was for Anne. He tried her home and cell phone and got no answer from either. He didn't leave messages. Anne could be with a patient or at a school and not want to be interrupted. But Chris didn't think so. On a sudden impulse, he got his car and drove to New Braunfels.

He was becoming very familiar with that fifteen-mile stretch of urbanized highway. The billboards didn't tug at his vision. As he drove, he began to feel that he might be making a mistake. If Anne had wanted him there, she would have called. But he wasn't thinking of Anne; he was thinking of Morris Greenwald, and what he might be planning. Chris didn't sense any great desire for his company from that direction, either, but not being wanted had very little deterrent effect on him. He and Anne were alike in that way.

Sure enough, when he reached the parking area in the

caliche lot above Morris's house, Chris saw Anne's Volvo. It sat in the lot very dusty from the tires up, only its windows and top relatively clean, like an animal struggling to keep its head above dirty water. Chris wondered how often Anne had made this trip in the last few days. She hadn't invited him along.

Before he knocked on the massive front door of the house, he glanced up at the fatal balcony. No one was standing there, but the door from the house was pulled aside; a flimsy curtain blew out. Chris had an urge to climb up those tall bushes to the balcony and either eavesdrop on the people upstairs or burst in on them. Instead he rang the bell. A long minute later the door opened and Anne stared at him.

"Chris!"

"Hello, Anne, sorry for intruding. I came to give your father some advice."

She stared at him strangely, still blocking the doorway. "Why?"

"Because he needs it. And because you and I know he didn't kill this man."

"But we know it for different reasons," Anne couldn't help pointing out. Chris noticed that she wore the remnants of her professional outfit, the blue skirt from a suit and a long-sleeved white blouse. She had washed off her makeup or it had worn away during the day, leaving dark streaks under her eyes. She looked tired and worried in a way her own patients never left her, as if she didn't know what to do. He wanted to hold her, but felt sure he was the only one of the two of them who wanted that. He would have wished this case away, not just because of Morris Greenwald's trouble, but because he felt it coming between Anne and him. When Chris touched her hand, she didn't seem to notice.

So he said in a businesslike voice, "He's got to hire a defense lawyer, and a good one," brushing past her and head-ing up the stairs. Anne followed him. Light spilled down from the upstairs sitting room. "Not just anybody. Maybe two. I thought I could give him some advice about that."

"Don't worry, he's already hired somebody."

"Who?" Chris asked over his shoulder, reaching the upstairs hallway and seeing the sitting room door standing ajar ahead of him.

"Margaret somebody. I'm sure you know her. What's her name? Margaret Hemmings."

Chris stopped, suddenly stiff. He turned back to Anne. "Please not."

"What's the matter? She's a good lawyer."

"She's a public relations consultant. She gives press conferences."

"Sometimes those press conferences come after I've beaten the prosecution in trial," said a languid, self-satisfied voice. Margaret Hemmings stood in the doorway of the sitting room, leaning against the jamb. She smiled, revealing a wide mouth and near-perfect teeth. She wore a long, deep-blue cocktail dress, as if she were on her way to a more formal event, but she'd taken off her shoes and was standing in her stockings. She had a casual, two-drinks-up-on-you style that went with the Southern drawl she occasionally employed.

"Hello, Ms. Hemmings," Chris said stiffly.

"I'd think you'd have high regard for my skills, Chris, after our last trial."

"Our last trial was our only trial, it was eight years ago, and it was a fluke. You happened to have some good facts, that you kept from me until trial. If you'd come to me ahead of time . . ."

"Come to *you* honey? You were the opposition, you might recall."

Chris broke off the discussion and went into the sitting

room. Margaret Hemmings, rolling her eyes triumphantly, moved aside to let him pass. Morris Greenwald sat on the edge of a love seat, leaning forward, staring down at the floor.

"Morris, I need to talk to you," Chris said brusquely. It was the first time he had used Mr. Greenwald's first name, and that seemed to get the older man's attention. But Morris answered, "I'm in consultation with my lawyer right now."

"That's what we need to talk about."

Chris walked past Morris toward that open French door. After a moment Morris followed. Turning to him, Chris looked past him to Margaret Hemmings, still in the doorway and watching with amusement. Seeing Chris glance at her, she raised her voice and said, "He's going to tell you not to hire me, Morris."

"Yes, I am," Chris said to her.

"Why?" Anne asked.

Chris replied to the lawyer. "When's the last time you tried a criminal case, Ms. Hemmings?"

"You may remember I represented Speaker Willis in his bribery trial, which ended with the judge dismissing the indictment at the end of the State's case."

"Yes, but you had nothing to do with that. You were one of about five lawyers that the speaker hired and you were in charge of spin. How many days of the trial were you in the courtroom?"

Hemmings came forward with a confident stride. "Morris needs spin too, Chris, as you call it. This case is about public perception and political reality. I can head it off before it ever reaches a courtroom."

"Is that what she told you?" Chris asked Morris Greenwald accusingly, but before Morris had a chance to answer, Chris also stepped toward Hemmings. "Nick Winston did everything he could do, *out*side a courtroom, to get Morris arrested and it worked brilliantly. Now he'll do everything in his power to get him convicted. When you talk about political reality, are you saying you can match Winston's clout with Andy Gunther?"

"And public perception, I said. Andy Gunther will drop the case once so many people believe it's bogus that he'll look like a fool taking it to trial."

"How do you plan to do that? You're not going to have Morris testify before the grand jury?"

Margaret Hemmings closed her mouth but smiled smugly. Chris turned to Morris. "Do *not* let her talk you into that. It's a trap. Prosecutors love to have the defendant testify before a grand jury. Then the defendant's locked into that story and the prosecutor can use it to cross-examine you at trial. People always change their stories a little—it's a matter of memory. But he'll use it to make you look like a liar. Trust me, I know."

Hemmings walked into the room. Chris stood his ground. Back near the doorway, Anne watched the two of them alertly, frowning. Chris hadn't glanced at her since he'd locked eyes with the other lawyer.

"I need to confer with my client now," Hemmings said.

"You need a defense. You cannot just try to prove him not guilty, or hurl accusations in all directions. You have to solve the crime. A jury won't settle for anything less."

"We'll see. I will need your cooperation. We want you to make a public statement. Dr. Greenwald as well. That's what I mean about molding public perception. Before the prosecution can even rise to its feet—"

"That's not molding. That's throwing out whatever you can to see what sticks. Does it matter to you that my story and Anne's contradict each other? That you'll be making all your potential witnesses look like liars before the trial even starts?"

"We'll have to work on that," Hemmings said, folding her arms and smiling at him.

Chris did turn to Anne then, raising an eyebrow. Anne nodded minimally. She too had her arms folded.

Silence lengthened. Chris turned to Morris, who still hadn't spoken. Chris said earnestly, "Morris, this isn't public relations. It's not making a business deal or losing it. It's a trial. You can go to prison for life. And, believe me, at this point that looks like a good possibility. I can find you a good lawyer. She is not it. Trust me—this is my field. Tell her you made a mistake asking her to come, and let me make a couple of phone calls."

Chris waited, standing over the older man. He could feel Margaret Hemmings's smile. Finally, Morris cleared his throat and said apologetically, "She has an excellent reputation, Chris. And a plan. I have to go with her."

Chris looked at him scathingly. He turned away from Morris's hangdog expression and Margaret Hemmings's triumphant one, and walked briskly to the door. He didn't turn at the doorway to make a last statement, but just walked out.

Anne looked at the woman standing with her father. Margaret Hemmings did great first-client interviews; she always impressed with her confidence. Anne had thought her very good until Chris's appearance in the room. Now she gave the woman a long, appraising look, then transferred her gaze to her father. But Morris was looking at the floor again, hands in his pockets.

Hemmings smiled a more pleasant smile than she'd displayed while Chris had been in the room. "Dr. Greenwald, if you wouldn't mind . . . ?"

Without reply, Anne quickly followed Chris out of the room. She caught up to him downstairs in the entryway. He was more obviously fuming now, glaring at the ceiling. "What's wrong with him?" he said angrily. "Doesn't he care about the possibility of going to prison? This is criminal law, my specialty. Why won't he listen to me?"

"They're both political," Anne said placatingly. "She got to him. He's heard of her through political circles—she's very well known in those circles—and he thinks that means she's good. Besides, he can afford her."

Chris stared. "Is that a consideration?"

"Daddy still puts up a good front, but he doesn't have the money he used to have. He was trying to put together a deal that would have recouped a lot, but now that's probably blown forever. Or maybe Margaret Hemmings promised she could fix that too. I don't know. I do know she's agreed to defend him for a very reduced fee." Anne knew the precise amount, because she had paid the retainer.

"A lot of lawyers would do that," Chris answered. "A lot of good lawyers, because the case will bring them publicity. He doesn't have to settle for her."

Anne's eyes strayed all over Chris's face. "What do you have against her? I take it she beat you in court sometime."

"A lot of lawyers can claim that."

"Not that many, I'll bet. And you remember every one, don't you? How many has it been, Chris? How many lawyers have won against you?"

He lost his indignation as a fleeting, self-deprecating smile crossed his face. "Four. But Margaret Hemmings . . . I was a young prosecutor, hadn't been in a felony court all that long. Only my second or third murder trial, but it seemed perfectly ordinary. Couple had a fight at a party, left still glaring at each other, a neighbor later that night heard them yelling at each other at home. You know, nothing unusual, except later that night when the man fell asleep his wife shot him in the head, the crotch, every place.

"She got arrested, of course. She was the only one there. Case seemed like a cinch—maybe that's why they assigned it to me. Then the defendant hired Margaret Hemmings. She was in Houston then, I think, and some women's group paid most or all of her fee. That should have told me something. She didn't try to deal in our pretrial meetings. Didn't even talk to me. That was odd, but I thought she was just some out-of-town snot. At trial I put on my case, then she put on one of the first battered-woman defenses anyone had ever seen. Testimony from the defendant about how her husband had beaten her in the past, threatened to kill her. Not in front of anybody, of course. Psychiatric testimony that a woman in her situation would never report the abuse, or leave the relationship, out of fear and shame. Classic defense now, but I hadn't seen it before.

"Then she had pictures." Chris turned his head upward again, as if he could see through the ceiling. "Pictures of the defendant bruised and scraped, with a black eye. Not the night of the murder, of course, because she'd been arrested and photographed that night and looked okay. These were from earlier occasions, she said. And she knew that when he woke up he'd do it again. Maybe kill her this time. It was so convincing I believed her. It was hard to cross-examine her without looking like a bastard. Everybody said I did a good job. Got a conviction for manslaughter. But the jury gave her probation, and when they said the words I was glad myself. Margaret Hemmings and I shook hands for the first time; the picture that got in the newspaper."

"There's nothing for you to feel bad about there," Anne said gently, but with an edge, because it sounded as if Chris now resented the idea of a battered-woman's-syndrome defense.

"I've given testimony like that myself. The syndrome is very real. Like you said, Margaret Hemmings just had good facts—"

"I'm not sure she did, Anne. I think she may have faked it all." Chris gave her a straight look. "She didn't try her case in the press that time. She kept it to herself until the time came to spring it. So I didn't have a chance to investigate the defendant's story. After the trial there wasn't any point to investigating. But one of the lady's neighbors, who'd been friendly with the dead husband, called me to say the woman had had a black eye sometime *after* the night of the murder. After Margaret Hemmings entered the case. While there was time in the months before trial to take pictures then let the bruises heal."

"You think she blacked her own client's eye?"

"I feel quite sure no one would ever be able to prove that."

"Chris—"

"That was one of her first big successes; now she's had others. But she hasn't tried a case in a long time. Do you think she'll be prepared?"

"What other choice does Daddy have?"

In the darkened entryway Chris and Anne looked at each other, both wondering what was going on upstairs, and elsewhere in the world.

"What can we do?" Anne asked. Chris shook his head slowly.

A few days later, Chris found himself the victim of a stalking.

For a stranger to get to Chris in his office, the stranger would have to make an appointment, have stated business that seemed important, maybe an introduction from someone Chris knew, and pass the scrutiny of his assistant Janie Garcia. But Chris didn't spend all his time in the district attorney's offices. About once a week he traveled to the old courthouse across the street to meet with county commissioners over budget and other matters. Sometimes he went to the police station a few blocks away. And often he descended the stairs in the Justice Center to check on the courts or visit a particular judge. So a patient person who knew the routine could reach Chris just about any day of the week.

On Thursday afternoon of an oppressively hot June day Chris came down the stairs to the third floor. Thursday afternoon felt like the end of the week; the building had cleared out to a large extent, emptied by vacation time and summer lassitude. Only a few people were congregating in the short third-floor hallway. The one nearest the stairs, a tall young man wearing jeans and boots and looking as if he belonged in them, smiled broadly at Chris and stepped forward with his hand extended. Chris took it automatically, wondering if the man were kin to a crime victim. The smile convinced him otherwise. He looked more like some brand of South Texas law enforcement officer on his day off.

"Hello, Mr. Sinclair. I've got somebody who wants to talk to you. Would you mind just taking a minute?"

Still holding Chris's hand and not waiting for a reply, the young man spoke quietly into the cell phone he held in his other hand. All Chris heard was a phrase that sounded suspiciously like, ". . . got him."

After a long pause during which Chris withdrew his hand but lingered close out of curiosity, the young man handed the phone to him. Quietly, he said, "The senator would like to speak to you."

Chris took the phone suspiciously. In his ear, slightly fuzzy, a hearty voice said, "Hello, son. This is Temple Lockridge. Sorry about the secret agent crap, but I'd rather there not be a record of me calling your office. Thought you might not want that either, in the long run."

"All right," Chris said slowly. The older man on the other end of the line seemed to hear his disbelief.

"Wonder if you'd do me the honor of coming to see me," the caller said. "We've got something that needs to be talked out, and it would best be done in person. Anytime this afternoon or tomorrow'd be fine. My young friend there can tell you the way, or bring you if you'd prefer. Ever been to Uvalde?"

"Of course, but—"

"I know it's a lot to ask," the voice said, growing softer and more cajoling. "Get an important man like you to come all this way without telling you anything. Let's just say it's about your recent trip to Austin."

"Mm-huh," Chris said, still noncommittal, thinking fast but speaking very slowly. This call began to make sense and seem real. "Senator, I'd like to accommodate you—"

"Then do, son." The voice took on an edge of authority. "I'd offer to come there or meet you halfway, but I'm an old fart and I've traveled more than enough in my life."

"That's all right. I'll come. How's tomorrow at about this time?"

"Thank you very much, Mr. Sinclair." The phone clicked off, and Chris pictured the man leaning back in a large desk chair and reaching for a cigar or a glass of bourbon or both. He pictured Temple Lockridge, legendary three-term Texas senator, retired two years ago but still very much a force in the state and beyond. From his ranch outside the small town of Uvalde he could place a call to the Kremlin or the White House and have it returned. Temple Lockridge rarely gave interviews anymore and when he did he claimed to be doing nothing more than raising cattle and enjoying his grandchildren, but anyone in Texas politics knew better. That included

Chris. If Senator Lockridge wanted to see him, he would go.

Chris handed the phone back to the young cowboy, who smiled and shrugged, seeming embarrassed now. He unsnapped one of the pockets of his shirt and handed Chris a folded piece of paper. "Here's directions to the ranch," the senator's employee said respectfully. "But it'd be no trouble for me to pick you up if you'd rather. It's a little complicated."

"I'll find it," Chris said.

The young man nodded, tipping an invisible hat. "We'll see you then."

He walked away, down the stairs, leaving Chris alone and feeling scammed.

But after ten minutes of investigation Jack Fine declared that the directions Chris had been given did lead to the address of the retired senator. And Chris believed in that voice on the phone, felt convinced by the sureness of its own power. He decided he would keep the appointment.

Chris spent the evening at home with Clarissa and didn't call Anne to tell her about his appointment. She didn't call him either, for that matter. Chris wasn't keeping anything from her; it's just that neither got around to calling the other. More and more often lately a day would pass without Anne and Chris speaking to each other. He thought she was making the drive to her father's house more often, but wasn't sure. Up until the recent past they had talked to each other nearly every day and seen each other most days of the week. Now they seemed to need a reason to call, and the intervals between coming up with such a reason grew longer.

The next afternoon Chris set off for Uvalde, a small town

fifty miles west of San Antonio. The drive was good for thought: not much traffic, good highway, few distractions. Somewhere along that road Chris got an impression of passing a divide into the real West. The land grew drier, scragglier, wilder. Fences had been built for keeping livestock in rather than people out. Houses stood farther apart, and back from the road. Sometimes a dilapidated house was surrounded by its leavings, from rusted-out farm equipment to last week's newspaper. But the landscape itself was beautiful, in a scraped, unshowy way. Chris had a pretty drive through some lonely country, the last few miles over narrow country roads. The senator's ranch comprised hundreds of acres, most of it enclosed by wooden fences, but here at the showpiece heart of the ranch the fence was made of good Texas stone. When Chris buzzed the intercom the gate jerked and opened. Chris drove over a cattle guard, parallel bars in the ground spaced tightly enough that a car could cross them but cattle wouldn't, and slowly up the rocky path toward the plantation-style house, two stories high with white pillars. A ranch house that could pass for a city mansion.

The house must have had security and servants, but neither announced themselves. The retired senator, a Democrat, obviously preferred a familylike atmosphere. The same young man from the courthouse yesterday opened the front door long before Chris reached it. "Hello again, sir. Thank you for coming."

Chris merely nodded. He wore a suit and tie and felt immediately overdressed when he stepped into the large foyer of the house. It had, unshockingly, a Western theme, with a cowskin rug on a hardwood floor and even a pair of horns mounted on the wall. An antique wooden pie safe served as an entry table. The young man waved Chris into a large living room, featuring a fireplace in which children could have sat and played Monopoly. In this room the Western motif was muted, as if the senator had to present it to the world at the front door but preferred not to live with it. A long, dented leather sofa faced the fireplace. A chandelier, wooden but *not* made of a wagon wheel, hung from the twenty-foot ceiling. At the far end of the room, glass doors gave onto a Spanish tile porch and a long, sloping vista of green land.

"Would you like something to drink?" the young man asked, after giving Chris a moment to look around and be impressed.

"No, thanks, I'm fine."

"Long drive. Sure you don't want something to cut the dust?"

"Ask me again in ten minutes."

The young man grinned. "In ten minutes you'll be in with the senator, and I dasn't interrupt."

Chris looked more closely at the young man, suddenly wondering if he was more than an employee, perhaps the senator's grandson. The young man just smiled an open, gracious smile, but it occurred to Chris that he'd never introduced himself. Chris stepped toward him and said, "I'm Chris Sinclair."

"Yes, sir, I know. Just call me Gordie."

A few moments later, without any signal that Chris observed, the young man abruptly led him across the living room, knocked at a door, and opened it into a large study. This room also boasted a fireplace, right beside the desk, so that Chris wondered fleetingly how many papers had been burned there.

The large desk that dominated the room was surprisingly ornate, with long carved legs, and gold-foil filigree worked through the desk's edge. It looked much more French than Western, and probably carried a story. Behind the desk, Temple Lockridge sat writing on a legal pad, wearing half–reading glasses. Thick white hair fell down his forehead. His hand holding the pen stopped moving. He concentrated, as if what he wrote would have immediate consequences, then wrote two or three lines quickly, without pause.

Chris couldn't help feeling as if he were watching a historical moment unfold. Temple Lockridge had been the dominant political figure in Texas most of Chris's life, first as governor, then senator, spending the last two decades on a national stage. He seemed to have been born for the part, with both a folksiness and an agile mind that he could deploy simultaneously, when necessary. He had retired two years earlier but had not remotely been forgotten.

Just as quickly as he had written, Lockridge looked up, dropped both his pen and his glasses, and came striding around the desk, hand outstretched. "Chris," he said in a rich voice that created immediate intimacy, and could do so just as well in a crowd of a thousand people. "Thank you for coming. I owe you a big one."

The senator was deeply tanned and creased and seemed oversized. He stood only slightly over six feet, but his crusty hand swallowed Chris's and his head was large, too, with pendulous ears. He looked well lived-in. Lockridge turned to Chris's escort and clapped an arm around the young man's shoulders. "Thanks, Gordon." To Chris he added, "We used to call him *Gordito* when he was a little fat one, but he grew out of that."

"Won't ever outlive it, though, apparently," the young man smiled, and left the room graciously, closing the door. Definitely a grandson, Chris thought.

Temple Lockridge gestured toward a chair, resuming his own. "You should have come two or three hours from now, when we could sit out on the verandah with a drink and watch the sunset. Well, maybe you'll be here that long. That chair okay? Two different presidents of the United States have parked their asses in that chair."

"If they didn't complain, I won't either."

The men smiled at each other, and Lockridge said, "I do appreciate you coming, Chris. I'm sure you thought about not, since I didn't give you much reason."

"You mentioned Mrs. Sorenson, and that made me curious. And of course I want to do whatever I can to help Morris Greenwald."

"Actually, I just said Austin. You put together the other. And in fact, you seem to have been the only person who's done that, outside of a select few who promised not to talk, who knew that Veronica was there that night. I suppose Morris told you?"

"No."

"Who did?"

"Nobody."

The senator watched him closely and shrugged.

"I figured it out because her state trooper bodyguard was on the scene."

"Don't tell me he was in uniform."

"No, sir. His face was his uniform."

Lockridge gave him a straight scrutiny that Chris took for a compliment. The senator seemed to follow Chris's reasoning. Questions occurred to him and he answered them for himself or dismissed them, all in a few seconds, and the conversation moved on to a different level. "If she'd asked me about it, I would have told Ronnie not to go to Morris's house that night." He shook his head. "Never go somewhere where you don't know why you're there."

"Like me today?"

Lockridge gave him another tight grin. "I'm sure you had some idea, or you wouldn't have come. I want to ask you for a favor. Keep the lieutenant governor's name out of this case." He poked the desk with a stern finger. "I give you my complete, one hundred percent assurance that she had nothing to do with the murder of young Ben Sewell." Lockridge said the name as if he'd known him, but he probably spoke the same way of Thomas Jefferson. "Veronica Sorenson cannot contribute to the investigation, she did not see anything of any evidentiary value and, as you know yourself, she was not in the house when the killing occurred."

"Why ask me this? Ask Andy Gunther. He's the prosecutor."

"Gunther will do what he's told. It's the defense in a murder trial that likes to bring up things like this, muddy the waters, sensationalize the story, and hope the defendant can slip away in the confusion. I'm asking you to tell the defense that that would be useless in this case, and it would be destructive."

Lockridge got up and walked around the room, touching various mementoes but always turning back to look Chris in the eye when he made important points. "Veronica Sorenson is on the verge of a very important career. She can take the next step quite easily. Governor, senator, maybe beyond. You know she was interviewed by the president when he was looking for a vice presidential candidate. She made the short list. And she's forty-two years old."

"And a Republican," Chris pointed out.

"This isn't about party, son. This is about power. Power for the state. I'd support a Texan for president or vice president even if he wasn't from my party."

"Or she."

"Exactly. So it is not a silly exaggeration to say that by keeping Mrs. Sorenson's name out of this, you will be doing a service for the state of Texas."

Chris couldn't help the *frisson* that ran up his spine. The setting, the words, and Senator Lockridge's earnest manner made the statement not seem silly at all.

Lockridge continued. "You know why she was there. She

wasn't using anyone, she was being used. She hasn't learned how to guard herself against things like this yet. She'll have to learn if she's going to go any further.

"But this would be too costly a lesson. She doesn't deserve it. If her name gets dragged through this kind of thing, it can dog her for the rest of her life. It can destroy her great potential. And I don't believe a man of your integrity will let her be used in this way."

Chris stood up. "Senator, I'm not in charge of either the prosecution or the defense. I'm trying to help Morris Greenwald, and I'm sure you understand helping a friend. This won't be my decision; it will be Morris's and his lawyer's."

"I'll worry about them," Temple Lockridge said in an assured tone. "I just don't want you holding any press conferences."

"I have no intention of doing that. I'll take your word for it, and hers, that Mrs. Sorenson doesn't have any evidence to offer. And if I'm convinced that her presence in the house that night had nothing to do with what happened, I'll never mention her name again. Is that good enough?"

Lockridge crossed the short distance between them suddenly, and gripped Chris's hand again. "It is. I'll take your word on that."

Chris felt he should thank Lockridge for the statement. The senator had almost patented that formula: extract a favor and make the giver feel grateful.

They lingered at the ranch, not mentioning their agreement again. Lockridge took Chris out on the verandah to show him the long vista of grassland that must have cost a fortune in water, and offered him a drink, as Gordie had earlier. Chris declined. Long before sunset he was on his way again.

On that thoughtful drive back to San Antonio, two things solidified in his mind. The first was that Veronica Sorenson had quite definitely been involved in what had happened at Morris Greenwald's home that night.

The second thought occurred to him about halfway home: the senator had called the event of that night "murder."

★ For years the Texas Folklife Festival in San Antonio was held in August, outdoors. In a month when rational people fled the region or stayed rooted inside air-conditioned enclaves, festival goers were expected to stroll the grounds of the Institute of Texan Cultures, listening to music, eating food on sticks, and dancing. All on black asphalt that caught the waves of scorching sunlight and splashed them back upward. Finally the sensible planners of the Folklife Festival had moved its date. To June.

On a Friday evening with sunset still hours away, Chris and Anne strolled slowly around the festival. Vendors sold chicken kabobs, sausage on sticks, corn on the cob, and turkey legs. Their stands sent heat waves sideways to clash with the sunlight streaming down and bouncing back up. Every tree or shade-giving edifice harbored little knots of people taking refuge as if from a storm.

Chris and Anne had come with Clarissa, theoretically. In fact, she had invited them. Anne made a very conscious effort not to impose herself on Clarissa as if she were an established fact of Chris's life, like the brand of toothpaste he used.

But sometimes Clarissa herself invited Anne to join them, for dinner or a picnic or an evening of Scrabble. This was one such occasion, and Anne had been happy to accept.

Chris was happy to be with her, too. As Morris Greenwald's trial approached, Chris and Anne spoke much less often than they had in the past, and on a much more shallow level. They felt themselves avoiding the one main topic, which somehow built a barrier over which it was hard for each to see the other. Anne grew more involved in her father's defense, which made Chris feel excluded. There also remained the burden of their conflicting views about what had happened, and Anne's refusal to involve Chris in her battle with Nick Winston. Anne and Chris had dealt with these problems that were driving them apart by not talking about them, which didn't make either of them happy.

So on this hot June evening they were content just to stroll, hands brushing, smiling at nothing, stopping to listen to bands, and silently agreeing to move on at the same moments. Clarissa, though she had suggested this event, for the most part stayed away from them. She was, after all, sixteen, very much her own person, and would undoubtedly be embarrassed to be seen with them.

Chris caught sight of her through the crowd, talking to a girl about her own age. They stood with their heads bowed close together, talking quickly, as if the exchange of information were vital and about to be interrupted. Feeling Anne close beside him, Chris slowly circled Clarissa and the other girl, at a distance. He was glad to see her with a friend.

He didn't recognize the other girl, and after giving them a few minutes of privacy he strolled over to be introduced. Coming slowly upon their conversation, he heard Clarissa say, ". . . here with my father and his girlfriend."

Chris immediately veered away. As Clarissa spoke she

tossed her head, throwing back her long blond hair. She'd said the phrase in an odd combination of tones, a teenager's contempt but also intimacy. Hearing her, Chris felt a powerful mix of emotions. The strongest was pride in the casual way she'd said "my father." That was him. That was how she thought of him, spoke about him to her friends. He was a fact of her existence, perhaps her only stability. From a distance he gazed at his daughter, feeling very close to her.

Clarissa wore khaki shorts and a short gray T-shirt, an outfit that made her arms look thin and her legs long. She also wore big, clunky sandals that showed off a toe ring. She had high cheekbones, a gift from her mother, clear blue eyes, and a rather small mouth that she often pursed. Cocking her hip, she looked as tough as she could have hoped, but obviously had no idea how vulnerable she also appeared. Life had already handed Clarissa worlds of pain, but she was enduring. Chris only wished she didn't have to build up such a tough shell to do so.

It looked as if Clarissa and her friend had run out of things to say. They began looking around. Just as Clarissa's eyes lit on Chris, he started forward and called her name. He reached her and unashamedly put his arm around her. Let her get embarrassed. That was what parents were for. "Didn't you want to hear that band that's starting up at seven? Hi," he said to the other girl. She ducked her head and drifted away before he could properly meet her—though Clarissa showed no inclination to make an introduction. "Who was that?" Chris asked.

"Francine. She's in a couple of my classes. I've told you about her," Clarissa added quickly, as if she'd been accused.

"Oh, yes. But she's not particularly a friend of yours, is she?"

Clarissa seemed inclined to argue, then shook her head. "I

was asking her if she'd seen Angelina. She said she might be here, but . . ."

That accounted for Clarissa's urging them to come to the festival: the possibility of seeing a friend. Angelina, as far as Chris could determine, was Clarissa's best friend, at least this week. When Chris picked Clarissa up at school the two were usually standing together, and as soon as Clarissa got home she'd get on the phone or the computer to let Angelina know something else she'd forgotten to say. They didn't see each other much outside school, so Chris didn't know the girl well at all. He remembered her as shorter than Clarissa but also leggy, with shoulder-length dark brown hair, small features, shy manners but an occasional boisterous laugh.

"She didn't come?" Chris asked casually.

Clarissa shook her head. "Francine said she decided to stay home. She's got a . . ."

Clarissa trailed off and Chris knew not to press. They walked toward a bandstand. Anne joined them. Clarissa's eyes roved over the crowd, even after the music started. Sometime later Chris couldn't help noticing how she stiffened and her gaze turned hard.

"What?" he said, having to repeat the question pretty loudly over the music.

"Him," Clarissa said.

Chris followed her stare but saw several people in the vicinity. None seemed to be looking Clarissa's way and none looked exceptional.

Clarissa turned suddenly and walked away. Chris and Anne followed, Anne glancing at Chris for reaction.

They caught up to Clarissa just as she said, "See, he knew she was coming."

"Who?"

"That boy," Clarissa said contemptuously.

"Who is he?"

"Nobody. Nothing." Clarissa was obviously angry all of a sudden, but she clammed up. Chris didn't think he'd get anywhere by pursuing it, at least not this minute.

Anne, though, walked around to stand in front of Clarissa. "It's not you, is it?"

Clarissa frowned. "What?"

"Who has a problem with the boy."

"No," Clarissa snapped quickly, then muttered, "It's Angelina."

"What's he doing to her?" Anne talked in her professional voice, quiet but not cajoling. She expected to be answered. Chris paid attention to Clarissa but also glanced curiously at Anne.

"Nothing." Clarissa frowned. "I mean, really nothing if you add it up or try to tell somebody about it. He's called her a few times, he says Hi to her at school. But then he's just—*there* when she goes somewhere. He doesn't do anything, or give her hate looks or anything. You could even say he likes her."

"Has he asked her out?"

"No. And Angelina'd say No if he did. He creeps her out."

"Is this boy new in school, Clarissa?"

Now Clarissa also caught Anne's tone and looked at her more attentively. "Yeah. He transferred in two months ago."

"What's his name?"

"Billy Stepple."

Anne took a deep breath. She seemed to relax a little.

"What?" Clarissa said. Chris wanted to know the same thing.

Anne paid Clarissa the compliment of answering directly. "You know I work with some kids like that. But I don't know that name."

She knew the pattern, though. Anne, too, looked around the

festival crowd, arms crossed. Now there seemed to be teenaged boys everywhere, wearing baggy jeans, "shorts" to their ankles, backward baseball caps. Suddenly it appeared conspiratorial that they all looked alike. Not one would meet an adult's eyes. They'd glance away, talk to each other, turn sullen shoulders. More people had arrived as sundown crept nearer. The boy in question could be close by or gone already.

"It's not fair," Clarissa said, "that he can be here and Angelina can't."

"No, it's not," Anne said quietly. "What do you think she should do about it?"

"I'm not sure," Clarissa said slowly, but she had obviously started thinking.

"He might be on juvenile probation," Chris said. "Maybe that's why he changed schools near the end of a school year. I could check if I get a little information on him."

Anne and Clarissa glanced at each other. Chris understood that he'd made a mistake, again, by offering to take care of the problem.

In downtown Austin, Nick Winston waited alone at a table in the Capitol Club, a well-appointed lounge on top of an office building. The place featured too-cool-to-care-if-you-get-it waitpersons and a high-tech decor, black metal tables with glass tops, no curtains on the windows, which consumed whole walls. The narrow end of the room afforded views of both the state capitol and the wide Colorado River in the opposite direction. Views of both came with only the best tables, of which Winston had one. He wore a tuxedo, smoked a thin cigarette, and appeared to lounge across the chair rather than sit in it. Twice while waiting he smiled and waved, but didn't work the room.

From his casual attitude, rising to his feet when his date arrived seemed endearing. Celine deserved the compliment. She wore a long, black evening dress with a demure neckline but a long slit up the skirt. She smiled at his attention, didn't offer a greeting, but took his cigarette and his attitude. Taking a puff, she said, "Is this going to be dull?"

"Yes," Winston said. Which was one of the reasons they'd met for a drink ahead of time, to buffer themselves against the reception that lay ahead. As an elected official, such events filled Nick Winston's calendar. He and Celine contrived to enjoy themselves anyway. Sometimes it seemed they were attending a different affair than the one where they actually were.

Winston gave a subtle signal, and a minute later a waiter arrived, setting beside Winston's martini a pastel, frothy drink in a tall glass. Celine sipped and air-kissed her thanks to her companion. Her fond expression removed only a bit of the sting when she asked, "You're not going to be arrested at this thing tonight, are you? Bad publicity."

"It's not funny. That dull-witted D.A. in New Braunfels is taking forever. In the meantime Morris and his lawyer are desperately casting around for other suspects. Nobody who was there that night is safe until Morris gets convicted."

"And for some strange reason people have a way of focusing on you."

Winston shrugged modestly. "Morris has no pull anymore. I'm not worried about him, and Margaret Hemmings . . ." He shrugged again, dismissively. "But your new best friend Christian Sinclair seems very busy, for somebody who's barely

involved. He's been to see the old man in Uvalde." Watching
Celine for reaction and seeing none, he added, "Or did you
already know that?"

Celine smiled, casting her gaze around the elegant room
while remaining aware of her companion's stare. "We call each
other every night just before falling asleep. Was this before or
after he saw Mrs. Sorenson?"

Winston didn't answer. He looked at his watch. Celine laid
her long-fingered hand atop his. When he looked at her face
again he saw a new intensity, underneath the playfulness. "It
sounds as if he's hopping all over the state but neglecting the
home front. I believe the case is in New Braunfels, not Austin
or Uvalde," she said.

Winston looked into her deep brown eyes, then his gaze
grew more abstracted. Celine finished off his cigarette and
took a sip of her drink, looking out the glass wall at the river,
placid and slow and beginning to twinkle in the dusk. She had
done her job, moved her lover's mind out of the course in
which it had been stuck.

She'd started him thinking. That was all it would take.

The following week in Comal County, the grand jury indicted
Morris Greenwald. The indictment arrived by mail at the
Greenwald estate and the suspect, who had become the defendant, opened it. He stared. He didn't understand. The
language of the relevant paragraph was simple, though: an
accusation that on the night in question "Morris Greenwald
did then and there intentionally and knowingly cause the
death of Benjamin Sewell by shooting him with a firearm . . ."
It wasn't the language that Morris didn't understand. He

didn't know how this had happened. He'd thought he had protection.

Face suddenly bright red, Morris threw the paper down and kicked the table in his entryway. He screamed inarticulately. That done, he grew calmer, though he still breathed heavily and his eyes darted around. He turned and slammed out his front door and walked heedlessly around his house. The balcony above Morris's head didn't draw even a glance from him. The killing was long gone, almost irrelevant. Someone was just using that event to attack Morris; someone smarter than that idiot D.A.

Morris felt cold fear and hot rage. If it came to it, he would take someone down with him—everyone, if he could. They must know that.

He walked and kicked at rocks and tried to understand.

Margaret Hemmings hadn't done her job. Chris took a secret satisfaction in that, though the news was grim. The grand jury process was always mysterious. Against Chris's strong opposition, Hemmings had asked that her client be allowed to address the grand jurors, and D.A. Gunther had readily consented. The defendant wasn't allowed to take a lawyer inside with him. Morris insisted he'd said very little, following his attorney's advice. Perhaps he hadn't said enough. Perhaps twelve grand jurors just hadn't believed what he had to say. That did not seem like a good omen.

"They're Germans," Morris said harshly to Anne. "They hate Jews."

"Oh, please." She looked around the New Braunfels restaurant where they sat, hoping no one else had heard him.

"You think not, my girl? You don't live here. I've had to deal with it for years. Some of them don't even bother to hide it in their faces. The others are worse. The ones who act friendly. Because they want something from you *before* they screw you."

Anne frowned and made a shushing gesture. She looked to her brother Bruce for support, but Bruce had his head down toward his plate. He had learned years ago to ignore most of what his father said, or seemed to do so. Anne had never been sure. Bruce had a great capacity for absenting himself while sitting there, a defense against being embarrassed by an emotional father who didn't mind sharing his most outrageous thoughts with anyone within hearing range.

Morris calmed down for the moment and took a bite of German potato salad. The three of them, along with Margaret Hemmings, were sitting at an early-American-style table at the New Braunfels Smokehouse, a popular barbecue and German-cuisine restaurant that drew tourists and locals alike. Morris hadn't wanted to come, saying it was too loud and garish, but Hemmings had insisted. She had fond memories of the restaurant from trips through town and, besides, she'd said, "Loud is good." As it turned out, during their lunch no one was louder than her client. Other patrons didn't seem to notice, though.

"Do you recognize anyone here, Morris?" she asked.

Morris turned and scanned the room in an obvious manner. The Smokehouse consisted of three dining rooms, introduced by a large entry room where items ranging from toys to jerky were offered for sale. Morris shook his head contemptuously. "Nobody I know. But I'm not sure I know anybody here anymore."

"Good," Margaret Hemmings said. "Let's talk."

"Yes, let's do that," Anne said, leaning forward and pushing aside the remains of her turkey sandwich. "You told us the case would never be indicted. What happened?"

"I said never come to trial," Hemmings corrected. She smiled a broad smile, as if everything were following her secret plan. Hemmings sat back, stretching out in a posture that emphasized the elegant length of her neck. She had a mane of dark brown hair, pale skin, and a firm but elegant chin. The lawyer seemed able to change her appearance from moment to moment, but always carried a knowing expression. Anne had begun to wonder if there was anything behind it.

"What about this call Chris got from Temple Lockridge? How are you going to follow that up?"

Morris and Hemmings answered quickly, their words a confusing mosaic of negativity. Hemmings put her hand on her client's arm and said, "We're not. We're going to let that lie very quietly in the background."

"Chris thinks it's important."

Morris looked attentively at his daughter. "When did he tell you that?"

"We still talk, Daddy. Not as much as we used to, but he's not going to keep something like that from me. He thinks it's important for your defense."

"It's not," Morris said offhandedly. "It was just a coincidence that she was there, like Temple said. I'm not going to inflict any unnecessary pain on anyone else just because of my problem."

"Since when is that your philosophy of life?"

Bruce said casually, as if to no one at the table, "It's too bad you don't have friends who could help."

Cutting off her father before he could answer and start an argument, Anne turned to his lawyer. "So the indictment was part of your plan. What's the next part?"

"Do you want to see?" Hemmings smiled. "Get the check,"

she said to her client, then punched numbers into her cell phone. In a bright, distracted-sounding voice, she said, "Andy Gunther, please . . . Oh, darn, I was supposed to meet up with him. Can you tell me where he went? Thanks so much, Darling."

She clicked off, gathered up the Greenwalds as if they were her children, and hurried them out to her car, a bright-red sport utility vehicle that could have been taken for a fire chief's car. "Anyone know where a restaurant called the Back Porch is?" she called over her shoulder as she gunned out into traffic. As she got directions from Morris, she made another call.

The Back Porch, only a few blocks from the courthouse, off Water Street, was the kind of café where a patron wouldn't have to ask how the chicken fried steak tasted. Just take a whiff and taste the odor of last week's from the grease on the walls. Or last year's. Its interior was dark and rough-hewn, like a log cabin, and at 12:30 on a weekday it was full of men who wanted to meet their friends, have a beer at lunch, and never ever be taken for a tourist.

A harried waitress in a checked dress and white apron said, "Just anyplace you can find, honey," and hurried on with her tray.

But Margaret Hemmings wasn't here to try the chicken and dumplings. She looked around the restaurant and in a moment spotted Andy Gunther, who had left his suit coat at the office, loosened his tie, laid his straw cowboy hat on the table, and fit right in with the ranchers and salesmen at the other tables. He appeared so slow and mellow that he barely turned his head as the click of Hemmings's heels approached his side. "Mr. District Attorney," she said icily.

"That has a strong ring to it, doesn't it?" Gunther said lazily. "They should make a TV show called that."

The two younger men at his table, possibly Gunther's assistants, laughed heartily.

"I want to know how you obtained that grand jury indictment," Hemmings said loudly. In a moment she had the attention of everyone in the restaurant. Andy Gunther bore up manfully under their attention. Morris, slumping in his attorney's shadow, didn't look nearly as comfortable. Anne hung back, watching. She noticed that Bruce hadn't approached the table at all. He had stopped at a table near the entrance, exchanging greetings with one of the men.

"You don't have the evidence," Hemmings went on accusingly to Andy Gunther, "so what did you tell them?"

"Grand jury proceedings are secret," Gunther said placidly, chewing on a toothpick. He hadn't risen, and let the lawyer talk to his profile.

"Yes, but your motivations aren't. You're a public servant. But you're acting out of your own private interest here, aren't you?"

That got the D.A.'s attention. "In what way?"

"In your private vendetta against this man. From the moment you got a call that someone had died in his home, you've done your damnedest to pin it on Morris Greenwald, haven't you?"

Gunther twisted around and pushed himself to his feet. "I don't have any grudge against him. Hello, Morris."

Hemmings put a hand on her client's arm as if restraining him. "In spite of the fact that he actively supported your opponents in both your campaigns for district attorney?"

Gunther laughed. "Oh right, that massive shift of power.

How could I have forgotten that? Listen, no offense to your client, but I think he gave a total of maybe $300 to my opponents. And since they were Democrats they didn't have much of a prayer of—"

"Yes, but Morris Greenwald also has lots of political contacts. Tell me you didn't resent his activities, and when you had a houseful of suspects you singled him out for persecution. I know politicians better than that."

She said "politician" with all the disdain most people usually bring to the word, but Gunther looked unbruised.

"I just presented the evidence. A grand jury—"

"Yes, but you decide what evidence to present. Why did you decide to ignore the evidence, the eyewitness accusation against someone from your own party, Nick Winston? And all the evidence of other explanations?"

"Because they didn't make sense. I've given you all the *Brady* material you've asked for. Read the reports. The grand jurors did."

"Bull," Hemmings said loudly.

Gunther turned to Morris, who had remained unusually silent. "Morris, you know I helped you get out on bail. I've got nothing against you. But you should know something. You've brought in this mudslinger here—"

Gunther jerked his thumb at Margaret Hemmings, and a light flared. Hemmings smiled. "That's the picture," she said.

While she and the district attorney had drawn everyone's attention, a young man with a camera had entered the restaurant and walked close to the confrontation. He'd just snapped a photo of an angry Gunther glaring at Morris Greenwald and pointing his thumb at Morris's lawyer, as if ordering them both away or inviting them to step outside. The young man raised his camera again, Hemmings changed her smile to a look of outrage, and the photographer snapped again.

Hemmings handed the young man, a photographer from the local newspaper, her card. "Anything you need to know, give me a call."

But the young photographer was saying apologetically to the district attorney, "Sir, I didn't know what this was going to be. If you have some objection, just call my editor and he'll . . ."

But Gunther had recovered himself with a smile. He clapped the young man's shoulder and said, "You run with it, son. I never object to having my picture in the paper. Just spell my name right."

Hemmings pulled Morris away, saying softly, "He won't like this one."

A moment later she stood on the front porch of the Back Porch with her client and Anne. Bruce was already waiting for them by the car. Hemmings smiled as if she'd just pulled off a brilliant cross-examination. "Wait 'til you see this day's work," she said, and gestured as if to indicate a headline: "D.A. PURSUING VENDETTA?"

Anne, arms folded, offered no comment. She looked hard and long at her father, but he didn't return her gaze. Bruce, across the parking lot by the car, appeared completely uninterested.

The next evening Anne stalked through her house. She'd come home at six, had a salad, and tried to work on the couch, reading her notes on a case and trying to write a report for the court. She tapped her cheek with a pencil, dropped the pencil, then the pad, paced back and forth in the living/dining room, washed her few dinner dishes, glanced at the phone, walked around again. She would have liked to talk to Chris, but decided she had no reason to call him. He must have decided the same thing. That, apparently, was the mutual decision they'd been reaching for days.

Anne went into the bedroom, changed into running shorts, and quickly went out her front door, though not so quickly that she forgot to lock it and set the alarm. She hung her keys on a loop around her waist. Carrying keys while running was a pain, and there'd been a time when she didn't bother. Now as she ran the keys jangled at her waist, sounding as if they were talking to her.

She ran hard for three blocks, feet pounding the street, then slowed down. At eight-thirty at night the sun was just setting. It shot out color like straining hands, making one last desperate grab at the world before it sank. Sometime later Anne noticed abruptly that it was gone. A streetlight buzzed and came on. She started walking. She took long strides, stretching her muscles. Usually this helped stretch her mind as well, but not tonight. Her thoughts remained coiled around each other; no single one would come loose. Anne breathed deeply, huffing. She swung her arms. She raced herself, trying to break free.

Eventually, she achieved a certain peace. She wore herself out, at least. At that point she turned toward home and found herself far away. Anne laughed. She'd pulled a good joke on herself. It seemed like the first time she'd laughed in weeks.

She arrived home to a house that looked empty. The sight set off a faint mental alarm. She had a little trouble with the lock, standing on the dark front porch. Inside, she hastily keyed in the alarm code as she snapped on the porch light and another light in the living/dining room. The house held an odd, crouching quiet, as if someone were waiting to surprise her. But she sensed its emptiness. Anne walked around, the sound of her steps making the house hers again, reassuring her.

She showered, letting the water hit her face and cascade down her hot body. June in San Antonio. Even after the sun went down, the earth wouldn't cool off for hours, and then only down to a temperature most places only reached at noon. The shower felt great. Anne's muscles thrummed. She began to think coherently.

Out of the shower, she donned a long white T-shirt that said across the chest, cryptically, "And how did you feel about that?" No attribution, no logo. Chris had given it to her. She didn't like wearing psychiatrist-appropriate attire, but the shirt was soft and cool. On the couch she folded her legs under her, put the report aside, and read a novel.

At about ten-thirty Anne looked up to discover that she'd missed the news, and her phone rang. She flinched slightly. Anyone calling at this time would have bad news. Or maybe it was Chris calling to say good night. Quickly she walked to the kitchen and picked it up. "Yes?"

"Dr. Greenwald?" The voice came hurried and jagged and hard to understand, as if the caller were moving his mouth away from the receiver. Anne couldn't even be sure of the gender.

"Who is this?"

"I ran away, Dr. Greenwald. I thought he was going to kill me."

"Troy?"

"Mm-huh. He found my letters. Remember, the ones we talked about?"

"Oh, Troy. I told you you needed to tell him. Not just let him find out on his own. Where are you?"

"A bookstore. Out at De Zavala, a Barnes & Noble. You know it? I was at the mall, but it closed." His voice came in and out. Anne pictured him staring around him, watching for a pursuer, almost forgetting the phone in his anxiety.

"I'll call your father, Troy. I'll talk to him. You need—"

"No! I can't go back. Not tonight, he'd—"

"Wait, Troy, don't hang up. Where are you going to go?" Anne felt an urge to run to the boy, but she wanted to make him solve his own problem. He'd have to do that for the rest of his life.

"I don't know. I could stay at my grandmother's, but it's across town and she doesn't drive at night. I guess—I don't have any money, I just ran out . . ."

Anne stayed silent, waiting for him to figure out a solution for himself, but the boy couldn't. In a moment he'd hang up the phone and make a worse decision. "I'll come get you," Anne said. "Just this once, Troy. I mean it. I don't do this for people."

That was a lie so blatant she thought the boy must hear it, but he only sounded immensely relieved. "Thank you, Dr. Greenwald, thank you. I'll wait for you out front. But I'm afraid he might come look for me here. But this is the only store open."

"I'll hurry, Troy. Don't wait out front. Stay inside. Close to the windows. Watch for me. I'll pull up."

He hung up. She wasn't sure he'd heard, or whether something had just happened.

Anne dressed hurriedly, jean shorts under the T-shirt, tennis shoes with no socks. Then she remembered the shirt's slogan, and hastily changed it. She grabbed her wallet and keys and hurried out the door.

It seemed like a long drive through the shining night, out Interstate 10 almost to the outer loop. The expressway still carried traffic; Anne didn't feel remotely isolated. She exited in the far northwest, driving past a row of restaurants along the feeder street and behind them a large shopping center. When Anne turned into its parking lot, she did feel she'd left the world behind. Nothing moved in front of her as she drove down on her rescue mission.

There was no boy standing in front of the Barnes & Noble. The store was closed by the time Anne arrived. Troy couldn't be inside. The center itself remained well lighted, and the parking lot dotted with cars. But no one was walking the sidewalks. Troy would have stood out. Anne parked at the curb right in front of the bookstore and got out. He might be hiding nearby, watching for her. She wanted to be very visible.

But her emergence from the car drew no response. "Troy?" she called, and a breeze carried the word away. Anne began walking down the sidewalk, looking behind pillars and in the entryways of closed stores. No boy. Nobody. Whose were these dozen or more cars in the parking lot? Again it seemed as if people were hiding from her.

She turned a corner of the shopping center and an evil-looking cat hissed at her. It was so white it could have been made of moonlight. Crystal-blue eyes glared at her. The cat wouldn't turn and run, but held its ground. Anne gave it a wide pass and felt a tingle when she turned her back on it.

That was the only sign of life she encountered. In a few minutes Anne returned to her car. She drove slowly around the whole shopping center, looking ahead, sideways, and in the rearview mirror. No one leaped out trying to grab her attention. She even drove around to the back, among the Dumpsters and loading docks. She wouldn't get out here. Too many places to hide, where people other than the one for whom she was searching might be lying in wait. Troy could have fallen prey to someone, in fact, if he had come around here. Anne began to think she should call the police, but had no idea what to tell them. She knew they wouldn't act tonight, before the boy had been missing for twenty-four hours. Troy could be anywhere. He could have called another friend or relative. He could have changed his mind and gone back home. Maybe his mother had found him here and promised to intercede.

Or maybe his father had found him and intercession was needed.

Anne didn't want to interfere. It wasn't exactly her business. She gave little credence to Troy's claim that his father wanted to kill him. The boy overdramatized; it was one of his tendencies. But he believed his own exaggerations. See how he had run.

Finally, nearly at midnight, she called. She had no other choice. A search might be already in progress. She could contribute information. Anne sat in her car in the lighted parking lot and called the number. She listened to two rings, expecting a frantic voice to answer.

Instead a sleepy, grunting one did so. "Mr. Burns?" Anne asked, and thought the voice grunted affirmation.

Uh-oh. He obviously didn't know his son was missing. But she was in now. "This is Anne Greenwald. Troy's counselor?"

"Oh." The man cleared his throat and became coherent. "Is something wrong?"

Anne hesitated. "I don't know. I thought—Is Troy all right?"

"As far as I know. Let me check."

The man put down the phone. Anne waited, expecting trouble. Mr. Burns finding his son missing. Blaming her. What could she say? But the man hadn't sounded angry. For someone awakened from a sound sleep, he sounded remarkably reasonable.

"He's fine." The voice was suddenly back in her ear. "He's asleep."

Anne didn't know what to answer. "Are you sure?"

"Dr. Greenwald, I haven't fallen for the pillow-under-the-sheet trick in a long time. Troy's asleep in his bed. He's fine. He's having a good week, in fact."

"No trouble tonight?"

"What do you mean? No."

"Damn!" Anne said.

The voice on the phone began to sound alarmed. Anne reassured him. "No. I'm sorry. Someone was playing a trick on me. I'm sorry. It has nothing to do with you, Mr. Burns. They just made me think . . . I'm sorry. I'll call you tomorrow and explain."

Anne hung up, hoping she hadn't left the man too worried, and she raced out of the parking lot. As she returned to the expressway, passing other late-night cars, she wondered if she should call the police. But again, what would she tell them? In the end, she just drove home and went in alone.

This time when she returned home her porch light was on. Anne stood at the front door for a moment listening. She heard nothing. Quickly she turned the key and went in. She started to punch in the alarm code to shut it off, but saw that it wasn't on. Anne still wasn't used to turning on her alarm, and she'd left in a hurry.

The living room light still burned, as well as a lamp in her bedroom. Anne walked quickly through the house, into every room. She even opened closet doors and pulled aside the shower curtain. No one leaped out at her, nor did she sense anyone hiding. But the house didn't feel right. Anne stood in the doorway between the bedroom and dining room, listening and trying to slow her breathing.

Damn him. Nick Winston had stolen her house from her. She didn't feel safe here anymore. He didn't have to do anything to accomplish that.

But he had done something. He had deliberately lured her out of the house. In retrospect Anne realized that she had never recognized the voice on the phone. She had simply accepted its identification of itself as Troy's. The voice had been soft and fading in and out, plus tinged with panic. It could have been anyone. But the caller had known something about Troy's problems, specifically that he held a secret from his father. Someone had found that out. Someone had been through her files, or her computer at the office.

Had she ever had Troy's file here at home? Had she made notes about his case on her home computer? The answer to both questions was "Probably." Anne's office and home often worked interchangeably.

Someone had gotten into her work, into her home, into her life. And something had happened tonight, but she didn't know what.

She felt very tempted to call Chris, or to check into a hotel. But then she would be abandoning the house. When could she ever return? She had concluded logically that Nick Winston couldn't hurt her. He couldn't take the chance: he would immediately be the primary suspect. At worst he was just trying to scare her. She was safe here.

But her body didn't know that. Adrenaline still made her shaky.

After checking the doors and windows, Anne undressed, putting on the long white T-shirt again. She gave up the idea of trying to read, turned off the living room lights, and went to the bedroom. Sitting on the edge of the bed, she began to relax. She took a deep breath, held it, suddenly felt sleepy. The body could be made to work. Smiling faintly, a little groggy from her drive and anxiety, Anne snapped off her bedside lamp and lay back on the pillow.

The next moment she bolted upright. She gasped aloud and leaped from the bed. In an instant Anne was across the room, turning on the overhead light, staring at the bed. It looked normal, but Anne had felt something hard and unyielding. Slowly she approached it and tossed the pillow aside.

Underneath, resting squarely on the bottom pillow like a gift on a cushion, lay a hard black plastic videotape case. As soon as Anne had lain back she had felt it through the pillow like the edge of a dull knife.

Now more curious than afraid, she picked up the case. It bore no markings. Neither did the tape inside. It looked like a blank videotape, one without even a label.

Someone had been here. No way Anne would have left this here by accident. A maid came once a week for half a day, but today hadn't been her day. Chris had a key to Anne's house, but he would never have done this; not at a normal time and certainly not now. If he did, she would kill him.

Hoping, though, that that was the answer to this puzzle, Anne walked slowly back into her living room. She turned on the lamp, felt observed through the front windows, turned it off again. She knelt in front of the television and turned it on by touch. The new videotape slid easily into her VCR. A late-night infomercial flickered off and a picture from the tape came slowly into focus.

A forest scene. Birds twittered. A ripple of water ran somewhere close by. An overgrown trail opened, hard-packed dirt with a scattering of pine needles. Someone was walking this path, the camera shooting the scene from the walker's perspective. Then it pulled back to show an attractive young woman in a lightweight spring dress. The dress tightened across her hips as she bent down, picked a flower, and put it in her hair.

The camera hadn't yet shown her face. Anne saw nothing familiar about her. She felt very bizarre as she watched this tape in her dark house, crouching in front of her television and keeping the sound low, as if she might wake someone. There wasn't much to hear, anyway. The videotaped scene had a homemade quality. It didn't seem like a commercially made movie.

A noise disturbed the young woman on the screen, she turned and Anne saw her face for the first time. No one she recognized. This certainly wasn't a big-budget feature, unless this young actress was only a bit part who wouldn't survive the opening scene. She looked alarmed. She turned and walked faster. Sounds pursued her. The woman ran. A branch caught her dress and tore off a sleeve and pulled the neckline down. So it was that kind of movie. Obviously panicked, the woman turned again and looked back.

Anne froze. The woman turned her face away and started running again, but Anne hit the rewind button and backed up to where the woman on screen looked back at the camera. She paused it.

Her own face looked out at her from the screen.

This had not been the actress' face from the beginning. At this point, just when the camera caught her most completely, someone had superimposed Anne's face onto the actress' body. It was expertly done, though. If Anne hadn't known better, she would have thought she were watching herself.

Anne let the movie continue. The woman ran. She stumbled, her dress tore some more. Now she began to look like a jungle heroine. When she finally turned, cornered, one breast lifted free of the dress. And again she wore Anne's face. She hadn't all the time she'd been running, Anne felt sure of that, but when she turned full face to the camera, the retoucher had done his work again.

The young woman wearing Anne's face stood with her back against a tree, chest heaving, her legs and one breast exposed. But her hair remained perfect.

A man wearing leather hunter's garb of an earlier century stepped out of the woods. The woman gasped. "It's you. Why didn't you call my name?"

"I didn't know why you were running, my lady."

Inane dialogue. It didn't last long. The man came forward, offered the woman his cloak, she pulled him close. In moments the movie became pornographic. Anne's face came and went on the screen. During much of the action the woman's face couldn't be seen anyway.

Anne knelt in the darkness blushing or flushed with rage. She couldn't have said which. Of course she'd never made such a video. That damned sure wasn't her body on screen. Very, very few people could say that with certainty, though, and she certainly didn't intend to prove it to anyone's satisfaction.

She continued to watch, her face becoming more and more stony. Anne became a strange sort of voyeur herself, staring intimately, listening to moans that seemed to come from her own throat. She hated what she was watching, and hated the mind behind it. Anne had no idea how much technical expertise would be required to create this vile misrepresentation. Maybe it took a studio, maybe a high school kid with a computer could do it. At any rate, this was much more elaborate than a note—letters cut out of magazines and pasted on a page. She caught a whiff of obsession. She felt a trickle of fear along her spine at the thought of how much time and work had gone into this.

She fast-forwarded to the end of the scene, and that was the end of the tape. Whoever had done this hadn't attempted to carry it on for the entire length of the film. Nor had he added a direct message to Anne at the end. The pornographic episode spoke for itself, but cryptically.

What was threatened here? This tape came from Nick Winston, Anne felt sure of that, but what was his message? She thought she knew: that he was watching her. That simple. Anne had had patients disturbed enough to do this sort of thing. They thought that obsession was tribute. The object of such attention should be flattered.

Nick Winston didn't have that kind of flattery in mind, though. By slipping into her house and leaving this tape that apparently chronicled an erotic adventure she had had, he was saying that he could be here at any time, he might be watching her at any moment of her life, and in any event that he could create moments that hadn't happened. Blackmail?

No. He just wanted to inspire fear. She felt certain of that.

But thinking of her former patients reminded Anne of what Andy Gunther had suggested before, that if anyone were stalking her it was probably a former patient of hers. Running the thought through her mind quickly, Anne felt surprised to discover how many such possibilities occurred to her right away. Winston would be sure to capitalize on that, if she accused him of making this tape.

And what exactly *had* happened here? Someone had left her a tape. There would be no trace of Winston's presence here. He certainly wouldn't have left fingerprints in her house or on the tape itself, and no one would be able to trace its origins, no matter how many experts might pore over it.

Her face went hot again at the thought of that scrutiny. She didn't appear on that tape, but anyone watching it couldn't help but think she did. People who saw it would carry these images of her forever. Once she put this into the investigative system, there was no telling how many such false memories might be created. And to accomplish nothing, she would bet.

Anne stored the tape among her recorded movies and went to bed. She felt safe from any further intrusion tonight, and finally fell into restless sleep. But she woke up resolved, as if she'd spent all night thinking about what to do. That morning she went about her routine and left for the office at the usual time. She didn't take the tape. She had decided not to tell anyone about the tape, at least not yet. Maybe Nick Winston would be frustrated when he heard no reaction to what he'd left under Anne's pillow. That was the tiny revenge she could take. At any rate, until she had a better idea what to do about it, the tape would remain a secret between her and him.

And so Anne began her collaboration with her antagonist.

Morris Greenwald received a trial date. August 3rd. The dead center of hell in south-central Texas. Trial participants could almost be assured of an otherwise empty courthouse during their trial. Court dockets grew sluggish in August, lawyers took vacations, judges disappeared. The trial might very well get postponed, but on the other hand the judge might have chosen the date deliberately, knowing very little else would interfere.

Chris Sinclair went about the business he'd been elected to perform. He oversaw prosecutions, set policies, met with the chief of police and county commissioners. He continued his exploration, with his Victims' Assistance coordinator Judy Darling, of the world of stalkers. He talked to Anne regularly, listened politely to her explanations of her father's trial preparations, and didn't offer advice.

On the day before the Fourth of July, as Chris drove to pick up Clarissa from a friend's house and wondered which of tomorrow's fireworks exhibitions he should take her to see, his mobile phone rang. The sound jarred him. Not many people had that number. That phone's trill usually meant bad news. He clicked it on and said his name.

"Chris? I thought you'd be here." Anne's voice, sounding anxious and something else. Mad at him?

"You told me about it, but no one invited me."

"You're not going to be like this, are you?"

Chris's jaw clenched, then he deliberately breathed deeply and said calmly, "I'm trying not to intrude. Too many lawyers screw up a case, and your father's made it quite clear whose advice he's going to rely on."

A silence descended on them—the same silence, though they were separated by miles. Chris pulled up in front of Clarissa's friend's house, a small mansion in Terrell Hills. At the top of a long, sloping front yard, the girls sat on a porch swing, talking animatedly. Clarissa saw him and waved.

Anne said, "I understand," and hung up. Chris wanted to call back and yell at her.

Clarissa got into the front seat beside him, calling something back to her friend. Chris smiled at her. She said, "What's wrong?"

Chris laughed at the anomaly of this insight emerging from a sixteen-year-old girl in blue jean shorts and a knit blouse that said "Bebe." Clarissa appeared to be in disguise. She was her mother returned to haunt him.

"What did Francine have to say?" He had learned to put questions this way. If he asked something like, "How was school?" she would inevitably answer, "Fine." He might pick her up from the rubble of a school that had been destroyed by fire and explosion, Clarissa could be bleeding or in tears, and the same answer would still come: "Fine." Half the time she would still say nothing, but at least he had come up with a questioning technique that required a more specific answer.

Yawning, she told him Francine's parents were going on a cruise. Nothing more personal. Chris looked in the rearview mirror, for a moment expecting to see someone following, watching Clarissa, but he didn't see anything unusual.

His mobile phone rang again.

Clarissa saw him hesitate to answer. Sensing possible entertainment, she picked up the phone, clicked it, and said Hello. In a moment the hint of merriment left her face. "Yes, sir," she said, and handed the phone to Chris.

"Hello?"

"Chris, this is Morris Greenwald. I'd appreciate it very much if you could join us."

Chris drove one-handed, bit back his first reply, and said, "Sir, you have an attorney. You should either rely on her advice, take her into your confidence completely, or fire her. I can't—"

"I'm not asking you to replace her. I would like to hear your thoughts. Please."

And Morris Greenwald hung up without waiting for a reply, just as his daughter had a few minutes earlier. Chris set the phone down.

"Where are we going?" Clarissa asked brightly.

So he took Clarissa along as he drove to New Braunfels. For a while they chatted, but halfway there Chris fell into a reverie, interrupted when Clarissa said, "What are you doing?"

"Nothing." He looked around for a landmark.

"Yes, you are," Clarissa insisted. "I've seen you like this once before, but I didn't know you then."

Chris turned to look at her, touched by her assumption that she knew him now. The earlier time she meant was when he'd been preparing for trial in the murder of Clarissa's sister. Now he realized he had been dropping into trial mode.

He put his hand on Clarissa's shoulder, then answered her questions during the rest of the drive. The girl peered ahead, eager to be involved. She grew her "thinking niche," a small furrow atop the bridge of her nose.

Reaching Morris Greenwald's acres, they parked and walked down the long path to the front door. Clarissa looked up at the balcony. "From here, in the dark?" she asked skeptically, shading her eyes.

It was five o'clock in the afternoon, nearly a hundred degrees. The sun hardly seemed to have descended from zenith. They were glad when the door opened and Morris Greenwald ushered them inside as if from a blizzard.

"Thank you for coming, Chris. Oh, and this must be—"

"Clarissa." She extended her hand. Morris became a host, but Clarissa politely declined his offers. "Would you mind if I just look around a little?" And she wandered away, hands behind her back, giving Chris a little wink.

Morris took his arm. "Come on up, Chris. Thank you for coming." At the top of the stairs, he added apologetically, "Margaret's here. We've been discussing strategy."

"I don't think I'll have much to contribute."

In the upstairs sitting room, the defense lawyer was lounging on the love seat. She wasn't holding a notebook or legal pad, nor did she display her usual animation. She looked up at Chris rather blankly. "Oh, good, our savior. Come in. Well, we've got a district attorney now. Maybe we can do a mock trial."

Chris didn't understand her evident hostility. He looked at Anne, who was standing across the room. Anne just looked back without giving him any kind of signal.

Margaret Hemmings threw herself to her feet. "We've been trying to come up with our narrative, but we're having problems. The first big one, of course, is that we can't reconcile your story and Anne's. It's too bad you didn't get a chance to talk to each other before you told your different versions to Gunther."

"Why? It wouldn't have made any difference. We both saw what we saw."

"Well, as a matter of fact, you didn't. Quite obviously you didn't. Maybe neither of you saw what you think you did. Maybe you're both partly right. Let's see what we can put together."

Chris stood his ground. He didn't sit down to be interviewed. "I've told you three times what I saw. I'm sure Anne has talked to you more than that. This getting together in a room to doctor our stories—this is the kind of thing prosecutors imagine defense lawyers doing. I'm not getting involved in this. You can ask me what you want at trial, you can emphasize any part of my story you want, but if you think we're going to sit here and you subtly suggest changes—"

"Nobody's saying that, Chris," Morris said quietly.

The defense lawyer swept her eyes around the room, her expression mixed of equal parts of irony and disgust. "I think we're done here. You need to talk to your family, Morris."

She picked up her suit jacket from the back of the love seat, twirled it like a cape, and stepped into her shoes. She walked out slowly, giving everyone in the room ample time to call her back or ask her a question. No one did.

After she was gone, and they'd heard the front door close, Chris said, "I told you I shouldn't have come here."

Morris Greenwald said, "Chris—" but Chris interrupted.

"Are you happy with her? Do you trust her?"

"Yes. She's doing a good job. You haven't seen every—"

"Good! Then go with her. Work with her. And tell her *every-thing*, Morris!"

"What do you mean?"

Chris moved suddenly, walking toward Anne. "This is what I hated about being a defense lawyer. Working in the dark, not trusting my client. The prosecution always has more evidence, they have experts collecting it, but they also always have problems in their cases, and you can exploit that if you just know the truth. But you so seldom get it.

"I prefer prosecution. On the way over here I was imagining prosecuting your case, and let me tell you, Morris, I liked my chances. Even with nobody able to put you exactly with the victim, even with two eyewitnesses saying other people did the shooting. In fact, if I were the prosecutor I'd love that part. I know Andy Gunther does."

Anne said quietly, "Chris, give us your opinion."

He turned toward her quickly. Now his voice began to rise. "Anne, did you think I could come in here and tell you some secret prosecutor information that would let your father dodge this thing? I can't. I cannot take over the defense and I wouldn't if I could because *I don't know!* I can't save this thing! Probably nobody could. There are too many lies out there. I don't know what happened, and someone is keeping something from me."

"Like Senator Lockridge?"

"For one. That one hardly counts, though, because I knew he was lying and he knew I knew. What I wonder is why he called me there to tell me something he knew I wouldn't believe."

"What?" Morris asked.

"That Veronica Sorenson was here but not involved. Please. When people gather and something big happens and a big person was here at the same time, it's not just coincidence. Things don't happen that way."

Morris cleared his throat. "I think Temple was sending me a message through you. He couldn't see me in person or even talk to me, but he could tell you and trust you'd pass it on."

"What was the message?"

"Leave her out of it and things will be okay."

Chris paced, shooting a glance at Anne as he passed her. He wanted to kick something. "Is that what your lawyer thinks? That somebody can derail this prosecution for you if you all just sit tight? Because that's insane. Criminal cases have a momentum of their own, let me tell you. If you're expecting a political savior, you'd be better off waiting for redemption in the afterlife. Because you'll—"

Clarissa slipped into the room. She stood with her back against the wall, her eyes wide, and said, "Someone's here."

She said it as if armed intruders might be creeping up the stairs. Chris hurried past her, out the sitting room door. At the top of the stairs he looked down to the entry hall and saw a man in a dark blue suit looking up at him. The man's posture and lack of expression were familiar. A woman stood with him. At the sound of Chris's steps she looked up too. "May I come up?" she said distinctly, her voice carrying.

She was Veronica Sorenson, the lieutenant governor of Texas. She wore a belted, blue dress with a loose skirt, halfway between being dressed for work or a garden party. Her dark hair hung free to her shoulders. Standing with her feet planted firmly, and gazing up at Chris steadily, she looked clear-eyed and in charge.

"Of course."

Sorenson's bodyguard touched her arm and murmured

something, but she said, "It's okay," and came up the stairs alone. "I'd like to talk now," she said as she passed Chris.

He followed her into the sitting room, where Sorenson looked around alertly. She spotted Clarissa, smiled sweetly, and walked over to her. "Hello, dear. You must be the hostess, since you let us in. Would you do me a big favor? Find me a bottle of water, please? Take your time."

Clarissa understood at once. She walked out, glancing back. Veronica Sorenson stood at the sitting room door and looked at Anne, waiting for her to exit graciously. Anne stood her ground and said, "Afterwards, one of them will tell me what you said, but they won't get it quite right, so it's better if I stay."

Sorenson smiled and shut the door. "All right. Does anyone have any questions for me?"

Chris had too many. Anne skipped ahead: "Why were you here that night?"

Sorenson smiled again. "You must be Anne. We met years ago, do you remember? I was a legislative aide. You must have been in high school. You came with your father to see my senator, and I gave you a little backstage-at-the-capitol tour. I thought then you were very quick." She turned her attention to Anne's question. "Why was I here? Morris, haven't you told them?"

"I haven't told anybody anything, ma'am."

Sorenson said bluntly, "I was here to be blackmailed." Morris began to protest, and she continued over him. "Not by you, Morris. Not directly. I came to meet people and because Morris and Ben Sewell needed some help with a project."

"Why did you come to them?" Chris asked.

"I was on my way back to Austin from a luncheon in San Antonio anyway. They worked around my schedule. When I got here and Nick Winston was here, I suspected a problem."

"Why?"

Morris turned and walked away, to the window. Only Veronica Sorenson glanced after him. Then she walked toward the center of the room. Chris and Anne moved closer to join her. Sorenson looked down, then studiedly raised her head and looked them in the eyes, one after the other.

"Nick Winston has something. He's had it for years."

"There's no need for this," Morris Greenwald said loudly, over his shoulder.

Sorenson ignored him. She looked at Chris as she continued. "It's something that is very embarrassing to me. Not criminal, but embarrassing. It's a videotape."

Anne grew suddenly red-faced. "Is it pornographic?"

Sorenson looked at her oddly. "Not in the professional sense. But I suppose you could say it is." She sighed. "I had an affair with Nick Winston, years ago."

Anne's lips tightened. She took a small step backward.

Chris looked nonjudgmental and puzzled, as if he didn't understand the relevance of this confession. It was an expression he had developed over the years of listening to potential witnesses, an expression that encouraged the urge to explain.

"We met in Austin through some charity event, and kept running into each other the way you do. We'd see each other at Republican events, which in those days in Austin was a very small group, let me tell you. But Nick had this way of standing back from things, as if he'd come there on a dare, and he had a smile that only I seemed to see . . ."

Sorenson waved her hand, sweeping that image away. "It doesn't matter. But I got married straight out of college, started working, became politically involved. I'd been married and very adult my whole adult life. I never had that time you're supposed to have, that crazy, fun . . . There came a time when I was getting even more active, about to run for office, and it was obvious I'd never had that time. My husband was very supportive but didn't see this need to—I didn't see it either, except when I was with Nick. One night we were the last two to leave a meeting, we went for a drink. Afterwards . . ."

She shook her head, tossing her hair. Sorenson still looked very adult. She didn't come close to crying while telling the story, her eyes didn't go faraway. She wasn't reminiscing in front of them; she was only trying to explain. Chris wanted to help her out by telling her she could skip ahead. Sorenson said, "It's a common story, I know. But it went on for some time. I got very comfortable with Nick, really intimate. One time we had a whole weekend together, we drank quite a bit. We even—Nick had some marijuana. I hadn't had any in years. Just a tiny bit hit me very hard. I began feeling freer than I ever had in my life. He had a videocamera."

She stopped. The rest of the story told itself.

"You were drugged," Anne said suddenly.

Veronica Sorenson looked at her soberly. "That may be true. I've thought about that. But what difference would it make? The tape isn't faked. I was doing what I'd done before."

"I'm sorry," Chris said. "This must be horrible for you. But is he holding this over you? I mean, I've heard much worse stories. Even if word of this got out . . ."

"Yes," Sorenson said. She had obviously given the matter much painful thought. "Everyone's had what Governor Bush called 'youthful indiscretions.' The trouble is, mine are on videotape. There's a big, big difference between hearing about something that happened and seeing it."

The lieutenant governor was poised, businesslike, and pretty in an unprepped way. Looking at her and hearing her story, Chris couldn't help the images that suddenly passed through his brain, of what lay beneath Sorenson's carefully tailored dress, of her smile growing broader and looser. Images of the event she'd described passed quickly through his head. Chris didn't think his face changed, but hers did as she watched him. Sorenson seemed to see the images in a balloon above his head. She looked angry, defiant, and resigned all at once. "You see what I mean? It might get shown at parties, but that wouldn't make me the Republican party girl."

Anne looked puzzled at this exchange. She glanced at Chris. He turned businesslike. "But what did this have to do—?"

"Nick has the tape. I've asked him to give it to me and he even did, once. I think he wanted me to have it."

Anne's face began turning red.

"But I know it was just a copy. He still has the original. He's never overtly threatened me. He's much too smart for that. The affair ended a long time ago, but we supposedly stayed friends. And friends do favors for each other. Except in our case it's always been me doing favors for Nick. They became political favors when I got into a position to do that. Nothing bad, no crimes. Finally I put forth his name for the Railroad Commission, and supported him for it."

"Then that night I came here and Nick was here. Just his presence here made me wonder. . . . I think that's what he was supposed to do."

"No," Morris Greenwald said, coming toward them. "It wasn't like that. We would never have threatened you, Mrs. Sorenson."

She didn't bother to respond. "So we discussed Morris's and Ben's proposed legislation. I said I'd consider it, and I left."

In a big hurry, Chris remembered. Her car had been speeding away that night as he and Anne returned to the Greenwald house, before the killing of Ben Sewell.

Sorenson turned to her host of that night and spoke to him for the first time. "Morris, you know this has nothing to do with your case."

"Yes, ma'am, I do know that."

"I was long gone before . . ."

"Yes. Believe me, Mrs. Sorenson, I don't intend to call you as a witness and I haven't mentioned your name to anyone."

She looked around at the three of them. "I'm not asking you to cover up. I will not lie—about anything. I've given a statement to the Comal County district attorney. They're convinced I have nothing to contribute to the case."

So Andy Gunther knew. But he wouldn't call Mrs. Sorenson, either. He was an elected official, and she was one of the highest-ranking members of his party. He wouldn't do anything to hurt her. *He'll do what he's told*, Senator Lockridge had said to Chris.

"All of you do whatever you think best," she said.

"Why didn't you tell me this sooner?" Chris asked. "Why wouldn't you talk to me?"

"I should have. That was a mistake. I was following advice, but now I'm not. I was absolutely not involved in this. I'm going to tell the truth, whatever happens."

"What about Senator Lockridge?"

"That was a mistake too, but not mine. I didn't know about it until afterwards. If I had I would have told him not to call you." She grimaced indulgently. "Temple is an old friend of mine. A mentor. He still wants to watch out for me, and he's from the old school where you try to hang on to every secret. I didn't ask him for help. In fact, that's one reason why I'm here. After I found out he had talked to you, I thought you'd be more convinced than ever that I had something to hide. Now you know."

"I know you were gone before the killing," Chris acknowledged.

Sorenson smiled. She turned to Anne, who had been

uncharacteristically quiet. "What about you, Anne? Do you have any questions?"

Anne considered. Finally she said, "Did Nick Winston ask you for anything?"

Sorenson shook her head. "No. We barely spoke to each other."

"He was just here. Watching."

Sorenson looked at Anne more closely. She hesitated.

There was a knock at the door. No one said anything, and the door opened. Clarissa came in carrying a bottled water, a glass of ice, and some nuts in a dish, all on a small tray. She looked so efficient and helpful and curious, Chris wanted to hug her.

Veronica Sorenson hurried toward her, re-donning her public smile. "Thank you so much, my dear. You shouldn't have gone to so much trouble. I'll just take the water, thank you. And what's your name?"

"Clarissa."

"Your father must be very proud of you." The lieutenant governor shot a glance at Chris as if she knew his secrets as well. "Could you walk out with me?"

Chris hurried to do so. No one followed them. They went down the stairs, where the stone-faced bodyguard was nowhere to be seen, but undoubtedly close at hand. Veronica Sorenson took the cap off the bottled water and drank. "Do you know why I've told you this?" she asked.

"No," Chris said, and immediately realized that if Anne had been there she would have answered Yes, and it would have been true.

"Because you're the only one who's not after the tape. You want to solve a crime. I believe you have a sense of justice. I'm counting on that."

She shook his hand, businesslike, and there was nothing sensuous in the contact. They had passed that. But Sorenson stood still for a long moment, looking into Chris's eyes. *This is a trick,* he thought. She's learned this, a politician's *faux* intimacy. But it was a good trick. He believed her.

She left quickly, and he turned to see three people on the stairs watching him. Now they had to get their stories straight. Lieutenant Governor Sorenson counted on Chris's sense of justice. But Morris Greenwald, perhaps, was counting on his violating it.

And what did Anne expect of him? She stared at Chris without overtones. He had never felt more remote from her.

★ Anne and Chris went about their lives, separately. Chris, to the surprise of everyone in his office, prosecuted an assault case. Aggravated assault—the victim's leg had been broken in the attack, and she might have a limp for the rest of her life—which made the crime a felony, but still a low-level case for the district attorney himself to try. He did it because he had learned that the best way to get to know a case and its characters was to take it to trial.

The victim and her attacker had at one time dated, though their stories differed on how involved they had been. Luisa testified that she had felt forced into a couple of dates and broken off the relationship as soon as possible. The defendant swore they'd been on the verge of becoming engaged. According to young Marcus, the "crime" had been nothing more than a lover's spat, albeit one that ended with permanent injuries.

Chris found the defendant odious. When he was handed over to the prosecutor for cross-examination, Chris just stared at him contemptuously. His direct testimony had left so many openings, so many ways to go.

Chris took a moment to decide a path. But he also with his stare invited the jurors to stare as well. Marcus Garment had burly shoulders and thick features he tried to lighten with a small smile.

"Mr. Garment, what was the fight about?"

"We weren't fighting, we were just talking."

"A peaceful discussion that ended with Ms. Garza having a broken leg and a black eye. How did that happen?"

"She turned away and caught her foot on something and tripped. I tried to help her up, but—"

"She *tripped*. That's how she broke her leg. Is that the story you want to stick with for this jury?"

"It's true," the young man said truculently.

"You said she turned away. Was she leaving you?"

"Just walking away."

"And you had warned her what would happen if she ever walked away, hadn't you?"

"No."

"Do you remember telling her that no one else would ever have her?"

"No."

"How *did* you express your tender regard for her?"

Near Chris, the defense lawyer shifted uncomfortably, trying to think of an objection, but there is no rule against sarcasm.

"I did tell her I wanted us to be together always," the defendant said brightly.

"Until death do you part. So you never threatened her?"

"No, sir."

"And yet, when the time came when she did want to leave you, the event turned out more like my story than like yours, didn't it?"

"Sir?"

Chris stood up and walked toward the defendant holding photographs. "You say you never threatened her, yet when she tried to leave you she ended up with a broken leg, a black eye—" He held up illustrative photos. "—multiple contusions, abrasions, and loss of blood. Terrible coincidence, wouldn't you say?"

The defendant tried to think of an answer, while Chris took a deep breath and felt himself expand into someone taller and broader-shouldered. God, prosecution was fun.

Andy Gunther was about to experience this same pleasure.

Chris had tried the case for another, secret reason, one that some would consider a disservice to the victim and his office: he wanted the practice. He would rather have been preparing the defense in New Braunfels, but he couldn't. Instead, he channeled his energies into doing his job.

A hand-addressed envelope containing two sheets of paper arrived in his office. One page was an official-looking document that Chris recognized immediately. The other was a note from Morris Greenwald: "The State gave us its witness list. Does anything pop out at you?"

A few things did. One, the absence of Veronica Sorenson's name among the witnesses the prosecution would call. Two, the case looked solidly prepared. Andy Gunther had listed two dozen witnesses, including the medical examiner, party guests, investigating officers—and Chris Sinclair. What was up with that? Gunther wouldn't call Chris as a witness. He knew Chris's story wouldn't help the prosecution. He just wanted to make the defense worry, probably.

Chris also saw some chances for good defense pretrial

work. Some of those State's witnesses might be sympathetic to Morris, including the woman who'd stayed after the party with Morris. Properly prepared, they could plant some land mines as prosecution witnesses that the defense would later exploit.

But that was a devious way to go about trial preparation. Margaret Hemmings would think of it. Chris didn't respond to the note.

Perhaps due to that lack of response, a few days later he had a surprise visitor as he left his condo complex to go for a run. He stopped in the courtyard below his front door to stretch. There in the shaded greenery Margaret Hemmings was waiting. She too appeared dressed for athleticism, in electric-blue wind-shorts and a tight white top with blue piping. She wore a white visor, too, over hair pulled back into a ponytail. Her outfit made Chris's faded running shorts and old gray T-shirt look ragged. She stretched as well, resting one foot on a wrought-iron table and laying her torso along that leg.

"You lying in wait for me?" Chris said. Hemmings's presence here meant she had researched his habits. More likely, Anne had told her the best way to catch Chris alone—something Anne herself hadn't done lately.

"I would have come up and knocked in another minute. I thought we could talk more freely than at your office, and I knew you wouldn't come see me. We've been having strategy sessions in New Braunfels and you haven't appeared for any of them."

"You're the lawyer, not me."

"Morris thought you'd be on the team, though. He won't let

me bring in another lawyer. Truth is, I don't think he can afford one."

"And that's a problem for you, isn't it?" Chris snapped. "It means you might actually have to try this thing."

He finished stretching and started running. Hemmings kept up with him through the condo complex, out a gate, and through the parking lot of the shopping center across the street. Chris stepped up the pace and she stayed at his shoulder.

"You saw the witness list," she said, not short of breath. "Do you know any of those people?"

Chris shook his head. "Just barely, maybe. I couldn't help you with any of them."

"There's somebody you could help with," Hemmings said, stopping for a car, then running again, out of the parking lot and across a street, into a neighborhood of pleasant homes and shade. The latter was inviting. At six-thirty in the evening, the sun remained tenaciously high, as if it had no plans for setting this night. The temperature was over ninety. Sweat darkened the neckline of Hemmings's pretty blouse. She finished her thought: "Andy Gunther. He'd talk to you. You can do that fellow prosecutor thing. I can't. He won't say a thing to me. I don't think he trusts me."

"Rightly so," Chris snapped. Then he almost fell as Margaret Hemmings grabbed his arm and jerked him to a stop. They stood in the corner of someone's yard, under a tall old oak tree. Red-cheeked, they faced each other.

"What's your problem?" Margaret Hemmings said angrily. "That I beat you once in trial? Get over it, Chris. You're acting like a child. Isn't it more important—?"

"That's not it. I got over that case a long time ago. But it showed me how you operate. You're not trying to prepare a case; you're trying to figure out how you can back-door it. Squirm out of it."

"I've taken a lot of cases to trial, and won more than my share."

"But in the last few years you've had more luck behind the scenes, haven't you? That's what you want to do this time, and you want my help."

She leaned in even closer. Chris felt her breath, and the heat of her body. "No, *Morris* wants your help! He thought he could count on it. Are you going to deny him that because you have some grudge against me? Is that really what you want? To see me fail, to see Morris in prison, so you can say 'I told you so'?"

"I'll give you all the legitimate help I can," Chris said tightly. "I'll tell my story in court, I'll be the best witness I can . . ."

"Whoopie," Hemmings said bitterly. Chris caught a hint of her desperation. Her fierce eyes darted over his face and past him, looking for a way out. "I need more than that," she said. "What do you care how I do it as long as I win the case? Don't you want that? Don't you know better than anybody that my client isn't guilty?"

For the first time, in spite of what he'd seen, Chris felt unsure. Gunther had told him Ben Sewell couldn't possibly have committed suicide. Chris didn't know how Gunther knew that, but if true it left open other possibilities. Margaret Hemmings seemed unsure, too. She had not seen Ben's death herself. She must inevitably doubt her client, as all defense lawyers do.

Chris felt a moment of sympathy for her. But the next moment she stepped on it. "Do what you want," she snapped. "But Morris needs your help. And Anne wants it."

Bullshit, Chris almost said. Anne would never send someone else as her messenger. He stared into Hemmings's red face, noticing lines and smudges of darkness under her eyes.

Hemmings had turned big-time; she was used to working with a team, where the work could be delegated. She'd taken on Morris's case because of the opportunity of great publicity for her, but now saw a great risk of defeat. Those were the signs Chris saw in her face.

But he couldn't help her. He couldn't come into the case, certainly not as Hemmings's assistant. Without another answer, Chris turned and ran, panting. Anger fueled him down the block. Hemmings made no attempt to follow.

Dr. Anne Greenwald listened, yet again, to her young patient describing his hopes for the future, including his hope that he could make up for his conduct toward the girl he'd stalked. He had planned his apology, including a letter to her parents. He sounded young and earnest and extremely contrite. Anne hated him.

She came around her desk, sat in the other visitor's chair next to him, and leaned toward Ronnie, her face almost in his. "Ronnie, listen to me. Stop making plans about this girl. Don't go near her, don't look at her. Don't think her name. Put her out of your mind. The only thing you can do for her is give her the peace of mind of knowing that you're not ever going to go near her again."

The boy's hair looked blown back. He leaned away from Anne and stared at her with wide brown eyes. Anne wore a white clinician's smock over conservative brown slacks and a long-sleeved yellow shirt. For Ronnie's appointments she wanted to look professional to the point of severity and completely unprovocative. She continued to stare at him, feeling herself losing it.

She got up and went around the desk again. She spoke more quietly. "I know you think you're pulling this off brilliantly, and your probation officer tells me you're doing great. But let me tell you, you're not doing great here. I'm not going to give the judge a positive report unless you show me some change."

"Like what?" Ronnie asked with a voice that cracked. His preppie shell had cracked as well. He locked his hands together, and his fingers looked long and large-knuckled. His Adam's apple bobbed prominently in his long neck.

"Like respect for someone's right to choose who she wants to be with. It's not up to you, Ronnie. You don't just decide someone is right for you and that's it—she has no say in the matter. She's had her say. She's made a decision. It's time for you to move on."

He blinked and pulled himself together all too quickly. "Well, I know that. I just mean I want to, you know, leave a good impression. But leave. Definitely. You don't have to worry about me, Dr. Greenwald. I'm never going to bother anybody like that again."

Anne sighed internally. She had just violated her own rules and the guidelines of her profession. She had told her patient to stop talking about the one subject most on his mind. In other words, she had instructed him to lie to her. The doctor-patient relationship had just ended.

Plus, she wanted to choke the little bastard.

Anne went to a charity reception, downtown at the giant Marriott on the Riverwalk. It would have bored Chris, she told herself, so she didn't ask him to go with her. Besides, she just planned to drop in. After a long day in the office she drove the few blocks across town. It was a little after six when she pulled into the parking garage of Rivercenter, the upscale shopping mall attached to the hotel. Anne wasn't a tourist; she knew enough to park on the back side parking garage, which was always less full. At this time of day shoppers had gone, diners hadn't arrived, and she almost had the garage to herself. She got out of her Volvo, clicked it locked, and stopped, feeling someone close. She could see nothing but concrete pillars and cars. No humans, but plenty of places to hide.

But why would anyone want to do that? Anne walked determinedly into the mall.

It had been three weeks since she'd found the pornographic tape in her house. She hadn't watched it again. It stayed on her shelf between *The Graduate* and *Out of Africa*. It stayed on her mind as well. Hearing Veronica Sorenson's story had convinced Anne absolutely that Nick Winston had delivered the tape to her. A man didn't change his patterns. One who worked with videotape didn't turn into a pyromaniac. He must have had other victims over the years, women he'd black-mailed with true or manufactured evidence. Or didn't black-mail but just kept in fear of him. That was usually the tribute a stalker demanded.

But she hadn't heard from him, hadn't seen him. She had only occasionally, as now, felt him near. And that feeling was false, she told herself.

She walked through the brightly lighted mall and into the equally modern but more low-key lobby of the Marriott, where stair rails gleamed like gold, the wooden accents were polished deeply, and the atrium gave a feeling of spaciousness. Anne had been to many receptions and seminars here; she knew her way instinctively. Up the escalator to the third-floor area of ballrooms and smaller meeting spaces. The reception for the Special Olympics was in one of the latter, a room that would hold about fifty people comfortably, or seventy-five intimately. Anne entered and found herself one of several dozen well-dressed people who looked as fresh as if the day were beginning.

She waved to a couple of friends, got a drink, glanced over the food, and tried to decide how many people she had to say Hi to so they'd know she'd been here before she could leave. Six, maybe seven, she decided. Anne went looking for those people.

Instead she found Nick Winston. On the far side of a banquet table featuring cold shrimp, crackers, and small cubes of cheese, a smiling man leaned against the wall. His black suit was expertly creased, his wingtips looked both conservative and expensive, but he carried himself with ease, one hand in his pocket, the other holding a drink. Anne saw him in profile across a short distance with people in between; she couldn't be sure it was him. She stopped and stared.

The man was talking quietly with a tall, striking woman with a mass of dark brown hair and a well-tailored, pinstripe suit. She looked animated and attached, keeping her attention on her companion, not glancing around the room. Anne had heard of Winston's girlfriend Celine, who had supposedly been at a political event with him the last time Anne had seen him. This must be she.

The man stood straighter, looked in Anne's direction, and before she could turn away his eyes fastened on her. Now there was no mistaking his identity. Nick Winston's intense brown eyes, staring into Anne's, seemed to pull her ten feet closer. For a moment his stare was cold as Arctic night. He wore no mask. His intention toward Anne glared plainly.

Then he smiled. He gestured with his drink and the woman with him turned to look at Anne as well. Winston murmured something to her. Celine laughed.

Anne felt herself turning red. She turned away quickly and crossed the room to the second bar.

Now Nick Winston knew her whole routine. This couldn't be a coincidence. Anne looked around for a friend, didn't see anyone she recognized. The hell with being seen; she wanted out. She gulped down a second drink and walked toward the door, feeling the crowd shift around her, parting to make a path. She felt a hand about to fall on her shoulder and braced herself to throw it off.

A voice had been speaking, but the microphone hadn't been working. Suddenly it boomed out over the heads of the crowd. "Oh, there we go. Well, most of you heard the compliments, so let's get on with the introductions. First one of our very special guests of honor, who agreed at the last minute to be here. Railroad Commissioner Nick Winston."

The crowd applauded. Anne didn't turn to look at the smiling face. She was just glad that the crowd's honor would hold him here. She hurried toward the door.

Nick Winston quickly took the microphone and the spotlight. "Thank you for that gracious welcome." He raised his chin, aiming his voice out into the hall. "But let's not forget who this is for." He waited a moment, and got no reaction. Dr. Greenwald didn't return. "The bravest, most special people I know," he concluded, to genuine enthusiastic applause.

Smiling, he handed the microphone back to the host and stepped down into the crowd. Celine took his arm and they both smiled brightly.

In Chris's condominium, the front door opened onto a short hallway, with a kitchen on the right. Above the sinks the kitchen had a wide counter and a view of the dining area, then the living room and patio doors out to a balcony. Clarissa's bedroom to the left of the living room, Chris's to the right. One night Chris stood at the counter holding the phone. After a moment he hung it up again, his call unanswered. Clarissa looked up from her homework on the dining room table. "Where is she?"

Chris shrugged. "I don't know." He walked across the living room, feeling Clarissa's eyes on him. A few minutes later she went out on the balcony. That was the first place he had ever seen her, without knowing it, thinking her image a reflection of her mother. Watching the young girl, Chris pulled out of his self-absorption. How strange Clarissa must feel about living here with him. They remained relative strangers—related strangers. Chris wanted Clarissa with him; he had arranged for it and talked her into it, but sometimes his life didn't hold room for her.

He watched the girl, dim and ghostly on the dark balcony. Her blond hair fell past her shoulders, which were bare from the tank top she wore. Clarissa's narrow shoulders moved. Chris got a sudden chill.

She had left the sliding door open a few inches. He opened it further and stepped out. Clarissa kept her face averted, but he was sure she was crying.

"What's the matter, Clarissa?"

"Nothing." She turned her face further away.

"Please. Don't tell me 'nothing' again. Is it—?" But he didn't want to guess and remind her of some other reason for sadness. God knew she had plenty.

Suddenly she turned to face him, tears down her cheeks looking defiant. "A boy at school asked me out."

Okay, this was a girl thing. He didn't understand. "Was it that boy who's been bothering your friend?"

"No. Just a boy. A nice boy."

"I'm sorry. I don't—"

"I can't have a boyfriend," Clarissa said angrily. "Don't you know that?"

For a moment he still didn't get it, then understood. At her old school Clarissa had had a boyfriend, one of the most popular boys in school. He and she had been the golden couple.

He was dead now.

"Oh, Darling." Chris went and put his arms around her. He could almost circle her double, she felt so slight. But hard. She was so clenched. No one pursued Clarissa now; she didn't have to fear gunfire again. But she probably thought she carried a genetic jinx. Her mother's history with men had been terrible. Sometimes fatal.

"I want to see her," Clarissa said suddenly.

They'd been thinking about the same person but in different terms. Chris drew back and studied her. Gently he began, "Baby, you know—"

"No," Clarissa said angrily. "I *don't* know. She's done this before, you know. Disappeared when she needed to. Maybe this is like that. Maybe she's hiding out, waiting until it's safe for her to come back."

Chris didn't know what to say. Clarissa couldn't believe this. She'd been there. Chris had not only been there, he'd seen the autopsy photos. "She's dead, Clarissa."

But even as he said it, he wondered if that was the right answer. Jean did live on. In her daughter and in Chris's memory.

He didn't know how to comfort the girl. Her anger and her tears were absolutely justified. It was a miracle that she didn't cry every day. Clarissa had seemed to have adjusted so well that he could forget how awful she must feel. And he couldn't return anything to her. He had no idea what to say.

Out of nowhere he began telling Clarissa about the night he had met her mother. He'd been a sophomore in college, at an outdoor party, and seen a girl dancing alone. By the end of the evening she'd shown him parts of Austin he'd never known, given him glimpses of a whole other world, and carried his senses away. He didn't say all this to Clarissa but his voice grew faraway and it became clear that that night had changed him.

"She had no fear. And a sense of confidence that included everyone near her. I know you saw that about her. But she also made the world seem less ordinary. Every day I spent with her was an adventure."

Clarissa said, "I know that feeling. Sometimes the adventure was where we were going to sleep that night."

Clarissa spoke harshly but with a tinge of fondness as well. Chris heard it, and when he looked at her again he saw her acknowledge the feeling. She smiled.

So maybe he'd done something right after all. For a moment he felt almost adequate as a parent.

"So do you think you need to tell this boy you can't date him because of your tragic history?"

"No." Clarissa's smile turned crooked. "That would really lure him in. You guys are such dopes for adventure girls."

He pulled her close again and felt her smile. He had no advice to give her. They went inside and he told her another story about her mother, a silly college story about a missed test and Jean's talking her way into a makeup exam. She *had* been fearless, not only about danger but about the ordinary fears that would wake other people out of nightmares ten years later, such as being late for a class. Clarissa had some of that same quality. That's what Chris was trying to tell her, and he knew she got it. Her tears dried. After half an hour or so she returned to the dining room table and whatever she'd been doing. Chris sat trying not to watch her, wondering if Clarissa's tears had been set off not only by memories of her mother but by the fact that they hadn't seen Anne for a while. Clarissa might have been able to confide in her. Anne was the only thing close to a mother figure in her life.

He wondered how Anne felt about that.

When Chris passed Clarissa on his way to the kitchen again he looked over her shoulder and saw that she had drawn, with a pencil on lined notebook paper, the front of Morris Greenwald's house. She had made the front door and the balcony slightly more prominent than was realistic, but otherwise the drawing looked very close to proportionate. She turned and saw Chris studying her work. Clarissa touched the pencil tip to the front door and then to the balcony, and looked up at him skeptically. She was calling attention to the angle, that would barely allow someone at the door to see people on the balcony. Chris nodded. He pointed. "Bushes," he said.

She drew them in. She had a facility. Clarissa sketched rapidly but the pencil marks became bushes, with branches stretching upward. Then she moved her pencil out from the house, downward on the paper. "There," Chris said, and she made a mark to indicate where he'd stood.

"You had a better view," Clarissa said carefully. "Farther away, but a better angle."

Chris wondered if anyone else had bothered to draw a sketch like this. Clarissa had made the problem so sharp.

"But Anne knew the people. I didn't."

Clarissa kept watching him. That was the problem.

"You want a summer job? I need you for a special assistant."

Clarissa smiled.

On Saturday morning Anne pulled up to the front door of her father's house. Her brother Bruce's car was parked in the driveway ahead of her. The front door of the house opened and Bruce came out, unaccompanied. He closed the door behind him and walked toward his car, head down, as if he didn't see Anne. Bruce wore a white polo shirt that stretched across his shoulders and stomach, khaki pants, and boat shoes. As always when dressed casually, he looked like he was wearing a costume.

"Bruce?"

Anne's voice stopped him just as he put his hand on the car door handle. He turned to her, unsurprised. Anne thought he'd known she was standing there, he was just going to walk on by without speaking. "Where are you going?"

"Florida," he said in a flat voice.

"What?" She walked toward him quickly. "Why?"

"I've got something going on there. A deal I can't neglect any longer."

"Are you kidding? The trial starts next week."

Bruce's shoulders slumped. He looked in Anne's direction but just past her eyes. She'd forgotten this expression. Bruce was hurt but wouldn't reveal it. He was in full retreat, not just from the house but from himself, the emotions he wouldn't express, didn't want to feel.

Their damned father had hurt him again.

"I know," Bruce said in a monotone. "I never planned to stay this long. I have a great opportunity in Florida. It could put me solidly on my feet for good. Here there's nothing I can do to help."

"Is that what he said to you?"

"No. I said it to him." A tiny smile crossed her brother's face and disappeared. So he wasn't slinking away without having gotten in at least one good shot of his own.

"Bruce, you know what he's like. But he needs you here."

Bruce looked up at the house, but then just shook his head. Anne understood. She had seen Bruce's reluctance to be too closely involved. He wanted to shake hands with everyone, make contacts. His father's arrest had ruined that, and the trial would make things even worse. It would blacken the Greenwald name all over Texas. Where once his father had been an asset for Bruce, now he would be an inescapable burden. Once he had provided his son opportunities. Now Morris would ruin them.

And the trade-off of having his father's gratitude wasn't enough for Bruce, especially since Morris was as likely to express that gratitude by yelling an insult as any other way. Bruce knew when it was time to fade away. He had a good instinct for survival, the same one that had finally saved their mother.

Nevertheless, understanding all, Anne still got mad. They were both such children. "You know what, Bruce? *He'll* forgive you for this. He'll understand."

Bruce understood her implications, all of them. For the first time, he looked at her. He looked younger, vulnerable, and for the first time Anne felt their old childhood connection. Once upon a time they had only had each other, and Bruce had tried to protect her. He spoke to her in a human voice: "Anne, you left him long before I did. Why did you come back?"

"Because he needs me."

Bruce stared at her, a crease down his forehead as he tried to gauge her sincerity. He reached a hand for her, obviously wanting to take her with him, or to tell her to run. But then his hand fell away. "Is that all it takes for you?" he asked, and turned and got into his shiny car. A moment later it roared away. Anne went inside to yell at their father.

"Oyez, oyez, oyez! The 207th Judicial District Court of the State of Texas is now in session."

As the tall, bulky bailiff, a sheriff's deputy in brown uniform, intoned this ritual, Judge Peter Younger stared out placidly at the crowded courtroom. Judge Younger was a slight man but didn't seem to know it. He had walked to the bench with a heaviness, his black robe billowing out around him, and he occupied the high judge's chair with great gravity. He might have been a formerly large man who'd lost a lot of poundage. More likely, he remained constantly conscious of the weight of his office.

Chris, standing inside the railing, watched him carefully. Chris felt very odd. He had literally no place to stand. He didn't belong at the defense table and he wasn't the prosecutor. He was just a witness. Both Morris Greenwald and Andy Gunther turned to look at him curiously. Morris wore a nice gray pinstripe suit and looked like a funeral director. Gunther wore a black suit and cowboy boots that pushed him even higher over six feet. He looked like a frontier sheriff; he should have had six-guns strapped on under that black coat.

Alice Pettigrew, Morris's lady friend, also stood with him, holding his hand. Chris wondered cynically if Margaret Hemmings had arranged that touch, but Alice's affection looked sincere.

"Does either side invoke the rule?" the judge asked, referring to the rule excluding witnesses from the courtroom. Andy Gunther nodded, and the judge called the trial witnesses forward. Chris joined the group. So did Anne, a few feet away. That was the closest they'd been in a week. For the last week the trial had technically been under way, with jury selection. Anne had been here for it every day, partly trying to provide psychological spin to the prospective jurors' answers, but mainly just to support her father. Chris had stayed away.

The group of a dozen or so people took the witness oath and the judge explained to them that the rule of seclusion meant witnesses could not be in the courtroom during other witnesses' testimony. They all nodded, and the witnesses departed, trailing backward glances. Alice put her hand on Morris's shoulder as she passed him. Chris remained in front of the judge.

"Your Honor, my name is Chris Sinclair, I'm the district attorney of Bexar County."

"The Court is well aware of who you are, Mr. Sinclair." Judge Younger gave him a slight smile that looked curious and impatient and not friendly at all.

"As an officer of the court, your Honor, I'd like to be excused from the operation of the rule." That meant that, unlike the other witnesses, Chris would be able to observe the trial.

Chris heard calculation going on behind him. Margaret Hemmings wouldn't want him here but could use his help. Besides, she expected him to be on the defense side. Andy Gunther was an elected official who wouldn't want to offend a fellow district attorney.

They thought too long. The judge was in a hurry. "Hearing no objection, the request is granted."

Chris thanked the judge and took a seat inside the railing, in one of the chairs reserved for attorneys. He had to choose a side then, and sat on the defense side, but in the seat closest to Andy Gunther. On Gunther's other side, an assistant sat with him, a very young man who hadn't said a word, but was leaning close to his boss, as if awaiting instructions.

Chris had a good view of the judge, the backs of the lawyers' heads, and the jury. The jury Hemmings and Gunther had chosen looked mean, or frightened. With a slight majority of women, they were dressed drably, most of the men in suits.

The average age looked to be over fifty, even including the young man in front and a very young-looking Hispanic woman on the back row.

"Mr. Gunther, would you like to make an opening statement?" Judge Younger said it as if he were discouraging the idea, but Gunther climbed to his feet.

"Thank you, your Honor." He walked over in front of the jurors, nodding at them as if he knew them. He probably did, in some cases. "You folks are lucky. I know you don't feel like it right now; you can think of two or three other places you'd rather be. But you're going to hear an interesting case, much more interesting than the usual criminal trial.

"I expect to prove that the defendant here, Mr. Morris Greenwald, had a party one night at his big house out off Ruekle Road. He invited some important people, and some of them came. Mr. Greenwald had a former partner named Ben Sewell, but they weren't working together anymore.

"Late in the evening, after most of the guests had gone, Mr. Greenwald and Ben Sewell got into an argument. Soon after that, Ben Sewell was shot and killed. By Morris Greenwald's gun. By Morris Greenwald.

"That's what I expect the evidence to show. Then the defendant tried to rearrange the scene, he washed his hands to remove evidence, and he tried, with the help of his daughter, to put the blame for the murder on someone else. But that other person could not possibly have committed this crime. Only Morris Greenwald was in a position to do so."

Gunther grinned at the jury. "Kind of a classic puzzler, but I expect to prove Morris Greenwald's guilt to your satisfaction."

Gunther turned and slowly resumed his seat. He moved as if he were crossing his own living room. He owned this courtroom. Chris watched him closely and saw no lack of confidence in the D.A. He was good, no matter what he thought of his case.

The judge asked Margaret Hemmings if she wanted to respond with an opening statement of her own. She hesitated, then said, "We'll reserve that right until the beginning of the defense case, your Honor."

Chris didn't move or blink, but inwardly he groaned. She hesitated. The first day of trial, the first move in the game, and Margaret Hemmings hadn't yet decided whether she would give an opening statement. Morris Greenwald turned and looked at Chris hopefully. Chris kept his eyes on the jury.

"Call your first witness, Mr. Gunther."

"Yes, sir, your Honor. The State calls Preston Furie."

Morris leaned over and whispered to his lawyer, who nodded. At least she seemed to know who this witness was.

Preston Furie turned out to be a tall man in his fifties with a deep tan and a quick smile. He looked like a very successful salesman, the kind who sold buildings or subdivisions or fraudulent bonds. Chris thought he remembered seeing him at the party, just passing through quickly.

"Yes, sir, I was there that night," Furie answered Andy Gunther's question. "I didn't spend much time at the party itself. Some of us were having a little meeting in a study or conference room downstairs."

"Was Morris Greenwald participating in that meeting?"

"Part of the time. He came and went. He was the host upstairs."

"Mr. Furie, did you find anything interesting in that study?"

The witness didn't have to be prompted further than that. "At some point I was looking for paper, a legal pad or something, and I opened a couple of drawers in the desk there. I guess I should have stayed out of somebody else's property, but I was just looking for paper. When I opened the bottom drawer I was a little surprised, because there was a gun in it. A handgun."

"Was Morris Greenwald in the room when you made that discovery?"

"Yes, only a few feet away from me. I looked up and he saw my face and realized what I'd found."

"Did you say anything?"

"I tried to make a little joke. I said, 'Watch out for her security, Morris.'"

Andy Gunther didn't ask the witness to identify "her." "There were security guards on the premises?"

"A few. There were some important people there."

"Did the defendant say anything or give you any explanation about the gun?"

"No. We didn't talk about it any more."

Everyone had seen the gun lying on the table in front of Gunther, a .38-caliber revolver, snub-nosed and compact but heavy-looking. Now Gunther picked it up and carried it toward the witness. Chris noticed that the D.A. didn't ask the judge's permission to approach the witness. Different local rules here in Comal County. Or the rules didn't apply to the district attorney.

"Mr. Furie, does this look like the gun you found in Morris Greenwald's desk that night?"

The witness glanced at the gun casually and sat back again. "It looks like it. I can't be sure."

"Oh, it is, don't worry," Gunther assured him. "It's registered—"

Margaret Hemmings finally found her feet. "Objection, your Honor. To the district attorney testifying."

"Sustained," the judge said in a bored tone. Gunther smiled boyishly.

So he was a cheater. Some lawyers try to follow the rules scrupulously. Others push them, making the opposition work to keep out improper evidence. Gunther obviously preferred the latter ploy. He would keep his opposing counsel alert, or he'd get in testimony that shouldn't be allowed.

"Pass the witness," he said with exaggerated courtesy.

Margaret Hemmings sat up straight. From the back, she looked stiff. Chris's own lips almost moved as he thought of what he would ask this witness. Some of his imagined questions and Hemmings's actual ones coincided.

"Mr. Furie, how many people were in the room when you came across this gun?"

"Half a dozen, maybe."

"Did any of the others see it as well?"

"I can't be sure. Maybe one or two. I didn't keep the drawer open very long, I'll tell you."

"What were the names of the other people in the room?"

The witness said a few names slowly, picking through his memory. He did not sound overrehearsed. He sounded so natural, in fact, that he must have been practiced. The names he said meant little or nothing to Chris, but Hemmings made a great show of writing them down carefully.

"Did you stay in that room very long, Mr. Furie?"

"In and out. Some of us would be there, then go out to another room to talk. That kind of thing."

"And other people would take your place in the study?"

The witness smiled slightly, as if he heard words being placed in his mouth but would play along. "Basically, yes."

"Was that room ever left empty, or with only one or two people in it?"

"I don't know. I wasn't there all the time."

"So someone else could have gone looking through that desk just as you did and found the same gun, isn't that true?"

"Objection," Andy Gunther said. He sat with his long legs stretched out in front of him under the counsel table. Judge Younger looked at him, and Gunther rose to his feet. "That calls for speculation, your Honor."

The judge gave the district attorney another look before sustaining the objection. So there was no love lost between the judge and Gunther. Chris wondered if Hemmings had noticed that.

She asked a good question. "Did you ever check that drawer again, Mr. Furie, to see if the gun was still there?"

The witness folded his hands comfortably over his abdomen, still smiling slightly as if in on the joke. "No."

Exaggeratedly, like a schoolgirl, Hemmings said, "Your Honor, may I approach the witness?"

The judge nodded. The defense lawyer stood up quickly and walked to the witness stand. The pistol still lay on the rail in front of the witness. Margaret Hemmings picked it up and said, "Pretty small gun, isn't it?"

"I guess," Furie drawled. "I'm no gun expert."

Hemmings popped open the cylinder, made sure the gun was unloaded, closed it again, looked at the witness intently as if formulating the perfect question, raising her left hand for emphasis, then turned away from him. Her back was to the jury for only a second, and by the time she turned to face the counsel tables her hands were swinging freely at her sides. Her skirt and suit jacket hung straight. She walked toward the district attorney, stepping like a model on a runway, then turned back to the witness. "Mr. Furie, would you tell us whether that gun has a serial number?"

The railing in front of the witness was empty. He looked down at it, frowned, bent to check the floor at his feet. Most of the jurors watched him. Two or three kept their eyes on Margaret Hemmings. After letting the witness search for a futile few seconds, she smiled, said, "Oh, here," and produced the gun from the waistband of her skirt.

"Hey!" Andy Gunther jumped to his feet. "I object to that, your Honor!"

"To what?" the judge asked.

Gunther had to think for a second. "To defense counsel interfering with the chain of custody."

"I don't believe I've ever heard that objection before," Judge Younger said with interest. "You mean you don't want her touching your exhibits?"

"I don't want her hiding them!" Gunther confronted the defense lawyer, clearly thinking of asking that she be strip-searched.

Margaret Hemmings smiled at him and opened her suit jacket. "If you like, I'll take the stand to swear I didn't switch guns."

Gunther glared, then resumed his seat, sitting up straighter than he had been. His assistant leaned over and whispered to him, but Gunther didn't reply.

Hemmings took some time to place the gun back on the rail in front of the witness and resume her seat. "Mr. Furie, based on what you've seen in the last few minutes, do you think it was possible for someone to slip that gun out of the study without you or anyone else noticing?"

Preston Furie knew his answer would be inconsequential. The jury had just watched it happen. The witness smiled and said, "I believe you could have done it, Ms. Hemmings. I don't know about anyone else."

Margaret Hemmings laughed, as did a few others. They had a nice chuckle. Some tension departed the room.

It had been a neat trick, one Margaret Hemmings had obviously come prepared to perform. She had known about the gun, and about the guest's finding it. So she had not come to this trial completely unprepared.

Chris had a simple question: Had Furie told anyone else at the party about seeing the gun? Hemmings didn't ask it, but otherwise she had done well.

Having scored points on her opponent, Hemmings passed the witness. Gunther asked him a few more questions just to try to reclaim the moment, but they were done with this subject. In three minutes Judge Younger was asking Gunther to call his next witness.

Which turned out to be another party guest, Mrs. Louise Peak, who described the scene upstairs in the main party room. Mrs. Peak, fifty-plus, dressed in a pastel suit that looked as if she knew her age but kept up with fashion magazines, smiled to show very white teeth. Her dark eyes remained watchful. Peak was in public relations, which meant almost inevitably that she had once been a newspaper reporter, and she retained her recording instincts. She testified in some detail as to who had been at the party, who had come and gone, which guests talked to each other, and the tones of their conversations, even ones she had only observed.

She gave an impressive demonstration of memory, but the jury began to look restless. Chris was surprised, too. Prosecutorial wisdom held that you led off with a strong witness. Kill the victim in the first few minutes. Show the fight that preceded the murder. Make it bloody and awful. Make the jury long to avenge this terrible crime. Lay it squarely at the defendant's feet.

But if Andy Gunther had a smoking gun, he was saving it. Margaret Hemmings let the witness talk. If the other side wanted to bore the jury, why interfere?

But Gunther may have been deliberately lulling her. After fifteen minutes he asked, "Did you overhear any conversations?"

"Several. I circulated."

"Did you hear anything that might be relevant to this trial?"

"I heard Morris Greenwald threaten to kill Ben Sewell."

Everyone in the courtroom sat up attentively. Judge Younger, who'd been staring out the windows, quickly swiveled his gaze to the witness.

"What were the circumstances?" Andy Gunther asked casually, but Chris felt his elation.

"I was behind them, moving from one group to another. Slowly." Peak smiled. Yes, she'd been deliberately eavesdropping. It was her job and her life. "I'm sure they didn't know I was there. Ben was trying to tell Morris something that had happened, I couldn't understand that. But Morris was impatient and didn't want to talk and said, 'If you—' Excuse me, I'll edit this part a little. 'If you screw this up, I'll kill you.'"

"Any idea what they were talking about?"

Peak shook her head. "None. Frankly, I passed on more quickly after that. I didn't want Morris to turn around and realize I'd heard. I didn't think anything of it—people say that kind of thing—but the next day when I heard what happened . . ." She shook her head again, this time sadly.

"You called my office?" Andy Gunther asked gently.

"Yes."

"Mrs. Peak, did you hear anything else that night that might be relevant to these proceedings?"

"No. I had another event to attend. I left soon after that."

Having sucked one party dry of informational value, she had moved on. Or so she'd thought. Chris thought how disappointed Louise Peak must have been the next morning when she discovered that much more had happened at Morris Greenwald's after her departure.

The witness passed to her, Margaret Hemmings went briskly to work. "Ms. Peak, you didn't take Morris Greenwald's threat seriously, did you?"

"No, I didn't, at the time."

"Well, you heard it and left. If you'd thought someone's life was actually in danger, you would have done something about it, wouldn't you?"

"Of course." Louise Peak held her chin high, as if fending off an accusation.

"Have you heard people threaten to kill each other before?"

"Yes."

"Often?"

"Well, once in a while."

"Have you ever known any of those threats to be carried out?"

"I've worked in the news business, Ms. Hemmings, so once or twice, yes, I have known someone to carry through on a death threat."

Hemmings remained composed. "But as an ordinary thing, a threat to kill someone is just a figure of speech, isn't it?"

Louise Peak looked at her with apparent sadness. "This wasn't an ordinary occasion, apparently."

Morris Greenwald had scribbled something on a legal pad. Hemmings glanced at it. Still sounding in control, she asked, "Ms. Peak, do you know Morris Greenwald very well?"

The witness cocked her head, considering her answer carefully. "That's hard to say. We've known each other a long time, but we're hardly intimate friends. Pretty well, I'd say."

"Have you ever heard him in the past say he was going to kill someone?"

"I can't say that I have."

"Really? You haven't known him to get angry?"

"Morris? Oh, yes." Louise Peak laughed. She did it in an elegant way, stretching her neck and showing her brilliant teeth.

"When he flies off the handle, is he known for watching what he says?"

"No. He's gotten in trouble a few times before for talking too quickly before he thinks. I can think of a few people who might have been at his house that night but weren't, because of Morris's quick tongue."

Hemmings nodded, satisfied. But Chris considered her tack a dangerous line of questioning. Establishing that her client was hot-tempered would play right into the prosecution's hands. Andy Gunther glanced over at the defense table, looking perfectly satisfied.

Margaret Hemmings moved off the topic. "Ms. Peak, you said you were gliding around this party for a while that evening, yes?"

"I don't think I put it that way."

"Well, put it your own way, then. You walked around quietly, participating in some conversations and listening in on others. Is that better?"

"No, that doesn't sound any better either," Peak said with some amusement. "But I guess it's about right."

"Here's my question, Ms. Peak. Did you hear anything else that would be embarrassing for the person who said it to hear in a courtroom later?"

The witness considered. "I saw some flirting, including between married people. I heard a possible political connection being forged between people who wouldn't want their alliance printed in a newspaper."

"You were a busy bee, weren't you?"

Peak looked back at the defense lawyer coolly. "I'd say it was a typical political occasion, at least while I was there."

"Exactly." Margaret Hemmings ended as if on a note of triumph. The district attorney looked at her curiously when she passed the witness back to him.

The judge glanced at the clock above the doors of the courtroom, which read almost ten-thirty, and declared a morning break. "Be back in these seats in ten minutes," he said sharply, and hurried from the bench.

Anne had been a witness many times in the past, as a psychiatrist. But on those occasions the judge usually made adjustments for the value of her time, allowing her to arrive, take the stand, and depart fairly quickly. Often she would be taken out of order, to fit the trial into her schedule. Today was completely different in many ways, but one was that she had forgotten the operation of the rule that excluded witnesses from the courtroom. She'd expected to be close to her father as the trial proceeded. Instead she found herself pacing the halls of the Comal County Courthouse, a space almost as restrictive as a prison day room.

And about as crowded. Prosecution witnesses waited their turns, many of them the guests from her father's notorious party. It was as if the Comal County district attorney had re-enacted the event. Most of the people sat in clusters chatting. They were old friends. Though they talked in low voices and wore serious expressions, a certain festive atmosphere began to prevail, as it does at funerals and wakes, just because old friends were getting together.

Anne didn't join in. She walked the halls, waiting. Her turn might not come for two days, but she couldn't be somewhere else. Leaning on the door of the courtroom, she wondered if her father felt her support.

Alice Pettigrew sat alone, composedly knitting. Anne watched her curiously, trying to imagine the reserved, courteous woman as a stepmother. Well, that wouldn't have much impact on Anne's life. But it made her think of another aspect of her father's life, something other than his business dealings. He had been alone a long time. Maybe Morris had hoped with the renewal of his fortunes to draw his family closer as well. That could have been why he'd invited her to the party that night. People had come up with stranger schemes for finding love, Anne knew.

A stir passed in the hallway. The two television cameramen moved to the far end. Everyone turned that way curiously. Reporters got their notebooks ready. A cluster formed. In spite of herself, Anne watched. Then, reaching the top of the stairs, Nick Winston appeared. A black suit draped his thin, stylish frame. A lovely woman, also well dressed but less formally, held his arm. Winston nodded soberly to the newspeople. His girlfriend swept her hair back from her face. Except for the absence of big, gleaming smiles, the two might have been arriving at the premiere of a movie in which Nick Winston was starring.

Anne folded her arms and turned her back. But she felt him. The character of the corridor had changed. The space grew even narrower.

Railroad commissioner Winston answered the reporters' questions politely. "Just a citizen here to do what the law requires."

After a short time they moved away. Winston would certainly have given them some answers that would appear in tomorrow's newspapers in New Braunfels and Austin, about his sober willingness but not eagerness to testify against an old friend. Subtly he would reinforce, for those following the trial, the idea of Morris Greenwald's guilt. He would play down their conflict. He would appear sympathetic but determined.

In this confined space, only Anne felt his hostility. She glanced back and saw the crowd slowly separate, and Winston come forward.

There is nothing more intimate than a stare. Anne felt his on her body. When she turned away, his stare cut a swath along her body, like the heat of a sunburn line. She felt his gaze crawl across her shoulders, down her back, beneath her clothes.

No. In spite of his damned video calling card, Nick Winston had never seen her naked. Anne turned and faced him. His dark eyes were on her, his mouth quirked sardonically, as if he had followed every twist of her thoughts. He saw her blush. But no one else would see him watching. He stood close to his girlfriend Celine, talking quietly to her, his gaze going just past her and stretching down the hallway to reach Anne.

There is nothing as intimate as a stare. For a moment he and Anne joined in one, enclosed in each other's thoughts. Then Anne turned away, walked quickly down the hall, and turned a corner. Because in the staring contest she had felt his triumph, because he had her attention. There is nothing more frustrating than an unreturned stare. She knew that. She cut him off.

Anne found a ladies' room and stood at the sink. She washed her hands and was looking into the mirror when the door opened and Celine entered. Tall, composed, the young woman seemed to pause between steps to strike a pose. Wearing a tight, dark green dress that ended a foot above her knees, she appeared dressed for a party rather than a trial. Celine stood just inside the door looking at Anne with an imitation of Nick Winston's sardonic smirk. "We finally meet," she said.

Anne turned. "Did he send you after me?"

The young woman glanced around the small room, even knelt and glanced under the stall door to make sure they were alone. Anne felt another chill. Celine was the scout, making sure it would be safe for Winston to come in. Anne also looked around the room, saw no windows. The young woman stood blocking the door.

"Some things are my own idea," Celine finally answered the question. She came toward Anne. "I have a really stunning suggestion. Why don't you just tell the truth?"

Anne stared. Celine continued, "No one's going to believe you, anyway. They'll know you're just lying to protect your daddy."

"Like you did to give your boyfriend an alibi for the night he followed me?"

In the echoing tiled confines of the ladies' room, Anne's response sounded weak, even to herself. Celine ignored it.

"Think of it," she said. "You could shock everyone, tell a different story than what they were expecting. Just that you're not sure what you saw. Which is true, isn't it? Otherwise you're going to look like a fool and a liar. I can't imagine anyone coming to see you for treatment after what they do to you on the stand. And after everyone in Texas hears about it."

Oddly, the threat relaxed Anne. It lessened the possibility that she was about to be attacked physically. She gave the attractive young woman a cool stare. Celine dressed and moved in a way to attract attention. She relished being watched.

"I'll bet you star in some of his video productions too, don't you?" Anne said.

Celine's eyes narrowed. She walked very close to Anne, until she stood right in front of her, and bent to almost touch Anne's nose with her own. Celine's brown eyes were wide and knowing. "Sometimes," she said softly.

Anne pushed past her and reached the door. She could feel her heart beating, and knew her face must be red. She turned at the door to see Celine still standing by the sink smiling at her. Anne went out without a retort.

She was furious, angrier than she'd been in a long time. She was mad at herself for running and hiding, for letting her tormentor dictate her actions. With long strides, Anne reached the main hallway.

Winston was no longer there. She looked around quickly, walked to the window at the end, and looked down onto the courthouse lawn. Winston stood near the steps smoking.

Anne raced down the stairs, along the first-floor corridor, and out the door. She reached the spot so quickly Winston hadn't moved. When she approached him he smiled and flipped his cigarette away. But Anne came up so fast and so close that he lost the smile.

Anne said in a level but rising voice, "You stay away from me and keep that bitch with you away from me, too."

Winston raised his hands as if in surrender. "I wasn't going anywhere near you, Ms. Greenwald."

"Are you really so smug you think you can intimidate me into lying for you? Why on earth do you think I'd do that?"

"I haven't asked anyone to lie."

Anne said firmly, "I saw you murder a man. I saw you put a gun to his head and pull the trigger."

The secret glint returned to Nick Winston's eye. "So you say, but no one believes you."

"That's not true," Anne said. "You believe me."

They stood close, staring into each other's eyes.

When Chris emerged from the courtroom for the morning break, he saw a small crowd clustered by the broad window at the end of the hall. The watchers included a television cameraman shooting footage. Chris looked around quickly and didn't see Anne. He had a sudden fear of what everyone might be looking at outside.

He joined the crowd, managing to get a spot at the edge of the window. The action was taking place down on the court-house steps. Anne stood very close to Nick Winston, obvi-ously yelling at him and poking her finger in his direction. Winston stepped back from her, raising his hands.

The crowd around Chris muttered remarks. Other people watched the confrontation from the sidewalk in front of the courthouse.

"Oh, hell," Chris said.

As Anne stormed away, Nick Winston remained on the side-walk, standing as if stunned. He shook his head, baffled. Then he glanced at a man on the courthouse steps who had obvi-ously been watching. Winston shrugged. He and the man exchanged a knowing glance.

Winston never looked up at the television camera filming from the second floor, but he knew it was there.

The last witness of the morning gave another account of Mor-ris Greenwald's party. This one, Lewis Purser, the treasurer of Comal County, a man who had probably ridden to political office on his name, had arrived late and stayed until the end of the evening. As he had gone looking for his host to say good-bye, he had heard Morris Greenwald's voice from behind the closed study door. He had heard the voice because it was raised in anger. Answering back rather meekly had been the soon-to-be-late Ben Sewell.

Margaret Hemmings sat up eagerly when her turn came and lit into the man on cross-examination, but so slowly and slyly that Purser must have thought she was trying to make friends with him. He sat in his wilted seersucker suit, pale eyes peering through round lenses, while she praised his insight and knowledge of the occasion.

"I guess after your years of political involvement, you must have known everyone in the room, isn't that right, Mr. Purser?"

"Most of them, I suppose."

"Do you know Nick Winston?"

"We'd met before, when he was running for the commission."

"So you would describe yourself as a friend of his?"

"Yes," Purser said slowly.

"Political allies?"

"Well, yes. We're both Republicans. Of course."

This brought a rippling chuckle from the Comal County audience, which knew that no other type of political creature could hold office in that vicinity.

"Has he talked to you since that evening?"

"Yes, he called me to talk about what happened."

Hemmings dropped that topic, deliberately leaving the jury to wonder why she'd asked.

"What about Ben Sewell—were you friends with him?"

"I'd just met him that evening."

"Really. How remarkable. And yet you recognized his voice through a closed door."

Purser had obviously been prepared for this question. "We'd spent quite a bit of time together that evening, including going to dinner. And he was one of the few people left by that time."

"But not the only man left."

"No, ma'am. But I recognized his voice."

"Could you hear what Morris Greenwald was saying?"

"No. Not the exact phrases. Just the tone. Angry."

"You said Ben Sewell answered rather quietly," Hemmings prompted.

"Well, by comparison."

"Yes. You characterized Morris Greenwald as 'yelling.'"

"Yes, ma'am."

"So you could hear Ben Sewell's soft voice well enough to recognize it, but you couldn't hear Morris Greenwald's much louder voice clearly enough to understand what he was saying. Is that your testimony?"

Lewis Purser blinked at her. Seeing his hesitation, Chris understood suddenly. Morris had yelled the name of Veronica Sorenson, the lieutenant governor of Texas. And Lewis Purser had been told very firmly, by the district attorney or someone else, that the name of Veronica Sorenson was not to be raised in this trial.

Margaret Hemmings probably understood that as well. And she used the forbidden topic to make the witness look like a liar.

"He was mad," Purser repeated. "He yelled something like, 'What the hell were you thinking?'"

"You remembered that just now," Hemmings said scornfully.

Purser licked his lips. Margaret Hemmings went at him for fifteen more minutes, but when the witness was passed back to Andy Gunther he had Purser reassert that he had heard the defendant yelling angrily at the man who would be dead a few minutes later. The treasurer left the stand slump-shouldered and not looking anyone in the eye.

Neither did Chris. Judge Younger granted a lunch recess,

and Chris remained seated while people around him rose and talked. Chris didn't want to join in the discussions at either the prosecution or defense tables. So he was surprised when a voice said almost in his ear, "Chris. Join us."

It was Morris Greenwald. After the invitation, he stood up. Margaret Hemmings stood behind his shoulder, trying to look completely noncommittal. Chris turned and saw Anne coming up the aisle, curiosity obviously eating at her.

"Please," Morris added. Chris looked up at him and saw a strange resolve in the older man's eyes. Chris stood up. "All right. Let's go."

★ "Not too bad, not bad at all," Margaret Hemmings said smugly.

She, the Greenwalds, Alice Pettigrew, and Chris Sinclair sat in a homestyle buffet restaurant near the courthouse, where they'd managed to go through the line quickly and find a relatively secluded table in the corner. They sat surrounded by food in small bowls, like gods to whom food offerings had been made, but the only person showing any appetite was the defense lawyer. She recounted for Anne and Alice the morning's work, including her "disappearing" of the murder weapon. Alice smiled as if enthralled, patting Morris's hand. He didn't smile at the story.

"Yes, that caught people's attention," Chris admitted. "You'd obviously prepared for that."

"All my life," Hemmings laughed. "I've been doing magic tricks since I was a kid. Now just in a different forum, eh?"

Chris lowered his eyes. He didn't want to call her on the admission she'd just made. But then, glancing at Morris, he saw that Morris understood, too.

"So the sleight-of-hand wasn't something you knew you'd need to do. It was just a skill you happened to have," Morris said levelly.

"Well, we've all got our bag of tricks. Listen, when we get back I'm going to talk to the reporters. Tell them how badly the prosecution's case is going. The judge tells jurors not to watch the news or read the newspaper, but let me tell you . . ."

"No," Morris said flatly.

His lawyer looked at him with puzzlement. Morris turned to Chris. "Can I fire my lawyer once the trial's already started?"

"What the hell?" Hemmings said loudly.

Chris shook his head. "Very difficult. The judge will think you're doing it just to stall for time, after you've already gotten a look at part of the prosecution's case. The only chance is if you had someone else ready to step right in, and you don't."

Morris looked at him imploringly, and Chris shook his head more firmly. "It can't be me."

Margaret Hemmings grabbed her client's arm. "What the hell are you talking about? We've got them on the run. Why are you saying—?"

Morris looked straight at her until she removed her hand from his arm. Then he said levelly, "Yes, you're good. You can cross-examine people, you can trip them up. But by my score-card, on the first morning of trial the prosecutor has proved that I intended to kill Ben, I had the murder weapon to do it, the opportunity, and I was in the mood. And I don't see any sign that you've planned how to deal with those things. You're just reacting."

"That's what the defense does in a murder trial!" Hemmings said, raising her voice enough that other lunchers turned to look at their table. "I don't get my turn yet."

"And what are you going to do when you do get a turn?"

The defense lawyer looked at her client blankly. They saw her wheels turn. "Oh, my God," Anne said.

Hemmings leaned forward and regained her focus. "Look,

by that time their case is going to be in such tatters that anything we give the jury will be the excuse they're looking for.
We may not even have to put on a defense. If I keep—"

"You're still counting on that, aren't you?" Chris said, his
worst fear confirmed. "For politics to come in and save you."

"If I keep making Andy Gunther stumble over the fact that
there's this big blank spot in his case that he can't mention,
he's going to start to get mad at people. He'll talk to people, say
he can't do it their way, and they'll tell him—"

"You don't get it, do you? It's too late for any of that. If politics was going to matter it would have happened before trial.
Nobody's going to derail Andy Gunther now. No prosecutor
takes a case to trial that he plans to lose. Andy's in this for a
big win. If you haven't seen that, you haven't seen anything."

Chris stopped talking and the little group all looked at Margaret Hemmings for reaction. She appeared composed and
businesslike in her blue blazer. Not one bead of sweat had
appeared on her face all morning. But her eyes were blank.

Chris's narrowed. "That woman who testified, Louise Peak.
How did she put it to you when she told you she'd heard Morris threaten to kill Ben Sewell?"

Anne turned to her father. "You did what?!"

Hemmings answered, "She didn't say that to me. She said it
during the prosecution's questioning."

"I meant ahead of time." Chris let a brief pause pass. "You
didn't talk to her, did you? She was listed as a State's witness,
but you didn't interview her before trial."

"My investigator did," Hemmings said defensively. "She
didn't say anything to him."

"No, sometimes they won't," Chris said. "If it's a big enough
bombshell, they only want to tell it to the lawyers. That's why
I always interview witnesses personally."

Chris sat back in his chair, his food untouched, and let the

Greenwalds stare at Morris's choice of defense lawyers. Even Alice Pettigrew looked astounded. Hemmings glared back at them. Morris turned and said, "Chris?"

"I don't know. You can ask for a continuance, but I don't think the judge will give it to you. If he doesn't, you'll just have to carry on. Like you said, she is skilled. She just needs some ammunition. A trial is the greatest truth-finding machine ever invented. Have you ever heard anything like that?"

Hemmings nodded wisely. Morris said, "Yes."

"Well, it's bullshit. You don't discover the truth during trial. You discover it while preparing for trial. You find it by doing the hard work of investigation."

Morris said, "Will you help?"

Reluctantly, Chris nodded. Immediately he turned to Anne. "And you. You're not doing the defense team any good."

"What do you mean?"

"Your confrontation with Nick Winston. What was that all about?"

Anne's green eyes grew hot. Clearly the first answer that came to her was that it had been nobody else's business. "I told him to stay away from me. He had his damned skinny girlfriend follow me into the ladies' room and threaten me with—"

"And you reacted just the way he wanted. You know at least one TV cameraman was shooting footage of you yelling at him? He looked more scared of you than you've ever been of him, I'll tell you that."

"Good."

"No, not good, Anne. Because part of your story of what happened is that Winston's been stalking you ever since the night of the murder, trying to frighten you out of telling what you saw. The prosecution's version is that you hate Nick Winston enough to lie to frame him. Which version of the story do you think you just gave a big boost to this morning?" He held his hands palms upward as if weighing.

Anne glared at him, then sighed. Her analytical faculty began to take over. "I'm not going to be afraid anymore," she said sullenly.

"Nobody says you have to be. But you do have to think. All of us do. This is a murder trial. Everything that happens, inside and outside the courtroom, has to be calculated. That's what they're doing. We have to do it, too."

"That's what I've been saying," Margaret Hemmings said triumphantly.

Chris stood up, ignoring her. "I'm going to be in the hallway this afternoon. The judge told the witnesses not to talk to anyone except the lawyers in the case. Maybe they'll think I'm one of the lawyers. I'll see if I can find out anything. Starting with Celine Banister."

Anne said, "Oh?"

Chris nodded. "Winston came to see me a day or two after the killing, and had her with him. I noticed something that day I should have asked her about before now." He turned to Hemmings. "Why don't you take this opportunity to ask your client about that death threat?"

He turned abruptly and walked out, leaving the other four to look at each other in silence.

Chris's opportunity to talk to Celine Banister didn't come until almost mid-afternoon. From lunch until then, she and Nick Winston seemed joined at the hip. The two of them did approach him and chat for a few minutes, but inconsequentially, as if two of them held secrets from the third. Chris spent the meantime talking to the other witnesses on benches and lounging against walls in the hallway. Most of them were eager to talk, and there was only one subject at hand. Chris asked one male guest, who turned out to be a Comal County commissioner, if he'd heard Morris Greenwald threaten to kill Ben Sewell. The man laughed.

"I didn't hear it, but it wouldn't have been a party without Morris telling at least one person he was going to kill them."

"Really?"

The man shook his head fondly, the way one tells stories about the uncle with the bad reputation. "Morris doesn't have small talk, and he likes drama. Hell, look at the whole party. What was that staged for?"

"What do you mean, staged?"

Now the county commissioner looked at Chris strangely. "I thought you were a politician. You think somebody just has a party for no reason?"

Time passed. Periodically a bailiff would emerge from the courtroom and call a name, and one of their number would disappear, as if to a game show appearance or an execution. A peculiar lottery. Chris began to feel a tingle of anticipation when the courtroom door would open. He had never seen a trial from this perspective, the perspective of the hallway. In a way, the corridor held more potential.

Eventually Nick Winston gave his girlfriend a kiss and went off down the stairs. Celine sought out a water fountain. When she lifted her head from it, Chris was standing beside her. She pushed her hair back and smiled.

"You don't smoke?"

Her voice sounded husky, as if she did. "We don't have much time," she said. "You want to spend it on small talk?"

Chris said, "That's a nice suit. Isn't it kind of hot for August?"

"You want to see me in something else?"

"I just wondered if you needed to wear long sleeves to cover up something."

Quickly, Celine unbuttoned two buttons and slipped the suit jacket off. Indeed, she wore a sleeveless top underneath, of a shiny color hard to pin down, between pewter and silver. She went from conservative businesswoman to flashy model in an instant. Chris looked at her upper arms, then pointed at the left one.

"You've healed."

She didn't seem curious enough to ask what he meant.

"The last time I saw you, you had bruises there. Just where a man's hand would grab you."

"Show me."

Chris declined. "Did Nick do it?"

"Nick would never lay a hand on me. Not in that way."

"That's what a lot of women think," Chris said. "That it's not abuse if he doesn't hit you. If he just squeezes your arm, or pushes you, well, that's controlling his anger. But eventually . . ."

"Never happened, never will."

"Then who did it?"

"I don't even remember it happening."

Celine kept smiling, deliberately enigmatic. She didn't want to be found out, but she wanted to be asked. "You're curious about our relationship, aren't you?"

"I'm really not," Chris lied. "I've seen a hundred like it."

"No, you haven't."

"What do you get out of being the girlfriend, Celine? What do you think's in the future? The governor's mansion? Washington? If he had those kinds of respectable ambitions, you two would already be married. Or more likely he'd be married to somebody more down-to-earth-looking."

"There's a compliment hiding inside there, isn't there?" Her eyelids grew heavier. "Anyway, I don't think about the future. I don't have that kind of impulse control."

She ran one long-nailed index finger up his white shirt front. Involuntarily, Chris felt the cold trail her finger left behind.

She glanced past him, her eyes changed, and Chris turned to see Nick Winston approaching, almost upon them. He, too, was smiling. They seemed to be the happiest couple Chris had ever met. Winston raised an eyebrow.

Celine hung her jacket over her arm. "Mr. Sinclair came over to remind me that it's August. I hadn't noticed until he told me."

Winston turned his smile on Chris. He looked inquisitive. "You've been in the courtroom," he said. "How do you think the trial's going?"

"If I were the prosecutor, I'd think it was going great," Chris replied.

Winston looked across at the courtroom doors. "That's too bad for Morris," he said, and sounded sincere saying it.

During the afternoon break Chris passed on to Margaret Hemmings the few things he'd learned from upcoming witnesses. He could see her sifting through the scant information for something she could use. Maybe Chris's warning that she had a whole case to try and so needed a strategy had begun to sink in. He sat in the courtroom for the rest of the day's testimony, but his mind stayed on Celine Banister's arms. Also her face. He wondered whether she really found life as amusing as she seemed, or if she had only adopted Nick Winston's pose.

Testimony about the party continued. More people had

seen Morris and Ben Sewell together and heard them arguing. Margaret Hemmings elicited on cross-examination that these witnesses had also seen the pair chatting amiably. And she had the county commissioner testify that he had heard Morris threaten to "kill" other people.

"He just meant get back at them, hurt them somehow. You know, financially or something. It was just an expression." The big man shifted in his chair, as comfortable as if having a conversation in a living room.

But when the witness was passed back to Andy Gunther, the D.A. asked, "These other people Morris Greenwald threatened to kill, they're still alive as far as we know, right?"

The commissioner's droopy face lifted into amusement for a moment. "Yeah."

"Did you hear anybody else threaten to kill Ben Sewell that night?"

The man stared levelly. "No."

"Did you hear him arguing with anyone other than Morris Greenwald?"

The commissioner took his time thinking, then shook his head. "I don't remember any other arguments."

"No more questions."

The prosecutor said it decisively, as if he'd just made an enormous point. Chris slipped a note to the defense lawyer. It said, "Try to keep Nick Winston here for a while after trial's recessed."

He rose and walked stiffly out of the courtroom, feeling the judge's eyes on him. In the hallway he passed Winston and Celine, heads close together, and Chris pointed back toward the courtroom. "I think Andy Gunther wants to see you when trial adjourns for the day."

"I'm sure he does," Winston said. Chris hurried on down the hallway and out of the building.

He trotted to his car and backed out quickly. It wasn't far to Interstate 35, and traffic wasn't bad in the small town of New Braunfels. The same wouldn't be true once he reached Austin. Chris drove as fast as he dared.

In recent years the city of Austin had finally come to resemble a real, high-energy capital city. There were other businesses than government and the university, and consumers with money to spend. Central city neighborhoods that had once been affordable for students had become gentrified and gotten expensive.

Nick Winston lived in such a neighborhood. Centrally located near 45th Street, it was an old neighborhood of mature trees and comfortable wood or brick houses, many of which had been recently refurbished. It looked like a placid, *Leave It to Beaver,* middle-class suburb, but in fact many of its longtime residents had sold out for profit or because property taxes had risen precipitously.

The lots were of average size, within yelling but not spitting distance of the houses next door. People could live here either in isolation or with friendly ties to their neighbors, as they preferred. Chris had a strong feeling Winston would be one of the former. Chris would have to get lucky to find someone who'd been watching his house on a particular night months ago.

Someone should have done this investigation back then. Chris hadn't, nor had he suggested it. Once Morris Greenwald had chosen his defense lawyer, Chris had tried to stay out of her way. He hadn't wanted her hearing that he had been talking to potential witnesses. He didn't want to intrude.

It had been a dangerous game on his part. He'd thought Margaret Hemmings would do a poor job of preparation, but he'd also known that if he criticized her course he would look like a troublemaker. So he'd waited, hoping that Morris would see when her trial performance finally came that she was counting on political intervention rather than doing her job. If he had criticized her too harshly or often, or tried to take over her job, no one would have believed him. He had had to wait until the trial started.

Now there was barely time for anyone to do that job. Chris found Winston's home, a pleasant-looking, three-bedroom brick house with a porch swing on the narrow front porch. He found the door securely locked. Even if he'd been inclined to break in, he probably couldn't have. Besides, he didn't expect there to be anything to find now.

Instead Chris knocked on neighbors' doors. The first house yielded no answer, the second a teenage girl who didn't even know her neighbor's name or when her parents would be home. "You shouldn't tell a stranger that," Chris warned her. She closed the door in his face.

Directly across the street from Nick Winston's house he found what he'd been looking for: a retired neighbor. The man was relatively young for retirement, mid-sixties, heavyset, with a bulbous nose and ruddy complexion. His eyes looked cloudy but lively. After he'd quickly established that he wasn't buying anything, and Chris that he had nothing to sell, Chris told the man his name but not the office he held. "I'm a lawyer," he said. "In the middle of a murder trial, and I'd like—"

"That one in New Braunfels?"

Chris looked at the man appreciatively. "How'd you guess?"

"Only murder trial I know of that involves anybody around here." He nodded toward the house across the street. "Him?"

Chris nodded. The man's face grew a grim smile. "Come on

in, it's too hot to talk on the porch. Name's Jimmy Dobbins."

They shook hands and Chris entered the man's living room. The room had a bare hardwood floor, a lounging chair next to a floor lamp, and a long, old couch against the wall to Chris's right. The room appeared underfurnished and underdecorated, as if descendants had already claimed some of the furnishings. Chris felt sure the man lived alone.

"The murder happened back in March," Chris began.

The homeowner nodded. "The nineteenth. Don't look so surprised. The Austin paper had that big story about it a week later, and of course I noticed my neighbor's name."

"Are the two of you friends?"

"I wouldn't say that. He's lived there for eight years or so, but he doesn't throw lawn parties, you know? I don't either, come to think of it."

"Do you happen to remember the night of the murder?"

"I sure do," Dobbins said positively. "Been wondering why nobody's ever asked me."

They remained standing, near the man's front window, which was uncurtained and gave a good view of the house across the street. They both kept looking at it as they continued to talk.

"What time did Nick Winston come home that night?"

Dobbins shook his head. "That's not the interesting question. The good question is who came to Nick's house *before* he got home." Chris looked both surprised and curious, which was enough to keep the man talking. "Big black car drove past about eight-thirty, nine o'clock. I sit here reading or watching TV, so I see what goes on. The car was going slow, like the driver was checking street numbers. It got even slower as it went by here, then speeded up again. Looked like the man had found the address he was looking for, then drove on by.

"Sure enough, a minute later a man comes walking back down the block."

"What made you think it was the driver?"

"We don't get a lot of pedestrians in this neighborhood. Yuppie joggers, you know, but not guys in dark suits walking along checking out the houses."

"Didn't he look in here and see you?"

"Maybe. He walked by but then came back, up onto Nick's porch. Seemed like he was in too much of a hurry to really cover up what he was doing. He rang the bell."

Chris had a sudden insight. "Celine was home."

Jimmy Dobbins nodded. He looked across at the house. Two large curtained windows appeared in its brick front. The presence of the lovely Celine may have accounted for why the neighbor checked the house across the street so often. Neither of them spoke for a moment, then Dobbins continued.

"She opened the door, they talked for a few seconds, then this man—"

"Grabbed her arm," Chris said.

Dobbins said irritably, "You already heard this story?"

"Sorry. Go on."

"Yeah, he grabbed her, pushed her out of the way, and went in. She was yelling at him, but it was funny . . ."

"How?"

"Like I had the mute on. She was yelling quietly. Then she stands in the doorway and looks around, like to see if any-body's watching, and she slams the door closed. From inside." Jimmy Dobbins looked at Chris to see if he understood the significance. "Now if it was me and an intruder shoved his way into my house, I'd go *out*. Go to the neighbor's house and call the cops. Y'know?"

Chris nodded. He looked at the house across the street.

"The man came back out in about fifteen minutes, with Celine still at him, but still keeping it quiet."

"Did the man have anything in his hands?"

"I don't know. He was wearing a jacket, he could have had something in a pocket. Nothing big, though."

"Maybe he just wanted to talk to Celine."

"If that was it, I can give you a pretty good guess what she told him. It wouldn't have taken fifteen minutes for her to get the point across."

Jimmy Dobbins smiled tightly, obviously still cherishing the little drama of which he'd seen only the smallest part. Newspapers and television didn't fill his days sufficiently. Chris wanted to suggest volunteerism to him. Think about that, at least, before buying a pair of binoculars.

But without people like this, some cases would never come to trial. "Can you describe the man who went in?"

"Black suit, like I said. Older man, fifties. Thick gray hair, curly. Broader shoulders. Like a block, you know?"

"Yes, I do," Chris said, picturing the man. "How long after he left did Nick Winston come back?"

"Maybe half an hour, forty-five minutes. He was in a hurry, too. Celine must've already called him and told him what happened. He ran from the car. She already had the front door open for him, but he just ran by her. Like he was mad at her, too."

"Did police come that night?"

"They never did."

Chris cocked an eye at Dobbins, who shrugged apologetically, understanding what his statement acknowledged. "You can check, but I'm pretty sure."

Chris mused over the information a little, then thanked his witness. "Anything else you think I should know, Mr. Dobbins?"

"Oh, lots, probably, if you're interested in Nick Winston's doings. Like a beer?"

August dusk had finally fallen, so warm the night seemed false. Chris said sure, sat down in Jimmy Dobbins's living room, had a beer with him and listened to another half-hour's worth of tales of life on Nick Winston Lane. Half an hour of listening was the only reward Chris could offer his witness. He paid it.

Chris still hadn't talked to Anne, just the two of them, in nearly a month. This period represented their longest separation since they had met. Chris felt the absence, and wondered if Anne did. He had lost touch with her to that extent, didn't know what she was thinking.

She was not the kind of person to throw herself wholeheartedly, unthinkingly, into a cause. Wholeheartedly maybe, but not unthinkingly. He doubted her complete devotion to her father, but understood that a family crisis changes relationships. Anne might not even believe her father, but no one else had the right to hurt him. She sensed that Chris didn't share that devotion. He was more interested in learning the truth, and in this one instance Anne didn't care about the truth. Most likely, Anne had seen Chris hanging back from devotion to the Greenwald cause, and that had made the distance between them grow. Once they start, such distances only widen.

On the highway, night had become real. Chris called Anne's house and got her machine.

"Anne, it's me. I'm on my way back; thought I'd stop by." He waited for her to pick up. "But if you're not there, I guess I won't." He let another pause pass and broke the connection.

Next he called home, checking on Clarissa and the possibility that Anne had gone there. She hadn't. "What happened today?" Clarissa asked. Chris could hear her bouncing. The trial excited her. She wanted to come watch. Chris promised she could the next day. Today he'd anticipated challenging Margaret Hemmings and hadn't wanted Clarissa along.

"Can I bring Angelina? If her mom says it's okay?"

The thought of that conversation made Chris smile inside his car in the grim night: "Mom? Clarissa wants to know if I can go watch her dad's girlfriend's father be tried for murder. Can I, please?" The possibility seemed remote enough that he said sure.

He also told Clarissa he'd be later getting home. In New Braunfels he took the Ruekle Road exit and swung around the curving street toward Morris Greenwald's house. As soon as he turned down the caliche lane toward the house the night seemed to grow blacker, even though the white caliche rocks still glowed like a holy path.

Chris parked in the parking area above the house. It was illuminated by one tall light, which made him feel very conspicuous. The house itself looked dark, except for two dim lights upstairs, which might burn all the time. Chris stood on the edge of the parking area wearing his suit pants and white shirt, looking down toward the house. He could see the balcony, but not clearly, and thought he wouldn't even have noticed it if it hadn't grown so significant in his life. He began slowly walking down. He wished someone would come out on that balcony, so he could try again to recognize the person.

Memory populated the balcony, but only for a moment, in flickers. In a few short months his memory of the event had grown unreliable, even as that memory was about to be tested. He would remember this phenomenon, he thought, when questioning witnesses about events months or even years in the past.

He'd left behind the light of the parking lot, and little replaced it. The front of the house wasn't lighted. Starlight made the grass purple. Chris looked over his shoulder and saw that the moon had been reduced to a nail clipping. As on the night of the killing, it gave only the feeblest of light. The sliver of moon hung high at the pinnacle of sky, in retreat from this scene. Chris looked around at the bushes and trees and couldn't even see the moon's influence. No moonlight shadows waved around him. The night felt still and warm and watchful.

He reached the spot from which he'd seen Ben Sewell's suicide. Chris still believed that was what he had seen. He looked at the tall bushes, which appeared thinner than they had in the spring. How many seconds had it taken him to get through them that night? Chris thought about re-creating his run now, with a timer, but couldn't think what good it would do.

Instead he looked to the front door. He couldn't see it from this vantage point, so he circled slowly to his right until he could. He tried to visualize the line of sight from the porch to the balcony. It looked as if that view would be blocked, at least partially, by the balcony itself. The angle was too steep to see much of what went on above. Chris walked slowly in that direction.

His dress shoes crunched quietly on the pebbles of the path to the door. When Chris stopped he heard a click, and froze.

It is a very distinctive sound, the one made by the hammer of a pistol being pulled back. It means the gun is ready, only a small further effort is required to explode its bullet out the barrel. Chris imagined leaping to the side, or spinning with a leg extended in a wide kick. He imagined in this position the bullet entering his groin, then traveling up his spine. His mind tried to imagine the pain, but couldn't.

Imagination, nevertheless, held him tightly in place. Unlike unthinking heroes on TV, he couldn't propel himself into action that he knew would be futile. Instead, he spread his arms wide and turned around to face whoever held the gun on him.

A light flashed into his face. "Chris!" Anne's voice cried. She threw down the gun. Chris winced as he thought of the gun discharging, but it didn't. Anne dropped the flashlight to her side. The light trembled from her hand holding it.

"What the hell are you doing?" she said, adrenaline making her voice loud and angry.

"Measuring. And I thought I might talk to your father. What are you doing?"

Anne's lips compressed, then she said, "I thought you were Nick Winston."

Chris stepped close to her, grasped her hand, and lifted the flashlight again so that it illuminated his face and blond hair. "Anne?"

"Sorry." She pulled her hand away from him. "I saw you from upstairs when you were in the dark. I thought it was him following me again."

Chris took a long look at her. It had been a while since he'd stood this close to her. Anne felt him studying her and resented it. She turned and walked away.

"You've been staying here, haven't you?" Chris said.

She didn't answer, which answered him. This explained why he hadn't been able to reach her at home. She'd gone into hiding.

And hated the thought of anyone knowing it.

She snapped out a "What?" when he said her name again. Chris waited for her to turn back to him, then said quietly, "What happened between you and your father? Why did you hardly ever mention him before all this started?"

"What does that have to do with anything?"

He didn't answer. Just kept watching her. He wanted to step close to hold her, and hoped Anne saw that in his face. This close, he could feel her tension, feel the night eating at her. He did take a step closer, to shield her from a large angle of possible scrutiny.

Anne didn't need him to tell her how she was behaving, or what that meant. She understood herself. Chris could almost feel the ground shift as she regained perspective. She drew a breath deep enough to lift her shoulders, let it out through her nose, looked at him briefly, then looked away again as she started speaking.

"He drove my mother away," she said. "Not that big a thing, really. It wasn't as if he abused any of us. In fact, he loved his children. We could feel that. He'd be there for school events. He liked to have his picture taken with us. He didn't really care if my mother was in the picture or not."

Anne stopped talking for a minute, let Chris watch her face, but didn't look back. "It felt like a happy family, because we were the kids and we were the center of it. I didn't understand for a long time, but my mother didn't even feel like part of it. It shocked the hell out of me when she left us."

"She left you?" Chris had never met Anne's mother, who lived three hundred miles away. Not that far, but it had always been too far to bridge.

"She left all of us. She left us with Daddy. We were teenagers; we were old enough to make a choice. If anybody had asked us, we would have said we wanted to stay with Daddy. My mother knew that. She wasn't as much fun as Daddy, she didn't cling to us the way he always had. I just thought she wasn't a very fun person. I didn't realize how completely unhappy she was. Because she hadn't had a marriage for a long time."

Anne sniffed but didn't look teary. She folded her arms, strengthened her voice, and said, "Anyway, she left. Back then I think she thought that would make her look bad with a court, that she was leaving her marriage for another man. So she let us go. And I hated her so much for that. I was fifteen, it would've been nice to have a mother around. The few times she saw me after she left, I let her see just how bitter I was at her. She stopped making the effort, and I don't blame her. Now I don't. But back then I thought, in my mean little heart of hearts, *You mean I'm not worth the effort of fighting through all these glares and shitty remarks to get to me?"*

Anne had always shrugged off questions about her mother, as if there were nothing of interest there. He had more questions now, but Anne had a way with a story. He'd already gotten the texture and tone of it. He also understood clearly that she didn't want to talk about it.

"That explains your mother, but . . ."

"Years later," Anne said in a faraway voice, toneless, as if she felt she owed him the end of the story but didn't want to be there for it, "I mean *years* later, I finally got to talk to my mother and I realized why she'd felt she had no choice. She'd lived there for years with a man who loved his work and his children and didn't have time for anything else. He had driven her out of the marriage long before she left. I'm not sure why, I didn't ask her, but there'd just been nothing there for her for a long, long time. Most of my life, probably. I don't blame her for finally leaving."

"Obviously," Chris said.

Anne laughed. God, she had a good laugh. Clear and heartfelt and open. He heard her come back. "That's it," she said. She dropped her arms from her chest and hooked her thumbs in her pants pockets. "I can say I understand and I forgive her, but I can't get those years back. They're what my father took from me."

They'd had a blow-up, then. Not as bad an estrangement as the one between Anne and her mother, but one that had driven her away from her father for years. So when Chris had met her she'd been a virtual orphan. She'd been on her own for years, independent by nature and necessity.

"What did Nick Winston have to do with it?" he asked suddenly. "What happened between you and your father."

Anne looked puzzled. "Nothing. It happened about the same time, I guess. Dad's declining fortunes. And I guess he and Winston were on opposite sides of some issues. I wasn't paying attention, to tell the truth."

Walking side by side, they had reached the front porch. Chris looked up at the balcony. Anne followed his gaze. The balcony stood dark and almost invisible. Anne read his thought.

"The light was on that night," she said defensively.

"Anne, a few minutes ago you thought I was Nick Winston."

"He's been following me."

"Yes. You saw what you expected to see."

Chris looked up there again and frowned. Anne uttered some vehement denial he didn't quite hear.

"What did you see?" Chris interrupted her.

"I saw Nick Winston put a gun to—"

"No, afterwards. I saw a man shoot himself, then go over the rail. Did you see him—"

"No. Ben slumped down afterwards. He didn't go over."

Chris thought rapidly. He started toward the bushes, then stopped himself. "I've got to get Jack out here. Damn, why didn't we—? Maybe those pictures the deputies took . . ."

"Chris, what is it?"

"I've got work to do."

Anne grabbed his arm. "Tell me."

The contact shocked him. He'd missed her touch. He stared at her soberly. "We're violating the rule against witnesses talking to each other during trial."

Anne smiled. He hadn't seen that in a long time, either. It wasn't her full, open grin, the one that immediately preceded a laugh. This was a sliver of a smile, a slight lift of the lips, but it was the best he'd seen her look in a while.

"Oh, darn," she said.

★ Clarissa thought it was all just so cool. To Chris's surprise, her friend Angelina's mother had let her daughter come, after a call to Chris. Summer had been going on for two months. The woman must have been ready to grasp at any excuse to let her daughter leave the house for the day. Chris didn't even ask if Angelina still had the problem with the boy following her. If so, that would have made her summer even more confining. But her mother felt safe releasing her daughter to the district attorney. Angelina was quiet with Chris, but on the way up to New Braunfels, the girls whispered and laughed in the back seat. After they exited the highway Clarissa climbed over and said, "We want to help."

Chris glanced at Angelina in the rearview mirror: a skinny girl with shiny brown hair and large teeth, which she flashed in a nervous smile; a girl who seldom spoke. She nodded, as eager as Clarissa.

"This is not a game," Chris began.

Clarissa sounded shocked. "A game? Are you kidding, Dad? Mr. Greenwald could go to prison for the rest of his life. Even if he just gets ten years it might be a life sentence for him. Just the shame would probably kill him. And Anne would probably blame you forever. She might not say it, but you know, it would always be there. He's got that lawyer who's not doing the job—it's horrible. Of course it's not a game."

Like verbal judo, her sincere, articulate expression of Chris's own position left him feeling as if he were about to fall over. Chris tried to regain his mental footing. "Okay. Well, I'm not sure what you can do. Just keep your eyes open. I can't be everywhere." He pulled into a parking place, and he and the girls got out. They both wore skirts, short but formal by comparison with their usual summer outfits. They'd gotten dressed up for this assignment. Chris talked to them in a low voice as they entered the courthouse.

"I have to be in the trial this morning. You can be in there, too, or you can stay out in the hall with the witnesses. They're not supposed to talk about their testimony, but people violate that rule all the time."

"Maybe," Clarissa said half to him and half to Angelina, "I can pretend I'm like a reporter from like my high school newspaper, doing a story on the trial. People . . ."

"How about if you don't commit any felonies while I'm inside?"

"Okay, Dad. Only misdemeanors, I promise."

They looked down the hallway. Already half a dozen witnesses were milling around. Chris quickly gave Clarissa thumbnail sketches of the ones he knew. Before he left her, she stepped close to him and said softly, "Of course it's a game. It's the best one, isn't it?"

Chris winked at her, then went to the clerk's office for a few minutes, and emerged with a subpoena. A subpoena can order someone to be present for a trial. It can also order him to produce evidence. In this case Chris wanted the latter.

He needed Margaret Hemmings's signature, since she was

an attorney on the case and Chris was officially nothing. He found her conferring with Morris Greenwald in the courtroom and held out his papers to her. "Sign this," he said. "It's a subpoena. I'm going to have it served in the hall during trial."

"To whom?" Hemmings asked. She looked weary, as if she'd been arguing with her client.

"Nick Winston. I want to see the jacket he was wearing the night of the murder."

Hemmings noted Chris's use of the word "murder," instead of what he'd always called the death. She gave him a quick, sharp appraisal. Their eyes met. Chris stared back at her. Margaret Hemmings was smart enough to know when she needed help, even if she wouldn't say so. She shrugged and signed the subpoena. Chris gave Morris a quick, sober look and squeezed his arm encouragingly, then sat down. In his gray suit, white shirt, and black, polished shoes, Chris took his place with the lawyers at the front. Margaret Hemmings and Andy Gunther turned from their tables and gave him identical suspicious looks, then quick smiles.

"All rise," said the bailiff.

The Comal County medical examiner reminded Chris not at all of his own favorite medical expert back in San Antonio, who could be counted on to catch anatomical details and usually remember the human element as well. Dr. Simon Wiesner, on the other hand, the witness who first took the stand that morning in trial, seemed disconnected from his testimony. A heavy man in shirtsleeves and a nondescript tie, he wore thick glasses that magnified his eyes on those rare occasions when he looked up from his notes.

"Dr. Wiesner, did you perform the autopsy on a young man identified to you as Ben Sewell?"

The doctor looked down at his notes before broaching an answer to this tricky question. "I did."

"Could you give us that case number . . . ?"

Gunther began the process of identification required for the record, but Margaret Hemmings stood up and said, "We'll stipulate that the autopsy was of the complainant in this case, Ben Sewell."

She sat back down with a hand gesture that seemed to tell the prosecutor to move along, and also indicated that she wouldn't pursue technicalities; she only wanted to get at the truth. At least Chris read all that into her responses. Hemmings looked weary this morning. He wondered what she'd been doing during the night.

"Could you please describe Mr. Sewell, Doctor?"

From his notes, the medical examiner informed the jury that Ben Sewell had been a white male in his mid-thirties, full-grown and well nourished, in healthy condition except for the injury that had killed him: details that did nothing to personify the dead man. Chris felt his own memory of the living Ben Sewell grow hazy as the doctor spoke in his uninflected delivery.

Gunther asked the doctor to describe the injury, and everyone listened closely.

"It was a close-contact gunshot wound to the head that entered on the right side, proceeded through the brain, and exited in a larger wound on the other side approximately an inch behind and an inch below the left ear. The wound was of such a nature that death would have been instantaneous."

"What does 'close contact' mean, Doctor?"

While the doctor explained that this meant the gun had been held almost against the victim's head when it was fired,

Chris took off on another word the doctor had used: "instantaneous." Ben had died in the moment after the shot had been fired. As soon as that finger squeezed the trigger, it had been too late to change anything. That, too, had been almost "instantaneous." This death hadn't been planned or thought out. Someone had reacted much too fast, pulled the trigger without thinking about the repercussions, or possibly without even realizing he'd fired the gun. It could have been done in a moment of fury or despair, but whatever the emotion that prompted it, the shooter hadn't had time to think. The quick reaction might have been followed by instantaneous regret, but that didn't make a bit of difference. As the bullet left the gun, in an instant, Ben Sewell was already dead.

Andy Gunther got to one of the main points of this witness' testimony. "Doctor, did you examine the deceased's hands?"

"Yes, I did."

"What would you have expected to find on those hands if he had fired the gun himself, held the gun to his head and pulled the trigger?"

"A paraffin test should have revealed gunpowder residue. When a gun of this type is fired, some of the force of the gunpowder exploding is blown backwards. It leaves tiny traces on the hand of the person who fired the gun."

"Is it difficult to get rid of those traces?"

"Not at all," said the doctor lightly. "Wash your hands and the traces will be gone."

"But you said in this case that death from the gunshot wound had been instantaneous, isn't that right?"

"Yes."

"Did you find any traces of gunpowder residue on Ben Sewell's hands?"

"No, none," Dr. Wiesner said emphatically, no longer needing his notes.

"And after he was shot, he damned sure didn't go wash his hands, did he, doctor?"

The heavyset doctor stared quizzically at the district attorney, who smirked back at him. After silence persisted for several seconds, the doctor turned to the judge and said, "I don't have to answer that, do I?"

With a sigh, Judge Younger said, "I believe it was rhetorical, Doctor. Any more questions, Mr. Gunther?"

"No, your Honor. I pass the witness."

Margaret Hemmings looked back at Chris. That testimony had been a preemptive strike against Chris's story to come. This was why Andy Gunther had warned him, as kindly as possible, that what Chris thought he had seen wasn't possible.

But Chris had been prepared for this. He had seen the autopsy report. Events hadn't happened that night exactly the way Chris had seen, or something else had happened that he didn't see. But he knew that already. No witness ever sees everything essential to re-create a scene. A trial isn't a painting; it's a mosaic, composed of pieces from different sources.

Margaret Hemmings turned to the medical examiner and said, "Someone else could have wiped away the gunpowder traces from the deceased's hand before you examined him, couldn't they, Dr. Wiesner?"

The doctor knew it wasn't his job to admit this possibility, so he sounded reluctant as he said, "I suppose so."

"You said the traces can be gotten rid of easily, didn't you?"

"Yes, I did. But I meant—"

"Thank you, Doctor. Now, did you conduct tests on anyone else's hands?"

As Chris listened to the testimony, he saw again his memory of the night of Ben Sewell's death. He had seen what he had seen. Ben Sewell raise a pistol to his head. In the courtroom Chris's memory became more vivid than it had been at Morris Greenwald's house. He saw again the body going over the railing, legs swinging around and over. He felt again the bushes tearing at him as he ran through them.

Hastily Chris wrote notes on a legal tablet, then tore the page off and passed it to Margaret Hemmings. She read it while asking the doctor a question, a trial lawyer's skill that sometimes gets one into trouble. Speaking and reading at the same time can be done. But it's impossible to listen to the answer at the same time.

Hemmings asked, almost reading from Chris's page, "Doctor, did the deceased suffer any injuries from the fall rather than the gunshot wound? Was the condition of the body consistent with having fallen about fifteen feet from the balcony to the ground?"

Dr. Wiesner appeared surprised by the question. He consulted his autopsy notes again. "One of the ribs was broken and another was cracked. I'd hesitate to call these injuries, though, since the victim was already dead at the time. There were contusions that didn't happen because the heart had stopped beating. Blood wasn't flowing beneath the skin, so it didn't bruise."

The doctor grew more expansive as he talked. He seemed to be spinning out theories as he listened to himself. "I would say Mr. Sewell would probably have suffered a concussion if he had survived, but of course he didn't."

"Did anything in your autopsy make you certain that Ben Sewell was already dead before he hit the ground?"

"Well, the nature of the wound . . . But yes, the condition of the body as well. Normally a person could survive a fall from that height without injury at all. If you landed on your feet and rolled, for example. But in this case the cracked ribs and the other internal injuries show that the deceased fell as heavily as possible, with absolutely no attempt to break his fall. I would say he landed flat on his back, like a—"

The medical examiner suddenly broke off, perhaps remembering that he was talking about a person. He blinked owlishly around the courtroom. Margaret Hemmings looked thoughtful, appearing to wonder why she'd asked these questions. Andy Gunther turned and looked at Chris, his expression questioning.

Chris wasn't sure what he'd learned. But the line of inquiry reminded him of the subpoena in his pocket. When the judge took a mid-morning recess, Chris approached one of the court's two deputy sheriff bailiffs, a short, stocky woman with her hair in a ponytail. After a brief conversation the bailiff took the subpoena and Chris followed her out into the hall. Discreetly, he pointed out Nick Winston at the end. Chris turned away as the bailiff approached Winston. Clarissa arrived to stand beside her father.

"I talked to him," she said. "He seems very nice. He already knew I was your daughter."

Chris had been about to tell her to walk away from him, because he expected to draw Winston's attention once the subpoena was served. Instead, he turned to Clarissa. Her eyes were clear and smiling and bright spots of excitement appeared on her cheeks. In other circumstances Chris would have been happy to see her so obviously enjoying herself.

"Stay away from him. He doesn't seem like anything special to you, but he's a dangerous man."

"I didn't say he didn't seem special," Clarissa said.

The deputy sheriff reached Nick Winston. He looked at her pleasantly, as if expecting a compliment or an invitation. The way he always looked. The deputy handed him the subpoena, which he took with the same air of expectancy. Winston made a gesture of signing, but the deputy shook her head, making her ponytail swing. She turned quickly and returned to Chris. "I'll fill out the officer's return and give it to you back in the courtroom, sir."

"Thank you."

At the far end of the hall, Nick Winston unfolded the subpoena and began reading. Then he obviously skipped the technical jargon and cut to the thrust, the line on which he was ordered not only to appear in court tomorrow, but to bring a certain sports coat, the one he'd been wearing the night of Ben Sewell's death.

Winston frowned. Celine leaned over his shoulder, reading, and she looked puzzled as well. Then they both looked at Chris. Winston shrugged a question. Then he turned from Chris to Clarissa and smiled. The smile made Chris want to hire his daughter a bodyguard. He stared heavily down the hall. If Winston got the message, it didn't bother him; he continued to smile.

"What's been happening?" Anne's voice came from behind Chris.

"Andy Gunther just proved that things couldn't have happened the way I said they did," Chris told her.

"I've been telling you that for months."

Down the hall, Winston stowed the subpoena inside his jacket and muttered something to his girlfriend that made her laugh out loud. Chris turned to Clarissa.

"Stay away from him."

"Okay, okay, but let me tell you what else I've found out. I was talking to the news cameraman. He says when he doesn't have the camera running people act like he's not there, or doesn't speak English or something. He's heard them talking."

"Like who?"

"Like that district attorney and his assistant. They were joking about the fun part coming up. How they were going to make somebody look stupid."

"Daddy?" Anne asked.

"No," Clarissa said. "Right now, this morning. But they're still putting on their own case. Why would they want to make one of their own witnesses look stupid?"

Anne and Chris looked at each other and shook their heads. A few minutes later Chris returned to the courtroom, which was dimmer than the hallway, like entering a movie theater from the lobby. As he walked up the aisle, Judge Younger had already resumed the bench. "Call your witness," he said, and Andy Gunther turned, smiled, and said, "The State calls Chris Sinclair."

It wasn't Chris's first time to testify, even in a murder trial. But on those previous occasions he was being questioned by one of his own assistants. The two of them had had the same goal. This was an entirely different proposition. He felt the self-consciousness of the witness stand descend on him even before he took it. He sat down carefully, not wanting to miss the chair, feeling all eyes on him, then stood up again hastily and held up his right hand.

"We'll waive the oath," Andy Gunther said easily. "Mr. Sinclair is an officer of the court."

Chris would just as soon not have had any professional courtesies extended. He sat down, unbuttoned his suit coat, glanced along the line of jurors, then turned to the defense table. He didn't feel any support there, either. If Margaret

Hemmings had his back, he needed to keep looking over his shoulder.

At the other table Gunther sat back in his chair, leaving the task of note-taking to his assistant. He smiled as if he and Chris were sitting across a card table from each other. "Tell us who you are, Chris."

"My name is Chris Sinclair. I'm the district attorney of Bexar County." He cleared his throat, hearing the stiffness of his reply. Andy Gunther had no such problem.

"That's a few miles away, isn't it? How'd you come to be involved in this mess?"

"I was at the party at Morris Greenwald's house the night Ben Sewell was killed."

"Do you know Morris?"

"Not well. I'm—I've been going out with his daughter Anne."

"So you were going to meet your girlfriend's dad? Was it that serious?"

"I'd met him a couple of times before that night."

Chris realized he sounded halting and suspicious, but he couldn't stop it. Andy Gunther's apparent friendliness didn't help. Gunther leaned forward confidentially and said, "Was this an engagement party?"

"No, it wasn't."

"Not that serious about her?"

Chris turned to the judge. "Can I object to relevance?" A few people in the courtroom laughed, including Gunther.

"Sorry, I'll withdraw that. Let's get to it then, Chris. Did you know Ben Sewell before that night?"

"No, I met him that evening, but just briefly."

"Did you know that *he* used to 'go out with' your friend Anne?"

"I heard that that night, yes."

"Did that make things uncomfortable for you?"

"I didn't spend any time with him after I heard that. I mean, I was with other people."

"But you took a good look at him, didn't you, this man who used to date your girlfriend?"

"I don't know what to tell you, Andy. I didn't spend the evening staring at him. It didn't seem like that big a deal."

Gunther nodded and smiled, apparently satisfied. "Gotcha. During the party, or afterwards, or anytime, did you hear this argument he and Morris Greenwald were supposed to have had?"

"No, I didn't hear anything like that. When I saw them they were getting along fine."

Gunther smiled. "You're not going to say anything damaging to the man who might become your father-in-law, are you?"

Chris would have expected a defense objection at this point, if not earlier. But he didn't glance at Margaret Hemmings, didn't want to look as if he were searching for help. "I didn't see or hear him do anything wrong. I wouldn't lie under—in a trial."

"In a trial," Gunther mused. "Well, tell us about what you did see. Anything else relevant during the party, or right afterwards?"

"I don't think so." Chris explained that he and Anne had separated from the others during dinner. Gunther let him tell the story, nodding along. They both felt Chris approaching the important part. Chris grew tense, then made himself relax. While Gunther asked another question, Chris rolled his head slightly, trying to ease the tension in his neck. He let his hands rest on his knees, and tried to re-create in his mind that night: darkness, cool breeze, thin sliver of moon hanging high above. He'd dropped off Anne and gone to park the car, having no idea they'd just made a critical separation. He looked at the jury, telling them the tale.

"I walked back down toward the house. The parking area is on a rise, so I was going slightly downhill. I couldn't see the front door from where I was, so I didn't know where Anne had gone. There were a couple of lights on at the front of the house, and light coming from that upstairs room where the party had been. I guess that's why I looked up there to the balcony." He frowned, trying to remember.

"Take your time," Gunther said kindly. At the other table, Morris Greenwald sat watching him like a spectator, no particular expression of expectation on his face. Beside him, his lawyer stared more intently at Chris. He had gone from being her witness to the prosecution's, and she seemed to feel that signaled a switch in Chris's loyalty.

"No, I heard something. A noise. Anne scream, I heard that."

"Didn't you run toward her, then?"

"I started that way, but then some movement caught my eye, and I saw Ben Sewell up on the balcony. He was standing at the dark end of it, the end closest to the front door."

"How did you know it was him?"

"I just recognized him. Besides, he was wearing this very distinctive yellow jacket. People had commented on it earlier. He looked very strange, very stiff. I saw him lift his right hand, and then I realized he had a gun in it. I yelled, and I started running toward him, but he fired."

For a moment Chris was back in that fatal night. He flinched. The instinct to look away had taken him over. He had turned his head and shoulders away, possibly crying out again, raising his hands as if to ward off this moment in time. When he looked back the body was going over the railing, face first, then bending in half and falling like a cat, hands and feet seeming to stretch down toward the ground.

"I ran into the bushes trying to get to him. The bushes were thick, they tore at me. I almost stopped and pulled off my jacket, but thought I needed it for protection. If I was thinking at all. I didn't really feel the cuts on my hands and face until later. I just pushed through as best I could."

"Did you hear Anne anymore?"

"No."

"As far as you know, did she go into the bushes?"

"No, she didn't."

"Who did?"

"When I got to the body, Nick Winston was there. He was bending over him. He looked up at me, looking scared."

Again Chris could picture the moment with magical clarity. Winston's face had been pale as the starlight. A thin cut crossed one cheek. He had blood on his hand, too. At first Chris had taken it for Ben Sewell's blood, but then had seen a slow dollop of blood swell out of the palm of Winston's upturned hand. Like Chris, he was bleeding from his push through the bushes.

"He said he thought he was dead, and asked me what to do."

"What did you tell him?" Gunther sounded much more serious now than when he'd begun his questioning. "Did you know what to do?"

Chris described his attempts to call for official help and preserve the scene. He'd failed somewhat in that, letting Winston go off to the bathroom. Gunther returned him to his overall view of what had happened.

"Chris, how long was it after you saw the shooting that you reached the body and found Nick Winston there ahead of you?"

"Maybe ten seconds."

"If he had been coming from the front of the house, from the other side from you, could he have gotten there ahead of you?"

Chris thought about it, as he had before. "Yes. There's a

path behind the bushes, he wouldn't have had to push through as much as I did. He could have beaten me there by a small margin, like it looked like he did."

Gunther let a pause signal the seriousness of his next question. "Chris, you heard the medical examiner's testimony, didn't you?"

"Yes."

"You know that Ben Sewell's death couldn't have happened the way you think you saw it?"

Chris answered slowly. "I know something else must have happened, something I didn't see."

"It was a dark night, and you were looking up at a dark balcony from some distance. Could you have missed something?"

"Of course."

"Could it have been that what really happened was that a hand reached from somewhere else, from the room itself, or from behind Ben Sewell?"

Chris thought about it. His memory resisted change. Could that hand he'd seen holding the gun have been someone else's hand? But no, he remembered the yellow sleeve of the gun hand. At least, he thought he did. It hadn't seemed important at the time.

"It couldn't have been an arm reaching from the room. That was still well lighted. But . . ."

"But someone could have been standing behind Ben Sewell, pointing a gun at him?"

"I suppose that's barely possible. But that's not what I saw."

Andy Gunther sounded as if he were probing for answers, not just trying to discredit Chris's story. "Was Ben Sewell a tall man?"

"Yes, pretty tall. Over six feet."

Gunther turned in his chair. "What about Morris Greenwald? How tall would you guess he is?"

"Shorter than that. Maybe five-eight." At the defense table, Morris nodded.

"Chris, is there anything else you saw that you think this jury should know?"

Chris looked at them, the individual women and men in the jury box. They stared at him as if listening closely. This was Chris's opportunity to wrap things up succinctly, save Morris Greenwald and explain exactly how things had happened. But he couldn't. He didn't have a theory that encompassed all the facts. "I guess that's all," he said quietly.

Margaret Hemmings didn't let him pass. She leaned forward and said, "Chris, are we to understand from your testimony that you think a man could have been standing behind Ben Sewell, completely hidden from your view, who shot him without your ever seeing him?"

"No, I don't think that."

"Why not?"

"Because as soon as Ben fired the shot he fell forward and went over the railing. Anyone standing behind him would have been exposed then."

"Could someone have fallen flat and hidden from your view for just a second, until you were running through the bushes, and then escaped back into the room?"

"I can't imagine that happening. It would have had to be split-second timing. I frankly can't imagine Morris Greenwald moving that fast."

"No more questions," Hemmings said decisively, sounding as if she'd made a telling point. Nonetheless, Chris had not done the defense case much good. He had sounded credible but confused. He didn't have the answers. On the witness stand he felt as if he were still stumbling through those bushes, flailing blindly in the night.

When his testimony ended, Chris stayed there a moment longer, looking at the defendant. Morris sat with his hands folded on the table, his face open and neutral, obviously trying hard to look as if he had nothing to hide. Chris had been in the middle of prosecuting someone in the past when he'd begun to fear that the defendant wasn't guilty, but would be convicted anyway. In this case, he'd been living with that same fear, that Morris was innocent but would be found guilty because he was the only available suspect. But from the perspective of the witness stand Chris saw clearly that Morris Greenwald was hiding something.

From the other counsel table, Andy Gunther gave Chris a wink and a friendly smile.

In the ladies' room, Clarissa and Angelina compared notes, literally. They'd both been roaming the hall with little notepads, pretending to interview witnesses while actually interviewing them. Angelina didn't like the task. She tended to end up standing behind Clarissa peering over her shoulder as she questioned someone. People smiled indulgently and asked them how old they were. Clarissa felt less like an intrepid girl sleuth than like a child pretending to be one.

"What'd that lady say to you?" Clarissa asked Angelina.

"She asked me what grade I'm in and the name of my newspaper."

"What did you tell her?"

"I didn't know what to say, Clarissa. I didn't even know the name of the New Braunfels high school, let alone the newspaper."

"Make something up, Angelina, for God's sake!"

"They live here, Clarissa, don't you think they know the name of the high school?"

Clarissa looked at her witheringly. "It's called New Braunfels High School, Angelina. Why don't you tell them you're going to the alternative school for dumbasses?"

Angelina looked extremely insulted. She got grumpy, they had a little spat, and Angelina said she wanted to go home. Clarissa made up with her by asking her advice, barely listening to the answer and disliking herself for the ease with which she manipulated her friend. "Look," she finally said, "that Nick Winston is the important one. We've got to get to him. He and his girlfriend are probably talking about why my dad had them served with that subpoena. Let's see if we can listen in."

"They won't talk about it in the hall. Besides, didn't your dad say to stay away from him?"

"Well, I'm not going to let him see me, obviously."

"He'll look for somebody following him."

"I know, Angelina. So you know what you do about that? You go out *before* he does. You get there ahead of him. That's how you follow somebody without them knowing . . . What?"

Clarissa asked the sharp question because her friend was looking at her strangely. "Nothing," Angelina said quickly, sounding a little frightened. Not of Nick Winston, either.

"He goes out to smoke every hour or so, and he always goes to the same place, this corner where it's shady. I'm going to go out there and wait. You stand by the window at the end of the hall and give me the signal when he leaves. Okay?"

Angelina nodded. The girls separated when they walked out of the bathroom and Angelina immediately took up her post. She stood there nervously, doing nothing but waiting. She grew alarmed when Nick Winston walked toward her, smiling, but she didn't see anywhere to hide.

"Where's your friend?" he smiled lazily.

"I don't know," Angelina mumbled. "We had a fight."

"About what?"

"She called me—I don't know. Nothing."

Winston smiled more broadly. He reached inside his suit coat, pulled out a cigarette, and stuck it in his mouth. Its other end danced close to Angelina's face. Winston produced a silver lighter from another pocket and snapped it into flame.

Angelina looked alarmed. "You're not going to smoke that in here, are you?"

Breaking rules frightened her. Mundane rules and major laws didn't seem very different to her. Winston grinned. He turned and walked away.

When he walked past Celine he raised his eyebrows. She looked back at the girl by the window.

It was hot as hell outside, already approaching ninety by ten o'clock in the morning. Clarissa felt sticky as soon as she stepped outside. In this sunlight people walked with heads bent, as if under a heavy downpour. Clarissa immediately sought out shade. She went and stood under a tree on the courthouse lawn, a spot from which she could see Angelina at the window above.

Dad would be mad at her if he knew what she was doing. Clarissa knew that. Nick Winston would be mad, too, if he caught her eavesdropping, and that was a very different proposition. But Clarissa knew something they didn't, that no one living knew. She was not this simple teenage girl she appeared to be. She'd had experiences like no one she knew, living on the fringe, responsible for herself and her sister before her age

broke into double digits. Her roaming, unstable childhood—
"Adventures with Mom," she sometimes thought of it wryly—
had marked her. She knew she wasn't a normal girl.
Homework and problems with boys were jokes to Clarissa.
She could play along—that was her life—but unlike her class-
mates, even the troubled ones, she knew what mattered and
what didn't. She stood in the shade under the tree, hip cocked,
unconsciously emulating the self-confident posture she'd seen
her mother adopt so often. This sixteen-year-old-girl look was
nothing more than the perfect disguise.

Up above, Angelina waved frantically. Clarissa nodded,
walked out of the shade, and took up her place in a little nook of
the courthouse wall, just around the corner from the spot where
she'd seen Nick Winston smoking twice already that morning.
Sure enough, a minute later she heard the swooshing click of
the cigarette lighter and smelled smoke. "What do you think
he's up to?" she heard a woman's voice ask. So Celine had
accompanied her lover. Perfect. They'd talk to each other.
Clarissa inched as close as she dared to the corner.

"I don't think so," Celine's voice came again. Clarissa wondered if Winston was standing on the other side of Celine, if
that was why she couldn't hear his responses. She wanted to
peek around the corner, but Celine sounded as if she were
right there. Then Clarissa heard a low rumbling tone, and
Celine gave a throaty chuckle.

Oh, please, don't get romantic. Talk about something.

"No, I think it's that girl," Celine said. "Why do you think he
brought her? She must know something . . . I don't know,
Nick, but somebody should find out, don't you think?"

Clarissa felt a slight unease, but quickly began to wonder
how she could use this. If they wanted to question her, she
could . . .

She felt more than heard something near, turned quickly away from the corner, and came face to face with Nick Winston. His eyes remained flat, inches from hers.

"What's new, Nancy Drew?"

But Winston's face looked as if he had completely lost his innate humor. Clarissa gasped. She jerked back, which put her back against the stone wall of the courthouse. Celine came around the corner and blocked her escape that way.

"What?" Clarissa said loudly, trying to sound angry instead of scared.

"Your little chum's lousy at giving signals," Winston said. "She's much too obvious. What were you hoping to hear? Me confess to murder? Or just hoping Celine and I would start making whoopie on the courthouse lawn?"

Celine smiled. Winston did not.

"Let me go."

"No one's holding you. That's going to be up to the authorities to decide. This is very serious, young lady."

Clarissa edged away from him. With a very small step, Winston cut her off. "I think we should speak to her school authorities, don't you, Celine? I'll bet she has a history of this sort of thing. She might already be on probation."

His voice sounded flatly authentic, and his face for the most part appeared solemn, but around his mouth he now had traces of his old smile. Anyone watching or listening would have thought Winston's reaction absolutely appropriate, but up close Clarissa saw him deriding her—and inviting her, as well, to join him in the game. She began to think seriously about screaming.

"If nothing else you should speak to her father," Celine said, staring at her.

"Go ahead. He—"

"I frankly don't think he has the parental skills to deal with this. In fact, I think probably Child Protective Services would be the better place to go."

"What about you?!" Clarissa shouted. "What are you two plotting out here?"

She didn't care about an answer. When they turned to look at each other innocently, Clarissa pushed through between them. Nick Winston's hand slipped around her waist and for just a moment he restrained her before she pulled free. She saw people watching from the sidewalk. Winston remained deadpan.

"It's all right, Cla-ris-sa. We know where to find you."

He said her name caressingly. Clarissa turned and walked quickly away, cheeks burning. She felt everyone watching her.

Nick Winston shrugged elaborately to the spectators, like taking a bow. Turning away, he said out of the side of his mouth to Celine, "Don't laugh, no matter what I say. Look serious."

"But I've never been able to resist your—sense of humor."

She was looking toward the courthouse, not at him, and her face looked grimly worried. But he saw in her eyes a sparkle reserved only for him.

Taking her arm and beginning to walk, he couldn't help saying, "God, I love you."

Without a sign of mirth, she said, "Ha, ha."

They went inside together, shooting nervous glances around, as if they didn't know who might accost them next.

Anne had to hold Chris back. When he found Clarissa huddled with her friend at the far end of the courthouse hall he immediately saw that something was wrong. Clarissa wasted less time than usual with her negative answers. Chris looked down the hall, saw Winston missing, and said, "It was him, wasn't it?" Clarissa nodded.

Without another word Chris started away, fists clenched. Anne grabbed his arm. Chris pulled her along with him, turned to rid himself of the burden, saw it was Anne. "Stop!" she said firmly.

Chris hesitated. Anne got a better grip on him and stood very close. "Isn't that what you said to me? Think what you're doing. Are we all going to threaten him?"

"He pulled Clarissa into this," Chris said tightly. "I'm going to tell him—"

"She put herself into it, Chris. Ask her." They both looked down at the girl on the bench, who blushed. Chris, suddenly deflated, sat next to her and put his arms around her. Clarissa pulled away.

"This is what he does," Anne said. She sounded more clinical. "If you run away, he's gotten what he wants because you're afraid of him. If you confront him he has your attention—"

"So he's gotten what he wants," Clarissa said, sitting up.

Angelina sat looking back and forth between them.

"He's just *there* all the time," Anne continued, staring down the hall. "Even when he's not. He wants to be the most important thing in your life. He's always there on the fringe. And there's nothing you can do about it. If you attack him, then you're the one who's done something wrong. But if you wait for him to make his move, it may be too late. Until, if he's really good at it, everything else falls away and there's just him standing there."

"My God," Chris said. Angelina stared at Anne, a tear running down her cheek. Even this strong, adult woman saw no way out of being stalked. Clarissa sat and put her arm around her friend's shoulder.

Anne turned back to them and her voice lost its faraway tone. "But I'm not to that point and I'm not going to get there. It's time to—" Anne stopped. She blinked. She seemed suddenly far away from them.

"What?" Chris asked and got no reply. Even Clarissa stood and said Anne's name. Angelina stared at her, losing her frightened look for the first time. The sight of Anne thinking was reassuring. Anne gave the process her full attention, her eyes going blank, lips parting. Chris and the girls glanced at each other, then stared at Anne as if watching a mechanism at work.

When she blinked and began to come to herself again, Chris said, "Don't you think you should share with the whole class?"

Slowly, Anne shook her head. She put her arms around the girls' shoulders.

"Not yet," she said quietly.

They had all forgotten about the trial, but after the break the prosecution had a surprise waiting for them.

Andy Gunther stood, an imposing but casual figure, slouching in his black suit and cowboy boots, and said, "Marie Withers."

Chris unconsciously slumped in his chair, prepared to be bored, and the name appeared to have the same effect on the pair at the defense table. They knew Marie Withers as just another party guest. Conversations with her in the hall, including an "interview" by Angelina, hadn't uncovered anything pertinent that she knew. Chris thought Andy was being unnecessarily thorough, filling in all the spaces.

The lady in question came up the aisle briskly, smiling around, looking very self-possessed. A nonauthentic blonde in her mid-thirties, Marie Withers was tall and athletic-looking, even in her blue suit. She had bright dark eyes, a wide mouth, and a shiny nose on this hot morning. From the witness chair she beamed at the jurors. Withers seemed more accustomed to the role of hostess than guest.

Gunther quickly established her name and status as a state employee. "I work at the Department of Health, but during the legislative session I work with the legislature."

"Is that why you were invited to the party at Morris Greenwald's house back in March?"

"I thought we'd just hit it off nicely the few times we'd met," Withers said disingenuously. She knew that being something of an insider in state government brought her invitations, and was obviously prepared to accept them.

"Was there anything you'd worked on for the legislature that you knew Mr. Greenwald had an interest in?"

"One project," Withers said, crossing her legs. "He and I hadn't talked about it in person, but I'd seen his name."

"And what was that?"

At the defense table, Morris began writing hastily on a legal pad, obviously informing his lawyer of this aspect of the case at the same time the witness did. Chris sat up more attentively.

"I was working on evaluating applications for a service contract. The legislature had called for bids for a recycling project to serve the capitol complex itself. Mainly paper. We use up a lot of paper in Austin." She smiled. "Some legislators were embarrassed that we'd never really gotten fully involved in recycling. They thought it was about time."

"And Morris Greenwald—?" Andy Gunther prompted.

"Had submitted one of the bid proposals. Well, he was one of a team on one of the proposals."

The district attorney tilted his head and looked off into the distance as if just now thinking about the implications of his witness's testimony. "And you accepted a party invitation from this man whose proposal you were evaluating? Isn't that a little unorthodox?"

Ms. Withers sat unflustered. "Frankly, I didn't think about that until I got to the party. The recycling project was just one rather small part of my job at the legislature. I was only looking at the health aspects of the proposals; I'd write a little report. I certainly wouldn't be awarding the contract, or even having any significant impact on who won. All the proposals came out pretty much the same on the health portion. Positively," she said, perhaps with a trace of irony, or perhaps this was just her ingrained way of speaking.

"Besides," she added, "Morris wasn't the only person at the party who'd submitted a bid for the recycling project. So I didn't think it was that big a deal."

"Who was the other person who'd submitted a proposal for the contract Morris Greenwald wanted?" Gunther asked, much too innocently.

"Ben Sewell," Marie Withers said in the same tone.

She seemed to change on the witness stand. She'd been friendly, casual, as if still being entertained at a party. But as soon as she gave this answer, Withers's mouth drew closed, her expression evaluating, and she stared across the room at Morris Greenwald. Morris had stopped writing and looked back at her, shaking his head slightly as if listening to nonsense.

"Did you have occasion to mention your knowledge during the evening?" Gunther continued his examination.

"Yes. I was talking to Morris shortly after I got there, and I remarked that it was nice that he and Ben Sewell could remain friends even though they were competitors."

"Did he appear to know what you were talking about?"

"No. He asked me. I told him that Ben had also submitted a bid for the recycling contract. It had come in just that week, as a matter of fact, right before the deadline."

"How did he react?"

"He seemed very surprised. He almost choked on his drink. Then he toned it down and said something like, 'That rascal,' but in the first few seconds he seemed very upset."

Morris wrote something on the legal pad in front of him in letters so large that even Chris could read them: "I OVERRE-ACTED."

Chris didn't get what that meant, and doubted Morris's lawyer did either.

Meanwhile Marie Withers wrapped up her testimony. She hadn't seen Morris with Ben Sewell again that evening after she'd given him her news. "It looked to me as if he was avoiding Ben, as if he didn't trust himself to speak to him."

"Object to that speculation," Hemmings snapped, and the judge sustained her objection, but the testimony was out there already.

"Pass the witness," Andy Gunther said smugly.

The defense lawyer sat tapping her pencil on the table, staring at the witness as if waiting for her to break down. Marie Withers looked placidly back at her.

"Ms. Withers, you don't know Morris Greenwald very well, do you?"

"I'd say not terribly. We're not big friends. In my position you try not to—"

"Yes, thank you. You haven't been around Mr. Greenwald, then, during any emotional crises in his life, I take it."

"I'd have to say no."

"So you have no way of knowing whether what you saw was a big reaction for him. For all you know, he could have gotten more upset over the caterers not having guacamole for the party."

"Yes," the witness said placidly.

"Ms. Withers, you've been in government service for quite a while?"

The witness gave the lawyer a smile tinged with acid. "Most of my adult life."

"Yes, that's what I said. Have you ever known anyone to kill someone else over competition for a contract?"

"Not that I remember."

"Don't you think you would have remembered an event like that? You have such a good memory."

Withers leaned forward, aiming the light of her smile. "I'm sure I would have."

"No more questions," Hemmings said dismissively. She looked down and wrote furious notes on her pad, as if she'd just learned a great deal. In fact, she was taking out her hostility toward her client.

They had a bizarre lunch, all of them assembled but not fully present. The defense team found an empty conference room they could use, and sent out for sandwiches. Clarissa and Angelina sat side by side near the door of the room, occasionally whispering to each other, not saying a word to anyone else. Chris paced, Anne sat and stared out a window, neither of them seeming to pay attention while Margaret Hemmings bashed her client.

"You all lie!"

"All who?" Morris asked quietly, his eyes narrowing.

"Defendants!" Hemmings explained, in his face. "Clients! You always hold something back, so the lawyer gets surprised at trial."

"It seems to me the same thing just happened. You knew this woman was going to be a witness, but you didn't know what she was going to say."

"And who could have told me that, Morris?"

He backed off and dropped into a chair. "It didn't seem important to me. What she said on the witness stand, that happened. But it wasn't the big deal she tried to make it out. I already knew before she told me that Ben had put in a bid on the project."

Hemmings stood up straighter. She wore a navy suit and looked very severe, like one's least fondly remembered elementary school teacher. "You did?"

"Of course. Ben and I were partners. We didn't do anything without telling each other."

"Something odd . . ." Hemmings trailed off. Morris acknowledged her meaning.

"Government projects like that, they look at so many factors in awarding a contract, plus there's so much influence being peddled, if you can improve your chances any way, well . . ."

"You colluded on your bids," Hemmings said softly.

"I don't know about 'colluded.' If either of us had gotten the bid, it would have helped us both out. If Ben had won, I'd probably have come aboard his team, and if . . ."

"Don't say any more. You know you're confessing to a crime?"

"It happens all the time."

"So does murder," Hemmings said angrily. "But it's still a crime. And your defense to this one is that you committed a different felony. I can't put you on the stand to say that."

"It'll be okay," Morris said lamely. "They haven't proven anything."

"They've proven that someone was killed, and that you had reason to be mad at him and had said you were going to kill him. The jury hasn't heard that anybody else had a reason to kill him."

"He killed himself! What about Chris's testimony?"

Margaret Hemmings turned to see just how caustic she could be in reply, whether Chris was paying any attention. Chris started speaking as if he hadn't heard a word they'd said.

"Morris, there was a copy of the tape there that night, right? The videotape Winston had been blackmailing Veronica Sorenson with? He brought it to you, right?"

Morris nodded.

"Why?" Anne suddenly said, from her perch by the window. "Was that going to be the party entertainment? Was that what you were showing behind one of those closed doors?"

"We weren't going to show it to anybody. We didn't even want to look at it. It was just a little—psychological advantage. Just let her know we had it, Nick said."

Anne laughed caustically at her father's idea of psychology. "You're lucky *she* didn't kill you."

The defense lawyer and the girls by the door looked more alert. But Chris continued his own track.

"So where is that tape? Do you still have it?" Morris shook his head. "Then what happened to it? Wasn't that important to you?"

"Ben being dead seemed more important, Chris. I don't know what to tell you. Ben had it before the party started. Then it just disappeared."

"Nick Winston took it back," Clarissa burst out. "That's why he killed Ben."

Chris shook his head. He'd had longer to think about this. "If he got it back, he wouldn't have had any reason to commit murder. Besides, there wasn't time. If he shot Ben, as Anne says, then ran down through the house, where would he have hidden the tape? I saw him a few seconds later. Those bushes and that room got thoroughly searched. The tape was gone already."

"Then why kill Ben?" Anne asked.

"That's what we need to find out. She's right." Chris nodded toward Margaret Hemmings, the only compliment he had paid her. "It's not enough that the State has a weak case. We've got to give them another suspect, and that means another motive."

In the spirit of cooperation, Hemmings said, "I haven't heard anything like a reason for murder that night. Your suicide story fits better—"

"I've worked on a thousand murders," Chris said. "More. Most of them are so stupid you want to cry. Arguing over the remote control. I prosecuted that one. Then there are the few where they try to be clever. But whenever you try to piece it together, afterwards there's a place where you can't make it work, where it doesn't make sense to you. Which is good; it means you're still sane. Have you ever tried to kill anybody?"

His eyes swept the room. He paused longest at Clarissa, who stared back at him. "It's damned hard to do," Chris said. "Only a very rare person can do it in cold blood. You have to be enraged, crazy.

"Somebody got furious that night. Angry enough to kill. Everybody'd been drinking, and that helps, and there was a gun close by. Somebody went over the edge. He probably came back a second later, but it was too late."

Chris ended up looking at Morris Greenwald. Morris shook his head very slowly.

Perhaps everyone in the room was thinking furiously, or

maybe they only felt the pressure to think. When a knock came at the door a minute later, no one had spoken again. Clarissa opened the door to a boy with bags of sandwiches. Morris jumped up and paid, appearing glad to have the opportunity. The girls passed out food around the table. Chris, still standing, unwrapped his sandwich, looked at it sitting on its plasticized paper on the oak conference table, then suddenly turned and walked out.

"Where are you going?" Morris called, but Chris only exchanged words with Clarissa, in a quiet undertone. She nodded, he laid a hand on her shoulder, then he was gone.

Moments later, her food also untasted, Anne left too. She and Chris went in different directions, and hadn't talked to each other, but were beginning to think about the same destination.

★ Before the lunch recess ended, Chris had tracked down Andy Gunther. The Comal County district attorney was coming up the courthouse steps on his way back from his office. He was walking with a long stride, empty-handed; one of his assistant's jobs was to carry Gunther's briefcase.

"I want to talk to you," Chris said.

They stood in the palpable heat reflecting up from the white steps, but Gunther in his straw cowboy hat looked comfortable. "Kind of busy right now," he grinned.

"We can do it in front of the judge if you want. It has to do with the trial."

"What, exactly?"

"Withholding evidence," Chris said flatly.

Gunther came up to Chris's step, so that he stood close and looked down at Chris. He bulked larger; sunlight seemed to expand him. Over his shoulder he said, "Tell the judge I'll need a few more minutes."

The assistant hurried inside. Gunther surveyed the world, turned his back on the courthouse, and nodded over toward a small grove of trees on the courthouse lawn. Chris followed, aware that he had just seen a small exercise of power: usually lawyers wait for judges rather than the other way around. Gunther carried that power like his size, casually but without letting anyone forget it. In the shade of the oak trees, at least fifty yards from the nearest observer, he lifted an arm to rest it on a branch and said, "So who's been hiding evidence?"

"You have," Chris said.

Gunther looked at him with no reaction. Finally he said, "Heard you got a subpoena. Want one to search my office?"

"No. It's not there. She has it back."

Gunther appeared completely unperturbed. "I know you're trying to appeal to my urge to confess, but this'd go faster if you'd just tell me what the hell you're talking about."

"The videotape, Andy. The bargaining chip that night at Morris's. I know somebody must have told you about it. Was it the lieutenant governor? She took it back, didn't she? Did she clear that with you?"

Gunther just watched him, waiting to hear everything Chris knew before he responded. Chris said, "Did she let you see it?"

Gunther's lips began a slow smile. "She offered. She described it to me. I stopped her. I said, 'Sounds like personal business to me, ma'am.'"

Chris had no trouble imagining this very private conversation between two politicians in position to do each other favors. Andy Gunther would have made something more of the encounter. While speaking very respectfully, adding fuel to his drawl, his eyes would have stayed on Mrs. Sorenson. Letting her see his imagination work. She was good at that, Chris remembered.

"And so you told her it wouldn't come up at trial," Chris said flatly.

"I told her that in my legal opinion there was no reason why it should. I couldn't see any way it was involved."

"Even if it gave someone else a motive for murder?"

"How?" Gunther sounded genuinely puzzled. "It was Morris who wanted to use it for blackmail. If she somehow got it back, that would have just made him madder. That tape goes against him, Chris, not for him."

"That's not for you to decide! You should have revealed that to the defense. Damn it, Andy, you know that. You were trying to protect someone, all right, but there are bigger considerations when someone's on trial for murder. If you know of some evidence that might show the defendant's innocence, you have an absolute obligation—"

"If I *have* such exculpatory evidence," Gunther answered, pushing off from the tree. His face had gone red; he finally looked something other than self-satisfied. "I don't have it, she does. Besides—" He stepped close to Chris again, right in his face, and lowered his voice. "I did."

"What?"

"I told Margaret Hemmings about the tape. Ask her. Morris knows too."

Seeing that he had shaken Chris from his high moral perch, Gunther regained his own ease. He stood tall, tucked in his shirt more tightly, and walked toward the courthouse.

Chris stood there wondering if Morris Greenwald was collaborating in his own prosecution.

Chris stayed outside making phone calls. When he returned to the courthouse he didn't see Clarissa or Angelina. Then he noticed Celine standing alone at the end of the hall. She gave him a long complacent look. Other people stood around, but Chris didn't see them. He only saw his daughter's absence.

Damn it, he'd told her to stay away from him. Clarissa was too bold. Chris waited outside the ladies' room, and after an older woman went in and came out he cracked open the door and called Clarissa's name.

Celine saw him crossing the hall again and kept watching. In a moment Chris would confront her, but he knew she'd lie, so he had to check the other possibilities first. He returned to the conference room where the defense team had met for lunch and found Anne on her phone.

"Where's Clarissa?" he said loudly.

Anne shook her head, still talking. Chris hurried out of the room again.

Feeling Celine's eyes on him, he crossed the hall again and slammed through the doors of the courtroom, intending to find official help.

Judge Younger, on the bench, looked up startled, then glared at him. Spectators turned to stare at him, as did the jurors. Every eye was on Chris. The only stare that didn't look hostile or surprised was that of Nick Winston, who sat on the witness stand.

"Please excuse me, your Honor," Chris said formally. The judge didn't respond except to turn back to the witness and nod.

On the front row of the spectator seats Chris had spotted two heads of long hair, one blond, the other brown. He walked up the aisle and sat down beside Clarissa. She gave him a nervous look, as if she'd done something wrong. Chris put his arm around her.

On the witness stand Nick Winston had transformed himself. In his dark suit he looked very serious. There was nothing of smugness or sly humor in his expression. He seemed to have gone even paler than usual. No one could have accused him of not taking this proceeding seriously.

"I'm not sure why I was invited," he continued his testimony. "I didn't know it was that important an occasion. It just seemed like a party. I get invited to a lot of parties."

Andy Gunther asked, "Did you ever see a gun in a desk drawer that night?"

"No, sir. I didn't see a gun at all, until I heard one fired."

"We'll get to that. Did you ever hear an argument between Morris Greenwald and Ben Sewell?"

"No. But I wasn't around them very much."

"Did you hear Morris Greenwald express any hostile intention toward Sewell?"

Winston sat silent and seemed to think for a moment. Then he shook his head. "No."

"Did you know Morris and Ben well?"

"I'd known them for years, let's put it that way. I wouldn't say I knew either of them particularly well."

"In fact, you and Mr. Greenwald are political enemies, aren't you?"

Winston appeared surprised. He looked at the defendant. "I don't think so. I don't even know of any political activities Morris had been involved in in recent years. We'd been on different sides of some issues in the past, but that's true of everyone who's active politically."

He gave Morris a friendly nod. Winston appeared to be a completely disinterested witness. He didn't even seem to know why he'd been called, what he could contribute. Andy Gunther led him through testimony that offered little of interest, until they'd reached the end of the evening.

"Did you ever see Ben Sewell go out on the balcony?"

"I didn't see him go out, but I saw him out there. I was outside myself by that time. I'd gone outside for a smoke." He shrugged apologetically to the jury. "Also just wanted to get some air. I was ready to go, but Morris had told me he wanted to talk to me about something after the other guests left. I walked around the house."

"When you returned to the front of the house, did you see anything unusual?"

"Yes. I saw Ben on the balcony."

"Was anyone with him?"

For the first time, Winston hesitated. "I think so."

"Who was it?"

Nick Winston looked very uneasy, the first time Chris had seen him appear less than sure of himself. He looked straight at Morris Greenwald. "I'm not sure," Winston said.

Gunther spoke seriously. "Commissioner, you think you have an obligation to protect a friend, I'm sure, but in this trial you have a higher duty. Who did you see on the balcony with Ben Sewell?"

Nick Winston looked down at his nervously twisting fingers. Then he looked up at the jurors. "Morris Greenwald," he said quietly.

"Liar!" Morris stood up at the defense table. The judge began banging his gavel. Morris shook off his attorney's restraining hand. One of the bailiffs started walking toward him. Gunther stood up as well.

Nick Winston gave Morris a look of entreaty. That drew a response from the defendant. With a snort of disgust he sat down again, just before the bailiff reached him. She stayed there, standing behind Morris's shoulder, her arms folded.

"As I said," Winston began explaining, "I wasn't posi-tive . . ."

Gunther held up his hand like a traffic cop. "Let me ask the questions, Commissioner." The D.A. sat again, scraping the legs of his chair along the wooden floor. "Were there any men other than Morris Greenwald and Ben Sewell left inside the house when you went out for your walk?"

"Not that I remember." Winston gave this admission as if it were dragged out of him. Watching him, Chris began to believe. Not Winston's words, but his performance. He looked so convincingly the reluctant witness that Chris began to forget what he knew about Nick Winston.

"What happened on the balcony?" Gunther asked sternly.

Speaking softly but clearly, looking down, Winston said, "They were yelling at each other. Then this other man pulled out something. I couldn't see what it was, but then I heard the gunshot. Ben fell."

"When you say 'this other man,' you mean Morris Greenwald."

"Yes," Winston said, almost inaudibly. But the jurors heard him.

Andy Gunther let a long pause gather, until Winston looked up at him. "Yes," he repeated, more distinctly.

"Was it dark at the front of the house that night, Mr. Winston?"

"Yes. There was very little lighting."

"But are you sure of what you saw?"

An expression of hope animated Nick Winston's face. He seemed to see his chance. "No. I said I wasn't positive. But . . ." His expression clouded again.

"There was no one else, was there?"

Winston shook his head. He looked downcast. "No."

Chris looked on in admiration. Winston's apparently reluctant testimony was much more damning than positive assertions would have been. His testimony seemed to be dragged out of him. Therefore it must be true. Listening to him, Chris began to picture Winston's version of events in place of what Chris had seen himself. He knew the jurors were doing the same thing. Winston made a much more convincing witness than Chris had.

Chris found himself surprised by Nick Winston's testimony. He shouldn't have been. If Winston were going to deny blame, deny what Anne had seen, he had to give the jury another suspect. Who better in that role than the man on trial for murder?

Gunther moved on. "Did you see what Morris Greenwald did after he shot Ben Sewell?"

"No. I was too stunned. I just stood staring for a few seconds, then I started running to where I'd seen Ben fall into the bushes."

"As you did that, did you pass the front door of the house?"

"Yes."

"Did you see anyone standing there on the front porch?"

Winston shook his head. "I think I heard the door slam, but I'm not sure of that. It might have been the gunshot."

"Did you reach the body in the bushes?"

"Yes. He was on his back. He wasn't moving. I knew better than to move someone who might have a spinal injury, but while I was standing there I didn't see his chest move. I just stood there. I didn't know what to do."

"If this jury has heard testimony that you were in fact kneeling over the body, would you dispute that?"

"No. Not at all. I was dazed. I'm not sure what I did. Until Chris Sinclair reached the scene and spoke to me, I wasn't even sure where I was."

Andy Gunther sat up straighter in his chair, folded his hands together, and said seriously, "Commissioner, did *you* have an argument with Ben Sewell that night?"

"What? Me? No. I don't even remember having any discussions with him."

Gunther nodded as if satisfied. "Pass the witness."

Chris stood up, not quite knowing what he was doing. He began walking toward Nick Winston. Winston watched him come. Chris pushed through the gate in the railing, still headed toward the witness stand. Winston looked more alert, less the bewildered chronicler he'd appeared as he testified.

Chris sat down beside Morris Greenwald. For the first time, he took his seat at the defense table. He reached for a legal pad and began writing.

Margaret Hemmings was slow to begin her cross-examination. Not because of Chris's interruption. She didn't even appear to see him; she just sat staring at Nick Winston. He composed himself, compressed his mouth, and looked back at her. Hemmings faced a lawyer's worst problem: a witness who would lie absolutely, without hesitation and completely convincingly. She was afraid to ask him a question.

"Mr. Winston, did anyone see you while you were out taking your stroll around the house?"

"Not that I know of."

"But people had seen you inside talking to Ben Sewell, hadn't they?"

"During the party, maybe, not afterwards. They couldn't have."

She tapped her pencil. "Did you see anyone leaving while you were outside?"

"No, I don't think so."

"You didn't see a black sedan with State Official license plates driving away at a high rate of speed?"

Nick Winston shook his head, staring at her flatly. Even Andy Gunther glanced at the defense attorney. At a loss for what to ask, she seemed to be circling the unspoken area of the trial.

Chris passed her a note. Hemmings read it and asked, "As you ran through the bushes, Mr. Winston, did you scratch yourself?"

"Yes, I did. I didn't realize it at the time, but I saw the cuts later, on my hands and my face."

"These bushes were very bristly?"

"I guess they were."

"In fact, once you went back inside the house, you went straight to the bathroom, didn't you?"

"Yes, but that wasn't because of the cuts. I thought I was going to throw up. I'd never seen a dead body before." Winston was easing back into his abashed pose. He looked embarrassed.

"Did you wash your hands?"

"I guess I did. I know I splashed some water on my face."

"You scrubbed your hands thoroughly enough to remove traces of gunpowder that would have been left there if you'd fired a gun."

Winston spread his hands. "I don't know. I hadn't fired a gun."

"Mr. Winston, why would—" Hemmings broke off that question. She tapped her pencil some more. Then abruptly she said, "Mr. Winston, you were served with a subpoena today, weren't you?"

"Yes."

"Ordering you to bring to court the jacket you were wearing the night of the murder."

"Yes."

"Do you intend to comply with that subpoena?"

"Yes, of course."

"Tomorrow morning?"

"Yes, if that's what the judge wants." Winston looked in that direction. Judge Younger nodded as if the subpoena had been his idea.

"No more questions," Margaret Hemmings snapped. She had no idea what she was doing, so she sounded very certain of herself.

Winston left the witness stand. He walked past Chris and

Morris, never once displaying his little smile. Chris felt it, though. Andy Gunther stood up and said, "The prosecution rests, your Honor."

Yes, of course, Chris thought. Bring on your best evidence, then rest. Make your strongest impression on the jury, then throw the ball to the other side.

Which should respond quickly. Margaret Hemmings sat as if she hadn't heard. The judge said to her, "Ms. Hemmings? Are you prepared to begin?"

Still she sat, looking over a list of names. Finally Chris took a pen and wrote one large word on the legal pad in front of her:

Anne.

He underlined it. Margaret Hemmings stood up and said, "The defense calls Anne Greenwald, your Honor."

The bailiff didn't take long to find her. Anne came striding down the aisle quickly, her eyes on the judge. She didn't glance at Chris or her father. Chris watched her steadily, though. He'd suggested that Hemmings call her, thinking the defense needed a strong witness to counter Winston's testimony as quickly as possible. But this also provided Anne with an opportunity—even an inducement—to commit perjury. She had admitted to Chris that she would.

Anne seemed unaware of his attention. She had testified many times; courtrooms didn't intimidate her. After being sworn in, Anne took her seat in the witness stand, turned to the jury box, and said, "Hello."

She ran her eyes down the rows of jurors. About half of them felt compelled to respond in some way, with a nod or a mumbled greeting. During a trial the jury is the focus of every-one's attention, but the participants tend to disguise their interest. The jury sits as if ignored, silent and watchful. Most of them like feeling unobserved. But Anne put them on the spot, brought them into the picture. By answering her, they had to acknowledge their presence—their complicity, in a way. Anne kept watching them, more than she did anyone else in the courtroom. She wore a pleasant but determined expression.

"Please state your name," Margaret Hemmings said.

"Anne Greenwald."

"Doctor Greenwald, isn't it?"

"Yes, I'm a psychiatrist."

"Where did you study, Dr. Greenwald?"

"My undergraduate degree is from the University of Texas. I went to medical school at Baylor in . . ."

Andy Gunther stood up. "Objection, your Honor. This witness is here because she's the defendant's daughter, not as an expert witness. Her training is irrelevant."

Judge Younger looked at Hemmings for response, who shrugged. She had already accomplished as much as she'd wanted, making Anne look more professional than the prosecution's eyewitnesses. She moved on to questions about the night of the party.

"Did you talk to Ben Sewell that night?"

"Yes. I hadn't seen him in a few years. We caught up."

"What did you talk about?"

"Personal things. Nothing of interest to anyone else."

Chris found that answer intriguing. So, obviously, did members of the jury, who glanced from Anne to him.

"I did ask him about his business with my father, and how they were doing, but his answers were very vague."

"He put you off?"

"Frankly, he seemed to want to talk about me instead." Anne lifted her chin.

"Did you ever see Ben and your father have an argument that night?"

"No," Anne said firmly.

"Had you seen that in the past?"

"Everyone who's known my father for more than a week has gotten into an argument with him at some time. And Daddy threatens to ruin them or hurt them. Five minutes later he's forgotten it." Anne looked at her father for the first time, fondly and indulgently, but with a hint of exasperation, too. A murmur of laughter rolled out from the audience, and several jurors smiled.

"But you didn't see that happen that night?"

"No. Ben and my father had been in business together off and on for years. They seemed to get along fine. Better than my father and I do, usually." She smiled.

Hemmings let Anne have her joke, then forced her into seriousness. "What did you see that night that this jury should know about?"

Anne described leaving the party to go to dinner, returning with Chris, and being dropped off in front. As a witness she grew more tense as she talked about walking up to the front door and realizing there were people up on the balcony.

"How did you notice them?"

"At first by their voices. They were arguing."

"What about?"

"I couldn't hear. But it wasn't a discussion. The other man was obviously furious at Ben for something. I think he was just insulting him. Then Ben stood up straighter. It looked like he was defending himself, which seemed to make the other man even madder."

"You've said 'the other man.' Did you recognize him?"

"Not right then."

"Was it your father?"

"No. Not at all. I'd know my father in the dark, and I would certainly recognize his voice. It was no one like my father."

Chris watched Anne, who didn't look back at him. She divided her attention between the jury and the defense lawyer. Now she sounded the way she did as an expert witness, not only very sincere but obviously wanting her audience to understand.

The defense lawyer's job was easy. Hemmings had obviously relaxed, secure in her witness. "What happened next?"

"The other man snapped. He jumped forward and from somewhere he pulled out a gun, a pistol. He put it to Ben's head and fired. Just like that. I screamed, but it was too late. Ben fell. But because I'd screamed the man turned toward me. He stepped back into the light coming out of the room and I saw his face clearly for the first time."

"Who was it?"

"Nick Winston."

She said the name clearly. The jurors stared at her. Frown lines grew on their faces as they realized they would have a job more difficult than most jurors have: deciding between two directly contradictory versions of what had happened. If anything, they watched Anne even more intently, some of them critically. She turned toward them and nodded.

"You're sure about that?" Hemmings asked.

"Absolutely," Anne said. "He stood full in the light and looked down at me. There was no mistaking him."

"What did you do next?"

"I went inside the house. I called for help. For a minute I stood downstairs and yelled. I was afraid my father or some other party guests were still upstairs in the sitting room, and

Nick Winston would come back through there with the gun and decide to shoot the witnesses."

"Did you find your father?"

"He came out of a downstairs room. I started up the stairs, yelling, and he came with me. We didn't find anyone up there."

"Including Nick Winston?"

"Yes. After another minute or so I even went out on the balcony, but he wasn't there."

"Dr. Greenwald, where could he have gone?"

"I've thought about this a lot," Anne said very seriously. "There's another stairway, a back stairs. He could have reached it while I was waiting downstairs, and gone down to the kitchen, out that way and around the house."

"Could he have done that and reached the body before Chris Sinclair did?"

"Possibly," Anne said, sounding unsure for the first time. "If he ran hard, and if Chris hesitated longer than he thinks he did." She looked at Chris for the first time, flatly. "Sometimes someone who's witnessed a shocking event isn't a very good judge of time."

Chris would have agreed. But the defense lawyer pressed Anne harder. "Does that seem very likely?"

"No," Anne admitted. "The only other possibility I've been able to think of is that he jumped down from the balcony to the ground after I went into the house."

"Anne, do you know of any reason why Nick Winston would have killed Ben Sewell?"

"No. Obviously, there was some kind of political business going on. I can only guess they—".

"Object to speculation," Andy Gunther said quickly, then looked as if he regretted his speed. Whatever motive Anne guessed at would probably have sounded like a lame reason for sudden murder. But it was too late, the judge sustained his objection.

Margaret Hemmings looked satisfied at that. Let the jury speculate rather than her witness. "Are you sure of what you saw?" she asked finally.

"Absolutely," Anne said. Again she looked to the jury, meeting their eyes.

Chris, who had heard her admit that she would lie to save her father, believed her. Which meant he didn't believe what he'd seen himself. Yet he could still see it, in his mind's eye. How could they be reconciled?

"Pass the witness."

Andy Gunther tried not to look eager. He didn't sit forward quickly and snap out a question. But Chris thought he could read the prosecutor's readiness, because he'd felt it himself, when about to cross-examine a biased witness whose story had significant weak spots. Chris grew more tense than Anne looked. He wished he could make objections.

He felt Morris Greenwald's hand clutch his arm, and turned to look at the older man. Morris stared at his daughter. But his grip on Chris's arm was the clutch of a frightened man. Was he frightened for himself or his daughter? Anne was his best hope in this trial. If the jury didn't believe her, it was all over.

"Dr. Greenwald," Gunther said, "you don't like Nick Winston, do you?"

"After seeing him murder a friend of mine? No, not much."

Anne spoke flatly, not making a joke. She stared at the district attorney as she had not at her own lawyer.

"I mean before the events of that night. You held a grudge against Nick Winston, didn't you?"

"I can't say I liked him. I didn't know him well."

"No, but you knew what he'd done to your father several years ago, didn't you?"

"No. I know they'd had disagreements, backed different candidates."

"And Nick Winston as a lobbyist helped restrict the sale of land your father owned, a move that cost your father a great deal of money. You knew that, didn't you?"

"I knew he was involved."

"That move even damaged your own financial prospects, didn't it?" Gunther insisted.

"I suppose it did, theoretically."

"Did you think what Winston did in that case was personal, revenge against your father?"

"I can't say I thought about it very much," Anne said dismissively.

"Really. You strike me as a more thoughtful person than that, Dr. Greenwald." He and Anne stared at each other. Gunther didn't mind that. If she grew angry she'd look vindictive, which would suit the prosecutor fine. But Anne just sat, waiting for another question.

It was a tough one. "Anne, if you'd looked up to that balcony and seen your father kill a man, would you be here testifying?"

Anne paused, which gave Margaret Hemmings time to stand and object that the question called for speculation. "No, it doesn't," Gunther snapped.

Judge Younger hesitated himself, then said, "I'll allow it."

Anne said carefully, "If I were called as a witness, I'd come."

"You'd testify against your father, if that were the truth?"

"Yes," Anne said firmly, but she no longer sounded as convincing as she had. Chris wanted to take her aside, out of the courtroom. He wanted to get her out of here.

Gunther began to sound sympathetic. "You understand that your father faces the possibility of life in prison?"

"Yes, I do."

"Would you lie to save him from that?"

Anne faced the jury again. "No," she said. She sounded very sincere as her eyes traveled along the two rows of people. But Chris knew she was lying.

Gunther obviously hoped some of the jurors saw that as well. He let his cross-examination end there.

Margaret Hemmings leaned forward. Hemmings had aged during the few days of the trial. She no longer appeared to be the exemplar of the well-tended socialite. She had begun to look like a working lawyer, even while demonstrating that she hadn't prepared to play that role. People on the defense team knew she hadn't worked up a strategy, but at least now she seemed to be looking for one. Lines had appeared in her cheeks that hadn't been visible a week ago. She looked intently at her witness and said, "Anne, have you lied to this jury today?"

"No, I haven't."

"Who did you see kill Ben Sewell?"

"Asked and answered," Gunther said casually, and the judge sustained him.

Hemmings shifted to the more mundane. "You said that when you went into the house your father came out of a downstairs room. Was anyone with him?"

And so they went over logistics and lines of movements. Hemmings had Anne move objects representing people around a chart of the house that the prosecution had introduced into evidence. She led her away from motivations for testifying. The afternoon wore away as the defense tried to bolster Anne's testimony and Andy Gunther tried to undermine it, using times and previous testimony. They drew back from the central question Anne had already answered for the jury: Would she lie to protect her father?

The main question of the trial remained whether the jury would believe her.

"I'll tell you one thing," Anne said angrily to her father. "Nick Winston wasn't doing you and Ben any favor when he gave you a copy of that videotape."

They stood near their cars in the parking garage adjacent to the Comal County Courthouse. Margaret Hemmings had gone her way; Morris and his lady friend were headed home. Chris stood nearby with Clarissa and Angelina. Clarissa clearly wanted to hear every bit of drama. Angelina looked around uneasily, arms folded. The parking garage seemed to make her nervous, with its angles and shadows.

Across the roof of her dark green Volvo, Anne continued addressing her father: "If you understood anything about her, you'd have known that. If she thought you'd seen that video, she'd never have had anything to do with you again. She'd do her best to destroy you. Winston knew that. When he gave it to you, he was trying to screw you all over again."

"Why do you think you know Mrs. Sorenson so well?"

Anne just glared at him. If the jurors could have seen her now they would definitely have believed that she wouldn't lie to save her father. They'd have believed she wanted to see him in prison.

Anne didn't answer her father's question, but it was plain on her face: she understood how Veronica Sorenson felt about that videotape. Anne didn't know Veronica Sorenson, but she could put herself in her place.

"You were all involved in something horribly sleazy," Anne said quietly. "I think you need to admit that when you take the witness stand. Otherwise you're going to look like a liar."

"You know I can't bring her name into it."

But Anne had finished giving advice. She came around her car, opened the driver's-side door, and got in.

Chris, who hadn't wanted to interfere in the confrontation between Anne and her father, stepped to the side of her car as she backed out. Anne just sat there for a moment, but then rolled down her window. Chris stared in. Anne gave him her profile.

The air in the parking garage was close and hot and fumy. Chris felt a little light-headed. Plus he felt observed, as he always did these days.

Keeping his voice low, he told her, "You know, I even believed you, and I was the only person in the courtroom who absolutely knew you were lying."

She turned to him. Her green eyes remained steady and watchful. He could see her emotions in the very flatness of her expression, in the grip of her hands on the steering wheel. Anne fought hard to suppress it, and she was good at that. "I did not."

"Sure you did, Anne. When you said you wouldn't lie to protect Morris. You already told me you would."

She shrugged and didn't bother to answer. Chris went on, leaning down to rest his arms on her windowsill. "I know you would, too. Even though you don't approve of what he did, even though you've resented him for a long time. Because you have this strange loyalty, Anne. To your patients, even the ones you don't like. Certainly to anyone you've ever loved."

She turned back to him. Her eyes had softened. It would have been a good moment for a kiss. If Anne would lean toward him, if Chris could put his head through the open window. But her expression wasn't that inviting.

"You'd lie for me, wouldn't you?" he asked half-playfully.

"Let's not test that." She put the car in gear.

Chris stood up again. Anne took off, leaving him in a stronger cloud of fumes.

Chris turned and saw the others watching him: Morris, Clarissa, her friend. They looked to him for answers, but he didn't have any. He did have an idea, though.

"Morris, can you do me a favor? Take the girls home for me."

Morris Greenwald gave him a strange plaintive look. When they'd met in the gazebo, they'd embarked on a conversation about the possibility of being related someday. The events of that fateful night had drawn them closer than relatives. Morris had come to rely on Chris's judgment; Chris had felt compelled to come to Morris's defense. But those were matters of necessity, not mutual admiration. Morris seemed to look to Chris for a sign of approval, even of fondness.

But how could Chris give him something his own daughter couldn't? Chris nodded as if to say things would be all right.

Clarissa protested. She saw that Chris was off in pursuit of something and she wanted to come along. But Angelina had to be brought home, and Chris didn't want to expose Clarissa to anything more today.

"You're going to see him, aren't you, Mr. Winston?" Clarissa said it accusingly, but the anger in her eyes wasn't directed at Chris.

"Stay at Angelina's until I come get you, would you? We'll have the ride home for me to tell you all about it."

Clarissa let herself be taken away. She would either eavesdrop on Morris's conversation or cross-examine him all the way home to San Antonio. It would be good practice for the old man.

Morris drove away with a wave. Chris turned back toward the courthouse. He wanted to see if all the trial participants had left. Then he had a trip to make.

He caught Margaret Hemmings coming down the courthouse steps. The glare of the late-afternoon sun matched the one she turned on Chris. "Come to give me a critique of the day's work?"

He forced himself to reply mildly. "Could we get out of the heat?"

That was more easily said than accomplished. The landscape appeared sun-drenched for miles around them. Hemmings descended the steps and Chris gestured to the sidewalk that led off to the right, taking them most quickly out of sight of the courthouse. He looked back up at the building, which Hemmings noticed. "Afraid to be seen with me?"

"Sort of," Chris said. "Look like you're mad at me."

That had been easy for her to do a moment earlier. Now she looked intrigued.

They crossed the side street, walked along it for half a block, and found a drugstore, its shade and air-conditioning inviting. Inside, Margaret Hemmings instinctively moved away from the other customers and turned to face Chris. She raised an eyebrow.

"I've been a jerk," Chris began abruptly.

Hemmings looked more than intrigued; she looked flattered. "Well, I—"

"There's a larger issue here than what I think of you."

"Ah." She understood quickly. The woman was not stupid. He'd never thought so. "Morris."

"Yes. And for you it's Morris too. You want to win, don't you?"

She didn't have to answer. Chris said, "I may need to get a concession or two from Andy Gunther, or the judge. With Andy, I don't think it will help if it looks like you and I are working together. But we have to."

She favored him with a long regard. A little smile glanced over her features for a moment—a smile with a hint of flirtation. But Margaret Hemmings was one of the few lawyers who had ever beaten Chris in trial, however she had done it. She may have grown lazy, but her skills remained strong.

"What do you have in mind?" she asked slowly.

"I'm not sure yet. And when I know, I may not be able to tell you. Can you handle that?"

Her smile returned. She looked again as confident as when he'd first met her again at Morris's house. But he thought that secretly she was glad someone else had something like a plan for this trial. Which meant he'd taken the burden of the defense on himself.

Nick Winston and Celine didn't speak much on the drive from New Braunfels to Austin. Long stretches of highway passed with only the sound of news on the radio. When they neared Austin, Celine reached across to cover his hand on the steering wheel. "Why didn't you want me to watch?" she asked about his testimony.

"Because I'd start playing to you. I'd go all sarcastic. I didn't want you to see my gulping, wide-eyed, puke-over-the-body routine." He smiled at her and lifted her fingers to his lips. She turned her hand over and he kissed her palm.

"But that's how it was, wasn't it?" she said.

Austin traffic was as bad as expected. Winston slowed and took the long, wide swing to the expressway home. Ten minutes later he drove through his own leafy, quiet neighborhood, and pulled into the two-car driveway where Celine's classic Kharmann Ghia sat. Without a word and without glancing at the house across the street, they walked up the sidewalk and into the house.

Inside they entered their own world. The interior of the house was more modern than the exterior, but in a subdued way. Blond wood predominated, in the furniture and the polished hardwood floor. Winston walked through the small living room into the den, where he opened a cabinet and put on a CD. A string trio played Mozart. Speakers throughout the living areas made Winston and Celine seem to be in the ideal seats at a concert.

Both the living room and the den in which Winston now stood had a stark quality. Only one built-in bookshelf in the living room held a small assortment of books. In the den, closed doors covered the entertainment center, hiding any sign of the owner's taste. No videotapes were in evidence, no books. Framed posters on the walls proclaimed the opera in Santa Fe, a Steppenwolf play in Chicago, ballets in New York and Washington.

Celine had gone directly to the spacious kitchen, where a long open counter provided a view to the den. She opened the refrigerator and took out a plate of sushi snacks and a bottle of white wine. While Winston started the music she transferred the bits of flesh and rice to a fresh plate and poured two glasses. She put them on the counter and came around to the den, taking the first drink of her wine. Her throat moved as she took a long swallow.

Winston left the room and returned a minute later carrying a sports coat on a wooden hanger. He displayed it to Celine, who shrugged. She came over to examine the jacket more closely. It was the one he'd worn the night of Morris Greenwald's party, the one Chris had subpoenaed. Celine ran her hand down the silk sleeve. The folds fell elegantly.

"It's perfect, isn't it?" Winston asked. It wasn't an idle question. Celine shrugged again, adding a nod.

But she didn't appear certain. "There couldn't be—blood in the fibers, could there?" she asked, looking into his eyes.

He didn't smile. With her, in private, Winston didn't appear so self-assured. He gazed straight into her eyes. "It's been cleaned half a dozen times since that night. I guess there might be, though. After all, I found the body. I touched him. I could have . . ."

He ran a hand over his own arm and chest. Celine nodded. "Give it to them," she said casually. "It couldn't prove anything."

Winston laid the jacket over a chair and joined her at the counter. They toasted and drank. Then stood looking at each other. They had no audience, no poses to assume. Celine stared into his eyes, willing him some of her own strength. When Winston started to turn away she took his wrist, pressing hard. Her fingers left marks.

Night grew closer to falling as Chris drove north. But it was only six-fifteen in August, a long way from sunset. From his left side the sun found a perfect angle to hit him in the face, under the visor he swung around to try to block it. He felt as if he were tanning, even through the ultraviolet-blocking glass.

Chris was running a little late. At the courthouse in New Braunfels, he'd made sure Nick Winston and Celine had left. He'd also managed to catch Margaret Hemmings, and their conversation had gone on longer than he'd expected. She had high hopes for the results of Chris's subpoena. He'd had to tell her not to rely on that source. When he'd left, Hemmings had remained sitting in the conference room, going over her trial notes, planning.

But a plan needed investigation. Chris had had another idea, but he hadn't shared it with anyone, not even Anne. He didn't want to raise anyone's hopes, because this trip didn't have a very good chance of producing evidence for the defense.

Nevertheless, he had to try. When he reached the capitol city, he drove by Nick Winston's house. He saw two cars parked in the driveway. Satisfied that Winston was not on the prowl this night, at least not yet, Chris headed for his real destination.

By the time he reached downtown Austin, the light had softened. The city had grown tremendously in the past decade. Most of that growth had been on the north side of town, the high-tech areas, but downtown showed evidence of prosperity too, in new office towers and increased congestion. By close to seven o'clock it was navigable, though. Chris made his way to the state capitol and parked in a slanted space along the drive around it.

The dome of the capitol remained well lit at night, floodlights aimed upward. The trees held lights as well. But the building must be almost empty by now. Chris wondered if he'd be denied admittance.

To his surprise, he got in without trouble. The rotunda stood open to tourists who wanted to come in and gaze up at the inside of the dome or at the portraits of past governors. Chris hurried through a wide doorway, up a staircase, and turned toward the Senate chamber. Far down the hall he saw a security guard, but Chris in his dark suit must have looked as if he were on his way to a late meeting. He encountered no challenge.

He had called ahead to see if anyone would be here, but that had already been after five o'clock. No one had answered in the lieutenant governor's offices.

The corridors were wide and echoed with his steps. The staircases he passed had thick balustrades and dark steps to which rubber treads had been added. Chris found the doors of the Senate chamber unlocked. He stepped into the round, dim room. He stood at the back of the room, looking past desks to the tall dais and podium from which the president of the Senate would preside. That officer was the lieutenant governor of Texas, and so her chambers lay behind the podium.

Chris walked around the outer edge of the room, feeling like an intruder, hearing ghostly whispers from those desks. Anyone with a sense of history could have populated them in his mind. Chris had no trouble. He also had no trouble imagining those historical wisps as real people who'd committed sins as well as history.

He reached the door that led to the rooms behind the podium area and finally found himself confronted—by the person he'd been unconsciously expecting. As Chris opened the door, a shadow stepped into his path, a sudden blackness in front of him like a failure of his eyesight. Then in the dim light the blackness resolved itself into a blocky man in a black suit. A man with gray hair, steely blue eyes, and a face that didn't move. He just planted himself in Chris's path and stood there.

"I want to see her," Chris said. "And you, too."

After a moment the trooper turned aside. Chris began walking again and the man fell into step beside him. They reached an office, passed through, and as Chris reached for the door-knob of the inner office the trooper's hand intercepted him. He knocked on the heavy wooden door. A voice from inside said a single syllable that Chris didn't understand but the trooper did. He opened the door wide enough for Chris to enter.

The inner office was large, forty feet by fifty, with lack of furniture making it seem even more spacious. In the middle of the back wall, with its chair facing him, sat a very large desk. Two lamps on its corners provided some illumination. Over-head lights had been turned down but not off. Veronica Soren-son, the lieutenant governor of Texas, stood behind the desk. She wore a dark suit and white blouse and looked as if she were late for an important dinner. Somehow she gave that impression, while moving nothing but her eyes. She didn't offer Chris a greeting.

Chris's escort began to withdraw, but Chris took his arm and pulled him into the office. The man could have resisted if he'd wished, but he came along so that for a moment they stood side by side. Then Chris approached the desk. He heard the office's door close behind him, but felt confident the trooper had remained.

As Chris came close to the desk, he passed the two high-backed visitor's chairs and saw for the first time that one was occupied. Anne sat in it. She remained dressed as Chris had seen her an hour and a half ago, in her trial skirt and blouse. Empty-handed, legs crossed, waiting, she looked up at Chris with a smile visible only in her eyes. Perhaps only to him. Otherwise she appeared very serious.

He couldn't tell which of the two had just been speaking. They both looked at him, waiting. Chris turned to the lieutenant governor and said earnestly, "Mrs. Sorenson, you have to come to New Braunfels tomorrow."

"Yes," Sorenson said calmly. "I plan to."

That took much of the wind from Chris's sails, but he went on. "You didn't see the murder that night, I'm sure of that. You didn't know it was going to happen. But you have vital evidence. You got the videotape back that night, didn't you?"

Sorenson folded her arms. She could look formidable when she chose, with a stern face and a penetrating stare. She hadn't risen in her chosen field, through layers of better-established men, by being demure. Sounding as if fending off an accusation, she said, "As I've already told the proper authorities, yes, I did."

"You may have told them, but they don't plan to introduce that evidence."

"That's up to them. I never told anyone to hide—"

"I'm sure you didn't. I'm sure you don't have to. Knowing mention of the tape would hurt you, Andy Gunther's not going to bring it up. Even Morris's lawyer won't. Even Morris. Because they see they can do you a favor. And they're not sure this helps or hurts either one of them, but they're positive it would hurt you. So they'll take that risk. Did Gunther even ask you how you got the tape back?"

Sorenson hesitated. For years she'd avoided speaking about this, even thinking about it if she could. Obviously it took a physical effort for her to make her tongue shape words about her long-held secret. "No, he didn't ask. He said he already knew."

"He knew a lie, then. Because Ben Sewell didn't tell him, and you're the only other person who knew. Ben gave it to you that night, didn't he?"

"Yes." This word came more easily to her. The lieutenant governor looked at Anne, who just watched her, unsurprised, as if she'd already known.

Chris had a mental stumble. He'd expected more resistance on this point.

"I don't know why he did," Sorenson said. She sounded reminiscent. "I'd spent an hour in that house waiting for the shoe to drop, for someone to demand something of me. But Ben just gave me the tape and said he knew I'd want it back."

Anne spoke up for the first time. "Ben had a different plan from my father or anybody else there that night. He just wanted to do the decent thing. Maybe he hoped that would pay off eventually, but that wasn't why he did it. He may have brought Nick Winston there just for that reason, once he'd learned about the tape."

"Did he tell you that?" Chris asked wonderingly. He found it hard to believe that Anne wouldn't have revealed such information sooner, but she had had a long chat with Ben Sewell the night of his death.

She shook her head. "That's just how Ben was."

Chris continued addressing the lieutenant governor. "Ben was naive to think the blackmailer would have given him the only copy of the tape. You weren't that naive. As soon as you had it you raced back to Austin. And then you—" He turned to the trooper who'd remained silent all this time. "—you went and searched Nick Winston's house. Hoping maybe he only had one other copy and he'd left it at home. Actually, he'd left Celine at home, but that didn't stop you."

The man didn't answer. He kept his eyes on his boss, not on Chris. Chris couldn't guess at their relationship, but it was obviously more than bodyguard and client. This man cared about Sorenson in a fatherly way, or in some other kindhearted way. Whatever the reason, he had obviously gone far beyond his role as a state trooper. Veronica Sorenson had let him, probably because she needed someone. A secret creates a hole in the holder's life, a vacuum into which someone else can be drawn. Sorenson couldn't share her pain with her blackmailer or her family. Her bodyguard had obviously stepped into that vacuum.

Chris looked at the man with new curiosity, and respect.

But Chris continued with his subject, saying musingly, "I asked myself why a man who'd had his home broken into wouldn't call the police, why a woman who'd been assaulted—"

The trooper's eyes widened and he said loudly, "I never—"

"I saw her bruises," Chris said. Sorenson and her protector exchanged a look. They would talk about this later.

"Anyway, they wouldn't report it to the police because they would have had to explain what you were looking for. I don't know whether you found it, either. I suspect yes."

Neither of them answered. Chris said, "It doesn't matter. But you have to testify that Ben gave it back to you. That's obviously what made Winston so furious. You've got—"

"I have a different idea," Anne said. "That's what I've just been explaining."

Chris suddenly felt like an intruder. Also, his sense of being the brightest student in the class abruptly vanished. He sat down in the other visitor's chair and listened, noticing that the trooper drew closer as well. Chris had only been telling him something he already knew. Anne was going to explain what to do.

"First let me just tell you that it's dangerous."

"To my life, or my career?" Mrs. Sorenson asked, with a touch of irony that made Chris like her again.

"Both," Anne said. The lieutenant governor sat down. The trooper stood by Anne's shoulder.

"You have to get rid of this thing. I don't mean the tape, I mean the situation. You're never going to get rid of this man by trying to appease him. Look how far he's already come on your back. Has anything ever satisfied him?"

"Some of it he's gotten on his own," Sorenson said defensively. "You don't understand Nick. He—"

"All the better," Anne said calmly. "But you'll never rise any higher, or even have any peace of mind where you are, until

you get rid of this baggage. You need to hold a press conference. Right away. And announce, yourself, what happened.
What's been happening all these years."

Veronica Sorenson sat not only silently but with no visible
reaction, as if Anne hadn't spoken to her. Her eyes were wide
and aimed at Anne, but not seeing. The planes of her face had
tightened. She looked beautiful but not quite human, a computer simulation of a beautiful woman. Then color poured back
into her face. "How can I do that?" she said. "I have children.
My husband . . . I'd be betraying them, not just hurting myself."

"Haven't you wanted to tell them? Tell them you made a
mistake years ago, but you're a different person now and you
need their help and understanding? Hasn't this been a barrier
between you for a long time?"

Sorenson sat thinking, withdrawn. Her trooper watched her
closely, his face still stony but sympathy in his eyes. He looked
as if she held his fate as well.

She shook her head.

"I can't," she said. "Not this abruptly. I have to prepare
them. I can't just—My daughter has to go to school. My God,
do you know what would happen? If I tell people this tape
exists, no one would stop until they find it. It would be on the
Internet. My children's friends would have copies. No."

Silence fell, accentuated by the dimness of the room. A
silent tug-of-war between the two women persisted for a
moment, before the lieutenant governor sighed and sat down.

"Then I have another idea," Chris said. Anne began nodding
before he even finished speaking. "Just announce that you're
going to have the press conference."

"Yes," Anne said, seizing on the thought. "Say you're going to
make an important statement about your personal life. That
you're going to rid yourself of a burden you've carried too long."

Sorenson smiled. "My husband will think I'm divorcing him."

"We'll work on the wording. As long as Nick Winston knows what you mean." She turned to Chris for confirmation. He nodded at her.

Sorenson began to catch on. "Let him know I'm going to out him. Because if I say I've been blackmailed all this time, he's the blackmailer."

Chris, the only lawyer in the room, said, "I'm not sure he could be prosecuted. You may have a statute of limitations problem. When's the last time he actually threatened you? It's just been implicit for so long . . ."

Sorenson said, "You don't understand Nick Winston. He's not afraid of prison. It's exposure. He won't permit that."

Chris and Anne looked up at the trooper. Sorenson didn't. He had her confidence.

"We'll need to have him followed," Anne said. "By someone less recognizable than Trooper Smith."

"I'll take care of that," Chris said.

"Can we put the trial on hold for a day or so?" the lieutenant governor asked. Again they looked at Chris, who shrugged. "I'll speak to the judge if necessary," Sorenson added.

They stayed half an hour longer, making plans, helping to write the statement, before Anne and Chris left together. As they passed through the dim outer office, Chris asked, "Why didn't we start doing this sooner?"

Anne's eyes caught what little light the room held, sparkling in the darkness. "Work together?" Anne asked. "I don't know. Why didn't we?"

Their hands brushed as they walked through the Senate chamber. At the door Anne reached for the doorknob. Chris's hand covered hers. She stopped, standing close to him. She grasped the lapel of his suit coat as if angry, and pulled him closer. They kissed in the darkness, a kiss that became fierce in a moment. Anne's hand found the back of his neck.

After a long moment she pulled back with an odd, smiling frown. Looking down, she asked, "Are you packing heat, or are you just glad to see me?"

"Both."

Anne pulled aside his jacket and saw the pistol in the holster on his belt. She had never known him to be armed before. "Clarissa?" she said.

Chris nodded. "He's not going to do anything to her."

Anne dropped the subject, though it worried her. They kissed again, in the darkness of the historic chamber. When they emerged from that room, they walked in step, unconsciously, heads close as they talked.

The next morning in court before the jury was seated, Nick Winston stood before the judge and formally handed his coat to Margaret Hemmings. The coat was protected by a plastic dry cleaner's bag. Hemmings took it carefully, holding it like evidence. Chris sat at the defense table. Judge Younger said, "Mr. Winston, I remind you that you're still under oath. Is this the coat you were wearing the night of the offense that is before this court?"

"Yes, your Honor, it is."

Hemmings immediately said, "Your Honor, the defense requests a one-day continuance to have this jacket tested."

"Can it be done in one day?" the judge asked.

Chris stood. "I'll get it done in Bexar County, your Honor."

"Why wasn't this done sooner?" the judge asked. He seemed

disinclined to grant the delay. Winston stood by neutrally, as if uninvolved.

Chris answered. "We didn't understand the necessity until we heard Mr. Winston's testimony."

The judge said, "What do you hope to prove?"

"Who was on that balcony, your Honor. Who's lied to this court and who's told the truth."

The judge pondered, then snapped out, "All right. One day. Bailiff! You'll accompany this coat to the Medical Examiner's Office in San Antonio. Turn it over to their evidence custodian."

"Yes, sir," the bailiff said, taking the coat from Hemmings.

"Everyone else, be here promptly tomorrow morning at nine. I won't grant any more delay."

He sounded angry, and left the bench quickly.

Chris had an idea Veronica Sorenson had made that call to the judge she'd suggested. The judge had granted her the favor, not the defense.

Chris leaned close to Morris and said, "I just lied to a judge for you."

Hemmings smiled. "Was that your first time?"

The little scene before the judge had been a ruse. It wasn't Nick Winston's jacket Chris was interested in testing. As he stepped across the aisle to make an arrangement with Andy Gunther, Winston stood in front of him, on his way out.

"What *do* you hope to prove?" he asked, his old smile back in evidence.

"Where you were that night," Chris answered. "And you'd better listen to the news this morning."

He walked past Winston and caught Andy Gunther at the side door. "Andy? I want something else. We can either go see the judge or we can make an arrangement ourselves."

Gunther looked at him with the beginning of a glare, but warily. "Sure, counselor. Want the shirt off my back?"

"No. The one off Ben Sewell's. His jacket, actually."

"His jacket? That yellow thing everybody's mentioned? Why?" Gunther looked genuinely puzzled.

"For comparison," Chris said. "I honestly don't know why. But it's something the defense should have done a long time ago. Think of it as a way to avoid an ineffective assistance of counsel claim when the case comes back on appeal or a writ."

The two men looked across the courtroom at Margaret Hemmings. She seemed to feel the weight of their attention, looked up from talking to her client, and walked quickly toward them. She wore her usual determined expression.

"Look," Chris said quickly to Gunther, "I spend most of my life in your position, Andy. And I hate it when defendants get sneaky. I could have gone behind your back to get this, ask the family to reclaim Ben Sewell's clothes from your medical examiner. They haven't been introduced in evidence—"

"Because they don't prove anything!"

"Then what's the problem? I'm trying to do this honestly, Andy. Wouldn't you rather be in on it than have me do an end run around you?"

Margaret Hemmings had arrived. She stood at Chris's shoulder with her arms folded and a challenging stare on her face. "Besides, if you don't agree, I'll put all this on the record, and even if the clothes don't prove anything else, they'll prove you were trying to hide potential evidence from the jury," she said.

Gunther returned her stare evenly, unperturbed, then said to Chris, "You were doing better before your team got here."

"Back off, okay?" Chris said. Hemmings's expression didn't change.

Andy Gunther gave the matter another moment's thought, shrugged, and said, "Let's go catch that bailiff."

As he turned away Chris glanced at Hemmings. She gave him a sly wink. She had played her part well, at just the right moment. Chris didn't much like being on her team, but there were larger considerations.

The two of them followed the big district attorney of Comal County down the back hall.

On Chris's way back to San Antonio he called his investigator Jack Fine. "Got somebody on him? Make sure, Jack. Use two people."

"Don't teach your granny to suck eggs," Jack answered.

"Where do you get these colorful country expressions? I'll be at the Medical Examiner's Office if you need me."

Clarissa had decided that morning to accompany Anne to the office. The girl acted as if she were so bored that even helping Anne's secretary get files in order would pass the time. But Chris knew his daughter: she wanted to be in on the action, knew Anne would be there, and thought Chris would be doing the boring stuff in the meantime.

She also may have wanted to avoid the Forensic Science Center, where autopsies were performed. The place had many other functions, though. It did not reek of death. In fact, the five-story building in the medical center area was one of the cleanest, best-lighted places Chris ever went. He caught a whiff of chemicals and cleaning materials, but also of excitement. Discoveries happened here on a daily basis.

That morning Chris met with a woman named Elaine Patterson, an expert not often used in court. Most days she taught chemistry at the University of Texas at San Antonio, occasionally consulting at the Forensic Science Center, and even more rarely being called upon by Chris or another lawyer to perform her unusual specialty.

"Hello, Dr. Patterson."

A woman in her forties, Dr. Patterson was thin, her hands always busy. She had her brown hair pulled back in a ponytail and wore large round glasses. Sometimes, Chris knew, she would break into a bright smile that completely transformed her face. This morning she wore running shorts and a blue T-shirt. "Did I take you out of class?"

She gave a small version of her smile. "I got a ride and I'm going to run home from here. At least that's the theory. Since it's August I might end up at a bus stop, though. What have you got?"

"A sports coat. A man was wearing it the night—"

"Don't prejudice me," she said. "Let me look at it and see what I can tell you."

She held the garment at arm's length, looked at it very slowly, then turned it. The jacket looked, as Winston had said, perfect. "Looks fine," Elaine Patterson concluded. "I'll look at it under the microscope, but nothing jumps out at me."

"I know," Chris said. "What about the others I already had you look at?"

She led him to a black-topped lab table in the small lab just off one of the main hallways of the center. Stretched out on the table's surface were a white shirt and a yellow sports coat. They had been removed from Ben Sewell's body after his death and, at the request of the defense, put into Chris's hands the day before. Margaret Hemmings had looked over the clothing weeks ago but had not had it tested. She had no theories a test might have proven or disproved. Neither did Andy Gunther, who had rested his case without reference to the dead man's clothing.

"All right," Dr. Patterson said briskly. "According to witnesses, the deceased was wearing this jacket when he fell one story through some bristly cedar bushes."

"Yes, ma'am. Possible?"

"Likely, I'd say. Look at it, it's ripped to pieces."

Relatively speaking, and compared to Nick Winston's pristine jacket, she was right. The yellow jacket had noticeable rips along the arms and breast. Chris turned it over. The back had a few tears as well. It was dirty, too, but not terribly.

"All right, I guess that's it."

"What about the dirt?" Dr. Patterson said, folding her arms. She had the straight mouth with a hint of mischief Chris had come to recognize on the faces of doctors or scientists who knew something he didn't. Anne had it sometimes.

"What about it?"

"The body was lying on its back when you found it, isn't that what you said?"

"Yes."

"And your doctor in New Braunfels said he fell on his back."

"Yes. So?"

"Didn't happen. At least not that way."

"Why not? The jacket's dirty."

"Sure," Dr. Patterson said, brushing at it. Some of the dirt fell to the table. "Loose dirt. Not embedded in the coat the way it would have been if he'd landed on it."

Chris thought hard. Everybody's version of events ended with Ben Sewell falling from the balcony to the dirt below. His, Anne's, Nick Winston's.

"Could he have gone down some other way?"

"There's something else about your story that bothers me. Tell me again how you saw him fall."

Chris had no trouble with that. The scene remained the last thing he pictured when he closed his eyes in bed some nights. Ben shooting himself, his body falling forward, headfirst over the railing, the legs coming up, swinging high, then turning . . .

"Stop," Patterson said at that point. "What do you mean by 'swinging high'?"

"You know." Chris tried to demonstrate by turning his hand into a stick figure of a man. It wouldn't bend all the right directions, but Dr. Patterson seemed to get the idea.

"So the legs went almost straight up?"

They tried to enact it. It wouldn't work using the lab table because they couldn't go over it. A few minutes later Chris and the professor were bent forward over desk chairs when they heard a small noise behind them. Dr. Harold Parmenter stood in the doorway watching. When they looked back at him, he smiled and didn't say a word.

"Hal, come here," Dr. Patterson said. "Listen to this."

Dr. Parmenter was tall, thin, sandy-haired, and looked absent-minded except when absorbed in a problem. That happened as he listened to Elaine Patterson describe what Chris thought he had seen. Dr. Parmenter was shaking his head after three sentences. "No."

Dr. Patterson raised a hand triumphantly. "Why not?" Chris said.

"Dead body would go over that rail like a sack of laundry, Chris. The muscles are slack, it's just guided by gravity. It doesn't swing its legs up and over. That's a protective instinct, trying to get your legs under you for the fall."

"You mean he was still alive at that point?"

That made it worse, somehow. Now Chris's imagination held Ben Sewell in his last few moments of life trying to break his fall, trying to save himself from further injury when he was already, essentially, dead.

"But that's not it, either," Dr. Patterson said. "Let me show you this shirt. By the way—" As they moved toward the evidence, both doctors studied Chris. "Why did you wait until now to talk to us, to have these tests done?"

"I'm not the lawyer!" Chris said exasperatedly. "Understand? This isn't my job!"

His answer obviously inspired more questions, but Drs. Patterson and Parmenter kept those to themselves.

Chris emerged from the center about four o'clock in the afternoon, having given all the clothing back to the bailiff from New Braunfels. Mulling over new theories, Chris listened to news on his car radio as he headed back to his office. The news ended with two sentences saying Lieutenant Governor Veronica Sorenson had issued an announcement that she would hold a press conference the next day to reveal long-suppressed personal information. "Since Mrs. Sorenson has been mentioned several times as a candidate for national office, speculation is rampant that this press conference will clear the way for perhaps a bigger political announcement in the fall. . . ."

Chris immediately called Jack Fine. "Yes," Jack drawled. "Commissioner Winston has a better network than you do. He apparently already heard the news. He took off. First he tried to get in to see Mrs. Sorenson. When she refused, he took off again. Guess where he's headed?"

"Here," Chris said, suddenly anxious to get to Anne and Clarissa. But Jack would have thought of that.

"Nope. I'll bet I could give you three more guesses and you wouldn't get it. He's on his way to Uvalde."

"Uvalde?" Chris asked wonderingly. There was only one person in the small town of Uvalde anyone political would travel there to see.

"And by the way," Jack added casually. "Anne called and I told her, too. That's okay, isn't it?"

★ As he drove west, Chris found Anne, theoretically. He found her out there in the digital network, a voice in his phone that could have come from anywhere. "What are you doing?" he yelled, as if his voice had to bridge that distance.

"Going to see an old family friend. And I've got one with me, too."

"Hi, Dad," a voice came faintly in the background. Clarissa sounded as if she were off on a jolly field trip.

"Damn it, Anne—"

"Chris, she literally would not get out of my car. And she's bigger than I am. Did you want me to have her arrested?" Chris knew she was keeping her voice light for Clarissa's sake.

"Just be sure you keep her out of it. What do you think you're accomplishing by going there anyway?"

A long pause told him the answer might be, *Nothing.* Anne finally said, "We'll stay out of the way," and clicked off.

"That was a lie, right?" Clarissa said. Her legs stretched long in Anne's passenger seat. Her body remained mostly thin and angular in her orange tank top, but not entirely so. In just the last several months, Anne sometimes felt as if she'd raised Clarissa from a child. "Because I wouldn't have come if we were just gonna 'hang back,'" Clarissa grinned.

"I can drop you off here," Anne said. But she kept driving, toward the setting sun. The highway was mostly two-lane, sometimes four, but remained relentlessly rural after they passed the town of Hondo. Smaller towns on this road appeared from the highway not even as wide spaces: a gas station and one or two other small businesses, at least half of them permanently closed. Anne felt as if they were traveling toward something that had blighted this landscape. But that wasn't true. Temple Lockridge had been the benefactor of his region as well as the state. If not for him, this road wouldn't have been paved at all.

But Anne knew the senator better than most voters. At least she thought she did. She'd met him years before. A child or a teenager sometimes gets glimpses of an adult that other adults don't see. Anne couldn't specify how she knew it, but when she'd found out that Lockridge might be even remotely involved in this business, she'd been afraid. Afraid that her blustery, self-assured father didn't know what a tiny bug he could be, simply squashed and swept out with the spilled coffee grounds.

Dusk fell before they reached the Lockridge ranch, making it look as if the old mansion were drawing a cloak over itself. A ranch hand, or a guard disguised as one, stopped Anne at the gate. He called the house, but either received no reply or a troubling one. "Maybe you'd better wait here, ma'am. The senator's got company now that—"

"I know. I'm meeting Commissioner Winston here."

The hand, a skinny, old, sun-cured wrangler who looked as

if he'd been pressed into this job because the real guards had business elsewhere, looked dubious. Anne turned on her dome light and let him look into the interior of the car, at her and at the teenager beside her. Clarissa said, "I really need to use the bathroom, Aunt Anne."

That was more than the gate guard wanted to hear. "I guess it'll be okay," he said, stepping back. "I'll call and tell 'em you're coming. If they want you to wait, they'll stop you up there."

"Thank you," Anne called, already driving up the caliche stone road. She looked askance at her passenger. Clarissa uncrossed her legs, smiled, and said, "Works about half the time. More than that if it's a man."

Inside the former senator's spacious den, where animal heads gazed down from the high, wood-paneled walls, Nick Winston stood with one bead of sweat trickling down his forehead. White-haired Senator Lockridge watched that bead. He had never seen the boy sweat before, and didn't think anyone else ever had either. It was a disturbing sight.

Celine, the girlfriend, a long-legged, sleepy-eyed playtoy, walked around the room admiring the decorations, including guns, photos, and old framed documents. "Is this President Nixon?" she called over her shoulder. "When was this one taken?"

"We need to talk," Winston said, his eyes locked with Temple Lockridge's.

He didn't have to gesture for Lockridge to know what he meant. After a long pause, the senator said from his leather wingback chair, "You can leave us here, Gordon. Leave the house to us for a while, all right?" Lockridge didn't move his head or his hands. If he gave a signal, it must have been by telepathy.

"Sir—"

"I mean it, Gordie. Now."

"Yes, sir."

Before he left, Gordon went to Nick Winston, who held out his arms and endured a thorough pat-down. Then the tall young cowboy, bodyguard, whatever-else-he-might-be, turned and walked stiffly out of the room. The people in the room heard the front door of the house close. Senator Lockridge inclined his head, giving Winston the floor.

"I want the tape," Winston said simply.

Lockridge didn't bother to deny anything. He folded his hands together and said, "I can't think what you'd have worth trading me."

Winston glanced at his partner. Another drop of sweat appeared beside his right eye.

"And," the former senator continued smugly, "you're not going to take anything from me because you're not armed, and I happen to be." He reached down beside his seat cushion.

Celine gave a short scream, a cartoonish sort of "Eek" that drew both men's attention. In the interval she opened her purse. She removed an efficient-looking silvery automatic pistol. Pointing it with what looked like excellent aim at Temple Lockridge's forehead, she said, "Oh, please."

Anne drove up to the ranch house in time to see a small band of young men walking away. One returned to confront her. "I'm sorry, ma'am, no— Oh, hello, Dr. Greenwald."

"Hello, Gordie. I'm supposed to be in on this meeting."

The young man calculated quickly the effect of throwing Anne into the mix. The senator could send a signal if he wanted her out. But he might enjoy the company. And the senator hadn't said anything one way or another about letting anyone else in. Gordon wasn't going to go back and ask him, after being definitively thrown out himself.

He looked Anne over carefully. She spread her arms. "Think I'm going to shoot anybody?" she asked with a smile.

"Maybe cut somebody with a remark. You alone?"

Anne glanced back at the interior of her Volvo, well lighted because she had left her door open. It sat empty.

She gave Gordon another smile. "Sure am."

He waved her away. Anne walked toward the house. When she looked back over her shoulder and saw no one watching her, she started to run.

Her shoes clattered on the wooden porch, so she slowed down. The porch was the covered, wraparound variety that circled the house. Anne did, too, glad that no one had turned on the porch lights. She passed old leather-and-wood furniture, two porch swings, and several ceiling fans, two of them turning lazily. She passed the window of a dining room and caught a glimpse through it of the den, where she saw Celine. If Celine was here, Winston would be too, but Anne couldn't hear anything out here. She retraced her steps to the front door of the house, opened it as softly as she could, and slipped inside. She hoped Clarissa hadn't already done the same. She hadn't seen a trace of the girl since they'd arrived at the ranch house. Anne crept across the entryway and peeked through a doorway into the large den.

She stood twenty feet behind Nick Winston. Past him she had an obstructed view of Temple Lockridge, seated, and Celine standing on the other side of the room, in front of the fireplace.

Anne thought at first that it was Celine who was speaking. The voice was high-pitched, edging toward panic. Then as Nick Winston threw up his hands, she realized it was him.

"Because I'm on it!" he shouted. "I'm on the damned tape! My face, my everything! It wouldn't be worthwhile if it didn't show everything. Now if she's gone crazy and she's going to tell the world about it, she's obviously going to say somebody was blackmailing her with it. And once anybody sees the tape, they won't have to guess who that was."

Temple Lockridge sounded amused. "It doesn't show you smoking pot."

Winston stared at him. "You've watched it."

From across the room, Celine said, "Well, duh. Probably every night, right, Senator? Or do you have the Playboy Channel, too?"

Lockridge gave her a long look, still not devoid of amusement. Celine continued, "But it's not the same as when it's somebody you know, is it?" She smiled, her mouth stretching wide. "Believe me, I know."

Winston, who appeared to have lost his place in the conversation, said, "I'm not going down with her. Without the tape she won't be able to prove anything. You've got the last copy. Give it to me."

"That's right," Celine said. "Nick hasn't asked her for anything in years. How is that blackmail?"

Nick Winston turned his head away from the room at large, wearing a strange expression, the first guilty look Anne had ever seen on his face. Then he looked up and gasped. The other two heads turned too, and Anne realized she'd been seen. So acting deliberate, she stepped out into the den. Her voice sounded terribly cool as she said, "Did you offer the senator a copy for some reason, Nick, or did he demand one once he'd found out about it?"

At the sight of her, Nick Winston appeared to regain his footing. "He seems to get a finger into most pies," he said, with his old smile.

"Oh, shit," Anne said. She had just stepped far enough into the room to see the gun in Celine's hand. Celine smiled at Anne but then ignored her. Her voice very flat, she said to the senator, "Now. Get it."

Lockridge kept his poise. "Go ahead and shoot," he said. "I've had a long life, and if you kill me you'll be nine kinds of dead before you reach the front door."

Celine walked toward him. Anne took a step and the gun swung toward her. Celine glanced at her for one second, said, "You're nobody," and pointed the gun at the senator again. The one second had been enough. Anne had seen absolute emptiness in the woman's eyes as she'd looked at her. In all her experience, Anne hadn't seen such lack of feeling. Anne couldn't offer Celine anything. Celine was just doing math now, and Anne had no place in the equation. She could be dead now or later. Anne froze.

She looked across the room to the wide windows, hoping to see the senator's men moving into place. She saw something much worse. Clarissa stood out there, trying to give Anne some kind of signal. She waved her hand. Anne wanted to scream.

But Celine's attention remained focused on the senator. She walked up to the wing chair where he still sat at ease, and suddenly thrust the gun down into his crotch. Lockridge made a sound between a grunt and a squawk, and the smile fell off his face.

Celine leaned down and said intimately, "A bull as old as you doesn't need these anymore, do you, Temple? I'll take them off now. I may go to jail, but everybody you see for the rest of your life, you'll know what they're thinking: 'There goes the ball-less wonder from Uvalde.' And you wondering if your plastic bag is starting to stink up the room."

She straightened up again. Lockridge began breathing again, heavily, but the color that had fallen out of his face didn't return. "Besides," Celine said, "I might not go to jail at all. Not after I tell people I did this because you raped me, you son of a bitch."

Her voice went up a notch; her face grew contorted. Anne watched, fascinated. She had no idea whether the woman was telling the truth, reliving a true experience, or acting.

"No one will believe that," Lockridge grunted.

"You don't think so? After the others start coming forward? What are you going to say they were, Senator? Forceful dates? They couldn't make up their minds but you could?"

"Celine—" Nick Winston said cautiously. It was strange to see him looking like the frightened, rational one. His fright scared Anne even more, because Winston knew Celine better than anyone. He stretched out his hand toward her. She pointed the gun at him. He cringed. But Celine had already swung the weapon back to Temple Lockridge's forehead. "Now get it," she said contemptuously.

Without another word of argument, the former senator heaved himself up from his chair. He crossed the room away from Celine, limping a little, looking like an old rancher who'd spent a lifetime doing hard work with occasional injury. Anne thought he was exaggerating his infirmities, and hoped Celine didn't think so as well.

Anne looked out the picture window again, then saw Celine looking at her and following her gaze. Anne coughed. She started following the senator, and Celine barked at her to stop. She returned her attention to Lockridge as he limped through a door into his private office. Celine followed him to the doorway, from which she could still watch Anne. Temple Lock-ridge swung aside some books and found a wall safe with a large combination lock.

"Not very original," Celine said.

Over his shoulder, Lockridge said, "Nobody's ever been in this room before without an invitation from me."

"Life is full of changes, isn't it, Senator?"

Nick Winston glanced at Anne. He no longer displayed his facial innuendo. He looked scared. Anne wondered whether he was acting, already planning a defense for himself if something went wrong. But his expression looked very real. Anne realized that, as is often the case, the relationship between the man and woman wasn't what everyone had thought. Celine was the driving force, the ruthless one.

She could be wrong, but in that moment Anne was certain of her diagnosis.

The wall safe door swung open, revealing a space about two feet wide and the same height, with quite a depth of darkness. Lockridge reached his whole arm inside, felt around, pulled out a videotape in a black case, looked at it, and put it back inside. He rooted around and produced another one.

"Maybe I should just take everything in there," Celine said jovially.

Lockridge slammed the door shut, spun the dial, and covered the safe again. He tossed the tape across the study and Celine caught it with her free hand. She turned her back on the senator and came back toward the center of the den.

"What do you say?" she said to Winston. "Should we watch it one more time for old time's sake, or just start cleaning up?" She looked at Anne, who had been edging toward the door, but stopped. Celine said musingly, "I think these two shot each other, what do you think?"

Winston walked toward her, reaching for the tape, but Celine ignored him. Very deliberately, she swung the pistol in a slow arc until it was pointed at Anne.

Chris drove right past the guard shack at the entrance to the ranch. He heard a yell behind him and speeded up, raising a cloud of white dust on the rocky road. He didn't mind a bit, calling attention to himself. In fact, as he neared the house he veered toward a small clump of men. Chris jumped out and recognized Gordon, the senator's closest aide. "What are you doing?" he shouted. "Why are you out here?"

Gordon came toward him, starting to explain, but Chris didn't listen. He ran toward the house. Men began running after him, to stop him or follow him Chris didn't know, but it didn't matter. Because before they reached the front door they heard a shot.

The men ran harder, stomping up onto the porch and through the front door. But Chris veered off, because he had heard something else. The crash of glass. He turned left, running around the house.

Every detail was vivid. The black night shone brightly. Chris saw the stone walls of the house, spots where flakes of stone had chipped off, the marks of the tools of the workmen who had laid in the mortar. The cedar posts that held up the porch roof also had strips peeling off. Chris heard his own breath and the thud of his feet hitting the ground. It seemed as though he had lived this scene before. He ran as if through memory, the strongest memory of his life, as in a life's last moments.

Ahead, coming around the corner of the porch, he saw someone. Running toward him. He recognized her instantly.

Moments earlier, Anne had stood frozen as Celine pointed the gun at her. "No!" Winston said sharply, but he obviously was no longer in charge of the situation. Celine stared at Anne, eyes glittering. All the emotion she'd carefully suppressed seemed to pass over her face: the jealousy, anger, insecurity; the enormous hunger for more than life could ever give her. All her greed and fury coalesced into a hatred Anne didn't deserve, but she was available. She could play the object of Celine's rage. The young woman raised the gun. Anne heard it cock.

Senator Lockridge hung back in the doorway of his study. He stood very watchfully, even fearfully, perhaps seeing a preview of his own death. Anne thought he must have some way of sending a signal to his men outside, but Lockridge stood frozen, lips parted in the voyeur's stare.

Anne looked steadily at Celine. "Tell me what you want," she said calmly. "I can help you get there. You've already got what you came for. Don't mess up your life now."

"I hate that shrink voice," Celine sneered. She pointed the gun.

But before she could fire, a crash startled them all. The sound of glass shattering was like an explosion. The body couldn't help ducking. The noise sounded like the first blast of an invasion. Celine spun around and aimed.

One of the picture windows lay in pieces on the hardwood floor. A wrought-iron porch chair sat on its side, still quivering from the impact of having gone through the window. Outside,

Clarissa stood looking rather tremblly herself. It had taken a huge effort to smash the chair through the plate glass, but she had done it in one try. She stared into the room, suddenly one of them.

Celine started toward her. Clarissa unfroze. She shouted, "It's her! It's Celine! She's got a gun." And she turned and ran.

Celine fired a shot at her, instinctively. Then she stepped through the broken window and ran after the girl. Anne screamed and started to follow. Nick Winston grabbed her arm. "There are men out there with guns," he said.

His expression looked strangely, morbidly hopeful. Anne shook free of him and ran toward the broken window. Men appeared in the den from the direction of the front door of the house. One of them yelled at her to stop, but she didn't.

Outside, enough light spilled from the house so that Chris saw Clarissa running toward him, and his face lit up. He held out his arms. But then he saw that she was being pursued. Chris reached under his jacket and pulled out his own gun. "Gordon!" he called.

Clarissa saw Chris and ran straight toward him. Behind her, Celine followed in hot pursuit, pointing a gun. She aimed and fired. The bullet zinged past Chris, ricocheting off the stone wall, leaving it scored. Chris screamed something and tried to fire back, but Clarissa was in the way, running awkwardly as she tried to duck, almost falling but then recovering, unfortunately. She was tall enough to perfectly block Chris's shot. "Get down!" he shouted. "Fall!"

That is a very hard instruction to obey. A running person is fighting for balance. To deliberately fall is to risk injury. The body resists it. Clarissa ducked her head, but that still didn't give Chris an open shot.

He could see Celine, though, running then stopping to take better aim. Her face looked insane. Chris saw everything clearly. His mind was racing, raising and discarding possibilities. In that fearfully dark night, he saw everything clearly but was unable to prevent the impending events. Everything was moving terribly slowly, including Chris himself. Everything except his mind. He saw all the consequences. The shot he couldn't take. Celine's range. Her raising and then lowering the pistol, sighting along its barrel. Clarissa's own expression of hope as she neared the corner of the house and her father. She thought she was free of danger. She couldn't see the gun aimed at her back.

Chris leaped to the side and up onto an ornamental hitching post at the edge of the porch, a railing for men to rest their feet on as they sat. The railing stood three feet off the ground—Chris could never have jumped that high a minute earlier. But adrenaline propelled him. He grabbed the upright post to steady himself and pointed his gun. Now he had a clear aim, over Clarissa's head.

"Celine!" he shouted. Anything to throw off her aim, draw her attention away from Clarissa.

But in the moment when he jumped, something had changed. Chris with his heightened senses saw Celine standing still for a moment, her gun no longer aimed so precisely. Its barrel went up minutely. Celine had obviously caught herself. A witness was watching her. And the girl hadn't seen anything to speak of.

Celine's mind was obviously racing as her rage began to drain away. She'd been reacting to the appearance of danger, but it was over now. Let the girl go. Celine could only get herself into bad trouble by firing now. She had begun thinking, not just reacting. Celine had passed the moment of insanity that leads to senseless murder, and instead begun to think she could still talk her way out of this situation.

Chris saw these thoughts reflected in her face. He held his own fire. Celine's gun hand started down. She was no longer staring so intently at the fleeing Clarissa. In fact, she turned a cryptic glance toward Chris. She shrugged, as if in apology or to say, "Oops."

Then Gordon, the senator's bodyguard, pounded around the corner of the house, revolver raised and cocked. He saw Chris on the porch rail, the frightened girl running toward her father, and beyond them a woman holding a gun. Without an instant of reflection, he aimed and fired.

The bullet took Celine dead center in the chest. She hadn't felt it coming, hadn't even seen Gordon. The impact knocked her back like a block from an offensive tackle. Her back and the back of her head hit the packed dirt hard. After a slight bounce, she didn't move again.

Chris jumped down from the railing and Clarissa reached him. He held her tightly, tightly, knocking her wind out. But that was what the girl wanted. She buried her face near his collarbone and tried to climb inside him. "It's all right," Chris said over and over again. "She's down. She's not chasing you."

Finally Clarissa raised her head and looked back. She saw the body on the ground but didn't ease her hold on Chris. Then she saw another figure emerging from the darkness. Anne approached the body, stooped beside it for a moment, and put her fingers on Celine's neck. After a long moment she stood up again. She came to join them.

Clarissa obviously felt reassured. She eased her hold on Chris just a bit. But she turned to Anne and asked warily, "Where is he?"

Anne knew she meant Nick Winston. She wasn't sure of

the answer, but said, "He doesn't have a gun, about a dozen cowboys have him, and I think one of them's tying a rope into a noose."

Clarissa smiled. Then she shuddered. Anne joined the embrace.

After a while Chris went to look at Celine. Cops and evidence technicians were on their way, and Chris knew enough not to move the body. But he wanted to see one thing. He lifted Celine's head just slightly and saw dirt ground into her hair and the back of her head from the impact of her fall backwards. Her blouse would be ruined as well. Chris let the body lie and looked upward, as if to see where her soul had fled. The moon shone thinly, revealing nothing.

In all the confusion hardly anyone saw another car arrive. A big black sedan with "State Official" license plates. It beat the police cars by a few minutes, pulling up right to the front of the house. Veronica Sorenson emerged from the back seat. She wore a long, midnight-blue dress with a deep neckline, and three strands of pearls. She appeared to have come from a gala. The ball was missing its belle as she strode across the hard-packed dirt of Temple Lockridge's front yard. Trooper Smith, in a black suit, had leaped out of the driver's seat and walked with his back to her, surveying the scene. The lieutenant governor left that to him, herself looking neither right nor left as she stepped up onto the porch and entered the house.

The front room held a blaze of light now. Sorenson walked through it as if through a dozen photographers, her chin high, mouth set in a tight line. Her bare arms emerged pale and strongly formed from the party dress.

At the doorway she almost collided with Nick Winston. Two men were bringing him out of the den, each holding an arm. The men stopped, and Winston and Sorenson looked at each other from a few inches apart. His face was white, his mouth shaky. He wanted a cigarette badly. He had been crying. Veronica Sorenson stared at him. No one who didn't know could have seen an intimate connection between them. If Sorenson's expression showed anything, it was contempt. To the men holding Nick Winston, it seemed as if she didn't recognize him.

She walked into the den, and took in its destruction as she walked: the broken window, the outdoor chair, a faint, acrid whiff of singed gunpowder. Sorenson's eyes moved minutely. Her heels clicked on the hardwood floor.

Senator Lockridge sat in his favorite chair, a cane resting against the side. A squat glass of amber liquid sat on a table at his elbow. No ice. Lockridge looked more shaken than anyone had ever seen him in public. He started to reach for the glass, then looked up at the sound of Veronica Sorenson's footsteps. She walked up and stood over him, tall and commanding. Lockridge seemed shrunken. He had turned old in the last few minutes. But as he looked up at his protégé he tried to regain his old control. He picked up his glass and toasted her. "I'm all right," he said. "Winston's girlfriend is dead, but nobody else got hurt."

Sorenson didn't respond. She suddenly bent and reached

toward him. Her hand went beside him, into the seat cushion, and she pulled out the videotape. She opened its case, looked at the label, then returned her eyes to him. Her eyes were cold and dark. Lockridge's faded blue ones went moist. "Got it back for you," he said gruffly.

Veronica Sorenson just looked at him. Her old mentor, who had brought her along and paved her political way, even though they were of different parties. She had done him favors in return. Certainly she had always paid him respect.

But when she had heard, through her trooper's law enforcement network, that Nick Winston was on his way to see Lockridge, she had guessed that they were in a sense collaborators. There could have been no good reason for her old mentor to have a copy of this video—especially for him to have obtained it but made no effort to wrest the original from its holder, her blackmailer. Either he wanted it for his own personal library, or for the same reasons Winston had made the tape in the first place: to own a piece of Veronica Sorenson.

Her sin had been uninhibited, indiscreet, joyful. Lockridge's had been furtive, calculated, and nasty.

In any case, her respect for the old man had died an ugly death tonight. Still watching the former senator unblinkingly, she pulled the thin ribbon of tape out of the videocasette and began tearing it into pieces. Lockridge did nothing to stop her. He looked at her fingers sadly.

She stared at him coldly the whole time she performed this operation, then she dropped the tape, turned on her heel, and walked out quickly.

Trooper Smith picked up the pieces.

★ Trial resumed the next morning, and no one was absent. New Braunfels lay a hundred miles from the scene of last night's confrontation, and seemed even farther, in the cool morning air of the courtroom. The spectator seats were absolutely filled, and more would-be observers lingered in the hall. Clarissa had a front-row seat, as did Anne. District Attorney Andy Gunther had agreed that she could remain in the courtroom as long as she didn't testify again. Clarissa sat very still, her hands in her lap, Chris looked back at her from his seat inside the railing, still fearful for her, but Clarissa looked alert and fearless. Not brave: fearless, as if nothing had happened. Chris glanced at Anne, who inclined her eyes to Clarissa next to her, then gave Chris a little smile, noting his pride. But Anne remained worried.

Even Nick Winston was in evidence, still appearing shaken. He looked like the most harmless man in the courthouse. Everyone knew part of the story from the night before. At the very least they knew that his girlfriend had been killed, and that she'd had a gun in her hand at the time.

After Winston had spent two hours at

the Uvalde County jail and by long distance hired an excellent Austin lawyer, he had been released because no one knew what to charge him with. Senator Lockridge refused to say that Winston and Celine had broken into his home. The Uvalde County sheriff had given up for the time being and let him go.

Judge Younger sat crookedly on the bench, casually, as if unaware of all those voters in the spectator seats. He nodded at Margaret Hemmings, who stood up and said, "The defense calls Morris Greenwald."

Morris jumped up from the defense table and took the witness stand with alacrity. He had waited for this chance. He expected his story to have the ring of truth, and to make a connection with this jury.

Chris, a veteran of hundreds of trials, could have told him that there is no such thing as the ring of truth. A well-rehearsed liar sounds more convincing than a stammering, forgetful truth-teller. And Morris, with his constant layers of strategy, sounded shifty at the best of times. But he took the oath with a loud "I do," and sat up straight in the witness chair.

Margaret Hemmings wore a more casual outfit this morning, an open-necked yellow blouse with wide lapels, a single strand of gold around her throat. She had obviously decided to go more feminine this morning. Chris hoped she had given as much thought to her examination of her client as she had to choosing her outfit.

She didn't beat around the bush. "Morris, did you kill Ben Sewell?" she asked abruptly.

"No, I did not."

He said it forcefully, then shut up. Clearly Hemmings had worked with him. Morris held his head high and looked along the rows of jurors. Their expressions were impossible to read.

"Did you have any reason to do so?"

"No. We were partners."

"Were you working together that night at your house?"

"Yes, we were. That was the whole purpose of the evening, to gather people who could help us and try to persuade them to do so."

"Did you ever threaten Ben that night? Specifically, did you ever say you'd kill him if he screwed this up?"

"I honestly don't remember," Morris said, looking across the courtroom at Anne. "But it would have been a rare evening if I hadn't said something like that. I must have said something like that to him once a week all the years we knew each other."

He didn't draw a chuckle from that packed audience. Anne's testimony had prepared them to hear this. That was one problem with the defense getting to go second, after all the State's testimony. Anne had sounded sincere. Morris sounded as if he knew what he should say.

Hemmings continued with a composed expression, as if she knew she were scoring points. "Did you know that Ben had put in a competing bid for this recycling project in the capitol?"

"Yes."

"Were you angry about that?"

"No. We had discussed the idea before he did it. I encouraged him to do it."

"Why would you do that?"

Morris cleared his throat. His voice began to take on those crafty overtones. "There are all kinds of different factors that go into submitting a bid. You have to make choices when you put together your package. You wish you'd get more than one shot at it. That's what Ben could do in this case, approach it from a different angle. If I got the bid, fine. If he did, good, too. Either way it would help both of us, because we were partners."

Obviously, Morris was trying not to say too much, not to subject himself to a different prosecution. He sounded as if he were leaving things out, but the jurors could understand why. The expressions of several had turned knowing.

"Did you see who did shoot Ben Sewell that night?"

"No, I didn't. I was downstairs seeing someone off. I thought the last two people left upstairs were Ben and Nick Winston, but when I went up there after I heard the shot, Nick was gone, too. Then he turned out to be outside. I don't know how."

The testimony continued. Morris explained how someone else could have gotten his gun. He described his movements during the party. He never mentioned Veronica Sorenson. The crowded courtroom grew warmer. Eyelids drooped. After an hour, Margaret Hemmings wrapped up.

"Morris, did you murder Ben Sewell?"

"Objection," Andy Gunther said, the first time that day he'd done so. "Asked and answered."

Meaning the defense was repeating itself. Hemmings had used up her best question as her opening shot. Gunther didn't want her to be allowed to repeat it. The judge sustained the objection. Morris sat forward on the chair, eager to answer.

Hemmings's tongue flickered at her lips. "Did you ever have any intention, at any time that evening, of causing the death of Ben Sewell?"

"No, I didn't," Morris said, forcefully and quickly, before Gunther could object again.

"Pass the witness."

Andy Gunther took his time. He sat half–turned away from Morris, his arms folded. Gunther continued to sit that way for a moment, then slowly uncoiled, turning toward the witness, sitting up straighter, and putting his arms on the table in front of him. Cocking his head to stare at the defendant, he waited until every eye in the room was fixed on him. Then he asked his question. "Mr. Greenwald, would you expect your daughter to lie for you?"

"No, I wouldn't."

"Maybe you should take your time and think about what I'm asking. If you were in bad trouble—"

"Objection," Margaret Hemmings said, standing up with obvious satisfaction at turning the tables. "The witness has already answered the question."

"Maybe if you'd just let me finish asking it, you'll see it's not the same question." Andy Gunther stared at her until she sat back down. It could have been a comic moment, except for the expression on Gunther's face. He turned back to the witness. "Mr. Greenwald, if you were in bad, bad trouble, and your daughter refused to help you, wouldn't you be devastated?"

Morris did take more time. "Of course, I'd want her to help. But I wouldn't ask her to lie for me."

Gunther's expression dismissed that answer. "You hate Nick Winston, don't you?"

"No, I don't hate him. I invited him to my house that night, didn't I?"

"I'll get to that. But a few years ago Commissioner Winston did you a very bad turn that cost you a lot of money, didn't he?"

"That's true," Morris said slowly. "But in my business you have to get over those things. There's always the chance you can work with someone like that in the future."

Gunther stabbed the table in front of him with a thick forefinger. "If you mean politics, that's my business, too, Mr. Greenwald, and nobody ever showed me that rule. The one they taught me is payback's a bitch. You know that one?"

"I've heard the expression."

"And revenge is sweeter the longer you have to wait for it. You believe that?"

"I don't know. I've never thought about it."

Morris was lying. He looked like he was lying. Chris lowered his eyes. There was no good way to answer the questions Gunther was asking.

"You invited Nick Winston to your house that night, didn't you?"

"Yes."

"You asked him to stay after the other guests left."

"Yes. I had something to talk to him about."

"What was that?"

Morris hesitated again. Fatal hesitation. For once Gunther was using to his own advantage the void in the trial where Veronica Sorenson belonged. Morris wouldn't bring her into this, either. "The things we'd been negotiating that night. I wanted to ask his advice."

Andy Gunther leaned forward. His large frame added bulk to his questioning as his eyes held Morris. "By doing that you managed to put him into a position where when you killed your partner, the only people who could testify about it were you and your daughter, didn't you?"

Again, no good answer. Morris blurted out, "No," in answer to the part of the question that asked whether he'd killed Ben Sewell. But people had been positioned as Andy Gunther suggested. Objectively, that part was true. Morris looked like a liar by denying it. Chris looked at Gunther with new respect. It's rare to be able to taint the other side's whole case with only a few questions, but he had done so. This jury didn't know Anne. They didn't know what she might or might not do out of family loyalty. They didn't know Morris, except by reputation and what they'd heard at trial, which cast him as a manipulator. It was a reputation of which Morris Greenwald had been proud before this trial.

And Anne couldn't take the stand to rebut this theory,

because with a casual agreement Andy Gunther had ensured that she wouldn't testify again.

Nick Winston sat on the aisle toward the back of the courtroom. Several people looked at him, and he did his part. He looked surprised, even stunned, as if he were just beginning to understand. He had the expression of a younger man, one who could be used. Everyone's knowledge of his recent loss didn't hurt in building this image.

Chris turned and looked at Anne. She appeared predictably surprised, and also outraged. Drop that expression, he wanted to tell her. It doesn't help.

The story Gunther suggested made sense. It explained the different versions of the story—except Chris's, and Chris planned to repudiate his own version if he got a chance.

Margaret Hemmings tried to do damage control when her turn came again, but once the prosecutor had planted the idea that Morris was not only a liar but a cunning schemer, there was nothing he could say to dispel the image. She finally gave up.

"Call your next witness," Judge Younger said neutrally. Hemmings looked weary. She had no others.

Chris stood up. "Your Honor, may I ask the court's indulgence to present two witnesses myself? They will be brief, and they're just to help the court get at the truth of this matter."

He didn't look at the judge, but at Andy Gunther. Everything hinged on the prosecutor's decision. Chris hoped that in front of this packed house Gunther wouldn't want to look as if he were trying to suppress evidence.

"What kind of witnesses?" Gunther growled.

"Medical," Chris said.

Gunther shrugged. He couldn't think how a doctor could hurt him, and he'd never in his career had trouble handling one on the witness stand, either in direct or cross-examination. "It's up to you, Judge. I don't object."

"This is very unorthodox, Mr. Sinclair. But if you promise to keep it brief—"

"Thank you, your Honor. I call Dr. Elaine Patterson." Chris spoke quickly, before the judge could change his mind. Letting Chris step into the trial was *damned* unorthodox. But Judge Younger knew this trial had passed out of the realm of the ordinary much earlier. And he may have been warned by a phone call about what was coming. Chris had no control over the other people involved in this case—some deep in the shadows.

Dr. Patterson had been waiting just outside the courtroom doors. She came striding down the aisle as soon as Chris said her name. She wore her large, round glasses, dark slacks, and a light-green blouse. She looked well dressed but not trying too hard to be professional. Her face did that. She took the oath with an expression of concentrated thought, then sat and turned the same look on Chris, who had taken a seat beside Morris Greenwald.

Andy Gunther sat up straight. Suddenly things seemed to be moving quickly, and he had the feeling he might have spoken too hastily.

"Dr. Patterson, what is your specialty?"

"Chemistry. Specifically the study of fibers and material."

"Could you tell us your qualifications, please?"

She did so quickly, a litany of degrees, awards, articles published, all of which made her sound very learned and consumed less than a minute of trial time.

"Dr. Patterson, have you testified as an expert witness before?"

"Yes. Many times."

"Your Honor?"

The judge looked at Andy Gunther, who shrugged. Judge Younger said, "The court accepts Dr. Patterson as an expert witness." He tapped his gavel for emphasis.

Chris continued to move quickly, laying out three items on the front of the judge's bench. "Dr. Patterson, these three items of clothing have already been identified to the jury. Do you recognize them?"

"Yes. These are the items you asked me to examine."

"Let's start with this nice silk sports coat." Chris carried it to Patterson, who glanced over it again just to be sure it was the same item. "This has been identified as the jacket Nick Winston was wearing the night of the murder."

"Yes. I examined this both unaided and with a microscope."

Dr. Patterson spoke in professional tones, not raising her voice, but not in a monotone, either. She was a teacher, and knew how to hold an audience in thrall with her voice. In the way she spoke there was a hint of revelations to come. The jury watched her with more interest than they'd shown their own county's medical examiner.

"What did you find?"

"I found very faint traces of blood. I found chemical residue showing the jacket has been dry-cleaned, probably several times."

"Did you find gunpowder traces?"

"No. Cleaning would have removed those traces, if there'd been any. Blood is more tenacious."

Chris said, "Let's talk about your visual examination. Dr. Patterson, let me show you a photograph, State's Exhibit 16, a picture of Nick Winston's face on the night of the murder. Do you notice anything?"

"Scratches, of course. The one on the cheek looks fairly deep."

"Yes," Chris agreed. "Now let me ask you. Could a man who ran through some very prickly cedar bushes, so that he acquired scratches such as those, have been wearing this coat at the time?"

"No."

A slight murmuring grew in the crowd, but no gasps of surprise. It wasn't that startling a piece of testimony. People wondered, in fact, what it meant.

"Why not?" Chris asked.

"Because this jacket is undamaged. There are a couple of very slight tears, that I had to use the microscope to see, but that's it. A man pushing his way through an environment such as you described, doing this kind of damage to his own face, would inevitably have torn the jacket as well. In fact, I think he would have held up his arms to protect his face before letting himself get scratched like that. But there are no corresponding tears to this jacket."

"Have you heard of invisible reweaving, Doctor?"

She smiled. "That's just an advertising expression. There's no such thing as mending so invisible it can't be seen under a microscope."

"All right, Doctor. There's been a second theory proposed, that Mr. Winston jumped down from a balcony, into these same bushes."

She was shaking her head before he got to a question. "Not wearing this jacket. Again, going down through branches like that, with that kind of force, without miraculous intervention he would have torn this coat. And his face shows the absence of miraculous intervention."

Chris held up the jacket and stared at it as if puzzled. So did nearly everyone else. Neither side's version of the facts fit the evidence of Winston's sports coat. Chris put it aside, as if the mystery could not be solved.

"Let me hand you another jacket, Dr. Patterson. This one would be identifiable from some distance, I think. It's the sport coat Ben Sewell was wearing when he was shot. What do you notice about it?"

Patterson was already busy examining the yellow coat. "You

see, this is what I mean. These tears here, over the breast and particularly on the sleeves, this is what I would expect to find if someone wearing this fell down through cedar bushes. See—" She stood up and donned the jacket to demonstrate. It was very large on her, but no one snickered. "The tears are on the undersides of the sleeves, as if someone held up his arms to try to protect his face. You see?"

She crossed her arms in front of her face, making a large X. The jurors could plainly see tears in the fabric along the arms of the X. When Dr. Patterson lowered her arms the jurors stared at her strangely. She did nothing to reassure them as she carefully removed the coat.

"Now, Doctor, if the jury has heard testimony that Ben Sewell fell dead from the balcony, landing on his back on the dirt below, can you confirm that?"

"Not while wearing this jacket, he didn't."

"How can you be so sure?"

"The back of the jacket would have been very dirty. The dirt would have been forced into the fibers of the jacket by the impact. Blood seeping out would have bound the dirt to the jacket material even more strongly. That didn't happen. Look. There was some dirt, still is, but most of it fell off just from lifting the coat. And this one has not been cleaned since the night of Mr. Sewell's death."

"Couldn't the dirt have just come loose over time?"

"No. It would have been embedded in the fiber. Under a microscope, I didn't find that."

"Can you show us what you mean?"

"Yes. With this shirt." She picked up the final exhibit in front of her, which had been identified as Ben Sewell's shirt. "The back of this shirt did have the kind of embedded dirt I would have expected to find if a victim had been wearing it when he fell on his back. I've prepared an exhibit." She held up a large posterboard holding a one-foot-square blow-up that looked like a science project exhibit.

"This is an enlargement of what I saw under the microscope when I examined this shirt. Ground-in dirt. It's almost become part of the material. Very difficult to remove."

"And what is this brown area over here, Dr. Patterson?"

"Blood."

Chris stepped back. He had sounded throughout his examination of this witness like a student, as if he were learning from her testimony. But in simply returning to his seat he regained an air of authority, just as he turned over the reins to Andy Gunther. "Pass the witness."

Gunther obviously hadn't formulated a question. After a pause, he said, "This is all rather theoretical, isn't it, Dr. Patterson?"

"No. There it is right in front of you. That's dirt. That's blood."

"But how it got there is open to question, wouldn't you agree?"

Now Elaine Patterson hesitated. "I didn't see how it happened, or who was wearing these garments. I can't tell you exactly what happened, only what the materials show."

"Exactly. Thank you, Dr. Patterson."

Chris dismissed Elaine Patterson with a smile of thanks and said, "Dr. Harold Parmenter, your Honor."

The lanky medical examiner also entered the courtroom quickly. It appeared that Chris had rehearsed his witnesses with the idea that the judge's or jury's patience might be wearing very thin before they got to testify. Or maybe they were just busy people.

"Dr. Parmenter, please identify yourself."

"Harold Parmenter, assistant medical examiner for Bexar County."

"Please tell us your training and other qualifications."

From his seat Andy Gunther said, "I'll stipulate to that, your Honor. I've had Dr. Parmenter as a witness myself."

"Thank you. Dr. Parmenter, are you familiar with the operation of the body's muscles and bones?"

"Yes." Hal Parmenter looked very serious as he answered the simple question.

"Have you studied how a living body reacts to stimulation as opposed to a dead body?"

"In my work, yes, I've had to learn that. I'd say, though, that a dead body doesn't react. Not in the muscular sense you mean. A dead body is an object. It's acted on by forces like gravity in the same way a rock would be."

"Yes. But the bones will only allow a body to move in certain ways, isn't that correct?"

"Yes, assuming the bones are intact." Dr. Parmenter crossed his legs. He spoke easily of dead bodies, which were his daily work. Chris often wondered, at times like this, if the affable, easygoing Parmenter's appreciation for people was enhanced or diminished by what he did at the office every day. Did he look at Chris and see an autopsy yet to be performed? How did he view himself when he washed his hands and brushed his teeth and took the health precautions to stave off death as long as possible?

Chris stood and moved between the witness and the jury box. "Doctor, let me give you a hypothetical situation this jury may have heard. A man is shot in the head, a wound that would cause death instantly. Would he become stiff immediately?"

"No. He'd still be as fluid as you and I. Even more so."

"Say a witness saw this man go headfirst over a second-story railing. His legs kicked up high—" Again Chris demonstrated with his fingers. "—then bent at the waist and went over the railing. Could that have happened?"

"No. Not as you describe."

"Why not?"

"Because that body is the way I described it, just an object. Nothing would make its legs kick up and then twist to go over. That's a protective instinct, to keep the head from hitting the ground first. A dead body doesn't have that instinct—or, of course, the power to kick up its legs."

"So the head wound didn't cause the almost immediate death we've heard?"

Hal Parmenter shook his head patiently. "It means more than that. With a head wound, he would have lost muscular function immediately, even if death wasn't instantaneous. He still wouldn't have had the power to do what you've described. The man you saw go over the railing was alive, completely."

Whispering did begin in the courtroom then. The jurors sat staring at the witness. Even Chris couldn't tell what they were thinking. But he certainly had their attention. He held it, putting his hand up to his chin as if he too were pondering this new point. He moved his hand again, apparently re-enacting the scene. Then he sat up abruptly and said, "Dr. Parmenter, are you aware of the failings of eyewitness testimony?"

"I've read some studies. I haven't conducted any of my own."

"From your studies or your own observations, are you aware of the concept that people see what they expect to see, rather than what's in front of them?"

Andy Gunther quickly and loudly said, "Objection. He's not qualified as a witness on this."

"Sustained."

Chris didn't care. Sometimes a question is as good as an answer. "Thank you, Doctor," he said quickly. "Cross?"

Andy Gunther wore a frown of concentration. He wasn't

used to a lawyer snapping out evidence like this. He was used
to those who took their time, went over things again and again,
circuitously and relentlessly. Who gave Gunther time to think.
Suddenly he had the ball and he wasn't sure where to go with
it. "Uh, Doctor, the body has certain automatic reflexes that
happen even if you're dead, doesn't it?"

"Certain muscle movements take place even after death, yes."

"Couldn't that have happened in this case?" Gunther stood
up to demonstrate, banging forward against his counsel table.
"The legs hit that railing, the torso goes forward, wouldn't the
legs automatically kick up behind?"

"Not as I heard it described. The legs would go up high
enough to clear the railing, certainly, dragged forward by gravity. But there'd be no reason for them to lift up as high as Mr.
Sinclair said. That's in part a protective instinct to avoid having the muscles behind your knees strained by stretching too
tight. But a lifeless body won't do anything to protect its muscles. Then there's the matter of bending at the waist while
going over the railing, so that the legs swing around forward.
Getting the legs back underneath you to break your fall. No
dead body has ever done that."

"Well, that explanation all depends on the body going over
exactly as you've heard it described, right, Doctor?"

"More or less as described, yes."

"It requires you to accept the description of an event from a
witness who can't tell one person from another, doesn't it?"

"I don't know what you mean," Parmenter answered quietly.
He knew he wasn't being questioned. Gunther was addressing
the jury.

"No more questions."

Chris stood. "That's all I have to present, your Honor."

Margaret Hemmings rose hastily. "The, um, the defense
and the friend of the court rest, your Honor."

The judge sat momentarily confused. The trial had taken a course he had never seen before. "Mr. Gunther, rebuttal?"

Gunther hesitated for a long moment, then said, "That's all right, Judge. We close."

"Well." Judge Younger still looked blank for a moment. Then he latched on to a legal phrase passing through his head and said, "The preparation of the charge. Yes. I must prepare the court's instructions now. The jury is dismissed for thirty minutes."

"Don't think it'll take that long, Judge," Gunther drawled, remaining on his feet. He proved correct. Argument over what should go into the court's written instructions to the jury took a minimal amount of time. The lawyers were more concerned with the factual contradictions than with legal theories.

Chris stayed out of the preparation of the charge. He walked over to the railing, to where Anne stood with Clarissa. Clarissa put her arms around his neck while he looked into Anne's eyes. *Thank you,* Anne breathed silently. "You solved it for me," Chris said.

"How?"

"When you made the same mistake I had. It made me realize—"

He was interrupted by Andy Gunther appearing at his shoulder. He cast a large shadow. His face was grim. "Why didn't you come to me with this stuff?"

Chris stood unmoved. "I just thought of it yesterday, Andy. Besides, what if I had? What would you have done?"

Gunther said, "We're gonna talk about this afterwards. Maybe with the grievance committee. Right now I've got to wrap this up."

When he left, Chris turned back to Anne and Clarissa. "What's Nick Winston up to?"

"He's still back there," Clarissa said quickly. "Giving a little press conference, I think. Want me to go—?"

"No. I want you to stay right here." He gave Anne an instructive look, but she didn't have to be told to keep a close eye on Clarissa.

Morris Greenwald and his lawyer were sitting at the defense table arguing in low but intense voices. After a minute of this Margaret Hemmings sat back, folded her arms, and stared straight ahead, absenting herself. Morris leaned toward Chris, who was sitting on his other side. Chris nodded.

The jurors took their seats, as did the judge. A greater than usual air of expectancy prevailed. The jury and the audience had heard a great deal of conflicting testimony. For once, perhaps, the jury looked forward to hearing the lawyers put it together.

Andy Gunther waived his right to open the argument, a usual prosecutor's move, saving his turn before the jury until last. On the judge's invitation, Margaret Hemmings stood stiffly. For a moment it looked as if, still angry at her client, she would refuse to speak. Then her face became merely stern as she walked toward the jury box.

"Does a man invite a houseful of witnesses to watch him commit murder?" she began. "Does he leave the weapon with which he intends to commit murder in a drawer downstairs, where anyone might come across it? Is he so careless that he lets slip angry remarks that could later be construed as a motive for the killing?"

She had reached the front of the jury box and stood there looking at each juror in turn. Clearly she was connecting. They watched her intently as she pointed back at the prosecutor. "He's going to tell you that Morris Greenwald committed an intentional murder. Not an accident, not something done in the heat of sudden passion. He carefully planned to kill his young associate, whom he'd worked with for years.

"He surely could have done it in an easier way, couldn't he? He and Ben Sewell saw each other every day. Morris probably had access to his home in Austin. If he hated him so much as to want him dead, why didn't he do it somewhere far away from his own home? Why didn't he make it look like a burglary, or a car wreck, or suicide?

"The prosecution can't have it both ways. They can't tell you that Morris Greenwald is a cunning killer and that he committed the crime in this blundering, stupid way."

She moved along the railing, spreading her arms wide. Chris wondered if she had practiced this move in front of a mirror. He vaguely remembered her doing something similar years ago in the case he'd tried against her. Most lawyers don't develop new tricks. They just refine the old ones. But if Margaret Hemmings's passion was feigned, it was feigned well.

"They can't even put Mr. Greenwald in the same room with Ben Sewell at the end of the evening. They can't prove that Morris fired that gun. Of all the witnesses milling around, they can't produce one who heard them arguing with each other.

"Well, one. How can I forget the star of the prosecution's show? Commissioner Nick Winston. Who saw everything and heard everything. How convenient. But we know why, don't we? Why he testified to every detail that would convict Morris Greenwald of this crime. Because Nick Winston is the real murderer. Anne Greenwald saw him do it. So he had to invent this story.

"His testimony has now been discredited. Let's say you don't believe Morris's story either. Of course he has an incentive to lie. He's accused of murder. So let's discard what he said. Discard Nick Winston's as well, because he's also been accused of the crime. Let's look at the other evidence. Anne Greenwald. She saw it happen. She had the best vantage point. And Nick Winston is someone she's known for years. She recognized him.

"Do you honestly believe she would lie to send a man to prison? She is a respected professional, a psychiatrist. Her whole career is on the line if she were ever charged with perjury. Just the taint of the accusation might ruin her credibility. You heard how many times she's testified in court. It's a weekly part of her job. She wouldn't risk that to lie, even to save her father. Or if she did—" Hemmings arrested herself, stopping straight and looking at the jurors with bright eyes, as if she'd just discovered this idea. "—maybe she would say something to try to save her father. Say she saw someone she couldn't identify commit the murder. Say it was suicide, as her friend Chris Sinclair did. They had time to get together and concoct that story. Anne didn't have to accuse an innocent man.

"She didn't. Her testimony was objective. The other objective testimony was Chris Sinclair's. Of course, he says something different, but again, he says the defendant did not commit this crime. The two objective witnesses, the two who are bystanders, unaccused, say Morris Greenwald is not guilty of murder. That's what your verdict should say as well."

Hemmings stopped and glanced back at her client, who was staring hard at her. Obviously not ready to quit, she cleared her throat and said quietly, "Your Honor, I'd like to give the rest of my time to the friend of the court."

Clearly Margaret Hemmings had great difficulty with that sentence, but she'd been instructed forcibly. She managed not to sneer over the phrase "friend of the court," but she did turn quickly and resume her seat, subtly pushing her chair away from her client. Judge Younger looked in surprise at Chris Sinclair, who was staring down at the floor. "Mr. Sinclair, would you like to address this jury?"

Chris was on his feet in a moment, in sharp contrast to his apparent lethargy of a moment before. "I feel I must, your Honor. Thank you for the opportunity." He, too, approached the jury box. "I should talk to you again because in this trial I was the worst witness you heard."

He shook his head. "Which really makes me mad at myself, let me tell you. Because I've tried hundreds of cases. I've watched thousands of witnesses, and like all lawyers I've always thought, 'I could do better than that.'

"And now it turns out I was wrong. I made the same mistakes I've seen lots of others make." He turned to the prosecutor and gestured at the witness stand. "You should try sitting up there some time, Andy."

No one chuckled. Chris turned back to the jury and said conversationally, "You know why? Because I wasn't prepared. Like most witnesses, that night at Morris Greenwald's house I had no idea I was about to be a witness. It was a party; I was just walking across a lawn. No idea life was about to throw me a pop quiz. I heard a noise, I walked to where I could see where it had come from, and I saw something horrible. A man I had just met put a gun to his head and fire. Then slump over the railing, swing over it, and fall.

"At least that's what I thought I saw. I began to realize my mistake a few nights ago when I went to Morris Greenwald's house. Anne Greenwald saw me. Anne, who knows me better than anyone else on earth—" He turned to look at her. Anne watched him steadily. Over to the side, so did Andy Gunther, expecting some revelation, and wondering how he could use it. "Anne saw me," Chris continued, "and thought I was someone else. She thought—"

"Objection," Gunther snapped out, angry at himself for waiting. "This isn't a time for testimony."

"Stick to the evidence the jury's already heard, counselor," the judge drawled. But he, too, appeared eager for Chris to continue.

Chris said to the jury, "You can also use your common sense and life experience. It's happened to all of us, seeing what we expect to see instead of what's really there. Thinking we see the salt shaker in its usual place even though this morning it's somewhere else. Thinking we recognize a person because that's who we're waiting for, only to realize this is a stranger walking toward us.

"So I saw a man in a bright beige sports coat, almost yellow, standing on a dimly lit balcony. I had even remarked on the color of that jacket earlier in the evening. To Nick Winston." He turned and sought out Winston in the audience. So did others. Winston tried his best to maintain an innocent expression. But how does an innocent person look? Winston appeared very interested, with no animosity. Chris didn't think that was the expression a genuinely innocent person would wear when he was about to hear himself accused of murder. And Winston knew what was coming.

"Let me tell you what happened that night," Chris said. "Not relying just on what I saw. This makes everything fit. Anne Greenwald was at the front door of the house. She saw two men arguing. Ben Sewell, an old friend of hers and her family's, and Nick Winston, whom she'd also known for years. Do you think it was possible she didn't recognize either one of them? No. She's a better-trained observer than I am, she saw what she says she saw.

"I was returning from the parking lot, coming from the other side of the house." He moved his hands, as if positioning the playing pieces. "I didn't have her same vantage point. I didn't see Anne. I heard a sound. That drew my attention, so I moved to where I could see the balcony.

"Morris Greenwald was inside, downstairs, seeing someone off. You've heard two witnesses to that. He thought Winston and Ben were upstairs. Then his daughter came running in. Anne had seen a killing.

"Back to me. That's the noise I heard, the shot Anne described. By the time I reached a spot where I could see the balcony, Anne was gone, already inside the house. And during those few moments, Nick Winston had moved very quickly. He knew he'd been seen. He knew that in a matter of seconds he had to create another suspect, or another scenario. But there was no one there except his fallen victim. So quickly Nick Winston took off Ben Sewell's sports coat, that very memorable jacket I had remarked on earlier, that everyone had noticed. Winston stripped off the jacket and dumped the body over the railing."

Chris pointed down at the ground as if the body had just fallen. "There's your physical evidence. Ben Sewell's body fell from that balcony, but not wearing his coat. Dr. Patterson told you it was impossible for the body to have been wearing that coat when he fell from the balcony. Because the jacket didn't have dirt pressed deep into it as it would have had if Ben Sewell had fallen that way. No, the dirt was ground into his shirt, not his jacket. He made that fall, but his jacket didn't.

"So Nick Winston kept the yellow sports coat but pushed the body over the railing. Then he dropped his own jacket over the edge. There's your second fit of physical evidence. Winston's jacket fell lightly to the ground. He wasn't wearing it as he forced his way through the cedar bushes. The jacket floated softly down to the ground. That's why it didn't have any tears, or only very superficial ones.

"And Nick Winston quickly put on the jacket that was left

and remained on the balcony, standing out of the light, wearing that yellow jacket. A tall, dark-haired man in that distinctive jacket. And he got lucky. I came along and saw him. But I didn't see Nick Winston. I saw what I expected to see. I saw Ben's jacket and assumed that Ben was wearing it. And I didn't have time to realize my mistake. Because as soon as Nick Winston knew he had another witness, he lifted the pistol, holding it just behind his head, and fired. It looked as if he'd shot himself. I screamed, he fell. He went face forward over the balcony railing.

"Unfortunately for him, he couldn't do it the way a dead body would do it, head first, unprotected. His instincts to protect himself took over, just for a few seconds. His legs flipped up and over and around. That's what I saw, a supposed 'body' falling, but in such a way as to protect itself.

"And that's how Nick Winston got to the body before I did. He didn't have to run from the side of the house. He dropped right beside the body. And used those few seconds to switch jackets again. So that I arrived to find him leaning over the body. And had no reason to suspect anything other than what I thought I'd just seen. Because everything fit."

Chris stared at the jurors and held up one finger. "Except that Nick Winston's face was scratched but his jacket wasn't. He had plunged through cedar branches on his way down, scratching himself and the yellow jacket he was wearing. You saw the photographs of the scratches on his face. You saw the tears to the yellow sports coat. Nick Winston went through those bushes. They scratched his face and his hands. But his own jacket remained unharmed. How could that have happened? And how could there have been tears in the yellow coat but no impacted dirt on its back, as there would have been if the victim had fallen to the ground from the balcony while wearing it?

"The only way those things could have happened is if Nick

Winston wasn't wearing his own jacket. He was wearing the victim's. He played the victim's role. And I fell for it.

"So don't believe my testimony. Don't believe what the witnesses think they saw. Believe the evidence that can't be changed. What I've just told you is what fits. The version of events that explains everything.

"What really happened."

Chris looked across the courtroom again. Nick Winston was shaking his head. He rolled his eyes. As clearly as he could from the spectator seats, Winston denied everything Chris had just said.

"Thank you, your Honor," Chris said, and took his seat.

No one else moved for a long moment. The courtroom sat silent.

Until an emphatic sound disturbed the peace. The sound of two beefy hands clapping. Very slowly, one clap, a pause, then another. Andy Gunther sat at his table and gave slow, sardonic applause to his fellow prosecutor.

"That was just fine," Gunther said loudly. "I don't know when I've seen it done better." He stood up, walked a few steps, and leaned down to face Morris. "Didn't he do a good job? Are you ready to welcome him into the family?"

Morris had the good sense not to answer or to smile, partly because Chris was pinching his leg under the table.

Gunther straightened up and strolled toward the jury himself, big hands in his pockets. He looked at ease, as if he were sitting with these folks on a porch. Undoubtedly, some of them knew him. Most of them had voted for him. They knew his reputation as a blunt straight shooter. "I'm not going to try to match wits with Chris Sinclair. To put together little bits of evidence the way he did. That takes a lot of time and thought, and I don't think this case requires that.

"I'm going to ask you to simplify."

Gunther actually leaned against the jury box, sideways. Chris had never before seen a lawyer do that and look natural, but Gunther did, as if it were his usual resting place. "He's told you in a mathematical, kind of scientific way one way this could have happened that clears the man he'd like to be his father-in-law someday. But he's left out one thing. He hasn't given you a reason."

Gunther paused as he looked along the two rows of jurors. Most were men, and most of those were of middle age or beyond, men who looked as if they worked hard for a living, in the dirt or not far removed from it. Of the four women on the jury, one was a young student, two were housewives, and one worked in a bank. Most of the jurors kept their eyes on their district attorney, though sometimes they would look out into the courtroom, seeking out participants in the night's drama. They were nearly all there: Anne, Chris, Morris Greenwald. And Nick Winston at the back of the room, looking on solemnly.

"What reason did Nick Winston have for killing Ben Sewell?" Gunther continued. "They weren't working on anything together, they weren't in competition. Winston had hurt Sewell's partner Morris Greenwald years ago, but that didn't affect Sewell personally. Winston didn't even know why he was in that house that night. He'd been invited and he came. He certainly didn't come to kill anyone.

"It was Morris Greenwald who set the stage. Who put all the elements together to get rid of the partner who'd gone behind his back to bid against him, and at the same time exact revenge on the man who'd cost him so much years earlier. He arranged to kill Sewell, then he and his daughter blamed the killing on Commissioner Winston."

Gunther became a little more animated, pacing along but staying close to the jurors. "Why didn't Morris go about this in a simpler way? Two reasons. First, if he'd just gone and broken into Ben Sewell's house and made it look like murder during a burglary, Morris couldn't have exacted his revenge on Nick Winston. And he might still have become a suspect, once his business affairs with Sewell started coming out.

"But the more important reason is just that Morris Greenwald isn't that kind of guy. He isn't a sneak. When he does something, he wants everybody to know it. He wants to make a big splash, the way he used to in the old days when he was a big-time political operator and contributor. He wanted to get rid of a problem and raise his own profile at the same time. Everybody would remember Morris Greenwald again."

Gunther turned toward the defendant. "Well, you accomplished that, Morris. Everybody's going to remember you. I don't think you'd be able to get together very many people for a party at your house after this, though."

No one laughed. Gunther didn't expect it. His face remained hard as he made the remark. Then he turned back to the jury offhandedly. "As for this last-minute physical evidence—that was impressive, wasn't it? Congratulations to Mr. Sinclair again. But it doesn't change the facts. What was there? Oh, yes, dirt on the dead man's shirt instead of the back of his jacket. Did anybody think of this?" Gunther turned his back to the jury and flipped up the tails of his own suit coat, as if he were mooning the jurors. The lining of his black jacket showed, as did his own white shirt. "Did anybody think that maybe when you go over a railing and fall twelve feet to the ground your clothes don't stay in perfect order? Maybe the wind lifts your jacket so you land on your shirt and that's where the dirt gets ground in. Nobody testified that the victim's clothes were perfectly straight when he was found. No dead body is ever perfectly dressed, I can tell you that. And did anybody ask whether there was dirt ground into the *inside* of his jacket? No.

"What else was there?" Gunther grew his most animated, leaning over close to the jurors, his face turning red. "Oh, yes, scratches. Scratches and lack of scratches. Nick Winston had them on his face but not his jacket." Gunther raised his arms in an elaborate shrug and made a dismissive face. "Come on. Is that what's going to decide your verdict? Scratches? Does anyone besides me remember Nick Winston testifying that there was a sort of path behind the bushes, and that he ran along that? That's how he got to the body first. So he found an easier way. He got a couple of scratches himself, but his coat didn't. Any of you ever scratched your face but managed not to rip your clothes at the same time? Of course you have."

Chris sat at the defense table feeling his carefully—but hastily—prepared case falling apart. Of course jurors had experienced that. But he hoped they also remembered the many, many times children had torn the knees of their jeans and left strawberries underneath. As a prosecutor, Chris was used to getting the last word with juries. He'd forgotten the hardship of being a defense lawyer, sitting and hearing his arguments refuted and being unable to respond.

Gunther stood straight before the jury, straightening his own clothes, becoming the district attorney again rather than a performer. "So I'm going to ask you again: simplify. Who had motive to commit this murder? Morris Greenwald. Whose gun killed Ben Sewell? Morris Greenwald's. Who threatened to murder the victim earlier in the evening?"

He let the jurors answer that one for themselves. "How much more do you need? I'll tell you, I've prosecuted a lot of murders, and most of them are harder to prove than this one. Murderers don't usually announce their intention like this one did. They don't usually let an eyewitness watch them like this one did. You need to go back to that jury room, review the evidence, and vote quickly. And vote guilty. If you don't, you're going to make me wonder whether we can ever again get a murder conviction in this county."

He stared hard at his townspeople, then turned and walked back toward his table. Chris waited and waited and finally leaned over and pushed Margaret Hemmings's shoulder. Belatedly, she jumped to her feet and said, "Objection, your Honor. He's trying to pressure the jury by putting the weight of every murder case—"

But her objection grew lost in a general stir that had begun at the back of the courtroom and quickly passed forward. The doors had opened and a newcomer slowly came down the aisle. The visitor made slow progress because he walked with a cane. He looked like an old man, or recently injured. Otherwise, Temple Lockridge made as impressive a figure as ever. He wore a white suit, which made his tanned, seamed skin appear darker. His hand holding the head of the cane looked strong and veined, as if from a lifetime of hard work. He nodded here and there to faces in the crowd. Some he might have known. To others he was just acknowledging their recognition.

Reflexively and quite unconsciously, Judge Younger rose to his feet as Lockridge came through the gate in the railing. "Senator, can we help you? Would you like to speak?"

Temple Lockridge smiled. He had a famous grin. It hadn't grown tired with age. "No, thank you, your Honor. And please forgive me for interrupting. I just came to offer my support to an old friend."

He had come to a stop beside Morris Greenwald. Lockridge reached down and gripped Morris's hand. A photographer got a picture. Lockridge held the pose for a long moment, then sat beside Morris, clapping a hand on his shoulder. Finally he waved a hand to the judge and the other trial participants. "Please. Don't let me interrupt."

The judge collected himself and sent the jury out. People stood and began milling around the courtroom, but few left. Temple Lockridge seemed to deflate slightly. Morris bent close and thanked him, but they had no conversation between them. After less than a minute the old senator rose again. His aide Gordon appeared and assisted him back up the aisle. It was a much slower process this time, as he had to stop every couple of steps to shake a hand or have a picture taken. He might have been campaigning again.

Chris had gone to stand beside Anne. "What was that all about?"

"Making amends. Or maybe someone ordered him to." Anne turned toward Chris. "Andy Gunther kind of took your case apart there toward the end."

"Yeah, I should have—"

"But you damned sure sold me. It's been a while since I've seen you in action."

She looked at him appraisingly. He smiled.

"That's true."

"And you are very damned good."

Clarissa said loudly, "Okay, okay. I'm leaving! You shouldn't talk like this in front of a child." She put her hands over her ears and walked away.

"What's she talking about?" Chris said.

"I have no idea." Anne had started smiling too. They stood there not touching, just looking at each other, expressions growing softer but with a certain eagerness as well. People came to talk to them but then veered away, leaving them a private zone in the crowd. It lasted maybe a minute. Long time.

Waiting for the jury's verdict is the least eventful part of trial. Usually. All the legal and investigative work is done. The only continuing work of the trial proceeds in private, while those who have been performing can only sit and wait. Opposing lawyers have been known to stand outside the jury room door and listen for clues. Curiosity compels this kind of behavior, but also boredom. There is nothing else to do.

But this trial took another unusual turn. The jury had been out only half an hour when another visitor arrived. Margaret Hemmings had gone outside to make a call, Anne and Chris were standing with Morris, Andy Gunther was chatting with his assistant a few feet away. A dozen or so spectators remained in the courtroom, including a reporter from the local newspaper. Suddenly the door of the courtroom banged open. Clarissa rushed in. She caught Chris's eye and made indecipherable hand signals. No one had to ask her to clarify, though, because a few seconds later Veronica Sorenson entered behind her.

The lieutenant governor of Texas wore a blue-and-white–striped dress and white summer heels. She carried a small, navy-blue purse, unusual for a public figure, who usually had her hands free while an aide carried things for her. But Mrs. Sorenson appeared unaccompanied, until Chris turned and noticed that her bodyguard in his inevitable black suit had entered the courtroom by a side door. Another must be waiting outside, behind Sorenson.

She smiled at Clarissa, who had stepped out of her way, but then the smile quickly fell away, as Veronica Sorenson came briskly down the aisle. The district attorney went to meet her. But after she passed through the gate in the railing, she spoke to Chris.

"Am I too late?"

He nodded.

"Damn," Sorenson said. "Well. There will be a motion for new trial, won't there? I can testify in that hearing. I can talk to the judge. He might—"

"Mrs. Sorenson, the jury's still out."

"Oh." She went blank for a moment, switching gears. Chris could see her mind work, weighing possibilities that all had her power behind them. Then she said authoritatively, "Well, we'll see. I wanted to get here in time to testify."

"What would you have said?" Gunther asked.

"You know very well what I would have said, Mr. Gunther. That Ben Sewell returned that videotape to me that night. I knew that would make Nick Winston furious when he found out. He'd been using that tape for years . . ."

"I wouldn't have let you testify to that," Gunther said quietly. "It's speculation. You weren't there to see Mr. Winston's reaction."

Sorenson stared at him coolly. "You think the judge would have stopped me? Mr. Gunther, I appreciate that you tried to spare my reputation in this trial. But I never asked you to do that. I think I had relevant testimony that you withheld."

"I made that decision." Andy Gunther looked uncowed. Sorenson continued to study him.

"What do you think of that decision now?" she asked.

He hesitated. Gunther looked at Chris, obviously remembering his argument. "I'm not sure," he said quietly.

"You want to make amends? Come with me. Let's talk to the judge."

Sorenson took Gunther's arm and led him away. They left the courtroom by the side door. Her trooper closed it and stood there.

Morris looked at Chris. "Is that allowed? Shouldn't we—?"

Chris said, "I have no idea."

Sorenson was back in the courtroom when the jury returned. She had never left after returning from seeing the judge. She sat in the row of chairs just inside the railing. Her trooper stood near the bailiff's desk. Another stood at the back of the courtroom.

Nick Winston sat in the back of the room again. Anne turned and looked at him. He didn't look back. His attention remained fastened on Veronica Sorenson. She never turned toward him.

The jurors filed into the jury box and remained standing awkwardly, until the judge waved them down. Then the fore-man, a thin man with well-creased skin, popped up again as the judge asked, "Do you have a verdict?"

"Yes, sir."

"Give it to the bailiff, please."

So Judge Younger was one of those judges who want a preview of the verdict. On the theory of checking the sheet to make sure the verdict was in proper form and had been signed in the right place, he looked for several seconds at the page on which the jury had decided the outcome of the trial. Then he returned the form to the bailiff. While the bailiff carried it back to the foreman, the judge looked expressionlessly at Morris Greenwald. Then he glanced toward the back of the courtroom, and finally at Andy Gunther. Gunther seemed to know what that meant.

"Read your verdict, please."

The foreman cleared his throat and looking down at the sheet in his hands, read, "We the jury find the defendant, Morris Greenwald, not guilty."

A moment of silence was interrupted by Morris leaning toward Chris and saying quietly, "'Not'?"

Then Anne stepped lightly over the railing and reached her father, throwing her arms around him from behind. The court-room erupted in noise in spite of the judge's banging his gavel. He gave up, leaned toward the jury, and said, "Thank you for your service. You're dismissed."

Chris reached the jury box before they could leave. Margaret Hemmings stood beside him, beginning to shake hands with the jurors. Chris said, "Was it just that you weren't sure, or did you think—?"

The jurors looked abashed. It appeared they wouldn't answer. Then the foreman, barely speaking above a mumble, said, "To tell you the truth, we didn't really follow all that stuff you were saying. But Senator Lockridge believing in him was good enough for us."

Chris stood still, abruptly deflated. Margaret Hemmings didn't seem to have heard. She went on shaking hands and receiving congratulations as the jurors began filing out. Chris was thinking that it didn't make sense. A lawyer could never tell what he did or left undone in a trial that would make a dif-ference to the jury. This one seemed to have based its verdict on a particularly irrelevant bit of theater.

But then one of the two housewives on the jury, a nicely dressed lady fifteen years older than Chris, leaned toward him and said quietly, "Some of us understood what you said, too."

She winked. Chris didn't know whether he felt better or not. He turned and saw Anne watching him, wordlessly asking a question that he couldn't answer.

In the tumult, Judge Younger said to Andy Gunther, "I'll sign that now."

Gunther went to the bench with a document. Veronica Sorenson accompanied him. The judge quickly signed his name. Gunther turned, caught the bailiff's eye, and gestured with his head out toward the audience. Sorenson stood beside him looking out that way as well.

Nick Winston sat at the back of the courtroom. He hadn't moved since the verdict was announced. But he felt observed. Lifting his head, he returned Veronica Sorenson's stare. Not liking what he saw on her face, he stood up. The bailiff, who had accepted the document from Andy Gunther, struggled up the aisle through the crowd that congested it. When he got closer, he held the papers toward Nick Winston.

Perhaps Winston recognized an arrest warrant. Perhaps he had read his fate on Veronica Sorenson's face. Or maybe just instinct took over. He stepped out into the aisle, made sure people were milling around between the bailiff and him, and took off running. As the bailiff yelled, "Hey!" Winston hit the courtroom doors and vanished outside.

The stone-faced trooper who had stayed within a few feet of Veronica Sorenson moved faster than anyone else. Calling to his counterpart, "Stay here!" he bolted out the side door of the courtroom.

Chris found that he had gravitated to Anne's side. She held his arm, looking from one exit to the other, then to the lieutenant governor, who stood between the counsel tables, staring at the exit doors as if she could see through them. She appeared to be following Nick Winston's flight, calculating his next move.

Chris said to Andy Gunther, "What happened?"

Gunther had his hands in his pockets again and looked pleased with the afternoon's events. "Mrs. Sorenson told the judge her evidence. She asked him to issue an arrest warrant for Mr. Winston. The judge said he'd sign it if the jury came back not guilty. He'd take that to mean twelve citizens were convinced someone other than Morris Greenwald killed the deceased, and that would be enough probable cause for him. Is that about right, Judge?"

Judge Younger listened to this recitation, then started down from the bench, unzipping his robe. He only said, "You'd better find that man. He's going to be dangerous." And he left the courtroom.

Veronica Sorenson said quietly, to no one in particular, "He won't be a fugitive. Nick won't live like that." Her voice saying his name had an intimate quality.

Anne and Chris stood with her father, all three of them looking nonplussed by the jury's verdict and its consequences. "I can go now, right?" Morris said.

Anne looked around. Her fist thumped Chris's chest.

"Clarissa!" she said.

They both stared frantically around. Clarissa was no longer in the room.

There was a hallway that encircled the courtroom like a belt. Two other straight corridors branched off from it to exits from the courthouse. And two staircases led upstairs, to another courtroom and conference rooms. The relatively small courthouse held too many hiding places to search quickly. Chris instinctively headed outside. If Winston had holed up inside somewhere, someone else would flush him out of hiding. If Clarissa had just gone to the ladies' room, Anne would find her. He wanted to stop Winston from taking her away from the area.

Chris ran out, into the glaring heat of a late afternoon in

August. He hurtled down the steps, his feet only touching two of them, and saw at the end of the long sidewalk Clarissa running toward him. He called her name, sped up, and caught her. He encircled her with his arms and tried to surround her, expecting a shot at any moment.

"He got away!" Clarissa shouted. "I saw where he parked this morning, and I went to check. His car is gone!"

She was raising her voice because sheriff's deputies and the gray-haired state trooper in the black suit were coming down the courthouse steps as well. They looked all around, as if they would see the car driving by. Two of the deputies got on phones, as did the trooper. "He won't get out of town," one of the deputies promised.

"Damn it," Chris said to Clarissa. "Don't you have any sense at all?" He hugged her, then pulled her inside.

The courtroom had nearly emptied out, as people realized the drama had moved outside. Even Morris had left, his arms around two of the jurors as if they were old friends. The jurors looked as if they might be reconsidering their verdict.

Anne stood close to the lieutenant governor. "He'll try to get to you," she said. "Maybe he'll just call, maybe he'll come to your house tonight." She gave Veronica Sorenson a more penetrating look. "Or is there someplace he'd know to meet you?"

Sorenson didn't look at her, didn't answer. Anne studied the woman even more closely. She saw the glitter of excitement in Sorenson's eyes, and realized the lieutenant governor knew more about the situation than she would share with anyone. The trial had worked out the way she wanted, but Morris Greenwald's acquittal had been merely incidental. Veronica

Sorenson wanted Nick Winston. After years of submission and fear, she had him gripped tightly in her own hand. She relished this moment. She would relish even more seeing him captured.

"Ma'am," said the other state trooper, a tall young man with prominent ears and a boyish face, "we need to get you out of here. We've called for reinforcements."

Veronica Sorenson didn't say a word, but let him guide her to the side door of the courtroom. She didn't glance back at Anne, either, as she stood waiting for the trooper to check out the exit.

The young man pulled open the door and eased halfway out it. A gun slammed into his nose, breaking it. Spurting blood, the trooper clutched instinctively at his face. Nick Winston kicked him in the crotch, then in the head, as the trooper went down. Winston grabbed Veronica Sorenson's arm, pulled her out into the hallway, and slammed the door shut behind them.

In the corridor he said, "You're going to fix this."

She said coldly, "I canceled my press conference."

"No, I think you'll need to have one after all."

Winston looked icy. He had no blood under the skin of his face. He held her arm as if he would break it, but Sorenson refused to cry out. Her own face remained stiff and immobile, too.

He dragged her down the corridor, looking both backward and forward. "You engineered this," he told her in a fierce undertone. "You told that judge something. Now you're going to undo it. Do you really think I'll go to prison? By myself? Darling, I know more than anyone suspects."

He stopped pulling her along the hallway and looked in her

face. His use of the endearment had brought a sneer to her lips, which made him smile. She said coldly, "They said you ran."

"Just to throw everyone off. I came back."

"You should have kept running, Nick."

They came around the curve of the corridor to where they could see toward the front door of the courthouse. "Damn it!" Winston said, and jumped behind his hostage, putting the gun to her head again.

The stone-faced trooper stood thirty feet away, feet spread and gun drawn and held in two hands. He made a good target. Winston could have shot him, but to do so he would have to step around Veronica Sorenson. Instead he commanded her, "Tell him to back off. Tell him we're just talking."

She didn't say a word. The trooper called, "There's all kinds of people outside. There's nowhere to go, Commissioner."

Use of the title was intended to recall Nick Winston to himself, to his position. It didn't work. "Sure there is," he said, looking at Sorenson's face. She finally looked back at him.

Staring into her cold eyes, Winston lost his smile. Then he looked startled. He had heard a small sound behind him. Looking back, he saw Chris Sinclair slowly approaching down the hall from the courtroom. Chris too had a drawn gun, aimed at Winston. Behind him, Anne Greenwald stood watching.

Winston instinctively jumped out to the side, away from Chris. Then he realized what he'd done, and slowly turned his head, flinching. The trooper was still aiming at him. He had a shot now, but not a good one, and Winston was still standing close by the trooper's charge, Veronica Sorenson. Winston smiled.

He brought his gun toward her face. "Let's give him some incentive," he said. He poked the gun toward her mouth.

"No!" Sorenson snapped. "Not ever again."

She slapped Winston. Her hand hit his face and her arm hit the gun, knocking it momentarily aside. He stared at her in astonishment, and with a look of betrayal.

And Sorenson suddenly slumped to the floor. Winston was still holding her arm, but couldn't hold her up. He looked down the corridor toward the exit. Behind him, Chris threw himself flat against the wall.

The trooper took the shot. He fired once, then again, the gun jerking upward, the trooper coolly bringing it back down, then he was running forward, aiming to knock the gun from Winston's hand.

But he couldn't get there in time. Winston looked down at Veronica Sorenson. "You know I—" he began, but those were all the words he could produce. He fell flat on the floor beside her. Blood leaked from two holes in his chest. Chris ran forward and kicked the gun from his hand, but the fingers were already lifeless. Winston lay with hands clutching his chest, as if he were cold, but he was clearly dead. His hand had released his hostage.

Veronica Sorenson raised herself on her elbows. She gave the body a long look, but one absent of expression. Ignoring the hands reaching for her, she stood up.

Anne had come forward and was standing close to her. Veronica Sorenson happened to be facing that way when she rose to her feet, looking back down the corridor toward the courtroom, perhaps wanting a moment to prepare a public expression before she turned toward the exit. Anne didn't allow her that moment. Arms folded, she stared at Sorenson.

Chris saw them both in profile. Sorenson paid Anne the compliment of a long exchange of stares. Then Anne's expression changed subtly. With a nod, she stepped back.

Sorenson turned and walked away down the corridor, the trooper following. She never looked down at the body.

★ The press couldn't figure how to spin the story, and finally settled on heroism. It made for such easy transitions. Start with courtroom heroics, ending in apparent cooperation between the two district attorneys to trap the true villain. Andy Gunther helped by promoting the "cooperation" aspect of the story, to the extent of taking it over. By the end of his news conference, the fact that he'd lost the trial had been overlooked in the general congratulations over catching the true killer.

Then, according to the news stories, several acts of heroism put that villain down on the floor of the courthouse with a gun by his side. Winston, unable to do his own spinning, fell naturally into the role of dead villain.

Reporters also made much of the heroic stamina of Veronica Sorenson, her poise both during the crisis and afterward when she faced them. That led naturally to stories that she had intervened in the trial to see justice done, at great personal risk. No one would ever bother to read the trial record, which would have shown that Sorenson's appearance had actually been irrelevant to the outcome.

Chris Sinclair shook hands with Andy Gunther. Even Morris Greenwald did. Chris and Anne and Clarissa returned to San Antonio and went about their normal lives. A few days passed. The weather cooled slightly, the press stories of the trial much more so. They now focused exclusively on Veronica Sorenson's rising political fortunes. She had become the best-known politician in the state, and had been called to Washington again for a private conference with the president. The idea of scandal in her past was played so far down that it disappeared into a vague notion that evidence had only been concocted to trap an attempted blackmailer.

School started again and Clarissa seemed content with that. She returned refreshed, ready to deal with the problems that awaited her there. Two weeks into the school year, she told Anne that Angelina had solved her problem with the boy who followed her around. Angelina just went about her business, occasionally staring stonily at the boy, otherwise ignoring him. "And then she stands with her friends and we all whisper and then look at him and laugh." Not many people can endure such treatment for long, and the boy soon slunk away. Anne thought the solution had been inspired also by Veronica Sorenson's treatment of her kidnapper. Angelina, too, had learned something from the trial.

And one day not long after the trial, Chris and Anne were sitting on a couch in the Marriott Hotel at Rivercenter Mall, having just finished lunch and not yet ready to return to work. Some kind of event was being prepared, nicely dressed people were bustling about, but ignored the two of them. Chris had his arm along the back of the couch. Anne sat close.

"Have you figured it all out?" he asked.

"You know what Mrs. Sorenson and I were doing that evening, before you found us in her office?" Anne said, not answering his question. "We watched the tape."

"*The* tape?"

"Yes. The one Ben gave her. She said she'd never seen it before, she wanted to know how bad it was, and she wanted someone else's opinion too. Not a man's, though, I think."

"How eerie."

"It was. We sat there in the dark, she had a little TV, we formed a triangle with it. She had the sound low, but not low enough. Sometimes I looked away, to tell you the truth, but she never did."

Chris gazed out into the second-floor lobby, out to the door where shoppers were walking by. "Was it bad?"

"I don't think Winston could have ever used it, except in desperation. On the tape she said at least three times, 'I don't want to do this.' Maybe she just meant the taping, but it seemed to me she meant what they were doing. It looked more like rape than anything else. She probably couldn't have accused him of that successfully, since she'd willingly been his lover before. But the tape made her look like a victim. I think it would have ruined her reputation—she was right to fear that—but it made me feel sorry for her."

"What did you tell her?"

"A little of that, but as soon as she saw how I was reacting she put it away. She said she was going to destroy it. Then you arrived."

Changing the subject slightly, Chris asked, "Why did Ben give her the tape? He must have known how that would infuriate Winston. It got Ben killed."

"Well, he wouldn't have expected that, of course. In politics you don't get mad, you get even, and by returning the tape to Veronica Sorenson he'd be allying himself with someone much stronger than Nick Winston. But I don't think that's what Ben was thinking. He just wanted to do the right thing. He may have agreed to Daddy's scheme just with that in mind. That's how Ben was."

Anne wondered for a moment if she'd always been attracted to decent men. It didn't seem a very sexy trait, but nonetheless . . .

They sat in silence for a moment in the elegant hotel. Anne began talking again. She had obviously been thinking furiously ever since that night. First she said, "Can you be my lawyer? Can I hire you so you can't repeat anything I say?"

"I don't think so. I already—"

"I'll tell you anyway." Anne turned to face him. "You know what happened there after the trial in New Braunfels? She killed him. Veronica Sorenson killed Nick Winston. I'm not sure how she did it, and damned sure no one will ever prove it, but she did."

Chris looked puzzled. "Because he still—"

"Not because he had power over her. That was over a long time ago, Winston just didn't know it. Everything she did for him, that he thought he made her do—She just created another ally for herself. She did the same for other people who didn't have any hold over her. Because it made her more powerful in government. That's what politicians do. And for Winston at the end, she lifted him high enough to make a good target."

Chris sat absorbing the theory, not commenting one way or another.

"And she used Winston. And Celine, without them realizing it. Sorenson knew Senator Lockridge had a copy of the tape. She used Winston and Celine to get it. She told Winston that Lockridge had a copy. That's something else nobody will ever be able to prove, but I'm sure of it.

"Now look at her. This has raised her image higher than

ever. Even the hint of scandal helps, I think, because she fought her way out of it. Who will ever mess with her again?"

Chris sat still for a few seconds longer. He turned on the couch to face her. As always, Anne had good theories. She had explained almost everything. But he had one question. She looked back at him, clear-eyed, and took his hand.

"Anne, that last look you gave her in the hallway of the courthouse, right after Winston was killed. What were you saying? She understood, whatever it was."

Anne hesitated, obviously deciding whether to tell him. Then she made up her mind, and continued watching him as she answered:

"I was offering her my congratulations."

about the author Jay Brandon is the author of a dozen novels. An Edgar Award finalist for *Fade the Heat,* Brandon has been called "perhaps the finest writer of legal thrillers in America." He's been a lawyer for a number of years, and lives in San Antonio, Texas.